THE
SHADOWED
ONYX

A Diamond Estates Novel

Nicole O'Dell

BARBOUR
PUBLISHING

Scripture quotations marked NKJV are taken from the New King James Version®. Copyright © 1982 by Thomas Nelson, Inc. Used by permission. All rights reserved.

Scripture quotations marked MSG are from *THE MESSAGE*. Copyright © by Eugene H. Peterson 1993, 1994, 1995, 1996, 2000, 2001, 2002. Used by permission of NavPress Publishing Group.

Scripture quotations marked NIV are taken from the HOLY BIBLE, NEW INTERNATIONAL VERSION®. NIV®. Copyright © 1973, 1978, 1984, 2011 by Biblica, Inc.™ Used by permission. All rights reserved worldwide.

Scripture quotations marked NLT are taken from the *Holy Bible*. New Living Translation copyright © 1996, 2004, 2007 by Tyndale House Foundation. Used by permission of Tyndale House Publishers, Inc. Carol Stream, Illinois 60188. All rights reserved.

This book is a work of fiction. Names, characters, places, and incidents are either products of the author's imagination or used fictitiously. Any similarity to actual people, organizations, and/or events is purely coincidental.

The author is represented by MacGregor Literary.

Cover photograph: dpproductions

Published by Barbour Publishing, Inc., P.O. Box 719, Uhrichsville, Ohio 44683, www.barbourbooks.com

Our mission is to publish and distribute inspirational products offering exceptional value and biblical encouragement to the masses.

ecpa Member of the
Evangelical Christian
Publishers Association

Printed in the United States of America.
Bethany Press International, Bloomington, MN USA; November 2012; D10003613

*This book is dedicated to the tireless parents
who stand in prayerful watch over their families,
and to the teenagers who appreciate it.*

Acknowledgments

Readers, you may be seeing a theme in these acknowledgments, in that I always mention my friend and critique partner, Valerie Comer. I have to give her top billing in this book though. Not that order of mention has anything to do with it. . . . Oh, I'm digging myself a hole, aren't I? Anyway, Val, at this very moment, is squinting at her computer monitor trying to finish the last of the critique a mere seventy minutes before the book is due. I feel guilty, but ever so grateful. I'm going to do my very best to never put her in that position again. But it's cool to know that she'll stick with me even if I do.

I also want to acknowledge my family. This book came as the wrap-up to a slew of book contracts that piled up at the same time. It was exciting trying to put together so many projects at the same time, but it definitely took its toll on the family. I appreciate them for sticking in there with me as I pursued something they won't even get to hold for another eight months. Talk about delayed gratification.

A huge thank-you to my friends and prayer partners who kept me and my family in prayer while I wrote this book. Researching and delving into the world of spiritual warfare and the paranormal is unnerving and downright scary at times. Your prayers kept me grounded in truth and focused on the goal. We definitely saw spiritual fallout from my efforts with this story. But we also proved over and over that our Daddy is WAY bigger.

As always, my writer-sister-friends: Jenny B. Jones, Cara Putman, Kim Cash Tate, Cindy Thomson, Marybeth Whalen, and Kit Wilkinson. Thank you for the prayers and the refocusing efforts. I love you all.

Chip MacGregor, thank you for your efforts in pursuing

this series, which was so important to me.

Friends at Barbour Publishing—you guys are amazing to work with. Every encounter I have is a pleasant one. From editors to designers to the sales team—you guys are awesome!

Special note to Kelly McIntosh. Thank you for working to bring materials to the YA audience and for going to bat for *The Shadowed Onyx* when it looked like it might slip through the cracks. You think maybe someone didn't want this story told?

Frank and Pam Smith, my real-life Ben and Alicia Bradley. Thank you both for your hearts of service—to have embraced me as a sarcastic teenager, with all my troubles, and to still love me today, as your adopted daughter. And thank you for teaching me about spiritual warfare by living it out right in front of me. I love you.

An old Cherokee once told his grandson about a battle that rages inside every person, no matter their age, ethnicity, or lot in life. Even their sex, their financial status, their heritage— none of it matters in this battle for souls.

That old Cherokee said, "My son, there is a battle between two 'wolves' that exists inside every one of us."

The little boy leaned in and listened closely, as he tended to do when Grandfather spoke.

"One of those wolves is Evil. It is everything bad in a person: anger, envy, greed, arrogance, self-pity, guilt, and lies. . . all lies. The other is Good. It is joy, peace, love, hope, serenity, humility, kindness, benevolence, empathy, generosity, truth, compassion, and faith."

The grandson pondered the concept for a moment. Then he turned his concerned gaze up to his grandfather's aged face, so full of wisdom, and he asked: "Which wolf wins?"

The old Cherokee simply replied, "The one you feed."

—a Cherokee legend

Chapter 1

"Are there any spirits in this room with us?"

Joy Christianson stared at Raven, whose face glowed in the candlelight from the black tapers flanking the game board on the floor between them. Raven's eyes drifted closed, and her fingers danced atop the same wooden triangle that lay motionless beneath Joy's.

The tallest candle flickered, casting a somber spotlight, illuminating the letters that would spell messages from beyond. The flame bent to the left as though a birthday child begged for a wish.

Peeling her gaze from the candle, Joy followed her new friend's instructions and squeezed her eyes shut. It was Raven's house, after all. Her house, her rules.

The game piece—that's all it was, right?—trembled and then slithered across the Ouija board. Joy's eyes snapped open, and she jerked back. "Very funny, Raven." Joy inched away as though gnarled fingers would reach from underneath, grab her ankles, and pull her to the great beyond. "I don't even believe in this stuff." She slid her hands under her legs. No way she'd put them back on that thing.

Raven raised one eyebrow and cocked her head. "Oh? You don't, huh? Then I suppose that's someone else's heartbeat I can hear all the way over there? What about the rapid breathing and. . ." She yanked on Joy's arm and inspected her hand. "Sweaty palms?" She returned to the ready position and waited. "People aren't usually scared of things they don't believe in."

Something *was* out there. Joy could feel it in her bones.

Something existed beyond the reality she knew. Something other than what she'd always believed in, other than God. But did she want to communicate with whatever—whoever—it was? "I don't know, Ray. I. . .I might not be ready for something like this. Besides, it's just a game." Joy needed to get out of there. Pronto.

"It is so not just a game." Raven shrugged. "You can think that if you want to. But then you might as well give it a try, if it's only for fun, that is."

Okay, now what? Joy could play along and pretend she didn't believe in that stuff, or she could admit her terror of all things supernatural and leave Raven's house immediately. The whole Ouija-board thing was probably totally fake, but then why the shivers, and, most importantly, why had that thing moved?

Perfectly explainable. The shivers were simply a product of her own nervousness, and the triangle thingy moved because Raven pushed it on purpose. Joy really didn't know Raven all that well. She certainly hadn't been someone Joy spent time with before. . .well, before. Until they locked sad eyes across a crowded lunchroom. Had it been a mistake to strike up a friendship with Raven just so Austin wouldn't bother her?

Raven flipped her dark brown hair behind her shoulder, though the top layers fell in front of her pale face like a dark curtain. She placed her fingers on the triangle's wooden edge and tipped her chin toward Joy. "Come on. What are you waiting for? There's activity here, and I'm going to prove it to you."

"What are you saying? You think there are ghosts or. . .what?"

One corner of Raven's mouth curled up, and she winked. "Or something like that. Let's go."

Joy pushed the sleeves of her fuzzy pink sweater up to her elbows and gathered her hair into a long ponytail, rolling a hair tie from her wrist to secure it out of her face.

Deep breath. Only a game.

She cracked her knuckles one at a time then reached her hands toward Raven's. Joy barely let her fingertips rest in position on her side of the piece. Her bright pink nails glared in contrast to Raven's black ones just inches away. The candle teased the black stone in Raven's skull ring with glints of light.

Joy trembled.

"Oh Great Spirit here tonight, will you identify yourself to us, please?" Raven slowly opened her eyes and gazed into the dancing candle flame nearest the door.

Joy begged her muscles to lift her fingers from the game's surface, but she couldn't move. What if something were there? What if—

Joy's fingers jerked an inch and then gently glided along the board as the triangle headed toward a letter. Raven again? Or did something more sinister propel it? She stared at the fingertips across from hers. They didn't appear to be applying any pressure to the planchette at all. Yet it continued to move.

"We mean no harm. Who is with us here?" Raven's voice sounded strange. Calm. Gravelly.

The bedroom door stood open only a few feet away, letting a bit of a glow into the dark room from a night-light near the hallway bathroom. Joy could make a mad dash, but she'd have to jump over the candles and the game to get to the door. And then what? She'd be out in the strange, empty house with all the worked-up spirits while Raven stayed back and made friends with the nice ones? No thanks.

The glass part of the triangle stopped over a letter.

"M," Raven whispered.

Was it okay to talk out loud? The thing paused for the briefest of moments then slid away, finally resting over the letter *E*.

"Me? Is that what it's saying? What does that mean?" Joy shook her head, blond wisps sticking to her lip gloss. "I'm done. Seriously this time." She stood and reached over Raven's head to twist the switch on the lamp beside the bed, dousing the mood with light.

"For now." Raven licked the thumbs and forefingers of both hands and squeezed the flames, extinguishing them with a sizzle.

"No, for good. I'm not messing with this stuff anymore. It freaks me out." Joy shivered and pulled her bulky sweater tight around her body. Never again. She'd have to find her answers another way. There *had* to be another way. But first she had to figure out what her questions were.

Raven shrugged as she folded the board and slid it under her bed. "There's not a lot you can do about it now. You've had a taste, and you'll want more."

෴

"Hey! Joy's back." Coach Templeton waved from the other side of the volleyball court.

Several players stepped aside as Joy jogged toward her, trying not to inhale the familiar gym aroma so she wouldn't totally lose it. What was it about smells that drove emotions harder than other senses?

"Good to have you back." Heather flipped her long brown ponytail behind her and patted Joy's shoulder as she passed. "Just in time for State next week. We could sure use you."

One foot in front of the other. Keep moving toward Coach. Don't look at anyone, especially Heather. Don't think about the

State Championships. Don't think about anything.

"Yeah. Glad you're here."

Who said that? Joy couldn't turn her head to see. She had to stay focused.

"Right. Me, too."

Joy nodded but kept her eyes on Coach. It was the only way Joy had a prayer of getting through the practice. Who was she kidding? It was the only way she'd get through the next five minutes. She ducked under the net and met Coach midcourt.

"How you holding up, kiddo?"

Way to go right for the jugular. Joy's eyelids were hummingbird wings as she fought back the ever-present tears. "I'm good, I guess. I mean, look at me." She gestured the length of her body. "I'm perfect. But Melanie. . .well, she's another story." The tears rolled down Joy's cheeks. She could do nothing to hold them back.

Coach slipped an arm across Joy's shoulders and steered her toward the gym office. "Go on in and have a seat. I'll be right there." She turned toward the team stretching on the court. "Lauren, time to do your job as the. . .um. . .newly appointed captain. . .so put everyone through some drills. I'll be right out."

Captain. Melanie's position. Mel had loved knowing that the team had thought so highly of her to vote her as captain. Well, why not? She was the best person Joy ever knew. And Melanie felt the same about Joy. They'd sure told each other plenty of times. Until a week ago.

And now Coach had simply handed Melanie's position over to someone else. As if Mel hadn't existed. No matter how deserving a player and teammate Lauren was, she wasn't Melanie. Never would be.

Coach Templeton closed the door, sealing out the sounds of bouncing balls and shoes squeaking on the gymnasium floor.

Noises that reverberated until they blended into one perfect sound called volleyball practice. Would Joy ever love the game again? Could she let herself love anything again?

"So. How are you, really?" Coached perched on the edge of her desk, inches from Joy.

Alone. Dead inside. "I don't know. What you'd expect, I guess." Joy shrugged her shoulders.

"Well. It's only been a week. I know how hard this must be."

Joy nodded. Coach couldn't possibly imagine. Not unless her best friend had committed suicide. Not unless she had been the one to find her dead and then have to break the news to her best friend's parents. No. Probably not. That stuff only happened in Lifetime movies. Or Joy's life.

"Are you seeing anyone?" Coach almost whispered.

Joy recoiled. "You mean dating?" What kind of question was that? Like Joy would ever date again.

Coach shook her head. "No. No. I mean like a counselor."

Joy shrugged. "My parents offered. But I think I'll be okay with the help of my church. I don't need a shrink." Yeah right. . . church. If anyone could help, it would be Raven. If Joy dared go there again.

"God is great, but even He talked about getting counsel from wise people and all that good stuff. You should really consider it." Coach peered into Joy's eyes. "I think you have what's called survivor's guilt. It's normal. But it stinks."

You think? Joy nodded. "I'll talk to my mom about it."

"That's all I ask. Now. You ready to play some V-ball?"

The thought of stepping out onto that court among her friends—Melanie's friends—without her there brought bile surging up Joy's throat. She whipped her head side to side. "I can't. Not yet. Can I try another time?" She searched the room for an escape. Great. One way in, one way out.

"That's fine, kiddo. Baby steps. You'll play next time."
Coach stood. "Do you have a ride home?"

Joy nodded. "I have my car." Her trusty VW Bug followed
her everywhere.

"Come on, I'll walk you out so you don't get a barrage of
questions on your way." Coach slipped her arm across Joy's
shoulders and steered her out the door.

Questions wouldn't be such a big deal, if only there were
answers.

Starting with: *Why?*

🌀

"I see dead people," Joy whispered to her reflection in the
laptop screen. What was the name of that movie? She scanned
the listings Google shot at her. "There it is. *The Sixth Sense*." Joy
shivered at the memory of watching that movie huddled on the
couch. Austin on one side, Melanie on the other.

Maybe she should watch it again, this time for educational
purposes. The little boy in the movie believed dead people only
saw what they wanted to see. . .and he had said something else
interesting. What was it he'd said? Joy snapped her gum and
drummed her fingernails on the desk. Come on, think.

Oh. Right.

They don't know they're dead. Could that be true?

Joy shifted on her bed and pulled her laptop closer.

New search. *Séances*. She'd heard the term, but didn't really
understand. Did people just talk at spirits, or was there two-way
communication? Or more?

Ooh. There was an interesting link. She clicked it.

Having had it drilled into her head to avoid stuff like spirits
and séances, even horoscopes, since she was a little girl, Joy only
wanted to know if they were real. In and out. No dawdling on
the website. She glanced over her shoulder as though someone

watched her every move.

Joy leaned in a little closer to study the images that popped up on the screen. Spirits. Ghosts. Humans sitting around talking to the spirits and ghosts. Come on. That couldn't be real. Did people actually fall for that stuff?

Ouija boards. She opened the page. Yep. That picture was exactly what she played with the other night with Raven. Was it just a game?

A clunky knock sounded at her bedroom door.

"Who is it?" Joy tried to keep the irritation from her voice.

"It's me."

"Bea!" Joy jumped from her bed, almost knocking her computer to the floor. She rushed to the door and threw it open to find her cousin on the other side. She pulled Beatrice into a tight embrace.

"Hi, Joy." Bea spoke in her typical monotone. "It's been so long since I've seen you. Where have you been?"

"I know. I'm sorry I've been. . .um. . .away." Since the funeral. No excuse for the time before that. Joy took her cousin by the hand and pulled her into the room. "But I'm glad you're here now."

"My mom said you're sad. Why?" Bea stuck out her bottom lip.

"Oh. I'll be okay now that you're here. Let's not talk about the sad stuff. Okay?"

Beatrice grinned her lopsided smile. "Good. I don't want to talk about sad things. Want to play UNO?"

More than anything. "Sure. I'll get it set up." Joy reached under her bed and lifted the game.

Beatrice wandered around Joy's room, checking things out before she settled down for a game. Joy smiled as Bea touched her clothes and tinkled her jewelry together. She picked up

Joy's bottle of Daisy perfume, sprayed the air, and then leaned in. She sniffed and wrinkled her nose as the mist tickled her. Beatrice lifted a pair of leather boots. "Can I try these on?"

"Of course." It so didn't matter that she'd stretch them out.

Beatrice slipped off her sneakers by the bed and bent to pull on a boot. She gasped and lifted her arm to point at the computer screen. "What is this?" She stumbled over her words like she did whenever she got upset.

Joy followed Bea's finger where it pointed at the images on Joy's screen. "Oh. That's nothing to worry about." She waved her hand hoping to brush off Bea's fears.

"Those are scary and ugly and not right." She scowled. "God is telling me they're not right."

Hmm. Beatrice was just a little girl in so many ways. Yet she thought she had an in with God that she could know when He was speaking to her?

"It's no big deal. Just research for school. Don't worry about it." Joy dragged her finger across the mouse pad, and then clicked twice to remove the images from the screen. One window closed, and the one behind it popped open to a YouTube video of a séance. No!

Beatrice gasped and pointed. Her hand clamped over her mouth.

"No. No. Don't worry. Look. I'm closing it." Joy shut the laptop.

Beatrice dropped her jaw and shook her head. She backed from Joy's bed toward the door.

"Look, Bea. It's fine. Don't worry. Don't leave." Now what? Maybe Joy could distract Beatrice with food or something.

"That stuff is bad." Beatrice stared at the closed computer.

Did she understand what she'd seen? She couldn't possibly. If she didn't really understand it, then where was her reaction coming from? Even with Down syndrome, Beatrice had always had an uncanny instinct about anything that had to do with Jesus or the bad guy, as she called them.

"How about we just play the game? Okay?" Joy grabbed the stack of cards and separated them into two decks. Come on. Play along, Bea.

Beatrice's eyes brightened. "Yes. But first we have to pray."

"Okay. . .um. . .about what?"

Bea clasped her hands together. She bowed her head and closed her eyes. "Dear Jesus. . ." She opened one eye and looked at Joy. Seeing Joy not in the accepted prayer position, Bea raised her eyebrow and waited.

"Oh. Sorry." Joy lowered her head and waited.

". . .please don't let any bad stuff into this room or into Joy's heart. And help me win UNO. Amen."

Joy fought back a smile. So insightful, yet so innocent. That was her Bea. Joy dealt the cards out between them and set the discard pile right in the middle. Hmm. What if it had been a Ouija board between them? What different scenes the two games created. Night and day—light and dark.

"You first, Joy." Beatrice stuck her tongue out one side of her mouth and clomped down with her teeth. Down to business.

Joy put down a yellow six. All was forgotten. Beatrice simply must have been reacting to the scary pictures and the sound coming from the website. But then why the prayer?

Her innocent cousin arranged her cards like it was the most important task she'd ever accomplish. Joy would bet anything they were lined up red, blue, yellow, then green—some things never changed. Beatrice glanced up and grinned a lopsided smile at Joy.

Joy smiled back. No. Beatrice couldn't possibly know there

was anything spiritually questionable about what Joy had been doing. Could she?

But then again, if Raven could hear from dead people, maybe Beatrice could hear from God.

Chapter 2

W hy don't you go on over to the coffee shop while I go to my Bible study class?" Mom sounded a little too hopeful as they left the sanctuary after making it through the sermon.

Joy grimaced. She'd planned on sitting with Mom in her class where they got serious about the Bible. Joy wouldn't have to talk. And no one would talk to her. Heaven.

Before Dad left for the office that morning, he and Mom stood in the driveway talking. He flung his red tie over his shoulder and leaned in to kiss Mom on the cheek. He'd whispered something in her ear before climbing into his Cherokee, ditching church to go sell houses.

Joy would bet good money that he'd whispered something about getting Joy to have some fun. She got it. They wanted her to relax and let loose a little. It had been awhile; they were right about that. But it wasn't easy. The pressure to strike a balance between being her normal, happy self and simply existing in some altered state of grief consciousness overwhelmed her. Impossible.

The coffee shop. Where the youth group went for *fellowship* during the adult Sunday school hour. A fancy name like fellowship didn't elevate it above hanging out at best, gossip hour at worst. But in better times, Joy loved it. Flashes of herself seated on a stool while her friends stood around her, waiting for her to make them laugh with some witty comment, flew through her brain. Gone just as fast as they'd appeared. That had been some other life. Some other Joy.

But today? The idea of unstructured socializing with random people where she'd be expected to make conversation, smile, even crack a joke now and then, terrified her. She would say something stupid, or worse, nothing at all. The last thing Joy wanted to do was bring everyone else down. Joy, boring? Never. She'd rather disappear than be boring.

"Go on." Mom nudged Joy's arm with her shoulder. "You need to go hang out with your friends, even if only for their sake. They're worried about you and want to spend time with you. They miss—"

Joy put a hand up. "Okay. Okay. I'll go." Anything to stop the whining. Joy took a deep breath and flipped her hair over her shoulder. Might as well get it over with. She walked down the long hallway from the sanctuary, past the kids' classrooms and the nursery, trudged up a ramp, and entered the airy new addition.

Common Grounds coffee shop was more like a giant sunroom with banks of floor-to-ceiling windows and lush greenery. Clusters of tables and chairs surrounded a massive fireplace in the center. A bonfire in the middle of a jungle. Except jungles didn't usually have four-dollar cappuccinos and frappés available made-to-order. At least regular coffee was free on Sundays.

Which reminded her, just before Halloween and Melanie's . . .death, someone from the Common Grounds staff had called in reference to the application Joy had turned in. Making coffee for the business-meeting crowd and stay-at-home moms would have been a good gig once upon a time. But now, the less Joy had to deal with people, the better off they'd all be.

Okay, here goes. Joy stepped through the vestibule and squinted against the sunlight.

"Joy!"

She heard her name several times.

"Awesome! Joy's here," someone called from the far side of the room.

"Ah. Now the fun can start." Tyler winked and patted the chair beside him, near the fireplace.

Perfect. She'd hide out with Tyler. She moved in his direction just as Wendy slipped into the seat. Lovely.

Tyler grimaced and mouthed the word *sorry*.

Knowing Tyler, it was probably true. Joy offered a weak smile and shrugged. No big deal. Whether he knew it or not, he was far better off with Wendy's bubbly cheerleader company than her own. She could join them, but the sight of Wendy giggling and batting her eyelashes at Tyler was way too much syrup for Joy to take.

An arm slid across the back of her shoulders. "Hey you. We sure have missed you around here."

Deena. Joy's tension abated at the human contact. She'd better not let her guard down or she'd be crying in no time.

The spunky youth leader had to stand on tiptoe to squeeze Joy tight. "I'm not going to bug you, but I'm here if you want to talk. Always." As if sensing Joy's wavering grasp on her emotions, Deena dropped her arm and patted Joy's hand.

Joy nodded, blinking away the sting in her eyes. "Thanks."

Deena held Joy's gaze with her deep brown eyes then flashed a bright smile. "You can do this." She winked and moved off to mingle.

Joy peeled her stare away. She needed a distraction. Food. Was she even hungry? It was so hard to tell these days. Blueberry or cranberry-orange muffins, her fave, or yogurt?

She paused and asked her stomach which she could handle. It responded with a churning gurgle. Yeah, food was not going to happen. Joy poured herself a cup of black coffee then added two packs of sugar and a dollop of cream. She blew on steam rising from the scalding brew as she searched for a place to sit down.

Kelsey lifted herself a few inches from her chair on the other side of the fireplace and waved, her auburn curls bouncing in front of her shoulders. "Over here, Joy. Sit with us."

That would work. Kelsey Martin. The least likely to meddle. Joy should spend more time with her. She approached the table, careful to keep her eyes averted from the other clusters so she couldn't be roped into a conversation as she passed.

Who were those new girls with Kels? The pretty black girl looked familiar, but she wasn't from school. And the freckled, tall girl—Joy had never seen her before. Joy slid into the empty seat and rested her forearms on the round bistro table, her coffee cup between her hands. She gave an effort at a smile. *Act natural.* "Who are your guests?"

"These are two friends from my school. They came to church with me today. This is Alicia and Paula."

Joy nodded at the tall girl, Paula, then at Crystal. "Nice to meet you guys." Wasn't too often new people showed up. Especially not from the private school.

"You'll love Joy. She's our resident sunshine. The life of the party. She always has good ideas, and we're never bored when Joy's around." Kelsey grinned.

Next she'll break out in a rousing rendition of "You Are My Sunshine."

Kelsey held up her fist for an oddly timed knuckle bump.

Okay. Joy returned the bump. Slightly awkward.

"We missed you at youth group this week. It's just not the same without our Joy."

Little did Kelsey know, it never would be the same again.

New subject. Joy cleared her throat. "So, can I ask you guys a question?" They'd probably think she was crazy, but she had to know. "Have any of you ever used a Ouija board?"

Kelsey's eyebrows shot up. "Oh, gross! No way."

Paula shook her head. "Not me."

Crystal nodded. "Oh yeah. Where I come from, people do that kind of stuff all the time. I'm from New Orleans, you know."

Paula gawked at Crystal. "What? I never knew this. You mean you personally have actually used a Ouija board?"

Joy got the sense that Paula would inch her chair away from Crystal if it wouldn't be so obvious.

"Oh sure, I have tons of times." Crystal shrugged. "I don't know where they are, or if we even brought them when we moved, but we used to have three or four in the house."

"How did I not know that? We've been friends this whole time since you moved here a year ago, and I didn't know you messed around with that stuff." Paula shook her head.

"What's the big deal, anyway?" Crystal sipped on her coffee.

Yeah. Joy could use an answer to that one.

"It's just scary, is all." Paula shuddered. "I've heard too many stories of people who start messing around with stuff like that— there's no turning back."

"So you don't believe it's real?" Kelsey arched a single eyebrow at Crystal.

How did she do that? Joy tried to lift only one with zero luck. Oh well, talentless eyebrows weren't such a big deal.

Crystal shook her head. "Oh no. I know it's real. Otherwise why do it?"

Exactly.

"What about you?" Kelsey turned to Joy.

"Me?" She'd done a decent job of deflecting to that point,

but now all eyes were glued to her. "Well, I think it can be real. I think any of that stuff is if you really believe."

Crystal nodded. "Yeah. You know, Louisiana black folk are kind of known for spiritual stuff like voodoo and fortune-tellers and all that. So it's never seemed like a big deal to me. I just think I know the power behind it. You just have to respect the power. Then you're fine."

"I think just like anything, it's what you do with it." Joy shrugged.

"Why did you bring this up today, first thing, like that? Did something happen?" Kelsey squinted at Joy. "Is this about Melanie?"

Joy winced. Hearing her best friend's name was like taking a bullet. "No. Nothing about. . .her."

"Then why?"

Joy needed to be careful how she answered. No sense stirring Kelsey up. "I don't know. I was reading about it in a book the other day and just wondered. I didn't know anybody who'd ever done it."

"Not me. Not ever." Kelsey shook her head, whipping those chestnut tendrils across her face. "I definitely think it's not something you should mess with. *Ever.*"

Joy smirked. *Why don't you tell us how you really feel, Kels?*

Crystal shrugged. "If you feel that way, then you definitely shouldn't."

"It's just. . .well, if it's a real thing, then it's part of our human reality, right? And if it's *not* real, then who cares if somebody messes with it?" Joy held Kelsey's gaze. "Do you see what I'm saying? If it's nothing more than a toy, then it's harmless. If it is an authentic tool to contact spirits, wouldn't you want to know?"

⑨

Joy had promised herself she'd never look through the memory coffin again. She'd lasted five days. Three whole days longer than last time. At least it was progress. But she couldn't resist any longer. Being at church had pushed her over the edge.

She pulled the blue plastic bin down from her closet shelf and kicked aside her large-animal biology books to make room on the floor. She popped open the latches on the sides and lifted the lid.

Deep breath.

Right on top where she'd carefully placed it after her last dose of her painful past lay his OHS basketball sweatshirt. Joy lifted it to her face and drank in the scent of Austin's favorite cologne. Eternity for Men. Fitting name.

What would she do when the shirt lost its smell? Well, hopefully by then she'd be able to keep her promise and leave the box unvisited.

Joy folded the sweatshirt into a puffy square and set it beside her on the area rug in the center of her bedroom. Next in the box was her movie stub key ring. She smiled as she thumbed through the dog-eared paper squares. The ticket from every single movie she and Austin had ever seen together since they were little. Nifty little hole punched in the right corner, slid onto the key ring, and she had her memento extraordinaire. How many times had she counted those tabs? One hundred eleven stubs spun around that key ring, representing hundreds of childhood outings that later became special dates. They'd provided her dozens of movie quotes to pepper her conversations and added up to two hundred plus hours of her life she'd given to Austin and could never get back.

She lifted out the wrist corsage Austin had bought her to wear to homecoming last year—now wilted and crushed. Like her heart. She'd looked so pretty in her eggplant chiffon bridesmaid's dress from her cousin Stacey's wedding earlier that year, a neat contrast to his dark suit. This year would've been their junior prom. Would've been.

She reached back into the box for the magazine cutouts of the prom dresses Joy had dreamed of wearing as she clung to Austin's arm. They had fantasized about being prom king and queen. Could have been a real possibility. But not anymore.

Nor would she need the stacks of wedding dress pictures she'd cut from *Bride* magazine in secret. She hadn't admitted even to Melanie that she daydreamed about marrying Austin and had every single detail of her future wedding recorded in her purple notebook. Where was that journal?

Joy shifted some trinkets and papers around in the box. Ah. There it was, stuffed full of notes, business cards, wedding pictures she liked and hoped to replicate with Austin. And. . .on the very back page. . .Joy had written her vows. She flipped to the end of the book.

I, Joy Christianson, promise to love you and laugh with you all the days of my life. I promise to honor you and uphold you as my husband. I give you my heart. I give you my life. I give you my joy.

Yeah. Loving and losing was way worse than never loving at all. Whoever had said the opposite had obviously never been betrayed. Joy put it all back in the box, secured the lid, and then made another promise. At least seven days this time.

That's it. She needed answers. Joy grabbed her keys and texted Raven:

You home?

Chapter 3

Joy sat on a pillow in the center of Raven's candle-lit bedroom. A spicy aroma from the burning incense filled Joy's nostrils. Why had she agreed to do this again? *Never* had only lasted three days. But sometimes the quest for knowledge beat out wisdom. "Um. What, exactly, do we hope happens here tonight?"

Lucas plopped down to the ground, crossed his skinny legs, and gave his signature grin—the same sneer he'd had since he moved to their sleepy Nebraska town of Ogallala in the middle of Joy's second-grade year at Progress Elementary. The big city had been evident in everything Lucas did and said—still was, actually. He'd never quite figured out how to fit in among the Ogallala natives. Or maybe he never tried.

Luc cupped his hand over the incense as though to capture its essence. Or was he simply warming his hands? Maybe Joy was taking her creeped-out qualms a little too far.

Laying his hands on his knees, Lucas closed his eyes, every movement he made was a measured step. "We are reaching out to the spirit who tried to talk to you two the other night." His voice droned in monotone. "It has something to say, so we're going to listen." He shrugged like it was the most natural thing.

A chill ran down Joy's spine like someone hammered a scale on a xylophone.

He opened the Ouija board and placed it in the center of their human triangle. The glass piece in place, he settled his hands in position and waited, peering from behind a wall of black, greasy bangs.

Raven reached her fingers to the board and laid them beside Luc's then scooted one hand a bit more until it barely touched his pinkie.

Joy cracked her knuckles and settled her hands in place. *Just get it over with.*

"Spirit friend, we know you're here with us, and we believe you'd like to talk to us." Luc's voice held no emotion, not even a single inflection. "We'd like to know who you are. Will you please tell us?"

The candle flame danced in his eyes. If he started chanting, Joy was out of there.

She felt movement as her arm was pulled along the board until the glass stopped over a letter. It couldn't be real. But it *felt* real.

M

Here we go again. Joy lifted some of the weight off her fingertips. She sure didn't want to be the cause of where the planchette moved. She glanced at Raven who stared at Lucas, as usual. When he was around, no one else existed. Not even a dead person. Joy's stomach churned. Never again would she care about a boy that much. Ever. Even if it meant not having a marriage like Mom and Dad. She'd rather be alone her whole life than risk the possibility of losing someone again.

Lucas cleared his throat. "Do you feel that?" He spoke in even tones and looked at Raven. "There's, like, a low rumble, a hum maybe, in the room."

Yeah. Probably the furnace, you idiot.

"I do feel it." Raven closed her eyes and lifted her face.

Oh please. What did she want? A ghostly kiss on the cheek?

In better times, Joy would have giggled at the thought of playing a trick on her. But not today. . .maybe never. Just too much effort.

The triangle continued its path on the board. Why hadn't she stayed home? That would have been so much smarter than her chosen alternative. She'd leave if her legs weren't superglued to the floor.

E

"See, Luc? That's what it said last time. *Me*. What is it trying to tell us?"

"Shh." Lucas shook his head. "It's not finished yet." He closed his eyes. "Are you still identifying yourself to us?"

With force Joy hadn't been expecting, the glass eye slid to the *Yes*.

What had just happened? It sure felt spontaneous. . . . It had to be Lucas or Raven making that thing move. It had to be. But it just didn't seem like it. Joy's eyes flew open, and she searched her friends for a clue to the truth.

Raven chewed on her lower lip. Was *she* nervous? Joy had kind of counted on her being the strong one.

"Okay. It's getting irritated. Feels interrupted." Lucas sat up straighter. "We're listening, spirit. Tell us who you are."

Back to the normal speed of death, their hands eased along until they revealed another letter.

L

What if it was actually real? Pastor Joel talked about the spirit world sometimes. It made sense that if God existed like she'd always believed, the dark side would, too. Joy watched in fascination as her hands were drawn to the next letter.

A

It paused for only a few seconds and dropped to the letter below.

N

Wait just a second. Was this some kind of sick joke? Joy looked from Raven to Lucas. Were they in on this together? How undeniably cruel to make that thing spell out. . . "Come on—"

"Shh," Lucas hissed, his eyes trained on the space above his gnawed fingernails.

I

Joy would never speak to them again. Simple as that. But then why didn't she just leave? Why let them finish out their ruse at her expense?

Lucas nodded at Raven and lifted his hands. He reached across the table and lifted Joy's fingers as Raven removed hers. Game over?

The planchette trembled and inched forward.

All. By. Itself.

Acid churned in the pit of Joy's stomach. Everything she ever believed about life, death, God, and heaven crumbled into purgatory as a game claimed her faith.

E

ⓢ

"I'm going to throw up." Joy scrambled through Raven's bedroom door and dove for the toilet in the hallway bathroom. Holding her hair back, she waited for the contents of her stomach to make a reappearance. It tried to empty, heave after heave. Guess it would have to have something in it before it could expel anything. Had Joy really not eaten all day long? Come to think of it, had she even had a drop to drink? Her cracked lips screamed that she hadn't. A shrink would say she was trying to kill herself.

Was she trying to follow in her best friend's footsteps?

She sat back against the bathtub, the cool porcelain

soothing her skin through her T-shirt. Her head thundered like a parade marched through.

"You okay?" Raven's muffled voice called out from the bedroom.

Took her long enough to bother asking. Joy's entire life, or whatever was left of it, had just been turned upside down, and Raven casually checked on her after an entire ten minutes had gone by? From the other room? Yeah, real concerned. She was probably in there making out with her boyfriend. Melanie would have been in the bathroom at Joy's side the whole time she was sick, holding up her hair and pressing a cool cloth to her forehead. That's what best friends did.

Wait a minute. Joy's head whipped from side to side. Was Melanie there with her? Had she been by her side ever since. . .since her death? Maybe she'd listened to all of Joy's conversations, counted the tears that fell, watched her sleep. Could Joy talk to Mel—like actually converse with her? Joy shook her head. Too much.

Placing her palms on the side of the tub behind her, Joy forced her body to unfold from its crouch. Her knees wobbled as she shuffled to the sink then flipped on the faucet. She let the cool water run between her fingers and over her wrists for at least a full minute. Leaning over the basin, she splashed some water on her face and let it drip off, stripping dried tears with it. Yanking a black, rose-embroidered towel from the hook beside the mirror, she pressed it into her eyes.

"Joy? You okay in there?" Raven's voice came through the door a little louder than the first time.

Hadn't Joy answered her? "Yeah. I'll just be a minute." Joy blotted her face dry, hung the hand towel back on its hook, then made her way back to the bedroom. Act casual. *Never let them see you sweat.*

Lucas lay kicked back on the bed, his size-twelve Vans rumpling the covers.

Raven sat cross-legged on the floor with her eyes squeezed shut. Candle flames still flickered in the circle around her.

What was that smell? A floral note mingled with scrambled eggs. . .or more like rotten eggs. Joy opened her mouth to ask Raven, but the scent was gone as quickly as it had appeared. Probably just her imagination. Looked like she really was losing it after all.

"You okay, Joy?" Raven's eyelids fluttered but didn't open.

Um. . .seriously? Joy stood rooted in position. She didn't know what to do, who to talk to, how to recover. How could she possibly be okay? Didn't they get it at all? "I have to know. Did all of that really happen? For real?"

Raven opened her eyes and held Joy's gaze. "Yes. That actually happened. For real." She smiled softly, like it was no big deal. Like a parent soothing a child afraid of clowns at a circus. This was far more serious than that.

"You're telling me that I just heard from my dead best friend?" Joy shot her glance from Raven to Lucas. "From beyond the grave?"

Lucas bobbed his head a single time. "Yes." He rolled onto his side, balled the pillow under his cheek, and yawned.

One fog lifted and another settled as a shiver ran from the top of Joy's head through the ends of her toes. No matter what, she couldn't let anything like this happen again. Joy had seen the movies. She knew what became of people like her who messed with this stuff. It never ended well. "Okay, I'm out of here. I can't handle this. Not that I even believe it."

Raven peered through her thick lashes, her eyes laced with something that looked like compassion. "You believe it. I can tell you do. You wouldn't be so terrified if you thought it was all fake."

Raven had her there. Joy shrugged. "Fine, but I'm out. I don't believe in this stuff—I mean, I guess I know it happened. But I can't embrace it. . . . It's not. . . I don't think it's right. It's not like, God's plan."

Eyebrow cocked, Raven waited.

The instant they'd left her lips, Joy's words had sounded absurd even to her. God's plan? What of the past couple of weeks was His doing? At the funeral the pastor had said nothing happens that doesn't pass through God's hand first. Well, if that were true. . .if He could have stopped Melanie from taking those pills, but didn't. . . . Unthinkable. Was that the kind of God she wanted to follow?

And on top of it all, now Joy had to deal with the fact her dead best friend could speak to her from the other side. If it had actually happened, then what did it all say about heaven and the afterlife? About everything she'd ever believed in? About her own eternal fate?

Too many questions. Not a single answer.

"I have to go." Joy scooped her purse, keys, and cell phone from Raven's bed then jerked the arm of her hoodie from under Lucas's sleeping body.

He twitched and let out a snore.

Raven opened the door for Joy then grabbed her wrist until Joy looked her in the eyes. "Don't worry about anything. I know this is tough to accept, but we can help you through it. Luc and I." Raven stretched an arm across the bed and shook Lucas's body. "Right, babe?"

He grunted what might have been interpreted as an agreement of some kind. Whatever. Not feeling all that reassured.

Raven reached out and patted Joy's back. "You have some

thinking to do first, then when you're ready, we'll teach you. There's no hurry. We're not going anywhere."

That's what Joy was afraid of.

Chapter 4

People didn't usually cut homeroom—why would they? No lectures. No assignments. No homework.

Well, most people didn't share their homeroom periods with Austin. Besides, there was a first time for everything. And after last night, Joy couldn't take sitting in that classroom for one minute. Joy pulled the hood of her black, threadbare hoodie over her head, stepped out of the stream of students, and ducked into the locker room. Thankfully, Mr. Cavanaugh never took attendance. If Joy skipped class and arrived at practice early, she could be dressed and on the court stretching before everyone showed up.

She spun the dial on her combination, settling on the familiar numbers she used for every pin number, password, and lock combination: Melanie's birthday. Which was coming up. What would Joy do on that day? The two of them had never spent a birthday apart since. . .well, for as long as Joy could remember.

She slipped on her spandex shorts and pulled her once-beloved black Indians hoodie over her head. It no longer seemed a badge of honor to wear her school colors. Now it was a sentence of doom that meant she was tied to that place for almost two more years.

Joy exhaled and slammed her locker door. The sharp crash

reverberated off the empty shower walls.

Time to get sweaty and out of breath before anyone else showed up with the prying looks and chatty questions. Joy jogged out to the court and started right in on jumping jacks to warm up her body before stretching.

Would Joy's efforts really keep her teammates from hounding her for info and staring into her eyes to see if she was losing it? Of course not. But it was something, at least. Way better than walking in past them all as they fired question missiles at her. Joy shuddered. No thanks.

How are you doing? How do you think?

What was it like? Death.

Do you have to catch up on all your homework? Was that a serious question?

What did the note say? Joy had to bite her tongue when someone asked her that. If she answered what she'd like to have answered. . .well. . .she'd have regretted it.

Heather appeared in the doorway, flashing her Zoom-whitened, glow-in-the-dark teeth for the world to see. Not that they could miss them. "Joy. Joy." Heather squealed and bounced across the room like a wet-nosed puppy. Except puppies were genuine in their affection.

"Hi, Heather." Joy panted. More than she needed to. Anything to prolong the arrival of the private moment they were about to have. Joy could feel it coming.

"So, Joy. I'm glad we have a minute or two alone before everyone else shows up." Heather bit on the white tip of her acrylic nail.

Oh boy. Me, too.

Heather grasped Joy's forearm. "Can you just tell me. . . How are you? Really?"

Sigh. People were clueless. "I'm fine, thanks." What did

she want to hear? Did she want Joy to admit she was falling apart? That she feared life as she knew it was over? That she was terrified of who she was becoming inside? Angry. Bitter. Sad.

"Well, I hope you're not just being brave. I sure don't want to arrive to the same scene in the locker room that you found at Mel's house that day."

Gravity defied Joy's chin. Had Heather really just said that? One thing Joy had learned in the past weeks is that some people had no class. And it was so much worse than she could have ever expected. She'd been so naive to think people cared about her, had her best interests at heart. She'd lived with that assumption for far too long. It was time for her to wake up and face reality.

Heather bent down, yanked up her kneesocks, and wriggled a kneepad into place. She bounced a few times then pulled on the other one. "What was it like, anyway?" Heather's eager eyes searched Joy's for info.

"What was *what* like?" Please don't be referring to finding Melanie dead. Please.

She glanced at Joy and raised her eyebrows.

Joy clamped her mouth shut and swallowed hard. "Heather. I don't know how to answer you." She spoke through gritted teeth. "Think about what you're asking."

"You're right. That was pretty rude. I'm sorry." She tucked a stray wisp behind her ears and did a perfect spike approach to the net, her feet squeaking on the polished gymnasium floor when she landed.

Yeah. She sure seemed sorry. But at least Heather was gone. For now. How could people not realize that Joy's horror wasn't fodder for their curiosity? Would she have been so insensitive if she were on the outside looking in? No way. In fact, there was a time Joy would have gone the opposite way. She'd have put her own feelings of curiosity, grief, anger, whatever, aside just to make other people feel more comfortable. No more. They didn't care about her; she didn't have to waste her time and energy on them.

Mom said the girls weren't curious as much as concerned. Suicide rocked a small town way more than drugs, sex, or any other stupid thing a teenager could do. They might even be worried that Joy would be next. The investigator had whispered that it was contagious, warned Mom and Dad to be on the lookout. Yeah right. If only Joy had the guts.

Wonder where they'd rank communicating with the dead compared to suicide. Joy smirked. They'd never believe her is what would happen. They'd lock her up in a straitjacket and slap a suicide watch label on her forehead.

Did they still perform electric shock treatments on people?

"Joy?"

She whipped around at the sound of Coach's voice calling from the doorway to her office.

"Can I talk to you for a minute?" She stood back, obviously expecting Joy to join her.

No? If only Coach could have let Joy slip under the radar, let her ease back in. She jogged across the gym, past the huddled groups of volleyball players, silencing whispers with every step. She ducked under the net and followed the scent trail of Coach's coconut lime verbena lotion into the office.

Act natural. "What's up?" Don't crumble. Joy leaned against the doorframe. She needed to look like she was ready to be out among people rather than strapped to a chair in the nut house.

Coach's eyes widened. She dropped her pen and leaned back in her chair. "You seem a lot better today than you did last week. Did you get some rest over the weekend?" She looked so hopeful, so proud.

Yeah. Not exactly. Joy could never tell Coach the truth about what'd been going on. "I'm good. Anxious to play." Joy held her gaze.

Coach tipped her head and narrowed her eyes. "Just don't push yourself, okay?"

Joy nodded. "I won't."

"All right. Get on out there. Let's have a practice." Coach stopped at the mirror on the wall beside her door and used a comb to perk up her blond spikes.

Joy jogged out to the back row of the far court and stretched her shoulders as Coach arrived at midcourt.

"Okay. Okay girls." She clapped her hands a few times. "Let's settle down and get this practice started. We only have a couple more before State. This is it." She glanced at her clipboard. "Go ahead and divide up for scrimmage. You know what to do."

Joy took her position as outside hitter in the back row. She wiped the tops of her shoes on her kneesocks and stood ready, waiting for the other side to serve the ball. Heather had the serve. She tossed it into the air and swung at it, making perfect contact with a solid thud. It sailed right over the net and dropped. Karen set the ball with the tips of her fingers, then Cameron bumped it to Joy. Joy leaped into the air and pounded the ball right at the apex of her jump. It whistled over the net and landed in the hole. A solid kill.

A cheer rose up from the stands at her right. Joy turned, expecting to see Melanie there cheering her on, but of course it was Lauren clapping and jumping in celebration of Joy's spike. That sequence had played out like an instruction video for volleyball students. Don't look at Coach. Don't let the team see excitement. They didn't need to know Joy had been concerned she might have lost her edge. Hmm. Maybe she'd gained an edge she hadn't even known possible. Rage might do that.

The serve sailed over Joy's side of the net and was volleyed back. The setter did her job, and Joy went in for another kill.

Beautiful. She was back.

Lauren jogged to Joy with her hand up in the air. "Nice one."

Joy slapped it and laughed.

"Feels good to be back, huh?" Lauren grinned.

"Yeah it d—" Wait a second. How could Joy be there having fun, laughing and talking to the new team captain, when Melanie was dead? How could she have allowed herself to forget? Even for a moment? She shut down the light in her eyes, closed her mouth, and turned away from Lauren's toothy grin. "Let's just play."

She'd play well—for the team's sake—but Joy wasn't going to forget again. She owed it to Melanie.

"Good practice, girls." Coach glanced down the list on her clipboard after the trial match ended. She flipped the page and nodded. "We've covered everything we need to about the State competition. You all know how vital your rest and nutrition is over the next couple of days. Let's be diligent so you're all ready for the meet on Thursday. Good sleep every night until then, you guys. Promise?"

Coach's eyes roved the group, locking with Heather and Lauren. Then Joy.

Joy nodded. She had every intention of crashing hard in her bed that night after she got back from hanging with Raven. In fact, it would be a bonus if she never woke up.

Chapter 5

"Hey sweetheart. You home?" Mom's normally singsongy voice held even more cheer than it usually did.

Mom was home? She and Dad usually had showings somewhere between Ogallala and North Platte on Monday nights. Or they spent the evening out working on their rehab project at the lake. Not that she was disappointed exactly. . .but. . .

Joy bent to pull her snow boots off and shook the November winter from her coat. Act natural. The computer and another Google search about the spirit world were only minutes away. "Yeah. It's me. What's up?"

A head poked around the corner. Mom raised her hand to her mouth and jerked her head toward the room behind her, blond, permed curls bouncing to her shoulders. "You. . .um. . . have a visitor." She spun and retreated back to the kitchen where the mystery person waited.

Mom's whisper had sounded too strained for comfort. Who could it be? Joy strode across the foyer and around the corner, stopping beside the refrigerator so she could peer into the breakfast nook without being seen. Mom faced Joy from the other side of the dining table, the guest's back was ramrod straight in front of Joy. But even from behind, she knew who it was. Those sandy waves. That heart-shaped mole on the back of his neck that he hated, but Joy had loved. His broad swimmer's back and long arms.

Arms crossed on her chest, Joy glared over his head at her mom. He shouldn't be there.

Mom shrugged and mouthed the word *sorry*.

Joy exhaled. "What are you doing here, Austin?"

His shoulders stiffened.

What had he expected? Joy wasn't going to open her arms and welcome him back or offer *him* comfort. Not after what he'd done to her. To them all. He deserved to suffer.

Mom looked at Austin, her eyes heavy with. . .what was that? Anger? Disgust? No. . .it was pity that flecked her blue eyes with gray. Figured. Mom stepped around Austin's chair, squeezing his shoulder as she passed. She moved through the kitchen and the same hand reached for Joy's and pulled her close. "Go easy. He's hurting, too," Mom whispered, her hot breath tickling Joy's ear.

For the entire year since Joy had started dating Austin, Mom had either complained that they were too serious or that they were spending too much time together. Every single day she said she wished they'd go back to the innocent, childhood friendship they'd enjoyed for ten years. Now she wanted Joy to show him sympathy and give him a chance? Mom should just stay out of it. Go back to her home renovation shows and fixer-upper magazines. Stop trying to repair what couldn't be mended.

Joy watched as Mom tiptoed toward the family room in silence and then continued on to her bedroom. Probably to pray. *Keep praying, Mom.* It would either work, or it wouldn't. Only time would tell.

Austin cleared his throat. "What can I do, Joy?"

He didn't face her. Not that she blamed him. After all, how could he?

Too weary to think, Joy rubbed her temples. "What can you do? You can erase the past month—or however long it's been since you and Mel first—." Not that Joy wanted to know. What if it had been many months? Or longer? "You know what? You can go back to being honest and good."

Austin's shoulders slumped lower with each suggestion.

"You can keep your promises." Joy took a shuddering breath. "Oh, no, wait. It's quite evident you can't."

Joy waited. Austin said nothing. He wanted more? She had plenty.

"You can go back in time and leave Melanie alone from the start. Better yet, you can just trade places with her now."

He flinched. "You don't mean that."

Oh? Want to bet? "Look. This is too much. Just leave."

Austin didn't move.

Okay. Fine. Joy had no energy to fight with him. Someone had to leave the room. If he wouldn't, she would. Flinging her hair over her shoulder, Joy huffed from the kitchen. It wouldn't be the first time Austin had sat by himself at her kitchen table. Hopefully he would see himself out and make it the last time.

If only she could get from the kitchen to her room without walking The Path. The journey to the safety of her bedroom was strewn with memories. The zillion times she and Melanie sprawled on the family room floor watching their favorite chick flicks and old classics over and over as they recited the lines. The hours and hours of late-night giggling and talking about boys. The junk food, especially Nutella Puppy Chow—their own concoction.

Oh, then there were the times she and Austin sat on the floor in front of the fireplace playing chess. He always won. Sometimes the victory was even deserved. And on the window seat across the room, where they'd shared their first kiss. And many more after that one.

Memories. Blinking didn't blot them out. Maybe more tears would wash them away.

But no amount of tears would wash away the moment she stepped from the bathroom, toweling her hair dry to find Austin and Melanie lip-locked in an embrace. She could still see the carpet imprint of their toes facing each other. Touching. Or maybe her mind was just playing tricks on her. Surely Mom had vacuumed since then.

Hurry. Joy felt ghosts nipping at her back as she scurried down the hallway. Finally safe in her bedroom, she closed the door and leaned against it as though holding back the crowds that wanted to press in. Wanting to invade her consciousness with more regret.

Why hadn't she just let go of Austin in that instant? Melanie could have had him if that's what it would have taken. If they were in love, Joy would have stepped aside. She was prepared to, once she'd thought it through. They didn't have to sneak around. The cost of betrayal had been too great. Too final. But would she have realized that then? Or would she still have raged against them?

What's done can't always be undone.

Well, look at that. Even holding the bedroom door closed with all of her weight did nothing to keep her pain from following her inside. Joy slid to the floor and wrapped her arms around her legs. What was she going to do? What could she do? She couldn't outrun the past. Eventually she'd have to face it.

Maybe that's where Raven would come in.

Speaking of Raven. . . Joy sloughed off the weight of the past and crawled across her shaggy area rug to the desk near the window. Slipping onto the pink-and-purple polka dotted chair pad, Joy tapped the touch pad, bringing her hand-me-down

HP laptop to life and went directly to Google.

Is it possible to talk to dead people?

Joy chewed on her thumbnail while the search engine churned out its results. A flake of pink polish chipped onto her tongue. She spit it over her right shoulder.

Over one hundred million results. Well, she could start with the first one. "How to talk to the dead." Nah. She didn't need a play-by-play after what she'd experienced.

Was it real? That's all she wanted to know. Because it sure seemed real.

Reading down the list of search results, Joy found that countless others had the same question. Click after click, she discovered that for as many people that asked the questions, three had a different answer, and everyone thought they were right. Hah. Sounded exactly like every other religion that existed. A bunch of beliefs backed up by nothing but opinion and emotion.

Except this time Joy had some proof. She'd seen it with her own eyes, yet she was having such a hard time believing.

Joy rocked back in her chair. What made this facet of the spirit world so difficult to accept? The Bible said there were all sorts of spirits. But it also said it was bad to consult any other than God. But what if *that* were wrong? The Bible had been written by people. What if they just didn't get how it all worked?

Is it dangerous to reach out to the dead?

Things like Occultism, Satanism, Wiccans, and other scary words popped up before Joy's eyes like the ticker tapes on Times Square. But none of that had anything to do with what she and Raven had been doing. At all. Joy wasn't following Satan. She had simply seen her friend's name spelled out from the beyond. Had Melanie reached out to her, or was it someone or some*thing* else? Had she sort of communicated with her best friend somehow? That couldn't be wrong. Not on any level.

Maybe it wasn't wrong at all. Maybe Joy had finally found something right for a change.

A knock jerked Joy from her thoughts. Mom cracked the door open and stuck her perfectly coiffed head into the room. "We're leaving, honey. Dad and I will be back in a few hours. This dinner shouldn't take too long."

Joy nodded. "I'll be fine."

The door clicked shut. Hmm. Mom and Dad off partying with the Realtors of America, or whatever it was called, meant she had the house to herself. Perfect. Joy scrolled through Netflix and selected three movies. She'd watch them all. It was time to find out if Hollywood depicted the supposed dark side the way she'd been experiencing it to really be.

Joy stuck a bag of popcorn into the microwave and poured a huge Coke while she waited. When the timer dinged, she reached in and pinched the corner of the bag, shaking it to spread the salt and butter evenly. She pulled on the seams to open the bag, careful to keep her face out of the steam. After dumping the whole thing into a red plastic bowl, she was ready.

Here goes nothing. Joy pressed PLAY on the first movie and settled down on the couch with her blanket and a pillow. She lifted a few pieces of popcorn to her mouth.

Hmm. The actors—if she could call them that—recorded supposed spirit activity while they slept. First of all, if that were real, why did they stay in the house? Secondly, why couldn't the guy get the woman to listen to him? One good conversation, a letter, a recording, something would have gotten her attention.

Yeah. That one had to be totally fake.

On to movie number two. A classic, the reviews had said. She munched on the popcorn. Okay, this one was pure

Hollywood entertainment—vomit, heads spinning in circles, bodies thrown against the ceiling. Really funny stuff.

Bang!

Joy squealed and slid to the floor, popcorn flying everywhere. What was that noise? She flew to her feet and spun in a full circle, searching for the source. She tiptoed toward the kitchen. Ridiculous because if someone, or something, were in there, it already knew she was in the house.

Oh. Her heart slowed, and she tried to rein in her breathing. Oreo lay in a heap on the floor by the refrigerator. The ancient cat must have climbed onto the counter and fell off again. The only cat on earth that never landed on her feet.

Joy strode to the kitchen and scooped her up. "You okay, Oreo?" She soothed the trembling kitty as she surveyed the room.

Well, so much for Hollywood entertainment. She wasn't quite as brave as she'd thought, obviously.

Didn't matter. It would have taken a crazy person to laugh off a bang like that. She hadn't completely lost her sense of reality. Yet.

Chapter 6

"It's Tuesday. You in for hanging out at the park tonight?" Raven sidled up next to Joy in the lunch line.

"I don't know about that." Joy glanced down at Raven's tray. "You seriously going to eat all of that?" Hamburger, fries, apple, and a candy bar? "Where do you put it?"

"I was going to ask you the same thing." Raven rolled her eyes at Joy's side salad and water.

"I'm not really hungry." Joy shrugged. She probably wouldn't even eat the salad. Everything sat like lead in the pit of her stomach. The more she faced the possibility that Melanie actually reached out to her from the great beyond, the more she didn't like it and the more difficulty she had doing normal things. Like eating. Why couldn't she go back to just before it happened? To the time when Joy just believed. Before she'd felt the need to put everything under a microscope. Or even better, to the moments before Melanie's death. . .or before the kiss.

Raven nodded and swung her leg over the bench and set her tray down. "I get it. But take it from a girl who's had her share of parental intervention"—she did air quotes with her fingers— " 'for my own good.' You don't want to raise any red flags."

Joy slid her tray onto an empty table. With Melanie gone, she hadn't cared where she ate every day. Or if she ever ate at all. "Red flags?"

"The more weight you lose, the more sunken your eyes get, the more strange stuff you do—you'll make everyone nervous. When parental-types get nervous, they come at you with doctor visits, counseling, medication even. Trust me. Life is much better when they leave you alone."

Oh right. Joy had forgotten that about Raven. "You had to go away to that place freshman year. Where did you go?"

Raven nodded, her mouth full. "Yeah. Colorado. Diamond Estates. 'Where the finest gems are pulled from the deepest rough.' " She rolled her eyes.

"What was that about?"

"Oh, you know. I raised too many red flags. Dad got a little nervous and sent me away to find God." Raven shrugged. "At least that had been the plan."

"What happened?" Joy poked at her salad.

"I got into some trouble over there. Was asked to either make a commitment or move out. I picked move out." Raven jabbed a ketchup-laden french fry at Joy. "That's why I said what I did about avoiding parental intervention. It can get pretty intense."

Raven made a lot of sense. Joy wanted to fly under the radar and get through as best and as privately as she could. "Point taken." She snatched Raven's candy bar, ripped the wrapper off, and shoved half of it in her mouth.

"Hey! That was uncalled for." Raven's eyes sparkled as she laughed.

"Just following orders." Joy bit off another hunk.

"You learn well, young student."

Joy laughed. "Very funny."

"So anyway, back to the point. Tonight? We on?"

Joy wondered what Raven had in mind. Not that it mattered anymore. "Sure. It'll have to be somewhat early though. Coach gave us a big lecture yesterday. Made us promise to get lots of sleep this week."

Raven made a talky hand in the air. "Blah, blah. Fine. Whatever. Meet me at the lake at six o'clock sharp. We'll hang out. I'll invite some people."

"It'll have to be six thirty for me. Practice doesn't get out until six." Joy forked a hunk of lettuce into her mouth.

"That's fine."

"Just no funny business, okay?" Hanging out didn't always have to mean some great big spiritual awakening.

Raven laughed. "What are you, thirty years old? What do you mean, 'Funny business'?"

"You know exactly what I mean." Joy sighed. "Let's just keep tonight's guest list to the living."

ᔕ

Joy flopped in her bed, the covers tangling around her feet. So much for a good night's sleep. She would drift off if she could only manage to turn off her mind. But if she slept, she'd dream. If she dreamed, she'd remember.

Still, her body ached for rest. That hollow feeling in the pit of her stomach warned she was running on fumes. She needed to shut out the day. Raven had been cool that night. Nothing scary or weird. That's what Joy wanted, right? Then why did she feel so empty?

Joy pulled the covers up and buried her head deep into the puffy pillow. Think of good things. Think happy thoughts.

What defined happy anymore? The only happy thoughts Joy could conjure were memories of the past. She could force thoughts of lazy summer days and busy vacations, but they all involved Melanie. Or Austin.

Well, that wasn't working. She could empty her mind. Try thinking of nothing. Joy stared at the ceiling fan as the blades circulated the stale air in her room.

She and Mel used to lay on the grass and find shapes in the clouds. . . .

No. Don't go there. Count the blades. Watch them go around and around. . . .

No memories, no dreams. . . .

Was it excusable to kill a best friend for stealing your boyfriend?

Joy sat in her car, idling in Melanie's driveway as little trick-or-treaters passed by. Buzz Lightyear, Woody, Jessie, and the whole gang, with bundled-up parents in tow, crossed the driveway. With one look at Joy's face, the dad grabbed Buzz's hand and pulled the group on to the next house.

Tinker Bell and Captain America were a little more gutsy as they marched right by her and rang the doorbell. No answer.

Next came a hobo with dirt smudged on his face, his daddy's shirt down past his knees, and a sack tied to a stick over his shoulder. Poor little boy's parents couldn't buy him a real costume?

One by one, kids approached the door and rang the bell, but the door never opened. What would Joy do if Mel came out to give the kids their candy and saw her sitting there? That would be awkward. Maybe it was time to face her demons. Not that she could expect Melanie to answer the door for her when she'd been blowing off the kids.

Joy's shoulders slumped as she plodded across the U-shaped driveway. Batman stepped from around the side of the house through the bushes and hopped on the porch. He looked Joy over. "Where's your costume?"

"What you see here?" Joy gestured to her body. "Trust me. It's not the real me at all. Not today."

Batman scowled. Unconvinced.

She pressed the doorbell.

Batman waited just behind Joy. After a moment, he stepped forward a few inches and looked her over one more time. He shook his head. He wasn't buying it at all. No way he would let her uncostumed body get to the candy first. He stepped in front of her and held his bag up to the door.

A minute passed. Two?

He lowered his bag. "I don't think they're home."

She nodded. "Yeah. I don't think so either. Better move on." She leaned back to let him pass. Time is candy, kid.

Batman stared. "Well? You going to go?"

"Yeah. In a minute."

He shrugged and jumped off the stoop, cape flying behind. He darted off through the bushes toward the next-door neighbor. Cute little boy. Someday he'd break someone's heart, too. They all did.

Joy shook her head, attempting to clear the only three-hour-old vision of Melanie kissing Austin. . .or Austin kissing Melanie. . .in Joy's family room. Not that it mattered who kissed whom. Neither looked to be trying to put a stop to it.

Joy shuddered at the sight of Austin's hands on Melanie's body. His body pressed up close against Melanie's as though they'd been in that embrace before. Would Joy ever be able to sit in that room, her own family room, again without hearing the kissing sounds coming from the two people she'd trusted most?

What had they been thinking? How could they have done that to her in her own house?

Joy stood on Melanie's porch. Her hand dangled like an anchor at her hip.

What would Melanie say? What excuse could there be for what she'd done? Oh, she'd come up with something slick—she'd had plenty of time to concoct a great story since she bolted as soon as it happened. To kiss your best friend's boyfriend and then say nothing? Of course she was embarrassed, but that was no excuse for fleeing *the scene of the crime. A drive-by heartbreak.*

Austin had stuck around at least long enough to beg for mercy. He had no excuse for what he'd done, but strangely, Joy was numb to him. The blinders had fallen off in an instant, and Joy saw him for who he was. A cheater. A liar. It only took her a year of dating and a decade of friendship to figure it out.

But, Melanie? That was different. A girl should always be able to expect more from her best friend than her boyfriend. Especially a lifelong sister-friend like Melanie. Those once-in-a-lifetime friends were supposed to bring healing when other people hurt, not heap on the pain. Joy was mad at Austin, but she was grieving for Melanie. She and Austin were through, but she and Melanie would have to find a way past this. To get back to the way it was. It would be difficult, but Joy would manage to forgive Melanie. Somehow.

Well, she'd wasted enough time. No point in pressing the buzzer. No one had come for the kids. She'd have to walk in just as she'd been doing for most of her life, no matter how grave the situation. It seemed too familiar to just walk in after what happened, but it was the only way.

Joy drew a deep breath. Was Melanie avoiding her? Or maybe she had her headphones on with music blaring and had no idea anyone had rung her doorbell. Joy stooped and fished under the porch mat for the front door key where it had been hidden for years. Stealthy. Mrs. Phillips could be CIA.

Joy fumbled to shove the key into the lock and turned the knob only to find the door opened easily. She stepped inside, listening for signs of life in the house. Television? Music? Conversation? But there was nothing. At least nothing she could hear right off. Joy kicked her shoes onto the mat beside the door.

Walking past the green-and-gold brocade sofa, Joy let her fingernails trickle across the back of the only piece of furniture in the formal family room. Mrs. Phillips always joked that she and

Melanie's dad had fought over who had to keep that sofa in the divorce. She lost.

Would Mel and Joy be able to laugh about something today? This week? Would it take a month? The closer the time drew to when she'd lay eyes on Melanie, the more confident Joy was that she'd forgive her. They'd only been divided by the chasm of betrayal for a couple of hours, yet Joy already missed her.

Footsteps soft on the carpeted hallway, Joy tiptoed to the kitchen. So quiet. No pop can on the counter, no Hot Pocket crumbs leading from the microwave. The first day since Joy could remember that Melanie hadn't eaten a ham-n-cheese Hot Pocket after school. Wow, she really must be taking this hard. Joy did a three-sixty. No cell phone on the countertop, no backpack on the floor. Melanie always left a trail as she shed her items and extra clothing on her way through the house.

Mel must not be home after all. Where could she be? Joy's stomach sank. Austin's? She wouldn't do that. . . . She couldn't. But then again, Joy had discovered that very day Melanie was quite capable of many things Joy had never thought possible. Should she go to Austin's to find out? If she didn't find Melanie in the house, she'd have to know. What if she did find her there? Joy would have to figure that out when, or if, it happened.

Joy peeked down the hall to Melanie's bedroom. The closed door and absence of light and sound made it highly unlikely that Mel was back there. But at least Joy would find out for sure before she tucked her tail between her legs and fled. After all, maybe Melanie was hiding herself away from Joy's accusations, from her pain.

Her socked feet fell silently onto the carpet. Melanie had to know Joy was there by then, but it felt better to be quiet. She passed the bathroom, then nine-year-old Matthew's room. Mrs. Phillips had the next bedroom, leaving Melanie with the master.

Arriving at the door, Joy pressed her ear against it. No sound escaped the door cracks. Then where had that music come from earlier? A passing car, maybe.

Joy twisted the knob and lifted the door up over the squeak. They'd practiced that move a thousand times in preparation for sneaking out while Mel's mom slept. Wonder if they'd ever do it again?

Ah. There she was, sprawled on her bed face down, sound asleep. Her luscious brown hair spread out in a wave across her back, her hands balled into fists beside her face like a sleeping baby.

Oh. Poor girl. She must have collapsed on that bed. Her feet rested at odd angles—like she'd fallen asleep on the way down. Her pants rode low on her hips, showing a bit too much of her somewhat ample behind. Joy chuckled. That would make a good picture for Facebook. Oh man, talk about getting even. But Joy had no desire for that sort of childish revenge.

She could sit at the desk and wait. Then she could talk to Melanie when she woke up. But staying there uninvited and unannounced somehow felt uncomfortable. Like it was no longer her home away from home and Joy was intruding on Melanie's privacy. No longer was Melanie's room as comfy and at ease as Joy's own. Joy longed for her bedroom at home. Mel had the right idea. A nap sounded like a great escape.

Boy, Melanie was awfully still. Joy peered a bit closer. There didn't seem to be any rise and fall of her back, none of the soft snores or twitching that Joy was so used to. Joy brushed a lock of dark hair off Melanie's cheek.

Her cheek was cold.

What was going on? Joy leaned over and shook Mel's shoulders and patted her on the back. Nothing happened. Could she just be passed out?

"Melanie?" Joy's hand trembled as she shook her friend's arm. "Wake up." She grabbed both of Melanie's upper arms hard enough *to bruise them and bounced her hard on the bed, shouting.*

Nothing.

Joy reached for her phone and fumbled to turn it on. Mom would know what to do.

Wait. Think clearly. Call for an ambulance first. Then Mom.

"911 emergency. This is Amber. Can I help you?"

"I don't know. I think there's something wrong with my friend. She's not moving at all. I thought she was sleeping. . . ." A sob escaped Joy's throat.

Reality came flooding in along with the sunlight that tried to pry Joy's eyes open. The same dream again. If she lay there with her eyes closed, maybe she could make it go away. Make it untrue somehow. Joy pulled her hand out from under the covers and felt the pillow beside her case.

Drenched.

No wonder she woke up exhausted since she spent the whole night crying.

Chapter 7

The wheels on the bus went 'round and 'round.

They bounced over the speed bumps as the driver steered into the parking lot of North Platte High School. Who'd have thought when she attended her first year of volleyball camp that her little-girl daydreams of playing in a championship meet like the big girls on TV would come true? And. . .here she was.

She kicked at the empty orange soda can that rolled against her shoe and tried to close her mind from the chaos of the small space narrowing all around her. The stale air—rank with gym clothes, sweat socks, and excited athletes—choked Joy. Why had she chosen to sit at the back of the bus? She wanted off. Even if she had to climb over people or claw her way out.

Joy stood from her window seat and ducked her head along the sloped ceiling as she searched for an escape. She shouldered her overnight backpack on one side and slipped the strap of her Adidas gym bag onto the other one. She picked up her water bottle just as the driver reached for the handle and yanked the door open. Finally. Joy stepped into the aisle. She'd fight her way to the door if she had to. There wasn't a player on the team who could hold her back. She lurched toward the door just as Coach climbed aboard the bus, blocking her exit.

Great. So much for fresh air. Maybe Joy could open a

window. If she didn't do something, she would pass out. Or vomit. She slumped into a spare seat halfway to the front.

Now, now. Calm down. Take a deep breath. If Joy didn't relax, she was headed for an all-out panic attack. Where had her patience gone? It had been replaced by a super-short fuse.

Coach looked up and down the rows like a farmer at harvest time. "You know I love you girls. It's remarkable that we're here, and I want you to be proud of what you've done and how hard you've worked. You're here to represent your school, but even more than that, you're representing your own commitment." She made eye contact with several players. "This team is a group of amazing people who know what they want and go after it even in the face of tragedy, disappointment, grief, loss, sadness, and everything else that's been thrown at you. I have so much respect for you all. Honestly? I admire you, and I've learned so much from you this year."

Nice words, but would it kill Coach to say them outside?

"Now it's time for us to go in there and fight our first team of this championship tournament." She consulted her clipboard. As if she didn't have the schedule memorized. "Gothenburg. When we win that, we continue on. We'll worry about what comes next one game at a time."

Heather raised her hand. "What if we don't win?"

Seriously? Joy rolled her eyes. Come on. What did she want Coach to say? *"Then we go to McDonald's?"*

Coach smiled. "Most of all, I am proud that we are here. I'm not going to say that I don't want to win. I'm not going to say we won't be disappointed if we lose. Of course we will, but I don't want you to forget we made it this far. Now go in there. Play this game with all your heart. Be a team, work together, and win it!"

The group erupted.

Joy saw her opportunity and stood up again. She sidled past the dawdling players and then the coach. Almost to freedom.

As soon as Joy's feet touched the top stair, she leaned her upper body out of the bus and felt the cool air on her face. She sucked in a deep breath of brisk Nebraska air mingled with diesel fumes as she climbed down to the pavement. Way better than sweat socks and hairspray.

Somewhat refreshed, or at least back to a socially functional level, Joy waited for the team to disembark and then fell in step with the rest of them as they headed for the school doors. Silent, except for nervous giggles that rang out every few seconds.

Warm air engulfed Joy as she walked through the double doors into the school lobby where the crowds milled around the entrance. Excitement and energy buzzed on the surface of Joy's skin like an electric charge. Of course, before they could find their gym, they had to squeeze past rows of merchandise tables with price sheets posted everywhere. Nothing like appealing to the emotions of high-strung teenagers and proud parents to get them to spend fifty bucks on a sweatshirt and thirty dollars on a piece of wood with their name scratched on it.

But the crème de la crème of State paraphernalia was the combo pack. One hundred and ten whopping bucks for a sweatshirt with or without a name on the back and the extra-large wooden plaque presumptively pre-engraved with individual players' names already on it, with a spot for the team photo and an individual photo to be slipped under thin sheets of plastic. Pictures not included. Of course.

Well. Joy felt her pocket. Mom had given her that blank check, probably hoping to buy her way out of guilt for not attending the game. She probably deserved the price of an extravagant souvenir purchase drained from her bank account. Joy checked out the rest of the team. Most were already purchasing something. Lauren and Heather had the combo pack tucked safely under their arms of course.

Should she do it?

Joy stepped over to the rows of wooden plaques, lined up in rows, sorted into alphabetical order. She flipped them forward as she read the names. *Marcus. Miller. Moultrie.* Joy was way past *Christianson*, but she had to know. *Parker. Peters.* And there it was. *Phillips. Melanie Phillips.*

Joy lifted it from the box and ran her finger over the letters.

"I'm sorry." A whisper in her ear made Joy jump. Coach squeezed her shoulder. "I should have checked to see it was removed before you saw it."

"Yeah I. . .I wasn't expecting it. . . . Yet, somehow I knew it would be there. Maybe that's how it should be. She was part of this team." Joy shrugged. "I'm thinking about buying it."

Coach nodded.

"I'll think about it." Joy handed the plaque over to Coach then shouldered her bag and headed off to find their locker room in the freshman wing. Her spending mood had crashed and burned.

§

"I can't believe we won!" Heather slipped her bikini-clad body into the steaming water. She settled into a bucket seat in the corner of the massive hot tub as Joy draped her towel on the back of a chair.

Coach lowered her book and looked up from her chair on the hotel's pool deck. "Hey Heather, I can absolutely believe we won. You girls played well. I saw lots of teamwork out there today."

Heather raised a fist and bumped knuckles with Lauren.

"Joy, if there was such a thing as most valuable player, you'd totally get it for this game." Amber shook her head like a

Labrador, water droplets flinging to the deck. "That one set. . . what a save. And your serve was a thing of beauty."

"Thanks. I just lucked out today." Joy shrugged.

"Well, tomorrow I want your position." Amber laughed.

She could have it, and the attention that came with it.

"Which brings up a really good point." Coach raised one finger. "Remember, this was only game one. We're on our way, but we have more work to do. Don't lose focus now, or we'll just hand them tomorrow's game. Okay?" She stood up from her deck chair and stepped around the puddles toward the restroom.

Joy dipped her toes into the bubbling water then slid her legs and body down.

Amber raised one eyebrow. "So, Heather, what's happening with you and Taylor? Because it looks like you two have gotten pretty close lately."

Heather giggled. "That's for me to know and you to find out."

"Real mature." Lauren splashed water at Heather's face.

"Hey, don't do that." Heather wiped water away from her eyes and pulled clumps of hair from her mouth. "This stuff is full of gross chemicals." She blinked and looked at Joy. "But how about you? Are you and Austin going to get back together?"

Lauren's mouth dropped open. Her brown eyes wide with horror. "Heather!"

Joy stared at Heather. Had her teammate really just asked something that stupid? How could she? Convenient she'd waited until Coach wasn't around.

"What?" Heather mustered up an innocent look. "Those two have had a thing for each other for like ever. She'll forgive him."

Don't count on it.

꩜

"Oh man. That was a total fail." Heather slumped onto the bus seat after the final volleyball game of the State Championships. Well, the final one their team would play, anyway.

"I totally wanted that State banner for the gym." Lauren sighed.

"Sure. Of course we all did. But we played a good game." Coach walked down the aisle and chose a seat among the players. "I'm so proud of you guys. Don't be down about your performance. You did nothing to be ashamed of."

Sure. Except for the three serves Joy messed up. No one said it, but she knew they were thinking it. Oh, and then there was the out-of-bounds dig that cost her team the ball. And the win. What a difference a day could make. But at least they weren't talking to her. That was a plus.

"I want to honor a player who is no longer with us. Melanie Phillips would have had a blast at this event. . . . She deserved to be here."

And they probably would have won with Mel at the helm.

Coach reached down to the space in front of her seat and lifted one of the large plaques. "This was Melanie's team plaque. I want Joy to have it, to commemorate Melanie's forever spot on this team."

The team broke into applause.

Joy accepted the engraved piece. It would have a spot on her wall, right beside her own. Joy traced her finger along the engraved letters on the gold metal square. How had life become so difficult? So sad?

The bus ride home was somber. The complete opposite of the ride to the State Championships. IPod playlists blared through headphones, and conversations stayed to a minimum. . . just the way Joy liked it.

"Talk about dropping the ball," Stephanie Powell muttered as she passed Joy's locker.

Joy rolled her eyes. The team statistician had been so snotty since they lost the State game. *Just ignore her.*

She came back around until she was directly in front of Joy. "You can't win them all, I guess. Apparently even when your team is counting on you the most."

What a jerk. Joy slammed her locker door and spun to walk away.

Steph chuckled and muttered, "Melanie would never have. . ."

Enough. "What was that? Got something you want to say to me?" Joy felt the rage boiling in her chest and extending out through the tips of her fingers. Must be what the Incredible Hulk felt like as his skin turned green and his clothes stretched then ripped.

Steph inched away from Joy, her face white.

"Just as I suspected. You're nothing but a coward." Joy jabbed a finger in her direction. "Keep your mouth shut around me. Understand?"

That's all it took to snap Steph out of her stupor. "Who do you think you are? You going to stop me?"

"Gladly." Joy threw her stack of books to the floor with a loud smack. She dove at Stephanie, yanking her by the hair.

"Ow!" Stephanie yelped, fingers clawing at Joy's hands. "Get your hands off me."

Joy gritted her teeth and threw Stephanie to the floor with a loud crash. The textbooks slid like dominoes from the impact.

Steph's eyes grew huge, and she stared at Joy like she was some kind of stranger.

Maybe she was. Joy didn't much care. She straddled Steph's body and sat on her stomach then reared back a fist and prepared to let it fly.

A strong hand grabbed Joy's in midair. "What do you think you're doing, young lady?"

Joy looked up to a pair of steely blue eyes. Oh great. Mr. Cavanaugh. "She started it!" Joy jerked her head toward Stephanie. The fact that Joy still sat atop Steph like a bull rider probably didn't help her elicit sympathy from the teacher.

"Physical violence is never the answer, nor allowed, no matter who provoked it. Come on. I'm taking you to the principal's office." Mr. Cavanaugh steered Joy down the hallway, directly into the empty office. "Have a seat. We'll wait."

Joy crossed her arms and stared straight ahead, unblinking. What a joke.

"What has become of you, Joy? You are so different. You used to be so happy. You were the life of the party, someone everyone could depend on for a kind word or a smile." Mr. Cavanaugh looked at Joy, his eyes sad. "Now you're. . ."—he gestured to her body—"always in black with the dark makeup. I don't get it. Plus the things I've heard coming out of your mouth lately. . .such morbid things. Where is all this coming from? I get that grief has a powerful effect on people, but this is really extreme."

Joy looked down at her clothing. Was it all black? Hmm. Black jeans, black T-shirt, black Converse. She hadn't made that change on purpose. Hadn't even noticed it really. She shrugged. "Sorry. I don't know. I guess I'm sad. I guess I'm in mourning." She turned a glare on him. "I mean, didn't people used to wear black and cover mirrors and never smile while they mourned the loss of someone they loved? Don't I deserve at least a little bit of time to get over the death of my best friend?"

Mr. Cavanaugh nodded. "Well, sure. As long as that's what it is. But something tells me it goes deeper."

You think? Joy slumped down in her seat. She just wanted silence while they waited for the judge and jury to enter the courtroom. Ridiculous. She was getting busted for something that wasn't even her fault.

The seconds ticked into minutes.

Mrs. Crosby burst into the office, panting and fanning her pink cheeks. She sank into her desk chair and unbuttoned the top button of her blouse. "I don't know why I wear this shirt on days I know I'll be back and forth across this school a thousand times. It's too tight."

Well alrighty then.

"Okay." She exhaled and turned to Mr. Cavanagh. "What's the deal? What happened?"

"Well," Mr. Cavanaugh said, "maybe we should let Miss Christianson tell the story."

Joy nodded and raised her chin. "Yeah, I'm all for it." Finally, she'd have a chance to say her piece. Joy uncrossed her arms and leaned forward. "You know, it's tough. It's really hard for me right now. People are picking on me for things and, you know, saying stuff to me that. . .I don't know. . .I don't even know how to explain it. But Stephanie pushed my last button. I had nothing left in me to restrain myself." Joy clenched her fists. "It was all I could do not to choke her."

Mr. Cavanagh jerked his head back and looked at Mrs. Crosby, his eyes wide.

Oh great. Now they were going to think she needed to be committed.

Principal Crosby waited for Joy to say more.

"You guys, I don't mean literally choke her. I just mean I came unglued. I'm human, and a lot has gone on in my life. How about cutting me some slack?"

Mrs. Crosby folded her hands under her chin and looked

into Joy's eyes. It took almost a full minute before anyone moved.

How awkward. Joy tried not to blink or look away.

Mrs. Crosby nodded. "Okay, I understand. But I have to address the fact you got physically violent with another student. You will be suspended for two days, which is minor compared to what could have happened."

"That's cool." Two days off. Sounded more like a reward than a punishment.

"But because I'm reacting so minimally to your actions, I want you to meet with the guidance counselor at least once a week for the foreseeable future, to talk about how you're doing."

Oh great. More emoting.

"Don't see the counseling as punishment. It's meant to help you." Mrs. Crosby smiled like she was proud of herself.

"Yeah, I can see that. I should tell you though, I'm already in counseling. Did you know I see a shrink every week already?"

"Well, I'm glad to hear it. I would hope so after all you've been through. I would really hope so. But here at school we need to make sure we're dotting our *i*'s and crossing our *t*'s."

Right. Not about Joy at all. Just taking care of business.

"There have been some changes in you we simply can't ignore. Your personality, style"—she looked Joy over from head to toe—"demeanor, actions, self-control. . .mood. . .all of those things signal there's something really deep going on."

Joy jumped from her chair, knocking it to the floor. She put her hands on Mrs. Crosby's desk. "What? Did you really just say that? You *think* there might be something deeper going on?" Joy stared her down. "Why can't you people just let me grieve in my own way instead of pressuring me so much to be this perfect person you think I'm supposed to be? Just back off."

Principal Crosby stood up. "The order for counseling

stands. The two-day suspension stands, and I will be talking with your parents because they need to know what's going on. I can't ignore all of this. I hope you understand."

"Whatever. Am I excused?"

"You're excused, but I really want you to realize you dodged a bullet here today. If I hadn't known you your entire life, you'd be facing some deep trouble for the way you acted in this school today." Principal Crosby shook her head. "I'd like a little gratitude for the light punishment and some recognition we're trying to work with you. Can you dig deep and find some?"

If it were in there, Joy would have already brought it out. "I'll do my best."

Whatever that meant.

Chapter 8

Joy's damp hair clung to her neck in icy strips. She stretched her arms above her head and yawned, her dry lips cracking like they did when she snored with her mouth open most of the night. Lovely. She squinted to see in her dark room. It felt like morning, but where was the sun? Pulling her covers tight around her shoulders, Joy rolled to her stomach and parted the blinds at the window behind her head.

Snowy mounds covered the bottom few inches of her garden-view bedroom, and judging by the sky, it had no intention of stopping anytime soon. Just what she needed. Now she could pull the covers back over her head and hide from the world all day long. No one would notice. With Mom and Dad already off for their day of Saturday real estate showings, Joy could probably make it for the next ten glorious hours without talking to a single living soul.

Then again, a day stuck in the house was probably the last thing she should be hoping for. She threw the covers off her body. She had to do something. But what?

Joy shivered as she slipped her arms into the fuzzy pink robe she'd gotten for Christmas the year before. When she'd first seen it, Melanie piped in with a Reese Witherspoon quote from *Legally Blonde*, "Whoever said orange is the new pink was seriously disturbed." Indeed.

No. Don't go there. The movie quotes would start filtering through her consciousness. Then Joy would pull out the DVDs and pop one into the player. Probably something like *Steel Magnolias*. Ugh. The scene where Sally Field is at her daughter's grave and her friends ask her how she's holding up. "I want to know why! I want to know why Shelby's life is over!" Sally had screamed with blood-curdling sounds of utter grief.

Ten minutes of a movie like that, and it would be all over from there. A box of tissues and a frozen pizza would be the extent of her Saturday. Yeah. Joy needed to avoid spending her day embroiled in the fictional misery of others at all costs.

Beatrice. Perfect. She'd go hang out with her sweet cousin. Joy fumbled on the nightstand for her cell phone. She touched the icon for messages and typed one to Aunt Sue.

OK IF I COME HANG WITH B TODAY?

The reply beeped within seconds. PLEASE. SHE'D LOVE IT.

That settled that. GR8. GIMME AN HOUR. C U SOON.

Now to let Mom know.

GOING TO HANG OUT AT BEA'S. WANT ME TO PICK UP DINNER ON MY WAY HOME?

Joy headed to the bathroom. Mom never replied right away, especially on a busy Saturday when, like all good Realtors, they usually had showings back to back all day anywhere between Ogallala and North Platte. At least Mom and Dad got to work together, their different personalities complementing their business. Mom loved paperwork, and Dad could sell diet pills in Ethiopia.

After showering off the sweat from her rough night, Joy used her blow dryer and round brush to smooth her hair. She'd leave it long and straight so Beatrice could play *beauty*, as she called it.

Joy stepped into her most holey jeans. One day the legs would fall right off of them. Until then they'd provide her the comfort, in more ways than one, she longed for. A black tee and her black North Face fleece over it, she was ready to go.

The phone buzzed and vibrated on Joy's desk. She glanced at the display to find a message from Mom.

Let's eat at Hoke's. 6:00. If you need $$ for the day, there's some in the drawer.

Cool. One great part of having parents who worked so hard was their guilt made them way more free with their money than other teens' parents. Little did they know, as much as Joy loved them, she didn't mind the time alone. At all.

Another text buzzed in. Joy? It's B-B. When are you coming?

Right now.

🌀

"My Joy!" Beatrice grinned her lopsided smile as she jumped from the porch, loped to the driveway, and reached into the open car door to help Joy out by tugging on her arm. Oh, that smile brightened Joy's day instantly. When Joy finally stood in front of her on the driveway, Bea threw her arms around Joy's neck and squeezed.

Beatrice wanted nothing from Joy except love and attention in return. Two things Joy was perfectly happy to provide. At least to Beatrice.

"What are we going to do today, Joy?" Beatrice linked arms with her hero, her grin never wavering, as she pulled her toward the house.

"I don't know. What did you have in mind?" Joy was game for anything.

Beatrice scrunched her face in confusion and tapped her chin. "Hmmm."

"Well, do you want to go somewhere, or do you want to stay home?"

"I know one thing. I want to get a taco with extra sour cream." She licked her lips.

Joy should have seen that one coming. "No problem. We can get tacos for lunch." Good thing she'd pocketed that twenty-dollar bill from Mom's cash stash in the kitchen. "But what else?"

Bea's eyes brightened. "Can we go play checkers right now? I have a new one called Trapdoor Checkers. It's so much fun. The pieces fall through the trapdoors."

Joy felt her heart rate slowing more and more the longer she was in Beatrice's presence. God sure knew what He was doing when He gave the world her innocent heart. "Perfect. Let's go." Joy smiled and stuck her hand out.

Beatrice grabbed Joy's hand and practically bounced with excitement all the way to the front door. "I missed you so much." She glanced behind her as she pulled, grinning.

"I missed you, too." Joy squeezed her cousin's hand, embarrassed by her selfishness. She should have thought of Beatrice's feelings during the past weeks. Of course it had been too long, and Bea simply didn't understand what might have kept Joy away. She took it as a personal affront. . .assumed Joy didn't want to be with her. The thought broke Joy's heart in two.

"What happened? Why didn't you come see me for so long?" Beatrice's lip poked out in a pout.

Be honest. But not too honest. "Like we talked about the other day, I had some hard things happen, and I stayed at home being sad."

"I'm sorry you were sad. I heard my mom say on the phone that your friend died. I'm very sorry about that."

"Thank you, sweetie." Bea had mastered the art of eavesdropping when no one thought she was paying attention or assumed she didn't understand.

"But I'm here now. I need to have some fun, so I'm just glad to be here with you. Let's be happy and play some games, and then we'll go get those tacos. If you win, you can have two. Deal?"

Beatrice beamed. "Deal."

"Oh, I almost forgot. I have something for you." Beatrice pulled Joy to her bedroom, dragged her inside, and shut the door. She pressed her finger to her lips. "Don't tell anyone. It's a surprise, okay?"

"I'm not going to say a single word about your surprise. What is it?"

Beatrice dove onto the floor and scrambled as she reached for something under her bed. "Got it." She stood up and handed Joy the sheet of construction paper with crayons and stickers and glitter all over it.

"Look, look." Beatrice pointed a stubby finger at a stick figure kneeling by a bed. "That's you praying. Look up here." She pointed above Joy to what looked to be an angel, as evidenced by the halo and the wings.

"This is great, Bea. But the angel looks mad. Why is she mad?"

"It's a he. Angels are boys. Turn the paper over and you'll see why he's mad."

On the flip side of the paper, Joy found a stick figure standing with her hands on her hips and a book on the floor. There were two devil-looking people standing behind her.

"This is you. This is a demon, and this is a demon. Oh, and this is the Bible on the floor."

Joy flipped the page back over. So that's what was going on in Bea's mind. "So the angel's mad because of the demons or because of the Bible on the floor?"

"No, the angel is mad that you looked at the demons." Beatrice shrugged.

Joy stared at the paper. Was she worried because of her own fears, or did Beatrice truly have some special connection to the spirit world?

Bea was a mind reader; that had to be it. Joy felt so exposed. "How did you think of this? What do you want to say to me with this picture?"

Beatrice shrugged again. "I don't know. Let's play checkers." Subject closed.

🌀

Joy steered her Bug into the driveway and hopped out, leaving it running. A quick stop at home to run a comb through her hair and brush her teeth before meeting Mom and Dad for dinner. She took the front porch steps two at a time and bounded through the unlocked front door, flipping on every light she passed on her way to the bathroom.

A quick glance in the mirror. Oh man. She looked ghostly. A little makeup wouldn't hurt if she didn't want to scare animals and little children. Joy riffled through her makeup pouch searching for the bronzer. A little bit dusted across her cheeks and forehead would take the paste out of her skin. She added some blush to pink her cheeks and a few swipes of mascara to open up her eyes so she wouldn't look like she hadn't slept in weeks. . .even though she *hadn't* slept in weeks.

Joy stared into her eyes as she brushed her teeth. Wait. That sounded like a chime. She turned the water off and cocked her ear toward the door. Was it the doorbell? It chimed again. Yep.

She jogged down the hall. Who could it be? Not anyone they knew well. Mom's open-door policy meant come on in. None of that doorbell nonsense. Joy looked through the peephole. Oh great. Investigator what's-his-name, the guy who'd asked her all the questions after. . .well, *after*.

Joy opened the door, but not wide enough to be considered

welcoming. "Hi. Can I help you with something, officer?"

Was he going to blindside her with more questions? Please not tonight.

"Hello, um. . ."—he glanced at the paper in his hand—"Joy."

Kind of rude he couldn't have checked out her name before ringing her doorbell. Whatever. "Yeah, I'm on my way out. What can I do for you?" She should be nicer to him. It wasn't his fault, after all. But he was a reminder. One she could easily do without.

"That's fine. I won't keep you. I just wanted to let you know that we're closing the investigation on Melanie Phillips's death, and I wanted to return your personal effects to you." He handed her a plastic bag full of things confiscated from the scene. Joy instantly recognized most of the things in the bag, including half of a best friend necklace and the suicide note Melanie had addressed to Joy.

Joy shook her head and squeezed her eyes shut. She'd deal with those things later.

"Thanks, officer." What was protocol for something like this?

He nodded, shifting uncomfortably. His body straining toward his vehicle. "I'm really sorry about your loss. Truly."

Joy nodded. *Me, too.* "Thanks."

"Well I'll leave you to your plans. You can trust you won't be seeing me show up on your doorstep anymore."

Thank the Lord for small favors. Or the universe? Maybe she should be thanking the universe.

༄

The little car tucked neatly into a parking space right outside of Hoke's. Joy hopped out and walked under the yellow neon signs out front to enter the retro diner.

"Hey, there. Haven't seen you in here in a while." Pat, the

redheaded waitress, flicked a dishtowel at Joy with a grin.

Joy tried to smile. "Hey. I know. It has been awhile. But I'm in the mood for a great burger."

The waitress's happy face faded. That always happened when people gave even a moment's thought to why Joy hadn't been around lately. Wonder how long that would go on? She sure didn't like to be a mood killer everywhere she went.

"My mom and dad here yet?" Joy looked around the dining room, hoping to avoid the twenty questions.

Pat pointed to the back. "In the booth."

"Oh, I see them. Thanks." Joy followed the wood paneling to the rear of the restaurant and slid into the empty side of the booth. "Hey guys."

"Hey love." Dad grinned. "We're ready to order, so go ahead and decide. Then we'll catch up."

The rumbling from Joy's stomach insisted on a burger, fries, and a shake. An appetite like that would be perfect for dispelling any kind of fear her parents might have about her health and nutrition.

"What can I get you folks?" Pat poised her pen above her notepad and waited. Mom ordered her usual salad, then the waitress turned to Joy.

"I'll have a cheeseburger, extra pickles, and an order of cheese fries." How many times had she and Melanie shared a plate of fries?

"I'll have the same." Dad folded up his menu. "Chocolate shakes all around, too."

Mom laughed and held up her hand. "Oh, not for me. Diet Coke, please."

Pat scooped up the menus. "I'll be right back with your drinks."

Could Melanie actually be with them there at Hoke's?

Almost like when little kids had imaginary friends. But, in this case, the invisible friend wasn't imaginary. Joy scooted to the right a few inches. Logically, she knew she wasn't sitting on Melanie, but. . .still.

"So how's business?" That should help keep the attention off herself.

Mom beamed. "Great. Dad and I made a big sale today. Should make for a good Christmas in the Christianson home."

"Congrats. What'd you sell?"

"You know that house out at the lake with the wraparound porch?" A grin pulled at the corners of Dad's mouth.

"Sure. The one a few doors down from our new-old house?" If they ever finished the rehab so they could actually move in.

"That's the one. We sold it for more than the asking price." Dad wiggled his eyebrows. Nothing made the man happier than coming out on top of a good deal.

"Wow. That's awesome." For them. Not so much for the buyer. Buyer beware and all that good stuff.

"Yeah. It turned out well for everyone." Mom spread her napkin in her lap. "As for the rest of the weekend, we still have a pretty full day tomorrow. We'll go to church, and then Dad and I have a couple of showings after."

Joy shrugged. "I figured. It's cool. I have tons of homework." But Joy at church? That would be interesting to say the least. Would some kind of spiritual alarm bell go off if she walked through the doors of the sanctuary?

Dad lifted his hands for the waitress to set the tall milk-shakes down. "We're just sorry we're not around much this weekend."

Or any weekend. But Joy would never say that to them. The mommy-daddy guilt would be too much for them to bear. They'd never believe that she actually preferred it that way. Or maybe they'd believe her, but then they'd worry what it meant.

Mom glanced at Dad with a question in her eyes. He gave a soft nod.

Oh great. Here it comes. The mental stability check.

"Okay, so your dad and I are very concerned about you, sweetheart. We want to know what's going on with you. It's time to be honest with us. How are you?"

Joy took a long draw on her straw, filling her mouth with the fudgy shake. How was she? The line from *Steel Magnolias* welled in her chest. Joy wanted to blurt out "*I'm fine! I'm fine! I can run all the way to Texas and back if I wanted to. . .but Melanie can't!*" But there was no way Mom and Dad could handle that kind of emotion. "I'm okay. I'm sad. I'm mad. I had my life turned upside down, so it's going to take awhile. But I'm going to make it." Joy shrugged. "I have no other choice."

Dad reached a hand across the table and covered Joy's. The warmth of the human contact drew her pain to the surface and tears welled up. She blinked rapidly, keeping the flow at bay.

"Joy honey, we're concerned about you." Dad squeezed her hand. "I just barely touched you, and now you're ready to burst. You're keeping your emotions in, and they're just bubbling at the surface ready to pour out at any moment."

As if to punctuate his point, a big tear coursed down Joy's cheek. Mercifully, Dad didn't point it out.

Pat saved the day. No one spoke as she set a perfect plate of greasy diner food in front of them. "Need anything else?" Pat wiped her hands on her white apron and glanced at each of them.

Dad smiled and shook his head. "I think we're fine. Thanks."

Easy for him to say.

Eyes back on Joy, Dad dropped the smile. "Your mom and I

think you need to see someone." He looked at Mom. "We think you need some professional help."

Joy dropped her fork. "Professional help? What do you mean? Like a shrink?" They couldn't be serious.

Mom shook her head. "No. Not a shrink—that's a psychiatrist. What you need is a counselor. Someone who can help you talk through what you're feeling. Help you come to terms with all you've lost. Melanie and Austin on the same day, and in tragic ways."

She forgot to mention faith, hope, and love. Those three were gone, too.

Mom reached across the table and squeezed Joy's hand. "It's been a horrible time for you. And you probably carry some misplaced guilt about the circumstances."

How did Mom know? If she could see it, then Joy was probably right in feeling guilty. Did everyone else think it was her fault? Did Maggie think it was Joy's fault her daughter was dead? Joy pushed her plate away. No point in trying to pretend she had it all together. They knew the truth.

". . .and your dad and I, we have to take care of you and protect you, and we can't know what's going on inside your head unless you let us in there. Right now, you're closed off, and I understand. Self-protection is natural to a degree, but we want you to see someone professional who can help you break through some of that stuff."

What stuff? Like how she'd never trust another relationship? How she'd probably never get married? How Joy's view of what it means to be a best friend is shattered into a million tiny pieces along with her heart? That kind of stuff? Impossible.

Dad nodded, and a crumb fell from his bushy silver mustache. "We love you. You're everything to us, and we'll do anything to make sure you come out of this strong. Right now, this is the best option we see. We're here for you of course, but we don't have the ability to really know how to help you."

Their words made sense. Joy would have recommended the same thing to a friend. It was so different when it was happening to her though. "Who will I see? And when will I go?"

"I'm not sure if you heard about this, but they hired a permanent family therapist at church, just this week. She moved here from New Jersey. Mary Alice Gianetti. She has an office at the church, and she'll be meeting with you once a week on Mondays for about an hour."

Mom's words tumbled over one another like they always did when she was nervous. It was why she didn't make a good salesperson. And why she wasn't selling Joy on the concept of therapy.

"You said Monday. Is that like two days from now?" How could Joy get herself out of it by then?

"Yeah. Why not get started right away?"

Joy could think of a few reasons. "Is this open for discussion?"

Dad shook his head. "It's happening, sweetie. Has to."

Joy nodded. Wow. Good ol' Mary Alice Gianetti from New Jersey wouldn't know what hit her.

Chapter 9

Mom thundered her Saab mid-life-crisis Turbo into the church parking lot Monday after volleyball practice. She pressed the satellite POWER button silencing Bill Cosby on the comedy channel. Did Mom think listening to the same comedian's spiel Joy had been hearing since she was a little girl would do the trick to help her forget about her best friend's suicide? She couldn't be that lame.

Joy closed her eyes. She'd have to walk across that big parking lot, through those familiar doors, sit down with the one stranger in the whole church—the counselor, Mary Alice Gianetti—and talk about her most raw feelings. Sounded like a party.

For once, as they left the car and walked toward the building, the parking lot seemed too small, the distance too short. Mom leaned her body into the back of Joy's arm. Was she trying to hold her up or make sure she didn't get away? Probably a little of both. Now there was a thought. Joy could take off. Run until she couldn't run any longer. Problem was, the demons that plagued her would surely follow close at her heels.

The double-door entrance rose up under the steeple that pointed to heaven. Like most churches, this one believed it had a special "in" with God. A fast track to the pearly gates. Maybe it did. . .but, if so, that meant so many other people who thought they were right, too, were going to be really surprised one day. Joy never heard the pastors address the beliefs of other faiths. They preached as though they assumed everyone understood and agreed that their teaching was right, so by default the others missed the mark. What if they were wrong? Someone had to be.

Joy had already mostly proven to herself the church was completely off about one very important thing she'd been taught, and had believed, since she was a little kid. Supposedly, people died and then beamed right up to heaven. Simple as flipping a switch. But even though she wanted more proof, Melanie made it look pretty likely that when people died, they didn't, or at least some of them didn't, immediately go to be with Jesus.

So the pastor was wrong. And so was the Bible. Now, what was Joy to do with that bit of knowledge? Where did it put her faith in everything she'd ever been taught?

Maybe she'd make that the first question she'd ask her counselor. What happened to people after they died? Or better yet, what do you do about your faith in God when you prove Him wrong? If even a professional gave the party-line answer to either of those questions, as Joy expected her to, then she'd know that Mary Alice Gianetti really was as clueless as the rest of them. Or that there was no answer.

Mom held the door open and ushered Joy through. Her eyes searched Joy's for signs of something. Poor Mom. The days of their carefree, chatty relationship seemed so distant. Now it was always somber with talk, or unspoken questions, about death, suicide, and betrayal. Joy shivered and pulled her arms tight around her body.

They approached the pastor's office where light crept from under the doorway. Don't knock, Mom. Just keep going.

Phew. She moved past the office door and zeroed in on the open door at the end of the hall. Mom poked her head through the open doorway. "Mary Alice? I'm here with Joy."

Last chance to run. Joy stared through the window at the end of the hallway. Those snow-covered cornfields looked inviting.

"Oh hey, Peg. Great. Send her in. If you want to, you can wait in the coffee shop. I'll send her down when we're through."

Mom nodded and held her hand out toward the office. "Go ahead, sweetheart. It'll be fine."

Whatever. Joy shoved her hands deep into her pockets and skulked past Mom through the doorway.

"See you in a little bit, sweetie."

Joy nodded. *Stop being so fake, Mom.* Didn't she know everyone could see through her? It was okay to be normal. Or at least some version of normal.

"Hi, Joy. I'm Mary Alice. Come on in and have a seat." She stood from her desk with her hand outstretched, bangles tinkling from wrist to elbow, and gestured toward the corner.

Well, at least Joy thought she was standing. Mary Alice Gianetti could not have been five feet tall. Joy stepped toward the stuffed chairs and sank into one. The counselor followed her and chose the blue one across from Joy's red one.

Mary Alice Gianetti crossed her denim-clad legs, her three-inch strappy gold heels dangling from her toe. So how tall was this woman really? And what was it about the counselor's name that made Joy say the whole thing every single time? Mary just wouldn't cut it. Mary Alice just sounded weird.

"So, Joy. . ."

Okay, if this lady was lame enough to say something like "tell me what brings you here today," Joy was out of there.

"We're actually going to do things a little bit differently than

I usually would at a first visit. What I'd like to do is talk about the future. The past is the past. It'll be there—we'll get to it, but there's a lot of tragedy in the past from what I understand about what you've gone through recently. More important is to try to rediscover what made you who you are. I'd like to help you find your purpose again and prove you're still in there." She tapped on her chest. "The real you."

Joy shrugged. The more she could keep Mary Alice Gianetti talking, the less she'd have to say herself.

"So let's start by looking ahead. What is the one dream job you could really see yourself doing one day?" The counselor waited with her pen poised over her yellow legal pad.

Joy looked up at the ceiling tiles. Some had rings of water stains. Two were missing completely. Surprising for a church where everything was usually impeccable.

The counselor kicked off her heels then drew her legs up into the chair and crossed them. Her bright purple satin tunic billowed up for a brief moment, and Joy saw a taut tummy—years of exercise, no doubt. The tan courtesy of the local beds.

"I don't know." Brilliant. All that buildup, and *I don't know* was the best Joy could come up with for her first words ever spoken in a counseling session?

Mary Alice waited.

"There was a time when I thought I would be a veterinarian, but I don't know anymore." Joy shrugged.

"Why don't you know? What do you mean you don't know anymore?"

Was she joking? Joy searched the wall for proof of a college degree. "Well, I think it's just with all that's gone on, I don't know who I am anymore. I don't know what matters to me." As she stopped and thought about it, where had the passion gone? The shelves of animal books lining her room. The National

Geographic DVDs and magazines piled on the floor beside her desk. The applications to the best vet schools in the country that she'd collected early and stacked on her nightstand where they'd been for the past year, completed and waiting until the first moment she could send them.

Oh, and she couldn't forget the animal first-aid kit she'd had beneath her bed since she was eight, waiting for a broken wing to splint. Time was, she hadn't gone a day, rarely a few hours, without thinking about the clinic she'd open near the lake after she'd proven herself by working for the Animal Clinic off of Route 30 for a few years.

Joy hadn't thought for one moment about that dream or any other since That Day.

"Aha." The doc held up a finger. "My point exactly. You're still Joy. What God put into you to make you unique is all still there. Who you were before your friend's death is still who you are after her death. Circumstances can affect the way you look at life, but they don't change who you are inside."

Not buying it. Circumstances absolutely did change a person from the inside out. How could this woman try to say anything otherwise? Joy opened her mouth to protest, but what would be the point of arguing?

The counselor nodded. "See what I mean? We need to spend our time focusing on how to reclaim the Joy you once knew."

Joy's deep questions about life, death, and eternity probably had to wait until next time. Though she had little hope Mary Alice Gianetti would have any answers.

All the talk of the future made Joy want to cling to the past.

She pointed her trusty Bug toward Ogallala Cemetery. The last time she'd been there was the last day she saw Melanie in her physical form. In her casket. That smell. Oh, it had been awful. She noticed it the moment she walked into the funeral home. "Where is that smell coming from?" she'd whispered to her mom.

"Oh, you know Maggie and her candles."

She'd been selling them for years, which was fine, but to subject all of them. . . ?

Joy had tiptoed into the viewing room, where they'd spent the day before greeting the family, shaking hands, and being squeezed by middle-aged women she'd never met. That day they were there to say good-bye once and for all.

The candles had been everywhere—every surface flickered with a tea light or votive. Maggie stayed near a glowing cluster and inhaled comfort of Melanie somehow. Joy would have to overlook the pumpkin spice that filled the room. At least it was better than roses. She stepped over to Maggie and put her arms around her. "How are you doing?"

"The best I can." Maggie's shoulders slumped.

"It's all anybody can ask." Great. She sounded just like the people who had driven her crazy with questions. Silly questions. Silly answers. Joy looked around the room. "The candles are a nice touch."

"Pumpkin spice was Melanie's favorite."

That was true. Joy had forgotten. Mel always loved the minute leaves started to fall because she knew the boxes would start coming from her mother's candle company.

"Pumpkin spice," mused Maggie. "Gingerbread spice, vanilla—and she didn't play with them. Remember the coffee beans? She'd smell the candle and then the coffee beans to clear her senses, and then another candle and more coffee. She would do that for hours."

Joy remembered. They'd inhaled a lot of fragrance that way.

The pastor stood at the front. "Gather around, everyone. Take your seat and let's start the service."

Maggie clutched Joy's arm. "You're family. Don't sit at the back. You're the nearest family she had."

Joy smiled softly and followed Maggie down the aisle. It couldn't have been any other way.

Later she stood beside the family as the coffin lid was lowered. She held Maggie's hand, squeezed it as they caught the last glimpse of their precious Melanie.

Joy shook her head. A touch of a smile teased her lips. Even in that dreadful moment at the funeral, the movie addiction she'd shared with Melanie bubbled to the surface. They'd have surely looked to M'Lynn, from *Steel Magnolias*, talking about the moment her daughter died for the quote-for-the-day.

"There was no noise, no tremble, just peace. . . . I realize as a woman how lucky I am. I was there when that wonderful creature drifted into my life, and I was there when she drifted out. It was the most precious moment of my life." Joy sighed. Shelby's death, in the movie, was sacrificial in some ways because of what she'd put her body through for her son. A tragic but natural occurrence. Melanie's was everything but that. So not precious. So unnatural.

What was it about cemeteries that drew people to them like magnets? Filing in for holiday visits and to bring flowers at the change of the seasons. Dead people didn't know they had a new plant or a basket of silk flowers or even a visitor—or at least that's what Joy had always assumed. Maybe she'd been wrong. Joy pulled in close to where Melanie was buried and turned the ignition off. She leaned against the headrest as rain pelted her windshield.

What was the truth? That question was what brought her there. She needed to reach out to Melanie with no one around.

To see if she could make sense of it all somehow.

Joy climbed from the car and shut the door with her hip. Her eyes went right to Melanie's grave. The only fresh mound in the cemetery. She crept out among the headstones, careful to step around where she imagined the people lay six feet beneath the damp earth, and approached the churned heap of dirt.

It didn't seem like a real grave without the headstone. Joy's grandpa had selected and ordered it as a gift to Maggie while he was in town for the funeral. It would still be several weeks until it was ready. Wonder what Grandpa had engraved on it. Here lies a life ended too soon? Nah. Here lies a stupid, selfish person? No.

Here lies someone who had no hope.

Had the concept of hope dissolved for Melanie like it had for Joy?

Was Mel there? Could she see Joy? Joy's head twitched as she sensed something. Someone? Don't look back. The palpable presence wouldn't be visible. Maybe if she spoke out. . .as long as Melanie didn't speak back audibly. Joy couldn't face that possibility out here alone in a cemetery at dusk. No way.

"Mel, you know me so well, I'm sure you know I can't handle hearing from you, at least not yet, but I want you to know that I believe you exist somewhere between the world of the living and the dead. I don't understand it at all, but it seems to be true. I want you to know that I love you. I hate what you've done to yourself, but I love you." Joy scuffed the dirt with the toe of her boot. "Honestly, I could care less about Austin and what happened between you two. I came to your house. . ."—Joy's voice caught with emotion—"that day to forgive you. And I do forgive you."

Joy waited. She listened to the wind whistle in the trees. Winter was on its way.

Could the acceptance of forgiveness and love release Melanie from where she was trapped in the world of in-between? "It's okay to let go, Melanie. I don't know how it works. I don't know if you're stuck, or if this is where you want to be. I don't know if you have a choice, but if you do, it's okay to let go. It's okay to release yourself to eternity if it's a better choice than the one you're enduring. I'll be okay, and your parents will be okay. We miss you like crazy, but we forgive you and we love you."

Joy collapsed onto the fresh dirt, her knees instantly damp and muddy. She scraped at the dirt and clutched handfuls as though hugging what remained of her best friend. Her tears mingled with the raindrops and landed on her mud-caked hands.

She fell forward onto the grave and sobbed. Her body wracked with the pain of tears withheld. She set them free. Her mind wanted to shout into the wind, "Why?" But she knew the wind had no answer. So she cried.

Hours later. . .minutes, maybe. . .Joy clambered to her feet, feeling much older than her seventeen years.

" 'Wouldn't it be lovely if we were old?' " Joy whispered the quote from *The Way We Were* as she let the mud drop from her fists. " 'We'd have survived all this. Everything would be easy and uncomplicated; the way it was when we were young.' "

Chapter 10

"Time for us to talk about taking you to the next level."
Raven pulled the wrapper off her straw and rolled it into
a tiny ball between her fingers. She flicked it and hit Ronald
McDonald in the eye.

A little blond girl covered her mouth and giggled. Her
mother grasped her hand and glared at Raven.

"Next level of what?" Joy had had enough of the stages of
grief talk from the counselor. Was that what Raven meant? She
pushed away her tray of fries.

"You going to eat those?" Raven nodded at the pile.

Joy waved her hand. "Help yourself. I'm done."

Raven pulled the tray across the table. She squirted a huge
pile of ketchup and then shook a flurry of black pepper over the
mound of fries and a heavy dusting over the ketchup.

Gross. Raven selected three very peppery fries, dragged
them through the puddle, and then shoved them into her
mouth. "Next level of your spiritual journey."

Joy looked away. The food was unappetizing enough on
the tray, but half-chewed in Raven's mouth? Disgusting. No
wonder they were never very close before now. Totally different
people. Something about that appealed to Joy now though.
No expectations. No memories.

What had Raven just said? Joy needed to focus. "Did you

say spiritual journey?" Her head whipped from side to side. "Um. No way." There would be no more journeying.

"Yeah. Listen." Raven stuffed four more fries into her mouth then pointed her finger at Joy. "You got a lot of shadows, a lot of demons chasing you." She took a deep breath. "Don't just reject the idea immediately. . . ." Raven laughed. "I can tell by the expression on your face that you're hating this idea, but hear me out."

Joy's stomach twisted into a pretzel. No good could come of this conversation. Things had gone so far already. She needed to just grab her things and get out of there, take control back. But she couldn't. It was like being stuck in a dream. She couldn't move.

Raven licked the ketchup off her fingers. Finally. "Look. I know what it's like to be confused and to have your faith blown to smithereens. Exactly what happened to me when my mom took off and my brother committed suicide."

Joy gasped. "What? You're kidding."

"Yeah. Which is when I had to come live here with my dad. It wasn't by choice. Before all that, I was a happy churchy kid like you were. Suddenly, I was face-to-face with being totally alone. Luc changed it all for me, and I can change it for you." She shrugged. "It's really not that big of a deal. If you could take the leap and believe in God without seeing Him or experiencing anything, then this jump is nothing. Especially since you've already seen the spirit world at work."

She made a great point. It was true. Joy had blindly believed in something that had never, not even once, come through for her or even revealed itself to her in any tangible way. Yet here she was, staring eye-witnessed truth in the face and trying to deny it existed.

"It's time for you to put aside blind belief in the unseen and embrace what's right in front of you."

Joy nodded. "I'm in."

§

A leisurely stroll down a grassy lane with a white puppy on a leash. Joy reached down and patted the fluffy pup on the head then scratched it behind the ears. "You like that, boy?"

The little dog looked up at her with loving blue eyes that spoke his name from the very depths of his soul. Silas.

They walked and walked. Along the familiar streets of town without a care in the world, like nothing had ever happened to either of them. They had been friends forever, as though born together. Maybe their souls had been united in an eternity past.

Silas led the way. Not quite a puppy anymore.

They walked on, not seeing a soul until a form appeared in the distance. A man. Joy would recognize those sandy curls anywhere. Austin.

Silas began to pant. Even older—changes happened with each step forward.

How did the dog know she and Austin had a history? It was as if Silas could read her mind or at least sense her heart rate.

Joy felt the anger toward Austin rise in her chest like bile. A low growl came from Silas's belly. He pulled at the leash, saliva dripping from his mouth, guttural growls coming at regular intervals. His strength magnified until he looked and sounded like a beautiful, full-grown wolf.

Austin didn't notice them at first.

Silas barked once.

Austin turned, probably expecting to see a dog walker.

Silas and Austin made eye contact, and Silas began to run, yanking the leash from Joy's hand.

Austin's eyes grew wide, and he half turned to run away. He couldn't seem to pry his gaze off of Silas long enough to really attempt an escape.

Full speed for a wolf was a lot faster than Joy could go, so she watched.

Silas was at Austin's heels in a matter of seconds, but Austin kept running. Joy could imagine how terrified he must be, but she couldn't bring herself to cry out for Silas to stop. Would he if she did?

Silas stayed at the heels of his prey, foamy saliva dripping to the pavement. Austin ran. . .and ran, and ran.

Joy heard a siren in the distance. Ambulance? Police car? It grew closer. . . .

Joy's eyes were dry. Blinking. Opening to reality.

Wait a minute. What *was* that sound?

Oh. Six o'clock in the morning. The siren was nothing more than her alarm clock interrupting her dream.

The dream had felt so real, almost like an out-of-body experience, which made no sense whatsoever. Joy shook her head. She was losing it. Hopefully it was nothing a hot shower wouldn't cure.

ᔕ

"Tell me about what happened after you found Melanie on her bed." Mary Alice Gianetti put down her pen and notebook and leaned forward, her elbows pressing into the tops of her thighs.

That day? The moments after she'd realized Melanie wasn't sleeping had become blurred in her mind. Like watching a movie on rewind. "I. . .um. . .called for help."

"Tell me what happened, if you can. Take your time."

Joy couldn't tell her counselor the details if she couldn't remember them. She searched her mind for the painful memories.

"I remember the dispatcher telling me help was on the

way. She promised they would be there in about six minutes, but it seemed like it took a lifetime." Maybe it was a lifetime. Melanie's. "She told me to stay with Mel. Which I thought was odd. What? Did she think I was going to leave?" Joy shrugged.

"She talked me through the steps to do CPR." Joy's fingers reached up to touch her lips. She had breathed into Melanie's mouth, pounded on her chest. Sobbed. Shook her. Breathed into her mouth, pounded on her chest. . .

Lather. Rinse. Repeat.

It hadn't helped.

"The worst thing was when they wouldn't tell me anything. They packed her up and sped off in an ambulance and left me behind to get in touch with her mom to tell her to go to the hospital."

"Tell me what's wrong with my baby girl! Tell me! I have to know."

Joy shuddered.

"What?" Mary Alice pressed. "What memory just re-pulsed you?"

"The sound of Maggie Phillips begging me to tell her the fate of her daughter. It was horrible." Joy bit her lip. "She was desperate for me to give details. I almost lied and said Mel was conscious when the ambulance drove away. Just so she'd let me off the phone. So I wouldn't have to say the words.

"I also remember they didn't really do anything. They knew she was dead, so they loaded her in the back and went through the motions of their procedures. But there was no urgency. No hope." Joy shrugged. "That's when I knew for sure. That's when I gave up."

Mary Alice nodded. "I know this is difficult. Let's try to go a little further, but we can stop whenever you need to. What happened next?"

"I got in my car and drove to the hospital. I think."

"You think?"

Joy nodded and rubbed her eyes. "Yeah. I honestly have no memory of the time between when they drove away and when I saw the doctor. None."

"That's actually pretty common. Those memories might come back or might not. It's your brain's way of sorting through the necessities and sloughing off the extra details that take up too much space and pain. At least for now."

Exactly what it felt like.

"What about when you got to the hospital? What happened then?"

"One nurse." A single tear escaped and ran down Joy's cheek. She let it fall.

"What do you mean?"

"One nurse. Melanie had a single person taking care of her. Waiting for us to come." Waiting for the grief to descend on the hospital room. "The tubes were gone, or maybe they'd never tried any sort of medical stuff on her. I never asked."

Joy sighed. "Dr. Sinclair had been both Mel's and my doctor since we were infants. In fact, she'd been in the room when we both were born." She stared off into space. "So Dr. Sinclair was the one who finally told Maggie that Melanie had died. I was just so glad I didn't have to do it." Joy remembered being slumped against the wall while the two women, two mothers, clung to each other and sobbed.

"What were you feeling in that moment?"

"I don't know. Mostly I wished I hadn't waited so long to go talk to Melanie. If I hadn't been so self-absorbed, Mel would still be here. I believe that with all my heart."

"Maybe."

What? Wasn't the counselor supposed to go on and on

about how it wasn't Joy's fault? How she couldn't know what would have happened? How she wasn't to blame?

"But even if that's true, even if she'd be alive, did you have anything to do with her death? Did you encourage it or drive her toward it in any way?"

Joy shook her head. "No." The word came out more like a croak.

"So we're going to work on letting go of the whole guilt thing."

Easier said than done. "It might not be guilt like a shared responsibility. It's more like regret, like. . .if only."

Mary Alice nodded. "If only. Two of life's most gut-wrenching words."

What is this place? Joy looked up and down the rows of antique-like trinkets and dark idols carved out of wood or jade. Ivory crystals hung from the ceiling, and the smell of incense flooded the room to the point where it was almost too much for her unaccustomed senses to take.

Raven smiled at the skinny, Gothic cashier taking money from a middle-aged woman draped in a muumuu and dripping with gold costume jewelry.

Joy peered at his name tag expecting it to say something like Zeus or Pegasus. Huh? It read KYLE. Really?

Kyle's dark eyes widened. "Hey Raven. How's it going? Haven't seen you in here for a while."

"Yeah, haven't really needed anything but to save money, so I just stayed away."

"I hear that." Kyle turned his gaze onto Joy.

"This is my friend, Joy. She's new. I just thought I'd show her around."

Why did she have to say she was new? How embarrassing.

"Great. Well, poke around—recent additions in the back. Let me know if you need anything." He turned back to his customer.

"So what is this place, exactly?" Joy whispered.

"It's an unofficial consignment store of sorts. People share, trade, sell, or barter for the things they need to help them get in touch with the spirit beyond. You can get Ouija boards, crystals, and other beads and things like incense and candles to help you connect."

Joy felt the edge of a leather journal. "But how do you know the difference between what's legitimate and what's commercial?" She picked up a furry rabbit's foot. Come on, seriously? A rabbit's foot?

"Good question." Raven seemed to think through her answer as she held up a silver necklace with a five-pointed star dangling from the center. "Well, you need to understand that connecting with the spirit world isn't about the actual game board or the bead itself. It has nothing to do with the individual crystal. It's all about the faith you ascribe to a specific token or trinket. So if you truly believe the incense wafting through the air and the crystal shining in the candlelight is going to help you clear your mind and release yourself over to what's beyond, then it will."

Joy nodded. That helped, actually. She didn't have to put her faith in a piece of glass. It was about her faith, not the glass. . .or whatever the item was. Made perfect sense.

"Remember the day we used the Ouija board and heard from Melanie?"

Joy winced. How could she forget?

"Lucas and I had complete faith we were being contacted by a spirit, so it makes it easy for it to happen."

"Yeah, but I had zero faith, so why was I able to see?"

Raven grinned. "That's the cool part. It was our belief at work allowing you to witness the truth."

That sort of made sense. But really, did Joy need to fully understand it in order to accept it? She'd seen the very principles Raven described at work right before her own eyes. Unlike the churchy faith she'd been witnessing all her life. Apparently from afar.

Joy picked up a pack of incense and a few long candles. Was she ready for her own Ouija board yet? No. The thought of being at home alone in her bedroom while contacting spirits made her skin crawl. Evidently she wasn't there yet.

Something told her it wouldn't be long.

Chapter 11

Joy pulled back the bright blue tarp sealing the dusty kitchen off from the rest of the once-abandoned house and peeked inside. She moved aside so Raven and Luc could follow her in. The three of them scanned the space with flashlights.

Wow. Joy had to admit someone had been working hard. Wallboard was up where it had only been studs the last time she'd seen inside. The floor had been laid, at least in the downstairs common area, and the fireplace was in. Her parents had made a ton of progress toward making the Lake McConaughy rehab the Christiansons' new home. But for now, it had another purpose.

She let the plastic fall and wiped the chalky drywall dust onto her jeans. She peered through the haze at the empty family room. Three ceiling fans hung from the rustic wooden beams of the vaulted ceiling. A huge fireplace with a stone chimney ran all the way up the back wall. Picture windows overlooked the private dock. Well, the space that would eventually hold their private dock whenever Dad got around to building it. Joy supposed the bathroom would come first—even though the dock would be way more fun.

Then again, the daydreams she and Mel had of languishing on a pontoon boat as they floated across the lake were never going to be realized. It wouldn't be nearly as fun alone. Nothing would. Maybe she and Raven could be friends like that one day. But would Joy ever be able to let her guard down enough to let someone in to the same degree she had Melanie?

"Will this do?" Joy spread her arms and glanced at Raven and Luc. Was it too risky to have brought them here for their meeting? Maybe the empty house was too creepy even for them. It should be for her. But strangely, she felt. . .um. . .expectant.

Expectant. Yeah, that was the word. With Raven and Lucas at the helm, Joy knew something big was going to take place tonight.

Raven's eyes explored the space from floor to ceiling. She grinned and looked at Lucas.

Lucas made a fist and punched it up in the air. "This is perfect. You have no idea how great this space is." He closed his eyes and stood still for half a minute. "I can feel the energy here. It's humming with activity."

Was that a good thing or a bad thing? If only her fear would catch up with her resolve.

Luc opened his eyes and searched Joy's. "You sure you want to do this?"

Surprisingly sure. Joy nodded. "I'm more positive than I've been about anything in a long time."

"Cool. Here's the deal." Luc surveyed the space like an architect. "We need to clear space on the floor. A circle big enough for the three of us, but not much more than that. You have the candles?" He turned to Raven.

She slid six black tapers from the sleeve of her jacket and held them up. "Of course."

"Great. Those will go around the perimeter of the circle along with the incense I brought."

"Uh-oh. Incense? That'll leave a smell, right?" What if Mom or Dad came out here before the scent wore off? They might assume it was pot or something.

Raven waved a dismissive hand. "We'll open some windows and turn on the fans when we're through. It'll be fine."

"Okay. Sounds good to me." Joy dampened a cleaning rag with water from the bottle she'd brought with her and dropped it on the floor in the center of what would become The Circle. Using the toe of her black Converse, she spread the rag in a wide arc, three hundred sixty degrees around her. When the perimeter was drawn, they set to work clearing the inside of dust and debris, leaving a gleaming bull's-eye on the otherwise pasty walnut floor.

Raven placed six golden candlestick holders evenly around the edge and set one long, black taper in each. Between them, she set a golden dish with a cone of incense in the center. She lit them, one by one, and the room took an eerie glow as the flickering of the candle flames danced on the walls and their faces. Soon the hint of cloves mingled with musk as the different incense buds let off their aromas.

Lucas's eyes reflected the brightest light as he crossed his legs and lowered himself just to the left of center in the shiny circle. Raven stepped over the candles and sat down beside Luc, their knees touching of course. Joy moved around the candle nearest her and sat just across from them, facing the center, careful not to let her leg touch the flames. The flickers reflected off the drywall dust and looked like a mist swirling around them, engulfing them.

"We have a few important things to do, a few items to dedicate, and then a special request to make for Joy." Lucas clasped his hands in front of him. All business.

"I have a question," Joy whispered. "Who exactly are we talking to when we make this request? Like, are we praying to God? Or what?" It was the *or what* that made her really nervous.

"We're talking to the universe, calling out to the spirit world that exists all around us. They've always been there just beyond your consciousness waiting for you to call on them." Lucas grinned and shook his head. "Oh, how your life will change. You'll have faith like you've never had it before. Your thinking will become clear as the blinders fall from your eyes. You'll come face-to-face with what's already been proven to you. What you accepted as true your whole life will manifest itself to you in ways different than you've known, but beyond what you could have imagined even in your dreams."

It sure made sense. So much more than the religion and church stuff Joy had had shoved down her throat her whole life. Something niggled at her though. Movies and stories of people selling their soul to the devil were considered horror films for a reason. Surely she wasn't doing that. How could something that felt so good and comforting be bad for her? Well, no matter, really. She was in far too deep to back out now. "Okay. I'm in. What's next?"

"Did you bring the letter?" Raven whispered.

Joy nodded and pulled a well-worn sheet of notepaper from her jacket pocket. It had been crumpled and wadded then smoothed out and reread many times during the past week since she got it back from the investigator. She smoothed it flat for the final time.

Every note like this starts off the same way, and apparently I'm no more creative than everyone else. So if you're reading this, it means I'm gone.

I'm sorry. I'm so sorry I had to do this. So sorry for so many things. I'd like to say I'm doing this for you guys, so you won't have to deal with how badly I've hurt you. But that's not why. I'm taking the selfish way out. I'm running from my problems and from facing the pain I caused everyone. I don't know how to make up for it. I've betrayed my best friend, and I don't know how to fix it. I can't look at the pain in her eyes knowing there's nothing I can do to erase what I did. I also can't live with the thought of not being with Austin, knowing the price we paid to get to this point.

What's wrong with me? Why do I have to hurt the people I love? And here comes yet another selfish choice of mine. . .the one I know will hurt you all the most. Yet, I can't help it. I'm making the wrong choice right now. . .but then again, that shouldn't really be a big shock to anyone, should it?

I'm so sorry to all of you. I'm so sorry that you'll be left with grief on top of everything else. I'm so sorry I couldn't face up to what I did.

I love you all,
Melanie

Joy balled the letter in her fist, her nervous perspiration dampening the paper. Her body reacted the same way it had every time she read it. Rage. The whole tragedy should have been avoided. It was unnecessary. Which was why it was so difficult. Melanie should be there. The thought was nothing short of maddening.

So senseless.

So needless.

So stupid.

Lucas put his hand on Joy's knee and squeezed gently, pulling her back to the present. "Would you like to say something before we continue?"

Talk directly to Melanie? That had to be what he meant.

Did she want to? If she spoke to her, how would she feel if Melanie didn't answer? What about if she did? But she had to reach out. She might not have the chance again.

Joy nodded. "Mel? Um. . ." Boy, this was hard. "I want you to know I love you. I already told you I forgive you for what happened. It's been almost a month since you. . .left. I want you to be free." *I want to be free.* "I don't know if you regret taking your life. I don't get how it all works. But I want you to know I've been so mad at you for leaving me. It's like a rage consuming me. You took *my* life when you took your own— and for reasons we'd have worked through. You didn't give me the chance to forgive you. You didn't trust that I would. But I love you. I always will. And I'm letting go of the anger. I'm letting go of you."

Joy spread the paper on her knee and glanced at the familiar handwriting for the final time.

So over.

She held the corner over the flame nearest her. The fire nibbled at the paper then took a bigger bite. Joy lifted it directly in front of her eyes and watched the words burn. The flame engulfed the last word on the page. *Melanie.*

When the paper burned down to the last fraction of an inch, Joy let the last tiny ember fall to the floor where it withered to ash.

"Perfect. How do you feel?" Lucas looked into Joy's eyes.

"Good. It feels good." Not exactly free, but on the way there.

"Raven has a gift for you. She will dedicate it now." Lucas nodded at his girlfriend.

Dedicate it?

Raven dangled a tiny black velvet bag from her finger and looked deep into Joy's eyes then clasped her left hand. "The black onyx is the stone of release. It will help you in confusing and difficult times. It's most useful when you need to let go of the past or release an attachment to someone or something."

She opened the bag and pulled out a silver ring with a black stone nestled in the center setting, flanked by two hands that appeared to be lifting it up. Raven closed her fist around the ring and raised it. "May the power of the onyx and the forces of the spirit world join together to release Joy from the bondage of the flesh. Help her to let go of the past and look forward to the future. Protect her from evil and danger, and guide her in the ways of self mastery."

Yes. This was exactly what Joy needed. Please be possible. Was an amen appropriate? Joy snuck a look at Lucas. His eyes were closed, and he swayed to a silent rhythm.

Joy closed her eyes, but they flew open again a second later when she felt Raven's fingers on her hand.

Raven held the ring on the tip of Joy's middle finger. "With the union of the physical and the spiritual, please send a guardian to be with Joy at all times. A protector. A companion. Guardian, present yourself to her"—Raven slid the ring onto Joy's finger—"now."

Peace and clarity washed over Joy like a tidal wave. She stared at the ring as her breathing slowed to a steady pace. Everything looked the same, but something had happened. What was it?

Joy felt heat, like puffs of warm air, on the top of her foot and glanced down.

She gasped. "Silas."

The gorgeous white wolf from her dream lay peacefully at her feet. Joy looked into the animal's beautiful blue eyes and saw all the grief and regret she once carried—now it was on him. She was free.

"Do you guys see him?" Joy stared at the animal, afraid to look away lest he disappear.

Raven and Lucas locked eyes. "See who?"

"The white wolf here beside me." Joy nodded her head in Silas's direction. "He's right here."

Lucas grinned. "He's yours alone. No one else can see him. He'll be with you always."

He was real? He was hers? Joy felt a mixture of gratitude, peace. . .and fear. The unknown, such a strange reality.

The tarp crinkled as someone pushed on it from the other side. "Who's in here?"

Silas growled, foam seeping from the corners of his mouth.

Joy squealed and reached for Silas's collar. "Who's there?"

"What is going on here?" Austin poked his head around the drape. "What are you doing?" He locked eyes with Joy.

Couldn't he hear that murderous barking even through the gulf between their worlds? Joy leaned down to whisper in Silas's ears. "It's okay, boy." Good thing it was pretty dark in there— just a few candles—so Austin couldn't see exactly what she was doing. Now, how to answer his question? She couldn't very well tell him about contacting spirits and talking to the dead. After all, Austin thought she was a Christian since she'd always drawn some pretty strong moral lines in the time they dated.

Deflect. That was the answer. "Excuse me? What are *we* doing? The better question is what are *you* doing here?"

"I saw the flicker of light and thought there might be intruders. I wanted to check things out in case you were being robbed or something." Austin looked pointedly at the incense. "Is this what I think it is? You're not letting these two mess with your head, are you?" His face scrunched in confusion and concern. "I don't understand."

"Well, guess what? You don't have to understand. It's got

nothing to do with you. In fact, it's none of your business."

Austin nodded. "I'm going to make it my business if you're messing around with this kind of thing. It's not a game." He gestured at the dark room. "Do your parents know you're here? They never let us—"

Joy watched a look pass between Lucas and Raven. Then Raven rolled her eyes.

"Austin, there is no 'us' anymore. I have nothing to say to you."

"That's not good enough for me."

"Look, even if Melanie hadn't died, things happened I can't just erase from my memory. We wouldn't be together even if she were still alive. But with her death, and all that's happened since, there's no way I can forget the truth. I have no interest in you, and I don't trust you." Joy took a deep breath. Might as well let him have it. "I don't love you."

"Fine." His eyes flashed. "But I'm still going to have to talk to your parents about all of this." He gestured at the circle.

"Ugh, since when did you become so boring? You know, if I had suggested we come out here alone while we were dating, you'd have jumped at the chance. With or without my parents' permission."

"Yeah, well, I've learned a lot since then. Apparently you've done some changing yourself. This is so unlike you."

Lucas jumped to his feet. "Man, you don't know her at all. Just leave her alone. It's not your problem to solve. In fact, like Joy said, it's none of your business. Which is probably what's making you mad enough to spit nails. You have no power over her. You gave that up the day you started up with her best friend."

Austin glared at Luc. "Who do you think you are?"

"Um. . .invited. Which is more than I can say about you. How about we say good-bye?"

Chapter 12

The doorbell rang, but Dad got to the door before Joy or her mother could get there.

Stella floated in ahead of Grandpa, her billowy shirt like a powder-blue cloud.

"We're here and ready for some turkey and dressing!" Grandpa stepped into the house, changing the mood with his first word.

"Not until tomorrow, Grandpa." Joy poked her head from behind Mom.

Grandpa smiled and reached his arms out for Joy as he'd done every time she'd seen him for seventeen years.

Joy fell into the Old Spice embrace and clung to the familiar wool of his favorite sweater. He held on a little longer than usual but, to Joy, not nearly long enough.

His wife tugged on his arm and grinned. "My turn. How's my favorite teenager?" Stella dropped her slouchy red bag and pulled Joy into a voluptuous hug, leaning in close to Joy's ear. "We have to talk. I have some things for you to read." She released Joy. "Looking forward to some girl talk. Your grandpa's hearing ain't what it used to be. Or so he says."

"Huh?" Grandpa cupped his hand around his ear.

"Just as I suspected. Selective hearing."

Grandpa's eyes twinkled, and Stella laughed as though they

hadn't had that little exchange every day since they married three years ago.

Stella held up a bright pink acrylic-tipped finger, and a dozen silver bangles clanked to her elbow. "I have an idea. Let's leave these old fuddy-duddies to catch up. You come with me. We'll have some of that girl talk while I unpack." Stella shouldered her Coach bag and ambled down the hallway toward the guest room.

Joy followed. Should be interesting. She dropped onto the double bed and bounced. The springs weren't quite what they used to be when Joy used the same bed as a young girl.

Stella shut the door in the bedroom and lifted her shirt, exposing her wrinkled belly, then lowered the waistband of her stretchy, shiny jeans.

What on earth was she doing? Joy felt the door beckoning from behind her back, yet she couldn't move. Joy stared, her eyes glued to Stella like rubberneckers driving past a car accident. She just couldn't take her eyes off the older woman. But please, no more reveal.

Stella pulled her skin taut and lowered her pants just a bit more. She raised her eyebrows and cocked her head, like waiting for a reaction.

To what?

The pants shifted a bit lower, and Joy saw it.

Orange and black peeked out above the top of Stella's jeans. Joy leaned in to peer a bit closer. "Is that. . . ?" No way!

Stella laughed. "Yeah. It's my latest addition. I got it since I saw you last." She leaned far over and pressed on her chest, trying to see her own pelvis around her ample breasts. Probably wasn't happening without a mirror.

"A tiger?"

"Yeah. Not just any tiger. That's my Kitty." Stella pulled her pants back into place and patted the spot where her tattoo lay hidden.

"What made you pick a tiger? Just curious." Why not a heart with a rose and Grandpa's name? Eww. Gross.

"I just wanted to make sure Kitty was with me everywhere I went. Now she is." Stella smiled. "If you remember, the last time I saw you was under pretty heavy circumstances."

"Uh. Yeah. I remember." Nice way to describe a teenager's funeral.

"When I got home, I just wanted something to make me feel better."

"I don't see how a tattoo could accomplish that. But whatever makes you happy, I guess."

"Kitty is real. She's mine." Stella stared at Joy like she searched for answers. "She, um, takes care of me."

Wait a second. "Do you mean your tiger is your spirit companion?"

Stella squinted. "What do you know about that stuff?"

"I don't know. A little bit, I guess." Meet Silas. "I've been looking into some things." Talk about an understatement.

"Wow. Quite a development since the last time I saw you. You and I have a lot to talk about, but don't let your grandpa know what's going on in your head. He'll go all prayer-time on you." Stella chuckled. "He's been all over me ever since I started exploring. Says I'm not the same woman he married." She shrugged. "I guess in a lot of ways he's right—this is a far cry from church secretary, that's for sure. So, don't say anything or he'll think I'm influencing you."

"Don't worry. I'm the picture of restraint these days."

Stella lifted some things out of her suitcase and lined them on top of the dresser, pointing each item in a different direction.

"What's this?" Joy lifted an oval-shaped crystal and looked

through the prism into the light.

"Those things are nothing more than tools. . .or they're everything." Stella shrugged. "All depends."

Like Raven had said the other day.

Joy sighed and lay back on the bed. "I'm getting it—a lot of it anyway. Talking to the universe. Reaching out. . .you know. . . to any that might be listening. But it all just seems so cosmic. . . unreachable."

"Oh, I know. Believe me, I went through the same skepticism you have. It's normal to resist releasing yourself to what's beyond all that you can see. Eventually. . .slowly, you'll let go of this piece of confusion and that fragment of doubt until you're wide open to truth."

Joy propped herself up on her elbows and watched Stella hold up her billowing sleeve as she adjusted some of her trinkets. "It's just hard to let go when you thought you already knew the truth."

"Right. When faith and doubt intersect, there has to be some kind of connection or explosion of truth that makes sense."

Silas.

Melanie.

Joy couldn't argue with those explosions of truth. "I like the way you put it." Joy held Stella's gaze. "I heard from Melanie."

"Hmm." Stella frowned. "I wondered. Tragedy has a way of opening people to the universe. The moment when a person is most vulnerable and open to be reached."

"Yeah, makes sense to me." Joy twirled her onyx ring around her middle finger. Get the focus off her. "So how did you get into all of this? What prompted you to dig into the spirit world?"

"Hmm. Good question. I'm not really sure it was any one

thing. Just lived a lot of life that added up to me searching for the truth. Once I started feeling unfulfilled by organized religion and opened my mind to other options, doors opened and walls crashed down until I could see clearly."

Joy nodded and crossed her legs, leaning forward on the bed. Stella made total sense. How strange. She was just the nice lady Grandpa married after Grandma died. Now Joy was coming to her for spiritual advice?

Grandpa poked his head through the doorway. Had he been listening?

"What are you two doing back here all alone? I miss my grandbaby. Come on out and see your ol' granddad."

Joy didn't miss the look that passed between Grandpa and Stella. Uh-oh.

ᔕ

"Can you pass the sweet potatoes, Joy?" Stella reached a hand across the table, holding the flowy sleeve of her pumpkin-colored silk blouse away from the green bean casserole.

Gladly. Anything to get them out from under her nose where the sickeningly sweet smell of toasted marshmallows gagged her. Joy rose a few inches from her chair and passed the bubbly concoction across the table. Aunt Sue intercepted, spooned a glob onto her plate, then passed it to Stella.

Mom dinged her fork on her water goblet. "I'm so glad you're all here with us to celebrate Thanksgiving. It's been a rough year in a lot of ways, but an incredibly blessed one in so many other ways. So. . ."—she looked around the table with a smile—"how about if we each take a moment to say three things we're thankful for this year?"

Or they could—may be a crazy idea, but—they could eat while the food was warm.

Mom's smile was frozen to her face. "Who wants to go first?"

She had to be kidding. What could Joy say she was thankful for? She supposed she could tell her family about Silas. Would Mom be happy for her? Um. . .no. Joy glanced at Beatrice. There would be no talk of Joy's new guardian spirit at the Thanksgiving table. They'd commit her for sure.

Maybe Joy could talk about her new friends who helped her talk to dead people. She could only imagine what Mom would say about that. No, she had to come up with some kind of acceptable answer. *I'm thankful for world peace. I'm thankful for food on the table. I'm thankful for a warm house to call my own.* Really. What kind of answer did Mom expect from Joy? It really wasn't the year for sunshine and rainbows.

"Me. Me." Beatrice beamed and waved her hand.

Mom sat down. "Okay, you can go first, Bea."

"Well, I'm thankful that I'm going to be an artist." Beatrice paused and looked around the table as though making sure everyone was listening. "I really am going to be an artist."

Joy smiled. "That's great. I've seen your work. You'll be a really good one."

"I know. And I'm thankful for my hamster, JoJo."

Aunt Sue opened her mouth to say something, but Beatrice shook her head and held up a finger. "Just wait. I have more. And I'm thankful for my books and for playing in the snow and for swimming."

Mom patted Bea's hand. "That's wonderful. I'm thankful for swimming, too."

What could Joy possibly say that would top swimming?

Dad raised his glass of Pepsi. "I'll go next. I'm thankful for a successful career, a healthy family, and the prospect of moving into our new home this year."

In that order?

And it might be their new home this year if they ever got

the work done. Wasn't it about time to hire more people? Maybe that could be Joy's answer. She could be thankful for contractors and construction workers and drywallers. . .maybe even painters. Wonder what Dad would say to that?

Joy ripped the corners off her white paper napkin. Mom had gone all out and bought the big ones that came something like forty to a pack. The supersized five-hundred pack was never good enough for Thanksgiving.

Mom's turn. "I'm so very thankful for the cross." Her hand rose to her neck, and she lightly touched the diamond pendant on the slender white gold chain. "I'm thankful for my eternal hope in Christ and that I can pass it on to my family."

Typical super-spiritual Mom answer. Joy tore another strip off her napkin and added it to a growing pile.

And now Grandpa's turn. "I'm thankful for my salvation and for a beautiful family who loves me." He placed his calloused, liver-spotted hand over Joy's pale one. "And I'm most thankful for my granddaughter who has just made it through the roughest moments in her life."

That's what he thought—the year wasn't over yet.

Mom turned to Joy. "Your turn."

Oh come on. Seriously? How about Stella? Or Aunt Sue?

Joy stabbed a bite of turkey and stuffing and popped it in her mouth, hoping to hold off the agony for as long as possible. Couldn't she just pass? Did anyone really expect her to come up with something to be thankful for?

Okay. Just get it over with. "I'm thankful for. . . I really don't know. I guess I'm thankful that we're together and for a family that loves and supports me." Wasn't that enough? Joy flattened the pile of napkin strips without making eye contact with anyone. Come on, peeps, talk amongst yourselves. Nothing to see here.

But they remained silent. Had they set this up ahead of time? Joy could picture Mom gathering them in the corner telling them she worried about her daughter's mental health and wanted her to realize there were good things in life among the pain. So like Mom.

Joy snuck a peek. Everyone stared at her, waiting. Okay. One more thing would get them off her back. She couldn't very well say she was thankful for Silas. And Mom and Dad sure wouldn't understand if Joy said she was grateful Melanie had reached out to her from beyond. How about napkins? She was thankful for napkins? No? Okay.

Ooh. She had it. "I'm thankful for new beginnings." Joy sat up straighter. That should do it.

Mom beamed.

Phew. Joy stuffed her mouth with cranberry salad so no one would ask her for more info.

"New beginnings are a truly wonderful thing, sweetheart."

Sure, but the beginnings of what exactly?

🌀

Raven had said the spirit world buzzed with activity on holidays, especially nights like Halloween, Christmas, but Thanksgiving, too. Wonder why? Joy raised her finger and pressed the doorbell. Three cars in Luc's driveway, but the house was pitch-black. Were they in there?

The door opened slowly, and Raven stood in the dark entrance, her face illuminated by the candle dripping into the golden candleholder cupped in her hands. The same holders they'd used the other night. The night of Silas. Joy looked down to her right.

He wasn't there.

She fought panic. Why had he left her? "Silas is gone," Joy hissed at Raven.

Raven nodded slowly. "He must believe you are safe here." She spoke in a monotone then turned toward the inside of the house.

Weird.

Joy followed Raven, mimicking her deliberate walk and silence. They passed through the threshold into the dark family room. The cloying scent of cloves and cinnamon attacked Joy's senses. A breeze swirled around her and made her shiver, yet heat climbed from her chest and up her neck.

People clustered in three circles, four to each one. One group hummed in unison as they swayed to a rhythm only they heard. The second group huddled in the far corner with an Ouija board open between them. The third had their eyes closed as they passed a pipe around the circle.

No question what was in the pipe they smoked. What had Joy gotten herself into? Austin thought he'd stumbled onto quite the scene the other night; he wouldn't believe this.

Raven beckoned to Lucas.

He passed the pipe and rose from his spot on the floor then approached with the same deliberate gait as Raven. "Hey Joy." He spoke in that monotone hush voice as well.

What was with these people? She should have stayed home and played UNO with Grandpa and Beatrice. Grandpa had seemed kind of sad when she left until Stella told him to leave her alone. "Teenagers want to be out, free," she explained as she twirled across the room. Then she'd promised him a few games of Yahtzee later. That part perked him up.

"Why don't you take my spot over there?"

"Yeah, I don't know if I'm ready for that."

"Check it out. You say that every time you face something new. . .then you try it and love it. Why don't you just go for it? You know you will eventually."

Luc had a point. She sure hadn't been exercising much resolve lately. But no drugs. Too far, even for her. "Yeah, I don't think I can, Luc. It's too much."

"Okay, well, do whatever. It's cool."

The Ouija board. After Joy's first experience with it, who would have thought it would seem like the least dangerous option in any room? She approached the huddle, recognizing only one of the two faces she could see. A boy in the grade below hers. What was that kid's name? The other one seemed way older. The, uh, silent type.

Joy lowered herself in one of the gaps between bodies then looked to her left to see the girl who'd had her back to the room.

No way. Heather? "What are you doing here?"

"You're into this stuff? Wow. I didn't see that coming at all." Heather grinned as she shook her head.

So glad to have amused her. If only the ground would open up and swallow Joy whole. She had to get out. Joy started to rise without bumping into the boy at her left, but Heather grabbed her hand and pulled her down. As she plunked to the floor again, the quiet guy bolted. Wow. That was fast. Something she'd said?

"Don't leave, Joy. Look, I'm sorry I've been insensitive. I've been going through some things, too. It's no excuse. . .just what it is." Her voice trailed off, and her eyes looked sad. "Stay. You don't have to say anything. Just join us. Maybe you'll like it."

Heather seemed almost normal. Almost human. All right, Joy would stay for a little bit, but the minute things got uncomfortable, she was out of there.

Something brushed against her leg. Joy looked down. Silas! He must have sensed her unease and reappeared. She reached down as if to stroke him. If only she could feel the heat of his body beneath her hand, but such was the limitation of the gulf between life and death.

The trio waited with their hands on the planchette. Joy rested her fingertips beside theirs. *Here we go.*

Heather opened her mouth. "Are you alive or dead?"

Well, that was an interesting way to start a conversation with a spirit.

The glass piece began to inch across the board.

B

This felt familiar. Not as creepy as the first few times though.

O

Joy stole a look at Heather. Her thick hair swung past her shoulders and draped across the game board. She flipped it back as the planchette slid toward the center. Her green eyes grew wide.

T

It took everything in Joy not to let go of the planchette to wipe her hand on her jeans.

H

Both?

Heather looked up at Joy and shrugged then back at the game board. "You're both alive and dead?"

The planchette hovered over *Yes*.

Joy cleared her throat. "Are you saying you died once and now you're alive?"

Yes.

"Do you miss being alive in human form?"

Yes.

Joy had to know, but she wasn't sure if either answer would soothe her. "Would you come back if you could?"

No.

"Why not?"

R
E
G
R
E
T

It was all Joy could do not to follow the skinny guy out the door. She should have never come.

Chapter 13

School was a complete impossibility. Joy couldn't imagine sitting in class, listening to lectures, working on group projects. She shuddered. Group projects were the worst, even at the best of times. But on that day, in that moment, Joy couldn't do something so normal. Not when her life had spun out of her grasp. It had become virtually unrecognizable to her.

Ghostlike memories haunted her around every corner. She darted in and out of rooms, before the bells rang or after classes started so she could avoid Austin. A spirit wolf followed at her heels most of the day. Was this her life, or was she acting in some twisted made-for-cable movie?

Escape. Joy needed time to reflect. Yeah. A reflection day. That's what she'd call it. It sounded way better than cutting school. She had to get out of Ogalalla no matter what. North Platte wasn't that far. Maybe a movie and a walk around the mall, just for a change of scenery.

After pocketing one of Mom's twenty-dollar bills for gas along with her stash of birthday money, Joy slung her backpack into the passenger seat of her car. She slid into the driver's seat then started up her yellow Bug. Shivering, she flipped the heat on full blast, backed out of the driveway, and turned toward the interstate. North Platte or bust. Shouldn't be that difficult to find, though she'd never driven all the way by herself. Her parents wouldn't have allowed it. But Joy wasn't in a permission-asking mood.

Once upon a time, she would never have dreamed of blatantly ignoring her parents' wishes like this. Rule follower. Girl next door. Dependable. All terms people might have used to describe Joy. At least in the past. Now though, it seemed like Joy was out for whatever Joy wanted, and it felt good. She hadn't thought about putting herself first before, but things changed so fast, it no longer made any sense not to look out for number one. In the end, she was the only person she could be sure of. So what if she had fewer friends? So what if people thought less of her? She didn't really care when she looked at the big picture.

Joy took her eyes off the stretch of flat interstate and looked beside her. Silas was sound asleep in the passenger seat, resting so he could be on alert when he sensed a change in Joy's mood. She'd really come to know her guide well. He'd never let anything happen to her.

She took the ramp into North Platte. Now, where was the movie theater?

On second thought, that was something she would've done with Melanie. How about something different? She'd been wanting to do some research, so she'd hang out at the library for a while. Cut school to go to the library—how lame.

After finding it right where it was last time she'd been there, Joy buzzed into a parking space.

"No school today?" The librarian lifted her glasses and looked at Joy over the bridge of her nose the instant Joy walked through the doors.

"No. I'm homeschooled." Not really a huge lie.

The disbelief was evident in the crease of the librarian's eyes as she slammed the staple through the stack of papers she'd been collating. She must've heard that one before.

Get a grip, lady. It wasn't like Joy had gone out drinking or partying. She was at a library for crying out loud.

Joy wandered to the religion section with no idea exactly what she was looking for. No way she'd go ask the Nazi up front. Joy scanned the rows of books about everything except what she'd been experiencing with Raven, Lucas, and Silas. . . and now Heather. What would she call it? Was it actually a religion?

She envisioned an old, leather-bound *Neverending Story*-type book called something like the *Guardian Spirit Bible* or something fancy like that. But no. She'd found better stuff at home with her Google searches. The closest it seemed she could get were the books on Wicca or Paganism, neither of which had anything to do with her. She was just being spiritual, not satanic. There was a difference, right? Maybe no one had written a book about that. She'd have to ask Raven later.

Okay. She was bored. Enough research. Time to face the real reason she'd come all the way to North Platte—even if she hadn't admitted it to herself. There had to be a tattoo shop nearby. Joy found an empty computer station and did a quick search. Flipping through the options, she liked the looks of Twizted Needle on its Facebook page. It seemed clean and professional. But, oh no, they required a parent or guardian to be present with minors. Well, Joy would just have to look like she wasn't a minor. At least she was wearing her Nebraska Huskers sweatshirt. The tattoo guy might believe she was a college student.

The next problem was how she could make sure the tattoo captured Silas's individual look. It had to be him. Not just any white wolf. Him. They had to get the eyes just right, which would mean she'd have to have a picture of exactly what she wanted. She typed *white wolf* in the search engine. So many pictures were just not quite right. She scrolled for miles through photos that came close, but missed the mark in the eyes.

Finally, there it was, the perfect picture of her Silas. Almost as though he'd posed for a portrait session himself.

Print.

Now, would she need an appointment? Could be a problem. She couldn't ditch another day of school to come back later, so it had to be today. Besides, if she didn't do it right away, she might lose her nerve. Maybe they wouldn't be busy since it was the middle of the day. She navigated back to the Facebook page of the tattoo parlor and entered the number into her cell phone.

"Twizted Needle. What's up?"

"Hi. I was wondering if you could get me in for a tattoo this afternoon. I'm only in town today."

The librarian gasped and dropped her stack.

Joy shot her a glare. Hopefully the tattoo shop wasn't owned by the lady's nephew or something. As if.

"Um. . ."

Joy heard the rustling of paper. An appointment book?

"Yeah. Looks like if you come over right now, we can get you in, if it isn't too big."

"Cool. I'm on my way. Should take about ten minutes."

ॐ

It wasn't too late to back out. Joy stared at the brown brick building. She didn't have to go in. If she did, someone would take a needle and shove it into her skin over and over and over. What was she thinking? She glanced to the right and locked eyes with Silas. No, it was important she do it. A final step in uniting them permanently. Eternally.

Time to face the music, or the needle, in this case. Joy

climbed out then slammed the door shut. She smoothed her clothes and ran her fingers through her long hair. Look older.

The door chimed as she stepped inside.

"Be right with you." The tattoo artist called from behind the white divider as he finished up with a client's back tattoo.

She wandered to the wall where photos of people who'd had tattoos done, and even of people receiving tattoos, hung on display. A coffee table held albums with even more samples of possible designs. Joy flipped through the pages, arriving at a section displaying tattooed body parts she could have gone her whole life without seeing. The heat crept up her neck and warmed her ears. Act cool.

Joy patted the printout of Silas she'd tucked into her pocket. Hopefully it wouldn't be a problem.

"Joy Christianson? Come on over here." The young, bald guy with head-to-toe tattoos slid back on his chair and leaned out of his cubicle to beckon her.

Prepared to plead ignorance about the age restriction, she stepped around the curtain and offered a wide, albeit shaky, smile.

"Hey Joy. I'm Mike." He stuck out a hand to shake hers. "Oops." He ripped off a rubber glove then shook her hand. "What did you want done today?"

So far, so good. Joy reached into her pocket and pulled out the folded picture of Silas. "This is what. Probably just the face. I'm worried about the eyes though. I need them to look just like this."

Mike nodded. "Oh yeah. This is a great shot. It won't be difficult at all. Except white can be kind of funny on the skin." He peered closer at the picture. "What if we did the wolf in black outline and only the eyes in color?"

Joy gasped. "That's so perfect. I love it."

"Great. Me, too. Where did you want to put it?"

"Well, tell me what you think. Originally I had thought about over my heart."

Mike grimaced and shook his head.

Joy shrugged. "But the more I think about that, the heart is kind of in the middle of the sternum, which would be weird."

"Uh, yeah. Assuming this is your first tattoo. If you were covered, it wouldn't be a problem."

"Right. And it doesn't make sense to put it somewhere I can't see it. So I think I'd like him right here on the side of my thigh where I can touch him if I need to or look down and see him. Plus right there, I know he is right in step with me everywhere I go."

"Sounds pretty well thought out and easy enough. Let me work up a stencil and we'll get started." He slipped the picture under a piece of tracing paper and set to work.

Joy's eyes remained locked on the paper. Get the eyes right. That was all she asked.

"Okay then, have a seat." Mike spun the chair so she'd be facing him.

Joy settled in the seat. This was it. She could still back out. Wonder how many people actually did at that point?

"Okay." Mike laid the stencil over Joy's thigh. "How's this, here?"

Hmm. If it were too high, she'd hardly ever see it. "Actually, could you scoot it down just an inch or two?"

"No problem." Mike wiped the design away with an alcohol pad and repositioned it.

She didn't want it to show when she wore regular shorts, but just above that would be. . . "Perfect."

"Great." Mike turned and fiddled with the tattoo gun and ink tubs. He whipped back around, gun in hand. "You ready?"

Joy nodded and gripped the armrests. The gun buzzed. Joy squeezed harder and clenched her teeth. She turned her head away as Mike neared her leg with the humming needle. Closer and closer—like slow motion.

Oh, come on already. Get it over with. Joy scrunched her eyes shut.

The buzzing made contact with the surface of her skin. The first instant it tickled like butterfly wings, then, not so much. Not as bad as she expected, but definitely not a nap in the sun. But the work had begun, and there was no turning back now.

A quick peek at the work revealed a bloody wolf murder on her thigh. Breathe in. Breathe out.

How strange that human beings not only asked for someone to shoot ink into their skin with needles, but even more that they'd actually pay for it. The price of beauty. . .or art. . .or whatever.

Ouch. That spot was tender. When Mike went back to areas he'd already started work on. . .zowie! Joy wanted to climb the walls, but she held tight.

Phew. A break. Mike changed the color in the gun. Time for the blue.

Joy watched closely as he went to work on those perfect eyes. The color pooled with blood on the surface of her skin, so she couldn't quite make out what lay beneath.

After ninety minutes of needles, Mike put the gun down. "That's it. Want to take a look?"

"Absolutely." Joy lifted her feet from the rests and placed them on the floor.

Mike put a hand on her elbow. "Steady as you go. It'll take a few minutes to get your sea legs back."

Joy almost laughed. She'd only been sitting for an hour and a half, but as she started to walk her knees wobbled. Wow. Yeah.

Sea legs—good term.

Mike helped her over to the mirror, and she turned sideways to look at her Silas on her leg. "It's exactly what I wanted. Beautiful." Now Silas would be with her forever. Joy looked down at the wolf's face staring up at her, panting. Silas approved.

Chapter 14

Y ou're a smart girl."
      So they've said.
The chair rolled across the floor mat.

Joy glanced up from counting carpet squares. What was Mary Alice doing?

"I think this'll help you to step back and see where you fit on the timeline of the stages of grief." Mary Alice Gianetti's orange bob bounced as she talked.

Real human emotions shouldn't be reduced to scientific stages. Shouldn't that have been part of Psych 101? Or maybe all shrink-types believed people all fit into nice, neat little boxes with bows. "Stages of grief?"

"Yeah, if you look back, you'll see that you've followed a pretty textbook pattern, as most people do." Mary Alice pulled a sheet from her printer and offered it to Joy.

Sigh. Joy cracked the knuckles on both hands before accepting the sheet.

"You'll see by the chart. . ."

She let her eyes trail down the page to see where she fit on the graph of human existence.

Denial and isolation? Check.

Anger? Check.

Bargaining? Check.

Depression? Check. Check.

Acceptance? Never.

Where did the list say *talks to dead people?* How about *goes Goth?* And what about *hates life?*

". . .there at the bottom. It's quite clear you feel depressed, but I'm already seeing signs of you moving toward acceptance."

Joy shook her head. No way. "I don't see how that's possible. I can promise you I'll never accept what's happened. Ever."

Mary Alice shook her head. "No. I don't mean you're becoming okay with the events that took place. More. . .you'll make the truths a part of your new reality and grow into a person who once experienced some horrific things. They become a real part of your past, but will no longer define who you are."

Hmm. Was that what Joy was doing?

"But in this process of evolving, we have to make sure you're still you on the other side of it."

Huh? That seemed a bit contradictory. "Well, if it's all like a natural part of the process, why not just let it develop? Why worry about creating some final outcome?"

"We have to make sure you're in a healthy place as you move forward because it will lay the foundation for the rest of your life. You're probably in the most pivotal moment of your life, and we have to manage it well."

Sounded like loads of fun. Joy twisted her head until her neck popped.

"So, for the next few sessions, starting right now, I'd like to bring in your parents. Okay by you?"

And the fun just kept on coming. "They're here?" No way they skipped work.

"Yes. They both arrived a few minutes ago and are just waiting until I invite them in." The counselor leaned in and waited until Joy lifted her eyes. "You can say no."

What good would it do? Joy shrugged. "I don't really care— nothing to hide."

Mary Alice paused. A flicker of doubt crossed her eyes but faded just as quickly. She stood up, though didn't gain much altitude over her seated self. Short legs made long strides to the door. She opened it and poked her head out. "Come on back, Mr. and Mrs. Christianson."

"Please. Call us Peg and Alan." Mom sat beside Joy.

Dad shook Mary Alice Gianetti's hand. "It's a pleasure to meet you. I've heard a lot about you. . .well, from my wife. My little girl's been a bit of a clam these days."

Joy rolled her eyes.

Mary Alice nodded. "That's fine. I've encouraged Joy to keep our sessions private if she wished."

Hmm. Was she on Joy's side for once?

"Okay. Let's dive right in. Joy, your mom and dad are concerned about what's been going on. From the mood changes, the dress, the suspension. . .it's worth taking a look at. I asked them to join us for the session today, but I want you to know we aren't here to dig up trouble or break your confidentiality. We're only talking." She turned to Joy's mom. "Peg, would you like to start? Share your concerns with Joy."

Mom nodded and turned to Joy, biting her lip. "I've seen some scary things going on with you. You're acting very strangely, you're hanging around with people who make me very nervous, and Austin said those new friends of yours are no good."

Austin. Seriously? Mom was going to listen to what he had to say? This was not good. Had he told her everything? "What do you mean no good?"

"He just said they are kind of known for making some bad choices."

Oh? Austin hadn't ratted her out completely. Which was smart, or he'd have sealed their fate for good. Well, it was sealed, but he didn't believe her. It was the hope he held that kept him from telling all. She could work with it.

Dad cleared his throat. "I guess what makes us very nervous is how much you've changed."

"You're just not yourself lately." Mom put her hand on Joy's.

"Of course I'm not myself." Joy turned to Mary Alice. "Does this make any sense? How am I expected to be myself?" She looked at Mom. "Don't you understand what's happened in my life? What I've gone through? My life got flipped completely upside down. I don't see how people don't get it." Joy shook her head. "You know, I don't think you guys are paying attention. I think you expect everything to return to your idea of normal within a short matter of time. In the meantime, you're just looking the other way hoping the time passes quickly."

Mary Alice nodded. "Good, Joy. Now tell us. What would you like them to know?"

Joy locked eyes with her mom. "I want you to accept that I will never be the same. I have to reinvent who I am, and you might not like me when it's all said and done. Who knows?" Joy looked out the window. "Facts. I would do anything to change them, but I can't and neither can you." Joy jumped up from her chair, knocking it backward. She ran out through the parking lot into the field behind the church.

Run. She fled as fast as she could make her legs move, not fast enough, not far enough. But at least it was something. The wind whipped her face, but she felt alive with Silas at her side.

🌀

"There you are. I hardly ever see you around anymore." Austin let his eyes roll from Joy's head to her toes. "Then again,"—he shook his head—"I don't know if I would recognize you if we weren't standing in front of your locker."

Whatever. So he didn't like her in black? So what? "Look, Austin, I don't have time to chat right now." She dug through her locker. Where was that textbook? She had to get away from Austin, even if meant leaving her book behind and missing a homework assignment.

Austin reached in front of Joy's face and blocked her locker. "Joy, look at me." He grabbed her face between his hands and forced her to turn toward him. "What's going on with you? I've heard some things, and I've seen stuff. . . . Those guys are messing you up. I can't just stand back and watch it happen." Austin dropped his hands and clenched them in fists. "Please don't ask me to do that."

How wonderful it would feel to fall into his embrace. So familiar. So comforting. Joy felt her body pulled like a magnet. His eyes reacted, like they knew.

Those same eyes had locked on Melanie's seconds before their kiss, maybe an hour before her death.

Oh right. Reality doused her like a bucket of ice water. What was she thinking? She spun around and reached in her locker for her book. Then turned to leave. Austin took a step toward her.

"You leave me alone." She jabbed a finger at him with each word. "I'm serious, Austin. Dead serious."

His eyes clouded.

She spun to walk away.

Austin followed. "Listen. I know I hurt you. But there's more to the story. . ."

Ugh. What part of "leave me alone" did he not get?

"The worst thing I did was kiss Melanie. I didn't kill her."

"You might as well have."

〄

"Guess who's here." Mom's voice sang down the hall.

Great. What now? Joy slid off her bed and stretched as she slumped to her door. She cracked it open. "What's up?"

"I have a surprise for you. Come on out."

"Oh goodie." Because Joy loved surprises so much. She shook her head. Why couldn't Mom get it? Surprises, no thanks. Meddling, no thanks. Joy approached the family room in time to see Kelsey shaking the snow out of her curls and handing Mom her coat.

Perfect end to a perfect day. Now smile. Don't be rude. "Hey, Kels. What's up?"

"Look who's here for a sleepover." Mom flashed a proud smile.

A sleepover. Mom took it upon herself to impose Kelsey on Joy for an entire night? Kels was great, but Joy wasn't really in the market for a new BFF. All she wanted was sleep.

"I hope it's okay I'm here." She stole a glance at Mom. "My parents had to. . . They had plans tonight."

What, you're too young to stay home alone? Not buying it. Lying doesn't become you, Kels. It was a setup if Joy ever smelled one. "It's cool. I didn't have anything going on." Joy shrugged.

What would she do with Kelsey all night? So much for reading stuff on the Internet and crashing early. She'd had so many weird dreams lately that all she really wanted to do was sleep, but now she'd have to play all-night hostess at a girly sleepover. Yay. Maybe they could do their makeup and hair and talk about boys all night long. Joy sighed.

She cocked her head back toward her room. "I'll lead the way."

Kelsey followed Joy into the bedroom. "So what do you

want to do tonight?" She bounced on the bed. Her expression was eager, but the twitch in her upper lip gave away her nerves.

"Why don't we just lay it all out? Who set this up tonight, you or my mom?"

Kelsey stared at the floor. "We're just worried about you. We care."

Joy nodded. "I get that. I really do. Even appreciate it. But I'm not really the best company right now. So we'll have to get through this, but I apologize in advance for the bad time you're going to have. It's not like I'm the life of the party."

Kelsey glanced up. "You sure used to be. I miss that." She sighed. "I'm sorry it had to change."

Yeah, me, too. "Well, how about we watch a movie?" That would at least occupy some time with no talking required.

Kelsey grinned. "Okay. What do you want to watch? You pick."

She sure couldn't pick one of her and Melanie's favorites. What other options would make Kelsey happy? Make her think everything was fine? "How about *Polar Express*? I know it's a kid's movie, but I watch it every year, and it is Christmastime. We can put a fire in the fireplace and turn off the lights. Make some popcorn."

Kelsey beamed. "Sounds perfect, actually. Love that movie. Maybe we could even make it a tradition."

Simmer down. There wouldn't be a tradition. "Never know."

⟲

Fire roaring in the fireplace. Popcorn on the coffee table. Joy handed out blankets, and they were hunkered down on the sofa with the movie playing less than thirty minutes later.

As the Polar Express roared, Joy stole a glance at Kelsey. Sound asleep. Joy tiptoed to her parents' bedroom and put her ear to the door. No sound from in there; they were fast asleep.

Alone. Finally. Joy crept back to the family room and knelt on the floor in front of the fire. She stared into the flames and let them overtake her mind. She closed her eyes, and the heat bathed her face with warmth.

"Melanie, are you here?"

The fire intensified with a poof, its bright light filling the room for a brief instant.

Joy nodded. It was time. "I have a few questions for you." Joy took a deep breath. "Number one. Do you like where you are?" The fire blasted another *yes*.

"Okay. My second question is. . .should I join you?"

The flames blasted like fireworks one time. Another *yes*.

Joy stared into the flames as they danced. She sat with Melanie, hanging out. It wasn't the same. Would it be the same if Joy. . .crossed over and went to her? Would it be like times past, or would it only be a shadow of the memory? If Joy knew for sure, if she could confirm that it would be the same, she'd go to Melanie.

Minutes. . .maybe hours passed, evidenced only by the tingling in Joy's legs and feet. Yet she couldn't pry her eyes off the flame that was quickly dimming into ash.

"What are you doing?"

Joy glanced behind her.

Kelsey had risen from the pillow, propping herself with her elbow. She looked from Joy to the nearly extinguished fire then back "What's going on?"

Joy turned her gaze back to the fire. "I'm listening."

"Listening for what?"

"Answers."

Chapter 15

If Joy could talk to the undead version of Melanie, could she reach others?

Grandma? It would be so cool to talk to Grandma. . .unless Joy found out something upsetting. Like if she'd been at unrest the whole four years since her death. If Joy found out her grandmother had never found peace, it would break her heart. In that case, maybe not knowing was better.

The shadows cast from the flames in the fireplace danced on the ceiling and blinked across the window. Joy shifted on the window seat, pulling her knees up to rest under her chin, and pressed the side of her face against the cold glass. Light scratches brushed against the glass. Hard to say which were the trees blowing in the wind and which were. . .um. . .visitors. She wasn't afraid of the dark anymore; in fact, she preferred it. Light was unnecessary because it only revealed half the picture, if that. It crowded out the truth rather than illuminating it.

So, she could reach Melanie, she knew that already, and maybe even Grandma. What about relatives she'd never met before? Was contact with the dead limited to only people she already knew? That kind of seemed logical. . .but then again, all those ghost stories about people who were haunted by the homeowners who had lived and died in their houses before them seemed mostly believable.

But maybe hauntings were different than simple contact with a spirit. Hah. A few weeks ago, Joy never would have thought contact with the dead was simple in any way. But contact wasn't necessarily sinister. Haunting sounded way scarier.

Bang.

Joy jumped as something slammed shut. A cabinet door? Bedroom door? No one else was home, at least no one living. She waited for another presence to reveal itself in some way. Why wasn't she terrified at the prospect of being alone in the center of paranormal stuff? Maybe because it no longer was outside the realm of her normal.

Wait. Where was Silas? As if on cue, he pranced into the room and dropped to his belly at Joy's feet. Not a care in the universe.

Whoosh.

The fire narrowed from a cluster of flames to a spark then fizzled. The room was cast into complete darkness.

Joy waited. What if she could glimpse the spirit world as it existed beyond her human existence? Would it comfort her or terrify her? Maybe certain things were best left unknown.

That's what had happened to Adam and Eve in the Genesis fairy tale. They got themselves in trouble because they knew too much.

She opened her mouth to speak to the unseen ghost who had doused her fire, but no words came. Silas offered a soft *woof* as he lay on the floor, unconcerned with anything happening around him.

Well, if he wasn't scared, she had no reason to be nervous.

What would Raven ask the spirit if she were there? First for identification. That's what she did when they began to hear from Melanie. Then she'd probably ask for purpose like Lucas had done. Okay then. Joy could do that. She opened her mouth again. Nothing. It felt too much like praying.

Obviously, she wasn't quite ready to go it alone, but something told her she would be soon.

Joy reached to the wall above her head and flipped on the light, morphing the room from a party of dark spirits to a bright, lonely room. Not that it changed a thing. What happened behind the shroud of light continued with or without her.

🌀

The little VW pulled itself over as though its driver wasn't actually needed. Supposedly out for a moonlight drive, just to think, Joy found herself steering into the cemetery. Why did she continually put herself through this torture? But some kind of force had propelled her. Could she have driven somewhere else if she'd decided to?

Joy stared out the window at the rows of gravestones. What was she doing there?

She gripped the steering wheel and twisted her hands a few times. *Don't get out of the car. Don't get out of the car. Just turn around and go.* If she took this whole thing further, if she explored beyond what she already knew, it would expand her boundaries and open her whole life up to the unseen world. There would be no going back. But maybe if she turned and ran away now, maybe there was still a chance she could chalk it up to a few weird experiences she couldn't explain and move on.

Not knowing might be safer, but Joy needed answers.

Joy climbed from the car and slammed the door hard behind her. Who was she angry at? Herself? No. That didn't seem right. The world? Maybe.

God? Yeah that was it. God.

The whole religious thing, the Bible stuff and all that junk she'd learned about Jesus. Those songs she'd sung as a little girl

. . ."this little light of mine, I'm going to let it shine". . .what a joke.

She crept toward Melanie's grave.

Vacation Bible School, summer camp, getting baptized. . . more ridiculousness. She felt stupid for buying into that garbage. For being as smart as everyone said she was, Joy should have known better.

Joy stopped dead in her tracks. She was going the wrong way. But how did she know? A gentle tug pulled her body in the other direction. She turned up the hill and plodded along the snowy earth, headed right toward the Christianson family plots beyond the northern rise.

There it was. Grandma and Grandpa's single stone they'd bought to share. Grandpa's just waited for a date. Oh, and a body. But what about Stella? Did she know Grandpa would be buried by his late wife of fifty-four years? Would Stella visit his grave as he lay eternally sleeping with another woman?

Three children, eleven grandchildren, and three great-grandchildren represented a lot of shared life. Considering Grandpa had loved Grandma for decades—almost half a century—and had created generations with her, Stella could never come close. No way. She had to know that. And it had to drive her batty.

"Nana?" Joy whispered into the night. "Are you here? Have you been watching all that's been going on?" Joy waited. The wind whistled through the leaves, and snow swirled around her feet. "Can you tell me what to do? Tell me you're happy?" Or better yet, don't respond at all. Then Joy could allow herself to believe Nana was at peace, not trapped between eternities.

Joy closed her eyes and let the breeze tickle her cheeks as she felt a spiritual embrace that squeezed her body deep into her soul.

Her eyes popped open. "Nana? Is that you?" Joy sank to her knees. "I've missed you so much." She lay on the grave and cried. The eight-year-old inside Joy wanted to huddle in her warm bed under a homemade quilt with her grandmother. Grandma would scratch Joy's back and tell her stories of when she was a little girl in the coal-mining camp in the Appalachian mountains. Her nails would be sharp, but Joy wouldn't twitch or wiggle, afraid of breaking the moment.

Joy could picture Grandma's description of the little chapel with its stained glass window where they held Sunday services. She could envision the antics of the Culver twins in their knee-socks and smudged faces. She smiled softly like Grandma always had when she'd talked about them. She could almost taste the apple pies that sat cooling on every windowsill in the old days.

Why couldn't Joy have lived then? Simpler times.

The cold wind chapping Joy's cheeks turned warm in an instant. She lifted her face and dried her tears with the back of her hand.

The cemetery had grown still. Warm. Silent.

"Nana?" Had Joy spoken that out loud? It was difficult to tell. . .almost as though the air around her absorbed the sound.

Joy felt a strange sensation come over her body—a sense of lightening. Her legs felt buoyant, and her arms tingled with weightlessness. She couldn't see for all the mist. She stretched her toes downward but felt nothing. How high was she? And why wasn't she scared? Her sight cleared for a moment as though in answer to her unspoken question. Joy glanced down to see she hovered just inches above the earth.

What was happening to her? She should be petrified, yet she was intrigued. Silas nuzzled her hand, his warm breath tickling her with heightened sensation. He would protect her like always. He'd never let anything bad happen to her. They moved in his realm now.

The cemetery had grown hazy as if entrenched in a cloud she could see, yet not, kind of like looking through Nana's lace curtains. Joy could see the scene outside if she stepped back from the window. But up close, she could only catch snatches of the scene through the holes.

Who is that?

A shadowy, billowing figure approached Joy. Not flying, yet not exactly walking either. It was familiar, though not recognizable. The form of a human. . .but it floated with an otherworldliness that gave it authority. It knew.

Again, the sense of familiarity washed over Joy as the being drifted nearer. A hand appeared and reached out. It clutched Joy's hand, and her body instantly relaxed. The feel of those bony, calloused fingers and loose, crepe flesh. It was her.

"Nana? Can you talk to me?"

Silence.

Was she unable or unwilling? "Can you show me something then?" As if in response to her question, Joy's body wafted toward the sky. Weightless. She wasn't flying, and she didn't feel like she could alter her direction. Yet, strangely, she felt in complete control.

Joy glanced down at the ground four feet beneath her. There she lay huddled on Nana's grave.

Wait a second.

Her body was there on the ground, yet her spirit had escaped. Was this it? Was this how Nana and Melanie felt?

"Nana, I have to know. Is this what it's like to be dead?"

No answer.

Joy felt a tug on her hand. Nana squeezed and pulled her higher and higher. They traveled a distance, yet it only took moments before they arrived in front of Joy's home. As if transported there, she could sense the journey but couldn't remember it. Would she be able to return to her body, or was this it? If she did return, would she remember?

Silas nudged her forward.

"What would you like to see?" Nana whispered the first words Joy had heard from her in years. The sound of her voice sucker punched Joy.

She shook her head. "It's too much. I can't take it."

"It's okay, my love." Nana squeezed her hand. The familiar callouses a comfort. "It's okay."

Joy nodded and drew in a shuddering breath. She could do this.

They entered Joy's house, not through the doorway, not straight through the wall. They just appeared there.

Joy turned in a circle, taking in the scene.

Austin stood in the family room facing Melanie, the shower ran in the background.

Oh no. Joy's stomach clenched. Would she have to watch the kiss? Her blood ran cold, and her body shivered. If only she could look away. She really didn't want to see the moment of the betrayal that changed her life forever. It was enough to have to endure its effects.

"Melanie." Austin's voice dropped to a whisper, his hand on the front of her shoulder. "I *am* attracted to you. I won't deny that."

That's nice. Big, fat jerk.

"I like you, but nothing could ever compare to what Joy and I have. I love her." Austin dropped his head.

Joy's cheeks warmed. He'd never said that to her face. They'd agreed to wait.

Melanie took a step closer to Austin. And another, until

they were so close their bodies almost touched. He held his hand on her shoulder and kept her at a slight distance. She reached up and removed his hand. Then leaned in, her face softened for a kiss.

Austin's eyes twitched, and his face turned red the instant Melanie's lips touched his. Austin's mouthed one word: *No.*

Hovering over the scene, Joy's heartbeat quickened. So many variables, if only she'd come out of the bathroom a split second later. If only she'd taken longer in the shower. If only she'd seen that Austin had tried to stop the kiss.

Joy stepped around the corner rubbing her hair with her towel. Austin's back to her.

Could she cry out to stop the scene from unfolding? Joy looked into her grandma's eyes. They were kind with knowledge, soft with understanding. "Is this real? Is that how it happened?"

Nana squeezed her hand. "Yes."

"You mean he tried to stop her?" What would Joy do with that information? Did she need to do anything?

"Yes."

She'd seen it with her own eyes. Austin had his hand in front of Melanie's shoulder, not on the back of it. He was pushing her away, not pulling her toward him.

Why hadn't he stuck up for himself before though? What if he did really love her? Even still, it simply didn't matter. Joy was done with love. Forever.

Nana took her hand and gently tugged her toward Melanie crying in her bed.

Joy whipped her head to look from one side of the room to the other. "What? How did we get from my house to here?" Joy's gaze took in the scene. One she'd been familiar with. One that haunted her dreams. "If this is what I think it is, I can't watch." Nana pulled her closer to Melanie's bed.

Gentle sobs shook the bed frame. Heartbreak. Melanie wiped her face on her pillow, her eyes red from crying, her sheets damp with tears. "Why? Why did I do it? Oh God, I would take it all back if I could. How can I erase what happened?" Melanie gasped and sat up with a start.

"I know." She talked to herself. "I can't erase what happened, but I can erase myself."

Joy searched her grandmother's face. "Please. No more. I can't take any more."

She blinked, her eyes opening to the cold. Dampness had seeped through her layers. Joy pried her body off the ground and stood to her feet. Her body trembled as she turned in a slow circle to confirm she was alone in the cemetery.

Her skin was numb to the cold. In shock? But that had to be a dream. It couldn't possibly have been real.

Could it?

Chapter 16

Talk. Talk. Talk. That's all everyone wants to do." Joy let her hair fall like a room-darkening drape in front of her face as she rubbed her temples. So the whole take-your-daughter-shopping-in-North-Platte thing was nothing more than a ruse. "I'm so tired of talking." In the five weeks since Melanie's death, she'd probably said a mere fraction of the actual number of words she normally did, but the topics sucked the life out of her. Her head throbbed.

Mom turned her eyes from the highway and glanced at Joy who sat slumped in the passenger seat. Her knuckles white on the steering wheel, she took a deep breath. "Are you doing drugs?"

"What?" Joy's mouth dropped open. "How can you even ask me that?"

"Sweetie, your father and I are so worried about you." Mom swiped at a tear. "Look at you."

Joy glanced down at her body. Okay, so the gray skinny jeans and black, threadbare tunic slung off one shoulder weren't exactly couture. And the black tank top had been dug from the bottom of dad's drawer. The unmatched socks were kind of a trend. Sort of. Even though one was black and the other was charcoal.

What about her Converse? Everyone wore those. Maybe

without holes in the bottoms, but Joy hadn't noticed. That didn't make her an addict. "So I'm not like some Barbie doll fashion maven—how does that make me a drug addict?"

"It's just that. . .you've changed so much. You'd have never been caught dea—" Mom blinked hard. "You'd have never worn something like that outfit you're wearing. It's not that the clothes are so bad, though they are kind of gross; it's just that it's such a change for you."

Joy shrugged. "I just haven't cared that much lately."

"Then how do you explain this?" Mom flipped down the visor and slid open the mirror.

Joy studied her face. Sunken eyes with heavy, dark circles beneath them. Cracked and peeling lips. Pale skin. Heavy, black eyeliner and mascara. Then there was the problem of the hair. Once long, blond, luxurious; now limp, dirty, and dull, clipped back into something that resembled a loose ponytail, or was that a nest of some kind?

She nodded. "I get your point." But that didn't mean she cared. She might have to start making an effort though, if she wanted to fly under the radar like Raven had suggested. "I'll take better care of myself. But I am not doing drugs." Joy chuckled. Best to make light of the situation. "In fact, I bet you have more chemicals in your system from those perms you get."

"That's good, but I want to make sure." Mom stared straight ahead.

Joy's heart beat faster. "What do you mean, make sure?"

"I'm taking you for a drug test." She turned the car into the parking lot of a red brick building with no signs out front.

"You have got to be kidding me." Joy's stomach flipped. Thank goodness she hadn't smoked the pipe the other day. Would it have shown up in her system if she had? "You can't just do this to someone. Where's the trust?"

"I do trust you, but I worry more. You show all the signs of drug use and, as your mother, I have to know. I, *we*, can't help you if we don't know for sure." She pulled into a narrow parking space and turned off the ignition.

Joy crossed her arms on her chest. "What did Mary Alice Gianetti say about this invasion of my privacy. . .of my body?" She felt her head bob side to side as she spoke, unable to pull the snotty tone that laced her words. She'd better be careful or she'd make it worse.

Mom turned and locked her gaze with Joy's. "She gave me the name of this place."

Traitor.

"What, they don't have anywhere in Ogallala where you can pee in a cup?" Maybe other than the back-alley urine-tester place they sat in front of.

"I'm sure they do, but I was trying to keep this private by taking you somewhere no one would know you."

Ever so thoughtful, *Mother*. "Fine. Whatever. Let's get it over with." Maybe she'd change her mind if Joy were agreeable. It would prove she had nothing to hide. Joy climbed out of the car, slammed the door, and stood at the curb, waiting.

Perfect time for Mom to give in. She had to.

Mom climbed from the car and slipped her purse strap over her shoulder. "Okay. Let's go in."

Seriously? She was going to go through with it?

Joy waited until Mom passed her on the sidewalk then fell in behind her. Okay, really, she could back out anytime now. Mom pushed the door open and walked through, holding it open for Joy to pass. It sure didn't look like she had any intention of changing her mind.

They approached the reception desk where a woman sat in blue scrubs. She looked up from her paperwork and smiled.

"Can I help you?"

Ack. That voice. Joy had never heard a squeakier voice on a human. It was all she could do not to laugh.

Mom smiled. "Yes, please. We're here for a test."

"Great. Do you have an appointment?"

Appointment? Oops. No. Sorry. We'll have to come back later, right, Mom?

"Yes ma'am. I scheduled it yesterday. It's for Joy Christianson."

Yesterday? What a betrayal. Joy shook her head. Sure, parents had the right to check up on their teenagers, probably a responsibility to do it, but it just felt weird. Like once that line of trust was crossed there'd be no going back.

The receptionist handed Mom a pack of papers on a clipboard. "I need you to fill these out for me, please. Oh, and since the procedure you requested isn't covered by insurance we need to collect payment before it's performed. The fee is eighty-nine dollars, and we accept cash, check, Visa, MasterCard, Discover, or. . ."

"Just put it on my Visa." Mom slipped it across the counter, and the receptionist slid the door closed.

Joy looked down at the stained carpet as Mom filled out the stack of paperwork. She could probably offer to help, but Mom had called this meeting, and she could take care of the details.

Mom turned the paper over and started on the other side. Finally, she scrawled her signature at the bottom and moved on to the next sheet. Joy shrugged. Lots of work for an elective procedure.

Mom held up a blank sheet and called out to the receptionist. "This is an insurance form. Do you really need me to fill that out since I'm paying myself?"

"No. We can do without that today, but if you ever do come

in for a procedure that requires insurance, we'll have to have you fill it out then." Mom nodded. A few moments later, she put her pen down and handed it all back to the receptionist.

The nurse worked her way through the stack. "Everything looks good. You two can go on back. Hand this to the nurse just inside." She gave Mom one sheet of paper.

Now for the fun part. Joy hung her head as she followed Mom to the door. How humiliating.

They stepped back into a lab area with curtained exam cubicles. Lab-coated medical people with needles worked at counter stations nearby. Reminded Joy of when Mike gave her the Silas tattoo. Not that she could tell Mom about it. Her hand reached down to cover Silas on her leg. Nice to know he was there even when she couldn't see him.

A nurse swiveled her chair away from the counter where she was labeling test tubes and approached Joy. Her nametag read JANET.

Mom handed her the sheet. The nurse looked it over and thankfully didn't shout out to the whole room that Joy was there for a drug test. At least it wasn't a pregnancy test.

"Mrs. Christianson, you can go have a seat right there." The nurse pointed at a waiting area then turned to Joy. "You can come right this way." The nurse smiled and beckoned. She held back a curtain and allowed Joy to step behind it. "Go ahead and take everything off and slip into this gown. I'll be back in a sec."

Joy glanced at the paper-thin blue hospital gown that tied in back. Seriously? Did Mom realize what a violation this was? Joy wriggled out of her clothes and scrambled to get covered by the gown as much as possible before Janet came back and caught her halfway in the act.

"All set?" Janet poked her head around the curtain. She could have asked before she looked. Sheesh.

Janet reached into a cabinet and pulled out a plastic-wrapped urine specimen cup.

Oh goody. Joy cringed.

"Alrighty. Come on with me." She led the way to the bathroom and motioned for Joy to follow her inside.

Wait just a second. Janet didn't plan on staying in there while Joy went to the bathroom did she? Gross!

Joy stood in the center of the small room. She looked overhead and at the walls. There had to be a privacy curtain or something. A sink. A single toilet. No curtain.

Joy stared at Janet. She had to leave. Joy glanced at the door. Anytime, lady.

"Sorry, hon. I have to stay to make sure the sample is really yours."

Was Joy being pranked? What did Janet think? Joy showed up with someone else's pee in her pocket? "Look, I didn't even know we were coming here until we were on the way. I couldn't possibly have prepared any sort of secret stash of urine."

"It doesn't matter. I have to certify that this is your urine." At least she looked like she felt bad about it.

"What if I refuse?" Joy would put her hands on her hips if it hadn't meant letting go of her gown and completely exposing her backside to do it.

"If you refuse to take the test, that'll be noted, and your mom will then have to decide what she's going to do." Janet shrugged. "I have to tell you, refusing makes you look guilty. If there's any chance your test will be clear, just take it so it'll be done." She looked Joy up and down. Didn't look like she had much confidence Joy would pass the test.

"I do not take drugs." Not that Janet would believe her. Or care.

"Then take the test."

Joy sighed. She had no choice. If she refused, Mom would never back down until she got it done, and Joy would look guilty in the process. But it was a matter of principle to not want to stand there in a room with a stranger and pee in a cup when she had done nothing wrong. It just wasn't fair.

"Does my mom know about all of this?" Joy gestured to the urine cup. Maybe she wasn't even aware of the level of humiliation she was forcing Joy to endure.

Janet nodded. "Your mom knows."

"I guess I have no choice. Let's get it over with." Joy snatched the cup out of Janet's hand and ripped off the plastic wrap. "At least turn your back or run some water."

"I will look in the mirror and run the water to give you some privacy."

At least that was something. Joy stepped closer to the toilet and lined it with toilet paper. After all, the types of people who had to take these tests probably weren't the type of people whose germs she wanted to swap.

Joy hovered over the toilet, her thighs barely touching the seat, and reached in with the cup. After filling it as high as she could, she put the cap on it and slipped it back into the plastic bag. Without a word, she handed it to the nurse who stayed facing the wall while Joy got dressed. Then she stepped away from the sink to allow Joy access. Joy washed her hands, dried them at the hand dryer, and they left the bathroom. Not another word passed between them. Some experiences were better left in silence.

"Okay, the humiliation is complete. You have your test. Can we go now?"

Mom stood up and put her *Family Circle* down on the magazine table, her cheeks pink.

It wasn't really Mom's fault. She meant well. But some

simple conversations should've been enough. She should've known Joy wasn't doing drugs.

Joy sulked to the car and climbed into her seat. She slammed the door shut and crossed her arms on her chest as she faced the window.

Mom got into the driver's side. "We get the results in about a week."

"I already know the results." Joy stared out the car window at a bird pecking at the snow.

Mom put her hand on Joy's knee.

She flinched away from the touch.

"Honey, I love you. None of this has anything to do with blame or accusation. It's simply that I love you, I'm scared for you, and I would do whatever it takes to keep you from going down the wrong path. Anything it takes." She cupped her hand under Joy's chin and turned her face until they made eye contact. "If we find out you're not doing drugs, I'll definitely be so relieved, but I'm still going to have to find some answers about what's going on with you. This test doesn't end the search."

Be careful what you look for, Mom. You might not like what you find.

Chapter 17

'Tis the season to be jolly.

Ho. Ho. Ho.

Bah humbug.

She wasn't feeling very much like Christmas Eve this year. Would it be possible to talk Mom and Dad out of putting up the tree? Hah. What a laugh.

Joy pulled herself from her bed. Better get ready for a typical Christianson Christmas Eve. Tradition had it they would spend this morning at the mall shopping for all the cousins and extended family. From there, they'd go get a tree and then come home to decorate it. Only thing was Mom would probably try to make it even more festive this year, thinking Joy needed to celebrate. Which would only make things harder. Less is more, Mother.

Joy shuffled to her closet. What could she wear? Maybe she should try and get in the spirit of things because if she didn't, Mom and Dad would have their antennae up. *What do you think, boy?* She looked down at Silas, happily panting beside her leg. "You'll go along with whatever, won't you?"

Might as well. She pulled out her favorite University of Nebraska sweatshirt and tugged it over her head then freed her hair from the back. Slipped into her favorite jeans and pocketed a warm pair of gloves. It would be cold out there in the forest, especially later, when they went tree hunting.

Joy opened her bedroom door and immediately smelled that mixture of bacon and cinnamon syrup. Yep. Mom had made her traditional Christmas Eve breakfast. Joy would bet money there was a French toast casserole cooling on the stove. Her stomach grumbled. Interesting development. She hardly ever felt hungry anymore.

"Hey Mom. Hey Dad."

"Hi, sweetheart." Mom spooned some scrambled eggs into a bowl.

Dad laid down his newspaper and looked up with a smile. "Morning. You're awfully chipper today." He seemed so relieved. Okay, Joy had been right. If she could pull off a happy Christmas, maybe it would be enough to get Mom and Dad off her back.

Joy went to the cupboard and grabbed a ceramic plate and a coffee mug. She piled her plate high with bacon and casserole, a little bit of scrambled eggs, and some cut-up fresh fruit, heavy on the grapes. "Looks great, Mom."

She filled her mug with steaming coffee, added two heaps of sugar and some milk. "I'm famished." Joy took a seat beside Dad.

Mom and Dad locked eyes. Joy could almost hear their thoughts. Dad would say something like, "I believe we've turned the grief corner." Mom would nod, "Yes, I hope so, but don't let your guard down for a second." Like a trained sniper, that one.

"So, we keeping tradition this year? Going shopping. . . going to get a tree?" Maybe if she reminded them of all the planned togetherness, her next request wouldn't raise any flags.

"Yep. That's the plan." Dad folded his newspaper and stood up from the table. He turned to put his dish in the sink. Mom reached back for it, seemingly sensing his movement behind her. Married for a long time, finishing each other's sentences, sensing the next move. . .sure would be nice to have a partner like that one day.

Joy stood and went to the refrigerator for the orange juice, Silas right at her heels. Joy smiled. That's right, she did have a partner like that.

She sat down and nibbled on a piece of bacon. Here goes. "Mind if I go hang out with Raven and some others after we're finished decorating the tree?" After Joy's good behavior, she was sure Mom and Dad would cave.

"It's Christmas Eve." Mom's eyebrows crinkled.

Dad scowled. "Yeah. We always spend Christmas Eve together."

"Well, we will spend the day together. But, you know, teenagers like to do stuff with their friends, too." Now don't say too much.

Dad shrugged. "I guess it's all right if that's what you want to do. I just don't want you rushing off at your first chance."

"I agree," Mom said. "I want to enjoy our time and play Christmas music and just be a family. I don't want to rush or feel like you're checking your text messages every five minutes, like you can't wait to leave."

"I promise it won't be like that." Now where was that cell phone?

⑨

Christmas Eve at the cemetery.

Who would have thought? Joy struggled to keep up with Raven and Luc as they crept among the tombstones long after hours. Lights glowed from behind the cluster of trees over the Northern Ridge near her family. But no, looked a little too much to the east to be where the Christiansons were laid to rest.

As the trio approached, Joy made out three other shadowy forms barely illuminated by the light of the candles in their hands. How did they keep the candles from going out?

"Come on, Joy." Raven tugged on her sleeve. "We've got to hurry. We only have a couple of minutes. Cops don't like teenagers in graveyards in the middle of the night."

Luc nodded. "You can say that again."

"Hey Joy." Heather called from the tree cluster.

"Hey. Haven't seen you in a while."

Heather looked Joy over. "I really like your jacket."

Joy fingered the black leather fringe hanging from the silver grommets. "Yeah, somehow I got my mom to buy me this a week ago. Must've been in a moment of weakness." She didn't have to admit to Heather that it was a guilt purchase after the drug test humiliation.

Heather chuckled. "It's totally cool."

"So what exactly are we doing out here?" Joy looked around the group. Nothing seemed odd that she could see right away.

"Beats me." Heather shrugged. "Lucas called this gathering."

Luc cleared his throat. "We're waiting for someone to bring something."

Well that cleared things up.

"Ah. There he is." Luc nodded toward a dark figure lumbering toward them.

Hey. Wasn't that. . . ? She peered closer. Oh yeah. Kyle from that store. What was he doing here?

Kyle approached from beyond the tree line behind them carrying some kind of lump wrapped in a burlap bag and stopped at what looked like a miniature grave with a blank headstone just a few yards away.

How had Joy not noticed that before?

Kyle scooted the sack into the hole, looked down, and

pulled back the edges.

Joy gasped. The baby Jesus lay in the grave wrapped in a sack. "You guys stole baby Jesus? Where did you get it?"

"It's from outside the Methodist Church. They won't miss it."

"You guys are crazy. Who steals baby Jesus from a nativity scene in front of a church, the night before Christmas?" Joy laughed. She had to admit, the absurdity made the risk worthwhile. "What are we going to do with Him?"

Kyle's mouth curled into a sinister grin. "We're having us an old-fashioned sacrifice."

Joy's chin dropped. She stared at Luc then turned to Raven. "Is he serious?"

"Why don't you think of it as a rite of passage? Here, you can write on the headstone." Raven passed Joy a black Sharpie.

Joy looked at the marker in her hand and then at the blank piece of wood standing at the head of the grave of the Christ child. Should she do it? Rite of passage, huh? She looked down at Silas. Did he approve or not?

He was panting and wagging his tail. Clearly happy.

Here goes. She knelt down and pulled the homemade headstone from the ground and laid it flat on the ground. What would she say at the top?

Jesus Christ, son of Mary and Joseph.

Leaves behind billions of followers.

Rest in peace.

That's all she could think of. It would do. She turned the slab up and stuck it back in the hole.

Heather backed away, her jaw unhinged. "Yeah. Guys, this is just too much for me. I'm out of here." She turned and fled the cemetery without looking back.

"Anyone else?" Lucas looked Joy in the eyes.

Her moment of truth. "I'm good."

Lucas gave Kyle a single nod. "Do it, man."

Kyle opened a bottle of Mountain Dew and sprinkled it all over baby Jesus and the burlap bag.

Why did he do that? Wait. What was that smell? Gasoline. He had gasoline in that bottle, not Mountain Dew. Smart. But did Joy really want to be a part of that?

Lucas lit a match and dropped it in the hole. Fire caught immediately.

Joy watched as the flames licked the baby's face. She glanced at Raven, who seemed to be in a trance as she stared into the fire.

Kyle stepped forward as he closed his eyes and raised his face toward the moon. "May our actions tonight serve as a symbol of our desire to separate ourselves from organized religion, matters of God, obligation, and accountability. Let this symbolic act serve as proof of our desire to be separated from all things of God and released to exist as the human spirits we were meant to be." He opened his eyes and stepped back into place in the circle around the grave.

Wow. That was deep. Joy looked around the circle. Everyone stood transfixed on the burning baby. She looked into the consuming flames, the image no longer recognizable.

Bright lights drenched the space and shone on their faces.

"Hold it right there. What do you think you're doing?"

Joy froze, her heartbeat stilled. Busted.

Kyle turned and sprinted into the trees like a shot. A cop tore off after him.

Raven and Luc stepped closer to each other, and Raven slipped her hand in Luc's.

Joy stood alone.

"Drop to your knees, and put your hands behind your head."

If only Joy could have an out-of-body experience now.

How was she to talk her way out of this one?

⑤

"Trespassing." *Bang.*

"Destruction of private property." *Bang.*

"Theft." *Bang.*

Dad slammed his fist on the kitchen table with each word. Joy slumped lower and lower in her seat with each jolt.

"You know, Joy Christianson, those were words I never thought I'd hear associated with you, let alone on Christmas Eve. I don't get it." Dad put his head down in his hands.

Mom wiped away a tear. "I don't understand either. Do you realize what you were doing? You and your. . .friends. . .were burning a stolen baby Jesus in a grave on Christmas Eve?" Mom paced across the kitchen.

"Oh!" She whipped around to face Joy. "I get it now. Those people you're hanging around with, the clothes you're wearing, your mood change. . .it's all making sense. How could we not have seen what was happening right before our eyes?" Mom hung her head and sobbed. She dropped into a chair and laid her face on the table, the weight of her realization too much to bear.

"Any of the possible things, Joy, drugs, pregnancy, anything you could have done would have been preferable to this." Dad glared at her.

Mom lifted her head and looked at Dad. "I don't know what to do. We have to do something. I don't even know how this would work." She jumped up and started pacing again.

Dad stared ahead, all his words gone. He looked beaten.

"What do you do, Alan? Ground someone for satanic sacrifice in a cemetery? Is that the standard protocol? I don't think there's much about this in a typical parenting manual."

What could Joy say? It sounded really bad when Mom put

it that way, but Dad looked ill.

"Daddy?"

Joy waited. And waited.

Finally he turned his face toward her. His eyes sagged. Defeated.

What had she done to them? But maybe if they understood. "You guys, you have to have an open mind. Listen, I just started searching. I needed answers about life and death and eternity and all of that. Some things happened and my eyes opened to stuff I'd never considered before. You've always taught me to study and learn and decide for myself. So I did."

Face red with anger, Mom pointed her finger in Joy's face. "Don't you dare turn this on us and suggest we encouraged you to go off on a search like this. I will not accept that, and don't you dare try to convince me you're right about this." She covered her mouth and ran from the room, her sobs growing even louder as she moved farther from the kitchen.

Dad shook his head. He didn't say a word.

"Daddy, trust me. If you would listen, you'd understand why I. . ."

He turned his pale face, eyes brimming with tears, toward Joy. "I love you with all my heart. That will never change, but I'm telling you right now I won't understand, and I won't listen to you justify why you sacrificed baby Jesus."

"But Dad. . ."

"I only wish I'd been a better example to you. I've let you down." Dad stared down at the floor.

Oh man. Yeah, it might've helped, but now she needed to feel guilty that he felt guilty? Too much.

Dad stared into Joy's eyes. "I feel like I don't even know you anymore. You're a shadow of the person you once were."

"That's way more than Melanie is. She doesn't even cast a

shadow anymore." Joy jumped from her chair. "There's nothing you can do about this. A person's spiritual journey is personal. I've chosen the path to walk mine."

Chapter 18

If Santa had made his list and checked it twice, there would be nothing under the tree for Joy that Christmas morning. All she wanted to do was pull the covers over her head and wallow in equal parts self-pity and embarrassment. But the flaw in her plan was the extended family. They'd eventually come knocking. Mom and Dad would drag her out of bed to socialize, pretending nothing happened and ignoring Joy's bed head and smelly breath. She'd be better off being proactive so she could face them showered, dressed, and on her own terms.

After her shower, Joy quickly made up her bed and tucked the covers under the mattress just like Mom liked her to. Today required extra effort. Clothes. What to wear? Nothing phony looking. Joy dragged her fingers over the pink sweaters and girly, flowery clothes. They'd see right through her if she wore something like that. She'd be better off in a more subdued choice, but a little brighter than black.

Oh, perfect. Joy tugged the charcoal cashmere sweater Stella bought her last year off the hanger. That over a red cami would be perfect. Maybe she'd even wear a pair of silver hoop earrings. Why not? Might as well go all out.

Joy paused for one last glance in the mirror and smoothed down some flyaways. Good as it was going to get. She pulled her shoulders back, held her head up high, and strode from her bedroom. If she didn't feel confident, at least she could look it.

"Good morning." Mom handed her a cup of black coffee. "You know where the sugar is."

"Morning, sweetheart." Dad looked up from his paper. "Merry Christmas." Almost an afterthought.

"Merry Christmas to you guys, too." If Joy held a knife, she'd be able to cut the tension in the room. No one seemed to want to address the big white elephant over there in the corner. Yet there it sat. Hungry. Looked a lot like a wolf to Joy, actually. An unhappy one.

"When's everybody coming over?"

Mom checked her watch. "Still have a couple hours before Grandpa and Stella arrive. Aunt Sue will bring Bea over at noon."

Joy nodded. "Smart." Always best to give Beatrice a chance to adapt to her surroundings on an exciting day, before throwing a crowd on top. She loved a party, but sometimes it was a bit too much stimulation for her. "You guys want your presents now?"

Mom shrugged. "Yeah, I guess this is as good a time as any." She plodded off to the family room.

Joy turned to pour a fresh cup of coffee. It was already exhausting having to choose every word perfectly, trying not to respond to Mom's clipped tone and dead short sentences. But they needed to give her a break. Didn't she have the right to explore her own spirituality? Didn't she? That would be something she asked Mary Alice Gianetti at their next session. Best guess? Mary Alice would commend her for finding a way to cope with her loss in her own way, but then go all Jesus on her.

Dad took a spot on the couch, so Joy curled up in his recliner. She pulled her heels under her thighs and tucked a blanket around her legs while she waited for Mom to take her regular role as Santa.

Mom smiled as she picked up the first gift. "Well, this one's for Joy." She handed a rectangular package to her. "Now before you open it, I want you to know I bought it months ago, not at all in response to what happened yesterday."

Joy shook the box. It was heavy, kind of dense. She lifted the corner and sliced the tape with her fingernail then peeled back the wrapper to expose two words. *Holy Bible.*

Silas stirred at the foot of her chair. He lifted his face and nuzzled her arm away from the Bible. How bizarre he'd react that way.

"Aw, thanks, Mom. We have a ton around here, so why this one?" Silas grew more agitated the longer she held the book.

"Well, I just wanted you to have your own engraved with your name. It felt like time." Mom shrugged. Her eyes looked heavy, like she'd been crying all night and just remembered why.

"Thanks, Mom. Thanks, Dad." Joy put the Bible back in its box and slipped it under her chair. Silas let out another growl then settled down.

Merry Christmas.

If only she hadn't gone to Raven's yesterday, she wouldn't have ruined her parents' Christmas, along with their hope.

"Okay, this one is for you, Alan." Mom gave her first real smile of the day as Dad accepted the gift.

"What could it be?" He shook the checkbook-sized box. Finally, he ripped off the paper and lifted the lid from the box. "Papers?"

Mom grinned and nodded.

Dad opened the top one and read. "Is this for real?"

"Yep. I can't wait."

"What is it?" Joy leaned over, trying to read the words on the paper.

"Your mom bought us a cruise. We're going on a cruise in the spring." He looked back at the travel documents in his hand. "Wow. Total surprise. Something I never would have expected."

"Yeah, you guys never take a vacation alone. It's totally time."

Dad stood up and walked to where Mom sat on the floor. He leaned down and gave her a kiss. "Thanks, honey."

"Now it's your turn, Peg." Dad pulled a small robin's-egg blue box from his pocket.

Mom giggled. "Oh, you're a sneaky one." She accepted the box and turned it over in her hand a few times. "Is this from Tiffany's?"

Mom had always said she wanted a box from Tiffany's, even if it had nothing in it.

"We've had a good year, and I wanted to celebrate."

Mom pulled the bow and lifted the lid on the jewelry box to find a gorgeous pair of diamond earrings nestled in a velvet cushion.

"Oh Alan, these are gorgeous." Her fingers shaking, Mom plucked the earrings from their nest and slipped them into her lobes. She hurried to the mirror over the fireplace and peeked at her reflection, her fingers wiggling the diamonds so she could watch them sparkle. "So beautiful."

Dad smiled as he stared at his wife in the mirror. "That's exactly what I was thinking."

Mom locked eyes with him in the reflection and smiled. "I love you, sweetie."

"I love you, too."

Joy cleared her throat. "You guys want me to give you some alone time?" But at least they'd made each other happy on what was destined to be an otherwise morbid day.

Mom laughed. "No. No. But here's your next gift."

Another small box. What could it be? Joy ripped off the paper, this time not even trying to be careful. She immediately recognized the item in her hand. "You have got to be kidding me. The newest iPhone?" Hot off the shelves, barely in stores. "Honestly, guys, you couldn't have picked anything better."

Mom lowered her eyes. "We just love you so much, Joy."

At least she hadn't said it in the past tense.

🌀

Joy's gurgling stomach and prolonged lack of appetite made it very difficult to sit before her plate of Christmas dinner. They were watching her; she just knew it. She'd have to eat enough to make them happy, but not so much she got sick.

As she nibbled on a deviled egg, Joy tried not to look as Beatrice piled more and more onto her plate and attacked it with a vengeance. That girl sure loved to eat. But how could Joy blame her? Bea didn't have much in her life but simple pleasures, and food was one of them. One Joy would never deny her, but the crumbs falling from Bea's lips and the smacking noises she made when she chewed were almost too much for Joy to take that day.

Grandpa reached around to his right to wipe Beatrice's mouth with a napkin. "You've got a little smudge there, Bea."

Beatrice laughed, exposing her mouthful. "It's so good."

Everyone laughed.

"So, Joy."

Oh good. Distracted by Aunt Sue.

"How are things going at school? How are you coping with everything? Are you able to stay up-to-date with your schoolwork?" Sue forked a bite of mashed potatoes into her mouth.

"Things are pretty good. I mean, it's not fun. It's been

a rough couple of months, but my grades are fine. I'll pull through."

Aunt Sue nodded then turned to her brother.

"How about you, Alan? How's work? Sell any houses lately?" She set her fork down and waited for his answer.

At least she'd moved on from Joy. What were the chances Joy would make it out of the house to hang out with Raven tonight? Yeah, slim to none. But she'd really wanted to see what they did on Christmas. Didn't look like this year would be possible.

Mom scraped some food from one plate onto another, and Sue stacked some dishes and gathered a handful of silverware.

"If you guys will excuse me, I need to use the restroom. I'll be back to help with the dishes in a second."

Joy stepped into the bathroom and closed the door behind her then slumped against it. Maybe she could just hide out in there for the rest of the evening. Would anyone even notice?

Rinsing her hands at the sink, Joy stared into the mirror. *You can do this. Just get through the next couple of hours.* But then what? There was no way she'd be allowed out of the house later. She'd have to see what happened. Maybe she'd just leave. She'd better get back in there though, or someone would come looking for her. They didn't give her a minute alone to catch her breath anymore.

Joy grabbed an armful of dirty plates and headed into the kitchen to help clean up.

". . . Joy. . ."

Huh? Had she just heard her name? She leaned her head a bit closer to the kitchen opening. What were they saying about her?

". . .suspended, fighting, grades are falling, and then what happened yesterday, and tons of other things I'm sure I don't know of." Mom sniffled. "I just don't know what to do, Sue."

"Have you considered that she might be doing drugs?"

"Yeah. That was my first thought. I had her tested, but she was clean."

"Good for you for doing that, Mama. Had to be a tough move."

"Yeah. It was. But I felt like I had to."

Joy rolled her eyes. Should she interrupt them or wait to see what they said? Curiosity got the best of her.

Stella came up beside her. "What are we doing?" she whispered.

"Shh." Joy held up a finger.

Mom coughed and blew her nose. "I don't know. That stuff from yesterday, it's a nightmare. I can't think of anything that would terrify me more."

Stella patted Joy on the arm. At least someone understood her.

Aunt Sue went on. "I should probably tell you. . ."

Or don't. Aunt Sue probably couldn't wait to gossip with her sister-in-law about Joy, but weren't Christians against that sort of thing?

"Beatrice said some stuff about satanic-looking pictures she saw on Joy's computer—Bea was pretty disturbed by them. And she drew a picture of Joy with some demons. I didn't know what to make of it at the time, but it all makes sense now."

"What do I do? I have no idea how to handle this. I'm scared to death. I'm so afraid I'm going to make the wrong move and push her away completely. Please pray that Alan and I make good decisions and find a way to help her."

That's enough. Joy pasted a smile on her face and flounced into the kitchen like she didn't have a care in the world. "This is the last of the dirty dishes. Want me to dry?"

Chapter 19

Joy pulled her Bug alongside the curb and parked near the mailbox. What on earth were all those cars doing in the driveway? The open garage housed the Saab and the Cherokee—so both Mom and Dad were home, odd for a Tuesday afternoon. Right up next to the garage door was Aunt Sue's Accord and a Ford with Colorado plates right beside hers. Two other cars Joy didn't recognize were pulled in behind those.

How strange. She couldn't remember a single time in her life when she'd arrived home to so many vehicles she couldn't identify, and without any advance warning that there would be guests. Maybe mom was having a Pampered Chef party or something.

Fine by Joy. She'd just get a snack and go to her bedroom. Hopefully people would leave her alone. Joy kicked her boots off in the foyer and laid her coat across the banister.

With every intention to slip unnoticed past the guests into the kitchen, Joy tiptoed into the family room and stopped short.

Seven pairs of eyes stared at her from unsmiling faces seated in a circle around the room. Mom. Dad. Mary Alice Gianetti. Aunt Sue. Kelsey. And some good-looking, middle-aged stranger with dark hair and bright blue eyes sat with the fireplace at his back.

Why so grave? She offered the group a hesitant smile, but

no one returned it. A chill ran through Joy's body. Silas inched closer, a low rumble filling his throat. Something was up.

"What's going on, you guys? Why is everyone so somber?"

The stranger stood up from Dad's recliner. He moved toward Joy with his hand outstretched. "Hi. I'm Mark Stapleton. It's nice to meet you, Joy."

"Uh. Nice to meet you, too. I think." Joy searched the faces of her family and friends for a clue.

"I'm here from Diamond Estates. It's a residential place for troubled girls."

"Yeah. I've heard of it. 'Finest gems from the deepest mire,' or something like that. My friend went there." She glanced at her mom. "What does this have to do with me?"

"I'm here to talk with you, and so is your family."

Oh no. Joy had seen this on TV. What did they call this? An ambush? No. An intervention. That was it. "I don't know what's going on here, but I'm feeling a little uncomfortable. I'll be in my room." She took a step back.

Dad stood up. "Joy, have a seat." He pointed at an empty chair.

"Excuse me?" Joy's jaw fell toward the floor. Dad hadn't ever talked to her like that. Then again, she'd never really given him reason to. "I prefer to stand. . . ." That came out more like a question than a statement. Way to be strong.

"This will be the last time I say this. We aren't playing games here. Joy, sit down." Dad jabbed his finger at one of the kitchen chairs that had been brought in for the occasion.

Joy scowled and sank into the chair. "I'm really confused. Would someone mind telling me what's going on?"

"You bet." Mark leaned forward and held Joy's attention with his intense gaze. "Your family has called this meeting out of concern for you. We're here to talk to you. This is all about choices you're making right now that have your parents very concerned. We've assembled a group of people, your team, people who love you and pray for you. Take a look around the circle. These people represent thousands of words spent in prayer before the throne of God, begging for your safe return to the fold, begging for your peace, your faith, your heart."

Mark slid off his chair and fell to his knee in front of her. "There is so much going on, there's so much at stake, and you've only scratched the surface of what can happen. We want to offer you some help. I'm going to start by giving everyone in the room here a chance to say a few words, and then I want to make you an offer."

Joy almost rolled her eyes, which would've been rude, but an offer? What? One she couldn't possibly refuse? At least he hadn't said those words. Because she would refuse it, Mark Stapleton. Put your money on that.

Mark returned to his chair then looked around the circle. "Who would like to start?"

Dad lifted a finger. "I would. I just have two things to say. Joy, I love you. That will never change. It's because I love you that I'm so worried about you."

Joy looked at the floor. If only the carpet could swallow her up.

"Number two," Dad continued. "You made a promise to me years ago, and to God, that you would follow Him. As that little girl who made that promise, you knew Him well. I want to find the heart of that little girl again."

Ouch. Joy remembered glimpses of that feeling. But the problem with the whole thing was emotion. You couldn't make a decision about faith based on emotion without any tangible proof. Joy learned that the hard way.

Aunt Sue lifted her hand. "I'll go next if that's all right."

Mark nodded. "The floor is yours."

"Thank you. Okay, Joy. . ."

Joy stared at the floor and twisted her ring around her finger.

"You know, I'm going to ask you to look at me. I'm an adult, and I'm here because I care about you. I've got things to say. I deserve your respect."

Joy couldn't believe Aunt Sue would talk to her like that. Did the new guy approve? She stole a quick glance at Mark. He nodded then dropped his head, his lips moving.

Joy sighed. Great. He was praying, and the rest of them were all against her. She glanced up at Aunt Sue.

"I only have a couple of things to say to you." Sue took a deep breath. "You're like a daughter to me. The day you were born was one of the brightest days of my life. I saw family when I looked into the eyes of my brother's baby. Honestly, Joy, it was the most precious moment of my life up until that time." Sue took a shuddering breath. "Six months later, my little Beatrice was born."

Good thing Bea wasn't here to notice her mom's tone of voice.

"From the moment of her birth, it was clear that Beatrice would face many challenges. And those first months, when I had this baby at home who looked different and I first heard the words *Down syndrome*, when I tried to imagine how our lives would be long-term. . .and then as I faced doing it all by myself when the pressure became too much for her father, and he bolted. . .I would look at you, Joy. I would feel so grateful that my daughter would have you in her life. I prayed you would be her best friend, her role model."

Joy scuffed her toe into the carpet. Bea sure did look up to her. Always had.

Sue took a deep breath. "The other thing I felt was jealous. I was jealous for my daughter because she wouldn't have the life you would. And I was envious of my brother because he had a healthy baby who would grow up to do amazing things, and my daughter wouldn't. At least as I saw it then in my limited understanding." Sue shrugged. "That jealousy consumed me for a long time until I truly learned to give it over to God. It wasn't all that difficult once I realized I had to turn it over to my Lord and Savior Jesus Christ. He'd already nailed those feelings to the cross."

Mom sobbed openly into a handkerchief, and Dad swallowed hard.

Mom rushed across the room, got down on her knees in front of Joy, and grasped both of her hands. "My beautiful daughter, I won't let this happen to you. The Word of God promises that if we teach you and raise you in the ways of God, it will stick with you in the end. That a good work was started in you, and God will be faithful to complete it. I'm calling on those promises right now. I'm not letting darkness overtake you."

Joy looked into her mom's eyes. If only it were that easy. She couldn't just wish to un-know what she knew and un-see what she'd seen.

Mark stood up. "Who else? Kelsey, did you want to say something?"

Kelsey's cheeks turned bright pink. "I don't know. I'm really just here for support. I want Joy back. That's all."

"Ms. Gianetti. How about you?"

All eyes turned to Joy's counselor. Mary Alice looked haggard, like she'd been run over. "I don't have a lot to say. I'm just sorry. Joy, Peg, Alan, I'm sorry I didn't catch this sooner."

"Okay. Then I'll take the floor now." Mark paced, his hand on his chin, finger tapping his lip. He looked into Joy's eyes.

"You are involved in the occult. Satanism. Demonic powers."

Joy cringed. It wasn't like that. Silas had been growling for a while. He was on his feet now, his teeth bared.

"I know you don't see it. But I would like the opportunity to teach you about demonic activity, paranormal experiences, and Satanism. . .and how it's worked in your life. Problem is, that will take time. I would like to walk you through the hard steps of shedding your deep personal connection with the occult, but that takes time as well."

Mark paced to the window then spun around. "Most importantly, I'd like the privilege of walking you through the steps of turning your heart back to Jesus. . ."

Silas barked and pawed the carpet. Foam dripped from his mouth.

"But that will take time."

What was he getting at? "I'm not sure I understand." How about moving this thing along?

"As I mentioned, I'm from Diamond Estates. It's a home for girls in Colorado, set in a beautiful piece of property, right in the mountains."

"Ah." It all made sense now. "You want me to go there." Joy crossed her arms. The cute old guy could say his piece, but he was absolutely insane if he thought Joy would be traveling with him to Colorado to live. It so wasn't happening.

"Girls come to Diamond Estates from all over. They live there and go through intense training, counseling, guidance, and everything else designed to turn you back to the Lord. They can go to school right there on the premises. I want to invite you to come."

"Do I even have a say in this?"

"Yes, you definitely do. Actually, we won't accept girls at Diamond Estates who don't want to be there. The work is too hard—it has to be something you want."

"Well,"—Joy stood up—"in that case, I think you've come to the wrong place. I'm finally coming to peace with myself. I'm finally in a place where I feel like I can move on and where I feel like I have purpose and hope and meaning. I'm not trading that for fairy tales."

Chapter 20

"Hey Bea. Want to hang out with me today? Let's go hike at Ash Hollow, maybe down to the canyon. Want to?" Hopefully Joy could repair all the weirdness that happened between her and Bea leading up to Intervention Day. And she had to do something to make up for not going to church with her parents that morning. They hadn't been happy. But they hadn't fought her either. Had they given up?

"Yes!"

Joy pulled the phone away from her ear and laughed.

"I want to so bad."

"Great. Grab all your stuff. Make sure you have your gloves and everything—it's cold out there. I'll pick you up in ten minutes." Thankfully, the weather report called for a dry, relatively mild afternoon. Just what they needed.

Joy hung up the phone and raced through the house to collect what she needed. She grabbed her coat from the closet and dug her warmest gloves out from under her bed. Leaving her bedroom, she snatched an empty backpack off her doorknob and stuffed everything into it.

She made a quick dash to the kitchen where she filled a pot of water and turned the gas heat on high. While the water heated for the hot chocolate, she dug a thermos out of the back of the pantry, never mind the smiley face stickers that dotted its surface except for where she'd tried to scrape them off, leaving a gummy residue. She scooped chocolate powder into the bottom then added the almost-boiling water. After she screwed on the lid, she shook it to blend the contents. Easy enough.

What else? Oh. Can't forget the cookies. Bea lived for Chips Ahoy! If she got tired or whiny on the hike, Joy could dangle them in front of her face like a carrot.

Okay. Winter gear, check. Hot cocoa, check. Cookies, check. Cell phone, check. Come to think of it, she'd better leave a note so someone knew where they were headed in case the cell service went out or something. She scribbled on a sticky note, *Hiking with Bea at Ash Hollow,* and stuck it to the fridge on her way out the door.

She got behind the wheel and backed the car out of the driveway. Now, she'd better hurry or Bea would unravel. No doubt she'd been watching the time since Joy's call, leaving her mother to scramble for her necessities. Not that Sue minded. She probably jumped at the chance of an afternoon to herself. Hmm. Joy probably regained another friend with this outing. Killed two birds with one stone. Nice.

Pulling her Bug into her cousin's driveway, Joy honked twice.

Bea waved from the window beside the front door where her face left a smoky shroud in the steamed glass. She threw open the door and ran out to the car. "Is it time to go, Joy?"

"Yep. Hop in." Did Aunt Sue know Bea was leaving? She'd better make sure. Joy turned toward the porch, but Sue was standing in the doorway.

"You girls be careful and have fun." She waved.

"I'll have her back in a couple of hours," Joy said from beside the car. "See ya."

Sue's eyebrows furrowed as she waved good-bye.

Not more than a minute later, Beatrice stared at the dashboard clock as the car pointed out of the residential area. "How long will we drive until we get there?"

Joy pointed to the digital display and smiled. Beatrice loved answers. Hmm, she was kind of like Joy in that regard. "Okay, you see the clock? It says 10:12. When it says 10:52, we'll be there. Sound good?"

"Sounds good." Beatrice got serious. There would be no talking now that she had a job to do. Distractions wouldn't be welcomed.

The minutes passed without conversation until Joy turned into the clearing by Ash Hollow's visitor's center where they'd leave the car. "We're here."

Beatrice held up one finger. "Just a minute." She stared at the clock as it changed from 10:51 to 10:52. "Okay. I'm ready."

They walked to the edge of the trail that would lead them down to the canyon.

"How long are we going to walk?" Beatrice practically panted with eagerness, already worried the hike would end too soon.

"I'm not sure. I figure we'll walk out an hour, find a place to rest, and have a snack. Then we'll come back. It'll take us an hour to get back, so that'll probably be two hours of walking."

"Okay, two hours." Bea looked at her digital watch. She tapped it to make sure it was working.

Joy smiled. Bea would keep careful track of the time to make sure they walked for exactly one hour before turning around. No more, no less, or she'd hear about it from Bea.

"What kind of snack? Oh, I know! Chips Ahoy!"

"Maybe. We'll see." Joy patted her pocket and smiled.

They plodded on. The snow crunched beneath their feet and tickled their eyelashes. The weatherman had said no snow for a few days, which showed how much he knew.

Beatrice pointed up at the top of the trees and scowled. "Don't you drop that snow on me."

Who knew? Maybe the trees did talk to her. Joy would believe anything these days.

Other than the time updates from Bea every five minutes, the two barely spoke as they huffed along the path, steam puffing from their mouths with every breath.

Joy shivered as the cold wind clawed through her zipper and attacked her bones. Only forty-two minutes passed, but the weather had begun to change. Should they turn around and head back? Bea would be so disappointed. How bad could it get? It wasn't even supposed to snow at all. Joy pulled out her cell phone and shielded it from the falling snow. Any chance of coverage out there? Nope. Not a single bar.

"Hey, can we build a snowman?" Beatrice dropped to her knees and used her mittens to gather armfuls of crunchy snow. She looked up at Joy, cheeks red with chafing and nose running. She grinned. "Come on, Joy, help me."

How could she say no? "Okay, I'll help, but we've got to move pretty quickly because the snow is really coming down."

"But we still have eighteen— no, seventeen minutes. So we'll be fine."

If only the weather could tell time. "Okay. But let's hurry."

Beatrice was all about her job of gathering snow for the big ball on the bottom. She gave no indication that she'd even heard. Okay, the faster they got that snowman built, the better off they'd be.

Joy began to pack on the snow to build out the bottom snowball. Then they rolled it across the snowy ground, gathering more.

Now for the snowman's body.

Beatrice gathered the snow and formed a sphere and then rolled it across the tracks made by the bigger ball until it grew large enough to mount on top of the bigger one.

Joy glanced up into the branches now heavy with snow. Maybe they should abandon the snowman building and get back to the car.

Beatrice picked up two rocks. "Look at these perfect eyes." She unwound the long scarf from her neck. "Do you think Mom would get mad if I left this here for our snowman?"

"Hmm. How about we put it on him and take a picture then take it back with us? You don't want to get cold on your way back to the car, do you?"

"Oh. That's true. I don't want to be cold." Beatrice searched the ground. "I'd better find some sticks for his arms."

Joy rolled the head then plopped it on top of the snowman. She stuck in two branches for arms.

Beatrice chewed on her tongue as she concentrated, making sure the rocks she'd found lined up perfectly straight and the eyes were exactly where she wanted them. She set the mouth into a big grin, added the eyes, then wound the scarf and tied a knot in front. She took a giant step back and tapped on her lower lip while she surveyed her work. Finally satisfied, Bea gave her creation one big nod.

How could Joy convey the need to hurry, without scaring Bea? She sure wasn't taking the subtle suggestions seriously. "Hey Bea. Want to go get a taco?"

Beatrice's face lit up. "With extra sour cream?"

"You bet."

"Well then we better hurry." She had no concern for the two-hour time frame Joy had set now that tacos were on the table.

"Cool. Let's take a quick picture then go." Joy brought

her phone to life and opened the camera app. But not before checking for reception again. No Service. "Why don't you go stand by him and smile?"

Beatrice lumbered over to the snowman. She put her arms around him and grinned as Joy took the picture and glanced at the display. Kind of tough to make out the image with the snow swirling all around them. Hopefully that wouldn't be the last picture ever taken of Beatrice, but if they didn't get out of there, it would be.

The snow blocked out the sun, making it appear much later than it was. "Beatrice, we need to go right now. We have to get to the car so we can get out of this storm."

Beatrice looked around in horror as realization of the brewing weather set in.

Joy watched the panic rise in her cousin's eyes. Oh no. Why hadn't she said snow instead of storm? "Now, don't worry. Take my hand. We're going back to the car." Joy turned to head north. Wait. Was north this way or that way? Joy turned in a full circle searching for something familiar. Anything. She scanned the area, but their footprints were long gone, buried beneath the snow.

GPS. She'd check her phone. Joy ripped her glove off with her teeth then dug in her pocket until her numb fingers touched her phone. She yanked it out and glanced at the screen. Of course. No service. Without service the GPS couldn't locate them.

Her heart raced as she tugged on her glove, fighting off the possibilities that attacked her mind.

Silas nuzzled her hand, his warm breath a real comfort through the barrier of her gloves and the boundaries of the flesh.

Silas! He would see them home. Wouldn't he?

"Are we lost, Joy?" Beatrice's hesitant voice warned Joy of

what she'd hoped to avoid. Her cousin looked around with wild eyes.

"Bea. Listen to me. You can't cry. Your face will get wet and then you'll be really cold. Just be a brave girl. We're going to be fine. We just need to start walking. . ."—Just take a guess. Joy turned her body—". . .that way."

Silas woofed and wagged his tail. He tugged her sleeve opposite of the way Joy had pointed. Really? Did he mean to lead them? Relief crowded out some of the panic.

"Oops. Sorry. I mean this way." Hopefully the renewed confidence Silas had given Joy would comfort Beatrice, too.

"Guide us, boy," Joy whispered. "We need you, buddy."

Beatrice scrunched her face in confusion. "Who are you talking to?"

She'd never understand if Joy told her the truth. "I didn't say anything."

"Oh, were you praying to ask God for help?" Beatrice wiped the snow off her eyes with her mittened hand.

"Yeah, something like that."

Silas howled and reared back. Joy stopped in her tracks. Were they going the wrong direction again? "Show me the way to go."

"That's really good, Joy. You're talking to God; that's really good."

"Yes, Bea, it's really good." Joy closed her eyes against the stinging snow. "Just get us out of here, Silas," she whispered.

Bea's eyes searched the space around them. "Something doesn't feel right. I want to pray out loud."

Joy nodded. Not that it would help other than calming Bea down, but it sure couldn't hurt anything either. "Okay. Hold my hands."

Beatrice thrust her hands into Joy's.

Joy took a deep breath. She could at least pretend. "Dear God. . ."

Silas growled. He pulled at Joy's clothes and tried to shove her away from Beatrice.

Beatrice stared at Joy. "Come on. Pray."

Joy kept one eye scrunched closed and the other trained on Silas. What was the matter with him? She just needed to squeak out one prayer to make Beatrice feel better so they could keep walking. "Jesus, we need Your he—"

Chapter 21

Joy's senses were yanked from the present and shoved into a dream.

Silas dropped his chest to the ground, ready to pounce at her, foam dripping from his bared teeth.

She tried to run, but her concrete-filled legs wouldn't move. What was wrong with him? He was supposed to protect her, take away her fear. Her heart thundered in her chest. Could he hurt her body from the spirit realm? Did she want to take the chance and find out?

She searched her surroundings. No way she could outrun him. Besides, if she ran, Bea would be an open target.

Silas gnashed his teeth and barked.

The tree? Joy peered up into the high boughs. No way she could get up there fast enough, besides. . .Beatrice.

The wolf bit a hunk of Joy's coat and pulled with angry animal strength, pulling her away from Beatrice. He ran in a circle around Joy, keeping her penned and separated from Bea. Steam from his breath shot out like flames.

Was all this just because she prayed? "Shh. Silas. It's okay. I won't do it anymore." She had to get him back on her side. Had to convince him. Then they had to get out of there before she lost her mind. Or before Silas got any angrier.

"Joy, you're really scaring me." Beatrice's voice teetered on the edge of high-pitched hysteria. "Keep praying."

Joy imagined what the scene must look like to Bea. She had no idea why Joy was huddled in the storm, terrified, her eyes searching for the raging wolf as he leaped around her.

Just act calm and fix this. She offered Bea a soft smile. . .at least she tried. "One sec." Joy turned her back and took a few steps away, Silas circling her, right at her feet. "I'm not praying for real, Silas. I have to do this so I can get Beatrice to calm down."

Silas stopped in his tracks. He let out a growl and one last huff as he backed away just enough that Joy felt free from him. For the moment.

Joy spun around to find Beatrice standing only a few feet away, her mouth agape. She'd heard everything. Tears coursed down Bea's face. "You lied to me. Who were you talking to? I'm scared. What are we going to do?" Beatrice threw the questions into the windy storm and covered her face with her hands.

What could she say to Beatrice that wouldn't cause more problems than they already had? "It's okay. Trust me. I'll get you home." Well, Silas would, anyway. If she could get him to calm down enough to lead them.

Beatrice shook her head. "No."

"No? What do you mean?"

"I can't trust you, and I'm not going anywhere with you. You're following someone who's not God." She shrugged. "So I can't follow you."

Oh, sweet, simple Bea. Her faith so strong, yet. . .ridiculous.

Joy couldn't very well leave her cousin to freeze to death in the snow while she ran for help, could she? But what choice did she have? Maybe if she went for help, Silas would stay back to protect Bea. But if he did, how would Joy find the car? And how would she find Bea again once she did?

"Come on. There's no time for this." She couldn't worry about scaring Bea anymore. In fact, she needed to terrify her. "Listen to me, Beatrice. You can be mad at me later, but right now we have to get out of this storm or we'll die. We'll freeze out here."

Beatrice shook her head. "God will protect me if He wants to. Burning in a fiery furnace or freezing in a snowy blizzard, He'll protect me because I'm not going to walk away from Him to follow something bad."

This was going nowhere. Time for a different approach. "Beatrice Pauline O'Malley, I am giving you a direct order to come with me right now."

Beatrice shook her head and sat on a stump. "Nope." She crossed her arms and turned her head away.

Lord, help me. . . . Joy shot a glance at Silas. The prayer had escaped her thoughts before she could stop it. Well at least she hadn't spoken it out loud, and Silas hadn't read her mind. Come to think of it, it didn't appear he could. That could be helpful to her.

Later she'd have to examine why her heart had cried out to God instinctively. Was that a leftover from her childhood faith, or was it something bigger? No time to figure it all out now.

A shrill ring pierced the stormy wind. What was that? It sounded like a phone. Not possible. Not in the middle of a blizzard at the bottom of a canyon. She bit her glove and jerked her hand out then touched the CALL button. "Mom? Are you there?" Keep the panic to a minimum.

"Oh, thank You, Jesus." Mom sighed. "Are you both okay?"

Define *okay*. "Yeah, we're pretty shook up, but we're fine."

"Thank the Lord. Where are you?"

"I might lose coverage again—the storm, you know." Joy searched for a landmark. "I'm not exactly sure, but we're down at the base of the canyon at Ash Hollow. I can't figure out how to get back to the car because I have no visibility and no GPS."

"Your dad and some rescue guys are up that way hoping for a lead. I'll let them know where you are. Stay put. Okay?"

"Don't worry. We're not going anywhere."

᎐

Time stood still as the snow pelted their bodies. A full hour had passed since she'd believed help was on the way. What if they'd gotten lost, too? Silas had disappeared, and Joy had no idea if he'd be back.

Beatrice wouldn't speak to her. She'd kept her back to Joy ever since the phone call.

Speaking of the phone, Joy checked hers again. Still no service. None since she'd spoken to her frantic mom, whose panic had to be intense now. Oh, and Aunt Sue. The poor woman must be beside herself.

Joy shivered and blew into her freezing hands, the gloves wet on the inside, frozen on the outside. Soon frostbite would set in. Beatrice huddled against a tree. Out of the line of snowfall, but still subject to the freezing cold. Joy inched over to her cousin and put her arms around her. At least their body heat could protect them for a while.

Bea shrugged Joy's arm off her shoulders, but Joy put it back. She could be mad, but Joy wouldn't let her die of stubbornness.

A brief flicker of light poked through the branches. The moon? No. Too early. What was it? Come to think of it, there was a rumble coming from somewhere. An engine?

Could it be her dad?

"Joy?"

"Beatrice?"

"Joy?"

Men's voices blended in with the roar of the wind and carried over to the spot where Joy lay covering her cousin. They'd made it. They were safe. "Right here," she croaked. Had they heard her?

Joy scrambled to her feet. "Daddy? We're here." If only she had a flashlight to shine toward them. Oh! Her phone. Joy scrolled through her apps until she found the one she wanted and touched it. The flashlight image on the screen shot a bright light through her camera flash. Perfect.

The voices were growing quieter. The rescuers were moving away from them. She couldn't let that happen.

Another option on the flashlight said SOS. Why not? She touched it, and the light intensified by at least three times and began to strobe. Joy stretched her arm and waved it overhead.

Nothing. Where had they gone? It was no use. They'd never be found in time. They would surely die out there. Joy scrunched her eyes closed. To have come so close to being saved and then lose it all. That was almost worse than if her phone had never rung, than if she'd never heard that voice call out her name.

Her eyes flew open. Was that what she was doing spiritually? What if she really was on the wrong path now? What if she'd been led the right way her whole life, but turned the other way when things got tough? What if the voice of God was silent to her, not because He wasn't speaking, but because she wasn't listening?

A crash to her left about knocked Joy off her feet. She spun around and gasped as a snowmobile skidded to a stop two feet from them.

"Bea! They're here." Joy watched as a man in a red snowsuit spoke into his radio.

"We've found them. Reconvene at the trucks." He turned to her. "You're Joy?"

She nodded.

"I'm Tom. That your cousin right there?"

Joy nodded. What? He wasn't going to take the freezing girl if she wasn't Bea? How about they get anyone they find out of here?

"Let's get you two on back so I can take you to the search crew. Your daddy is going to be one happy fella."

Beatrice eyed the stranger. Was she going to refuse to ride with him? After all the drilling into her head about stranger danger, there was a good chance she wouldn't. Beatrice was relentless when it came to rules. How to handle it?

The man slid off his seat and approached Bea. He knelt in the snow and removed his mask so she could see his eyes. Smart move. "Beatrice?"

She nodded, shivering.

"Someone wants to talk to you." He pressed a button on his radio. "Go ahead, ma'am." He held it up to Bea's ear. Aunt Sue's voice came through loud and clear.

"Bea baby?"

"Mama?" Beatrice sobbed.

"Yes. Beatrice. Listen to me. This man is not a stranger. He's there to help you. You can get on his snowmobile and take a ride with him. Okay? Mama said so."

"Okay. What's his name?"

"What?" Sue sounded perplexed.

"If he's not a stranger, he must have a name."

Uh-oh. Bea had her there. If Sue didn't know. . .

"His name is Pete." Sue held back her panic.

Joy shot a glance at Tom. As long as he didn't correct Sue, they'd be fine.

"Come home with him, Bea."

"Okay, Mama." She walked to the snowmobile, and Tom helped her climb on. "Thanks, Pete."

Tom winked at Joy and got on.

Joy straddled the back of the bench, put her arms around Beatrice, and clutched Tom's jacket. Well played.

"Here we go. It's going to be a bumpy ride, so hang on."

Chapter 22

Joy put her ear to her parents' bedroom door, part of her hoping they were sound asleep and she'd have to come back tomorrow. But television sounds buzzed through the wood. They were awake. She took a deep breath, then knocked.

"Come in."

Joy pushed the door open a few inches and spoke through the crack. "Mom, Dad, can I talk to you guys for a minute?" She opened it a few more inches so she could see their faces.

Mom put her Bible down on the nightstand and sat up against the headboard.

Dad flipped the TV off with the remote and set it on the bed beside him. He removed his glasses and glanced at Mom, then motioned Joy into the room.

Guess they were waiting for the next bomb to drop. Could she blame them?

"Come on in and have a seat." Mom patted the floral comforter beside her.

The mattress squeaked as Joy sat on the corner. It slumped toward the floor. She'd have been more comfortable standing, but it was too late now. "I have some things I want to say, but mostly. . .oh man, I don't know how to say this. . . ." Joy looked up at the ceiling.

"You're making me really nervous. I don't think I can take

anything more." Mom's voice shook.

Dad reached for her hand and squeezed it.

Joy jumped up and paced across the room. It was too much responsibility to have as much power over two grown people as she did over her parents. Everything she did affected them so much. She hadn't asked for that.

"You need to spill it. What's up?" Dad raised his eyebrows, waiting.

"Well, with all that's gone on. . .it's hard for me to explain. . ." Just say it. Joy took a deep breath. "There's the stuff you know, but there's a lot of stuff going on that you don't even know about." That you wouldn't want to know about. "If you could see inside my head. . .well. . .I'm scared."

Mom maintained her stoic expression. Was she even breathing?

Dad nodded. "Go on."

"There's been some weird stuff happening." How far to take it with them? Too far, they'd freak. Not enough info, and they wouldn't know what kind of help she needed. "Um, I've been messing around with some spiritual things, like a Ouija board. . ." She could never just come right out and tell them that her spirit guide tried to kill her after she prayed a pretend prayer to God. They'd lock her up in the psych ward for sure.

Mom gasped. "No. Joy. That's dangerous stuff."

Joy nodded. If they only knew. "I know. I need help with it all. At least, I think I do." If help were even a possibility. "I guess I'm going to need someone who knows what it all means. Do you think we can find someone or do something to help me figure out this mess I'm in?" Joy wrung her hands together. If only she'd let that Mark guy tell her what to do while he'd been right there in her house.

Why didn't they say something? What were they waiting for?

Joy needed help. But then again, did she truly want it? "The thing is though, I want someone who can tell me what's going on and answer the questions I have that sent me searching in the first place." Joy threw her hands up. That sounded hopeless. It probably was. Maybe she would spend her whole life searching for meaning, but never find it. "I mean, I can't just empty myself of everything again and have nothing to fill the hole. But I can't go back to what I was before all this either."

"That is the wisest thing I've ever heard you say." Dad put his glasses back on and stood up from the bed. He reached his arms out and pulled his daughter close. She let her arms hang by her side while her daddy squeezed. Too spent to move.

"I love you, sweetheart." He stroked her hair. "Your mom and I will move heaven and earth to help you through this."

That did it. Heavy tears plopped onto his light gray thermal. She reached her arms around him and breathed a sigh of relief. She wasn't in it alone. Then again, they had no idea what they'd signed up for.

Mom sat up straighter. "So are you leaving this up to us? Will you do what we think is best?" She held up a finger. "No. Better question. Will you embrace what we think is best?"

Interesting distinction. Joy stared out the window at the still falling snow. Embrace did hold a completely different meaning than simply doing. But, if she wanted true and lasting results, she'd have to give herself over to whatever process. No matter how scary.

"You tell me what I need to do, and I'll do it." At least she'd try. Joy dropped her head. "I'm really sorry all this happened."

Mom gave two sharp nods. "Your Dad and I love you. We forgive you of course. Now, just so you know, I'm jumping on this without looking back. It can't wait another day." Mom eyed her with intensity. "Agreed?"

Joy nodded. Oh boy. She knew that look. Circumstances were going to spiral out of her control faster than she could imagine. Like when Adam Samuelson followed her into the girls' restroom in eighth grade. She almost hadn't told Mom about it. But then she did, and everything turned upside down within minutes. Mom didn't fool around when she got it in her head to take care of something. And Joy's mess was likely to get the full-scale treatment.

"Then with the first light of day, I'm on the phone with Mark Stapleton from Diamond Estates. I'm going to get his advice, but I'm pretty sure I know what he's going to say. You ready for that?"

"I think so." What other choice did she have?

"No matter what?" Mom pulled her glasses off and chewed on one of the arms.

Joy nodded. She'd do her best. Hopefully that would be good enough.

"Good." Mom put her glasses back on and picked up her Bible.

She'd better get out of there before Mom started reading out loud. "I'll see you in the morning. I've got to get some sleep." Joy pulled the bedroom door closed. If only she could hear the conversation they were surely having on the other side.

Now what? Bed? No. She was too pent up, too anxious. She needed air.

Joy slipped into her coat and boots, felt the pocket for her gloves, and grabbed her keys just in case. She stepped through the front door and breathed in a gulp of the crisp air. Inhale. Exhale. Her body relaxed with each breath.

Would she get in trouble for leaving the house? Definitely, but really, what could they do to her? Besides, they'd never allow her to leave, but there was no way she was staying inside. In this case, forgiveness was easier to get than permission.

She moved off the porch and turned right at the bottom of the driveway. Just walk. The powdery snow kicked off the tops of her boots with each step. The moon reflecting off the snow made the night bright.

She'd promised herself she was ready to do whatever they said, no matter how scary. Did she mean it?

No matter how scary. The sight of Silas chasing her with foam dripping from his mouth, the fury in him as he ran in circles around her to trap her in, the fear she'd felt caused by the one who was supposed to always protect her.

What would he do to her if she pulled further away?

But he wasn't real, right? He couldn't actually, physically get at her from the spirit realm, could he? She'd felt his warm breath before, but hadn't ever ruffled her fingers through his fur. And he hadn't touched her when he was all worked up—even though he looked like he wanted to kill her.

Wait a second. He had tugged on her, she felt the pressure of his strength, and it did move her body. Did that mean he could get physical with her? Or not? Who would know the answer?

Joy reached down to the hem of her coat, just near the zipper where he'd clenched his teeth to pull her.

She gasped as the bottom corner of her coat dangled in four-inch-long shreds.

About exactly what it would look like if a spirit wolf crossed into the flesh and attacked her.

☼

OUTSIDE UR HOUSE CAN U COME OUT 2 TALK?

Joy touched SEND and dropped the phone onto the passenger seat beside her. She rested her head on the headrest. One o'clock in the morning. After the past two days she'd had, she should be cuddled up in her bed sound asleep. But she needed to see Raven. Now.

Her phone buzzed.

B RIGHT THERE.

Still warm from her midnight walk, Joy tugged at the collar of her coat and fiddled with the knob to turn down the heater. She stared at the front door. Come on. Where was she?

Movement caught her attention as a shadowy figure crept from around the back of the house toward the car.

Who was it? Joy fumbled in the dark and pressed the LOCK button as she squinted at the form. Where was Silas when she needed him?

The face glanced up, and moonlight reflected off Raven's pale skin. She pulled her winter coat tight around her as she clomped to the car in black sweatpants and what appeared to be her father's shoes.

What was she doing coming from the back? Almost gave Joy a heart attack.

Raven slid into the passenger seat and turned to Joy, her eyebrows furrowed. "What's going on? You okay?"

Joy shook her head. "No. Nothing is okay. I'm in big trouble, and I've got to get out."

"What do you mean? What kind of trouble?" Raven chuckled. "Can't be any worse than the other night at the cemetery. I mean, really."

"No, not that kind of trouble. Worse. Look, I tried to take Beatrice for a hike yesterday. We got stuck in the blizzard out at Ash Hollow."

"Yeah. You told me. It must have been really scary." Raven's concern was laced with annoyance.

"Well, what I didn't tell you is. . ." Joy glanced around her. No sign of Silas. Was he there, but invisible to her now? Maybe he'd always been able to go invisible. Or hopefully he just wasn't there at the moment. "I spoke out loud and asked Silas to guide us to the car."

"Smart. Did he?" Raven yawned, exposing the fillings in her back teeth. Gross.

Joy held up a finger. "Just wait. Beatrice heard me and totally freaked out. It was like she knew I was praying or talking to a spirit, but not God."

Raven rolled her eyes and stifled another yawn.

"Seriously, she freaked out and wanted me to pray. So I started to say a supposed prayer to God, and Silas came totally unglued. He was like foaming at the mouth and having a fit. . . and Beatrice wouldn't follow me because she thought I was evil. What do you make of all that?"

"Of what? Your cousin is a little nutty about that God stuff, but we knew that already."

"I mean about Silas. Why did he turn on me?"

"Why? Well, you turned on him first." Raven shrugged. What, that was supposed to explain it?

"I didn't. Unless a five-word prayer is turning on him." Joy tried to tone down her own irritation. She needed Raven's help.

"Apparently it is, or he felt like it was." Raven grinned. "Spirit wolves have feelings, too, ya know."

"I'm glad you can joke around about this. But I'm scared."

"Oh, you have no reason to be scared. Just tell Silas you're sorry and make up. It'll be fine." Raven patted Joy's leg. "Everything will go right back to how it was before you messed up."

"That's the thing. What if I don't want it to?"

Raven waved her hand. "Oh come on. You don't mean that. You're just a little freaked out. That's normal. You made a commitment. It's a for-better-or-worse kind of thing."

Trapped. That's what Joy had been afraid of. "But Beatrice. . ."

"Beatrice doesn't know what she's talking about, and it's not like she's the sharpest tack in the box. You can't go making decisions based on what she senses."

Joy blinked. How dare she insult Beatrice? "Ray. Don't even go there with me. You should know better than that."

Raven nodded. "Yeah, I'm sorry. Shouldn't have said it. Beatrice is awesome. You know how I feel about her."

Did Joy know? How could she? It wasn't like Beatrice and Raven spent all kinds of time together. "I guess. I don't know. I'm just saying she's not a target."

"Point taken. Again, sorry. But back to your problem. . ."

How to describe it? "Well, I thought I'd gotten answers. But now I just have more questions." She couldn't tell Raven about going to her parents for help. Not now.

"Okay. What kind of questions?" Raven slid down in her seat and pulled her jacket up around her chin.

"Starting with this. Can you explain this?" Joy lifted the tattered corner of her jacket.

Raven's eyes grew wide. "Who did that?"

It was a *what*, not a *who*. "Silas."

Chapter 23

Joy pulled the covers over her head to block out the sunlight. And the noise. What was that banging, and why was it so close? Wait a second—was someone in her room?

She threw back the quilt and popped up on her elbows. Mom stood hunched over Joy's dresser, rummaging through her underwear and sock drawer. "Mom? What are you doing?" Joy stretched her arms over her head and yawned. Was she dreaming?

"I'm packing."

Was she serious? Where was she going? Come to think of it, why was she in Joy's room packing? Joy glanced down to find the green Samsonite suitcase spread open on the floor with her belongings already filling most of the space.

Mom was serious. But she wasn't going anywhere. Joy was.

Mom looked at anything and everything in the room. . . except Joy.

"What's going on?" Joy sat upright.

Mom neatly folded a sweatshirt and tucked it inside the suitcase. She reached back into the depths of the sock drawer and scooped out an armful then dropped them into the zippered pouch on the side.

"Are you kicking me out or something?" Joy threw her legs over the side of her bed and stood up, instantly shivering in her tank top and shorts. She reached for the sweatshirt Mom had just put in.

Mom beat her to it and pressed her hand over the UN logo. "Let's leave this one packed. Just grab something else." Why wouldn't she make eye contact?

Joy pulled a sweater off a hanger and yanked it over her head. "Mom. This is scaring me. Would you just tell me what's going on? You're kicking me out, aren't you?" Where would Joy go? She had no real friends. Maybe Grandpa's?

"Okay. Here's the thing." Mom blinked. "I wanted to talk to you about this when your dad was here, but he had to run out to pick up a few things for you, and if I wait, we'll run out of time." She sat on the bed and pulled Joy down beside her. "I took what you said last night to heart, and we're getting you the help you need."

Silas appeared at Joy's side. Calm, but watchful. Alert.

Oh boy. This was going to be interesting.

"I talked with Mark Stapleton, and he's on a plane right now." Mom fiddled with a rip in Joy's quilt. "He's coming here so he can bring you to Diamond Estates."

"What about school? You do know that yesterday was the end of Christmas break, right? I have to leave in. . .oh. . ."—Joy looked at her bedside clock—"less than an hour."

"They have school at Diamond Estates. You'll only miss today."

Joy shook her head like marbles were rolling around in there. Maybe she'd misheard something. "I'm confused. How did this happen so fast? And how long will I be going?" Joy jumped from the bed. "Why didn't I have a chance to talk to you about this? I mean, I thought you were getting information. I didn't know you'd be packing me and sending me off today." The tears spilled down Joy's cheeks.

Today? She had no more time to make sense of it all? What if she'd changed her mind? What if she wanted to back out?

Mom nodded. "I had a lot of those same questions, too. But I have to agree with Mark. We're dealing with some serious stuff, and it's not time to play games. I also agree with Mark coming to get you because we're not about to risk sending you off on the plane alone."

"Well, why couldn't you just take me there?" She couldn't travel that distance beside some stranger, a super-Christian nonetheless, trying to make conversations about the weather. Come on.

"Honestly, sweetheart, your dad and I are simply not equipped to handle this with you, and we don't want to mess it up. Mark says. . ."

Something told Joy she was going to get really sick and tired of those two words before this whole thing was over.

". . .you're under an intense spiritual battle. I just think it would be doing you a disservice if I were the only one there fighting with you. I'll be on the sidelines praying for you every moment of every day, but you need real help. Help I can't give you." She twisted her hands together, but not before Joy saw them tremble.

Mom was scared. It all made sense. But could Joy really blame her? After all, Joy was terrified herself, and she was the one who'd caused the whole mess.

She let her body fall back onto her bed. Couldn't really argue with Mom's logic, if only it could be some other way.

"So how long do I have?" She had things to do and friends to say good-bye to. Well actually, maybe not. Maybe some things were better left alone. She could call Grandpa and Stella at least.

"Mark will be here in about two hours. You have time for

a shower." Mom turned back to the packing then looked up.
"Oh, almost forgot. Grandpa's coming in to see you. He'll be
here in about an hour."

Joy nodded. "Stella, too?"

"No. We thought that's probably not a great idea." Mom
offered a soft smile. "I mean, your dad and I feel that Stella
might not be the best influence on you right now."

Duh. You think? "Yeah. . ." Joy hoped Stella didn't feel hurt.
"I feel so bad that I've upset everyone's life so intensely. I'd undo
it if I could."

"Don't feel bad. Just get help. That's the only way to undo
it. Now go jump in the shower. I'll finish packing so you have
time with Grandpa, Dad, and me before you leave."

Joy slumped off the bed and inched her way to the door.
Her hand on the frame, she turned around. "How long will I be
there?" Week or two. . .three, max?

"That will all depend." Mom looked at her hands. "No less
than six months. Probably a year."

A year. The words fell like a lump in Joy's gut, and tears
filled her bottom lids. Mom and Dad were okay with Joy
moving out for an entire year. When she came back, she'd be
close to graduation. Then what? They were giving up the end of
her childhood. And they were okay with that? What about next
year's volleyball season? Not that it mattered.

She could still say no, right? What if she backed out? She
could tell Mom she got too nervous to be away from home.
Raven said girls had to want the help at Diamond Estates to be
accepted into the program. So she'd say she didn't want to go.
Send Mark home, unpack her suitcase. . .

But she wouldn't do that. If she did that, there'd be no hope
left for her. She'd be forever locked between two worlds. One of
them growing scarier by the day. No, she'd go. Make it easier on

everyone. She could always change her mind later. Couldn't she?

Those famous words from *Casablanca* filtered into her mind.

"You'll regret it. Maybe not today, maybe not tomorrow, but soon and for the rest of your life."

Fine. But regret what? Going or staying?

Chapter 24

We're going to need everything in your house that's in any way associated with the occult—books, games, DVDs, a Ouija board—anything you have. I need you to go collect them so we can burn them." Mark rubbed his palms together like he couldn't wait to get them on Joy's stuff.

"Burn them?" He couldn't be serious. That stuff cost real money.

Silas growled.

"Yes. We need to take care of that before we go." His eyes searched the family room. "I don't want to leave those things here to cause any problems for your parents." Mark strode to the bookshelves that lined the family room wall and ran his finger along the spines looking. . .for what? A witchcraft bible?

Mom nodded. "I think that's a great idea." Her eyes never left Mark as he searched her books.

Dad coughed. "Is this going to be like an exorcism?" His face paled.

Mark shook his head and turned back toward them, two dog-eared paperback novels in his hands. Joy strained to see the titles, but couldn't make them out.

"No. An exorcism is what's done when someone is possessed. I don't believe Joy is possessed because she's not manifesting a spirit through her body—that we've seen evidence of.

But she's clearly being affected by the satanic world—oppressed. So, while we don't need to exorcize spirits from her body, we do need to break any association between her and that realm." Mark looked around the room, making eye contact with each person. "And, like I said, we want to be sure that when Joy and I leave this house today, there is nothing remaining here to affect you guys or for her to come back to later."

Joy's shoulders slumped. It hadn't even crossed her mind that other people could suffer under the weight of her decisions. She sure didn't want her parents to be haunted or whatever. What if they got assigned their own wolf. . .or lion, tiger, or bear? Oh my.

"I'll be right back." She went to her room and lay on the floor by her bed. There wasn't much under there, most of her reading was done on the computer. She pulled out a few magazines from Kyle's store, a box of incense, and a picture book of white wolves.

She hopped up and strode toward the door with her findings. Oh! She'd almost forgotten Raven's Ouija board. Joy hurried back to her closet and pulled the old string hanging from the single light bulb then felt on the top shelf among her sweaters where she'd hidden the game. Ah. There it was. She pulled out the well-worn box held together by rubber bands.

Should she call Raven and get it back to her? Joy couldn't very well burn someone else's property, could she? And at least it would be out of the house. But she really didn't want to have a confrontation with Raven. She just wanted to disappear.

Speaking of Raven. . . Joy looked at her hand, the onyx glinting on her finger. She should probably turn it over to Mark. But it was hers. It had been a gift. She'd keep it as a memento of all she'd been through. It didn't mean anything unless she gave it meaning, right? Well, it was only a ring. That's all the power she'd let it have. A piece of jewelry.

Joy pulled the onyx off her finger and slipped it into her front pocket. No, that wouldn't do. She might lose it. How could she keep it with her but concealed? Ah! She scrambled over to her dresser and plowed through her unpacked socks until her fingers found what they searched for. She pulled out a long chain, slipped the ring onto it, and then clasped it around her neck. She dropped the ring down her shirt and felt it bump against her sternum. It would be safe there.

Better get back to the others. Joy hurried back to the family room where she set everything down on the floor in front of the fireplace. "This is all of it."

Mark looked the pile over. "Are you sure? No other books, movies, magazines?" He searched her eyes while he rattled off the possibilities.

"Nope. Nothing."

"What about jewelry? Any trinkets, necklaces, bracelets?"

Joy shook her head. "No. I'm not withholding anything on purpose, if that's what you mean." At least he hadn't said rings.

"Okay, because this is very important." Mark waited again.

What? Did he think she was lying? "I can't think of anything else there would be. But I do have one question. What about something that's borrowed? Don't I need to give it back to the person I borrowed it from since it's not my property?"

"No, in my opinion, this stuff is so dangerous that even if someone did own it, it's okay and even good to destroy it. You're doing them a favor."

Seemed like convenient logic to Joy. But whatever helped him sleep at night was fine with her.

Mom peered down at the contraband. "Um. You have a Ouija board? I don't understand how you could have something like that going on in our home." She sighed and shook her head.

"Would you believe it's not mine?" Not that it mattered whose it was.

"It's in our house. . .might as well be yours."

Mark cleared his throat and raised an open Bible in front of him. Where had that come from?

"I want to read to you from Acts nineteen. It says, 'Also, many of those who had practiced magic brought their books together and burned them in the sight of all. And they counted up the value of them, and it totaled fifty thousand pieces of silver.' "

Whoa. It was like whoever wrote that could see them standing around the fireplace.

Mark glanced at Joy. "Any doubts now that God is against all of this?" He gestured to the floor.

Joy shook her head. Oh, she already knew God would be against it all—if He existed. But if He *were* real, then she and God were on a what-have-you-done-for-me-lately basis. And it didn't look good for Him.

Mom rubbed her temples. Her eyes drooped like she might nod off to sleep right there in front of the altar of evil. Dad put his hand on her neck and squeezed. Joy stood alone. Except. . .

"Well, if this is it. . . ?" Mark turned to the fire.

"Wait." Had she said that out loud?

Mark spun around. "Yes? Did you think of something?"

Oh no. Joy's heart thudded like a drum. Her parents were going to kill her. But worse, she was doomed with Silas's face engraved on her body forever. She couldn't get away even if she wanted to. "I did something I don't think can be burned away. And I don't know what to do about it." Then again, maybe it was a good thing. Maybe she should keep it to herself.

"What do you mean?" Mom's eyebrows furrowed.

"Well. . ." What could she say instead of what she'd

intended? Nothing else seemed to fit that description. "I mean, I made promises. You know?"

Mark nodded. "Go on."

"Just like a commitment, kind of."

"You're right. It's definitely a commitment. That's what we're doing here. Severing those ties. Breaking that bond." Mark watched Joy's expression. "You okay with that?"

The doorbell rang. Saved by the bell?

Mom glanced at Dad. "That would be your father. Want to let him in?"

Joy, Mom, and Mark stood silently waiting. They heard the door open and a loud voice boom down the hallway.

"Dad. I'm so glad you could come." Then a moment of silence.

Joy could picture the two men embracing. She imagined Grandpa's eyes laced with sadness.

"Come on back. Everyone's in the family room. It's kind of somber—we're sort of in the middle of something."

As Dad and Grandpa arrived in the room, Mark clasped his hands together. "Well, let's do this thing."

Mark stood before the fireplace and lifted one of the Duraflame logs in the box beside it. He turned it over in his hands and tried to read the instructions. He was probably used to real wood for his fires. He flipped the flap up at the seam to see the instructions beneath.

Dad lifted his head out of his hands and gazed at Mark's attempts. He stared for a moment then shook his head as if snapping out of a thought. He jumped to his feet and took three strides toward Mark. "Here. Allow me."

Mark nodded and turned back to the group. "Okay, Joy, last chance. You've collected everything I suggested?"

Eyes on Dad, Joy watched as he lit the two arrows and

waited for the log to catch, brightening the room almost instantly. Joy shook her head. "No, that's it."

Mark turned to Mom. "How about you? Can you think of anything in the home that could have attachment to evil? Anything?" He waited. "I'm sorry if it seems like I'm driving this point too hard. I guess I just don't feel a release to move on. In my heart, I feel as though we aren't ready for the next step."

Oh great. He was psychic, too.

Mom shook her head. "No, I can't think of anything. . ." She gasped and held up a finger. "Just a sec. I'll be right back." She tore off down the hallway to the guest room.

Joy looked at Grandpa and shrugged. What could Mom be up to? Grandpa and Stella were the last people to stay in that room. Oh. . .unless Mom thought Stella. . .

Mom came back in the room holding a few of the little statues Stella had lined up on the dresser. "These are going to have to go."

Joy peeked at Grandpa. He closed his eyes and nodded. Hmm. He was in the thick of it, too, wasn't he?

"Okay, well here's what we're going to do, folks. I'll pray, and if anyone else would like to say a prayer, you're free to do that. Know that the power of God is in the name of Jesus. . ."

Silas barked. The hair on his back stood straight up.

". . .and every spirit bows at the very mention of His name, so we're *claiming* authority in the name of Jesus. We're not hoping for victory, we're claiming it."

Joy fought the urge to roll her eyes. It just sounded so ridiculous. Cage fighting made so much more sense. Put two guys in a cage; the stronger one wins. The spirit world was probably the same. Put a demon in a cage with an angel. . .

Mark lifted his hands into the air. "Father God, Holy Spirit, we invite Your presence into this space. We claim victory over the evil that assails this family. In the name of Jesus I command evil spirits to leave this place, amen." He lowered his hands and waited.

Dad cleared his throat. "Lord, as the father and the husband in this household, I repent of my weakness and my blindness and ask You to forgive me for lowering my guard and allowing this to happen under my watch. Please give me the strength to see what's going on around me with my family. Lord, please heal my daughter and bring her back. We claim victory, and I command all evil spirits to leave the presence of my family in the name of Jesus Christ, amen."

Mark nodded and turned to Joy. "In agreement with what's been said, take each of your items and toss them into the fire one by one."

In agreement with what's been said? There was the rub. If she threw the magazines or the incense into the fire, she was saying that the prayers Mark and Dad had prayed were her own. Such a tough call. Was it? What if she wasn't sure? She wanted her answers—like she'd told Mom. She wasn't going to run from one side unless she had somewhere else to go.

Problem was, they all stood there staring at her. She had to do something. She couldn't very well say she wasn't going to burn her stuff because she had doubts. If she didn't throw everything in the fire, they would freak out, but if she did, Silas would freak out. Joy looked at Mark and shrugged her shoulders.

Mark leveled his gaze and locked eyes with Joy.

Silas stood panting. Waiting.

Joy shook her head.

"I can't."

Chapter 25

The Explorer turned onto I-76 and pointed toward Colorado. The next three-plus hours were sure to be awkward.

Joy stared out her window and watched the mile markers fly by. One at a time.

Who'd have thought she'd be riding in a car next to Mark Stapleton, a relative stranger, whom she'd just thoroughly disappointed and probably embarrassed, on what would've been the most emotional day of her life—who left home at seventeen? But she had to keep it together. No way she'd start emoting in front of a stranger. At least he didn't seem bent on filling every moment with some spiritual conversation like he might have done if he weren't so angry with her. Ooh. Hidden bonus to the fire debacle: Maybe he would let her travel in peace.

Joy pulled out her iPhone and plugged in the headphones. She pressed the ear buds in and set the playlist to random—all she needed was the noise. Joy could read to fill the time. She toggled to the Kindle app.

Studying Mark out of the corner of her eye, Joy felt him inch a bit closer and peek over the console at her screen. What would he say if he noticed she was reading *Twilight*? Mom and Dad both read it, but it was one of those unspoken things they didn't admit around their churchy groups. But if Mark could tell what it was, Joy was sure he'd have some kind of comment. Or at least he would have before she shot him down at the bonfire.

Ugh. She'd really made a mess of that experience. The others might have thought she enjoyed their discomfort as she whispered "I can't," but the disappointment on Mom's face wouldn't be something Joy soon forgot. Mom had gasped and covered her mouth when Joy said she couldn't go through with burning her things. Mark had said it was normal, that they shouldn't worry. He offered to take care of it.

What had he said when he reached his hands out to Joy and asked her to surrender her things to him? *I will take care of them, but this is not symbolic of you turning them over. This is simply me taking them from you. Eventually, you'll have to make the choice for yourself before you'll be able to reunite in fellowship with God.*

Reunite in fellowship with God. What did that even mean? It didn't sound fun at all. But none of that really mattered in the moment. At least she'd avoided making the choice that day. And Silas was happy. At least for now. Maybe she could figure things out better before she'd have to deal with making Silas mad again. It would be great if her final spiritual awakening was some kind of combo platter of all the good stuff from every belief system, with Silas right in the center.

Speaking of her wolf, was he with her in the car? Her eyes roved the small space beneath her feet. No Silas. Where had he gone? Did his absence mean he wasn't coming with her to Colorado? On one hand, that would free her from a lot of issues, but on the other. . .what would she do without him?

Silas appeared in front of her and put his chin on her leg. He looked up at her with sad eyes. *Is this an apology for Ash Hollow, boy?* Joy spoke with her thoughts even though he probably couldn't hear them. She smiled. *Good boy.* Sure would be nice to have him with her on this adventure. At least she wouldn't be alone.

But now she'd better figure out what happened with Bella before they arrived at Diamond Estates. Thank goodness Mark didn't seem bent on drawing her into conversation for the entire drive. Probably figured he'd get her back to his lair before he spun his web around her, trapping her forever in his world. Too dramatic? At one time she'd have thought so, but not anymore.

Joy raised her phone to eye level and scrolled to the spot where she left off. Something told her books like that wouldn't be allowed at Diamond Estates. So if she was going to learn all about eternal love, vampire-style, she'd have to do it now.

"We're headed up the mountain and will be at Diamond Estates very shortly."

Joy blinked as her eyes tried to focus on her blurry surroundings. Mark Stapleton tipped his head up a snowy lane as the car's wheels gripped the pavement through the slush. How long had she been asleep? Had she snored, or worse. . . drooled?

Mark smiled. "Welcome back to earth. He handed her the iPhone. "You dropped this when you nodded off."

So, had he scrolled through her pics and read her texts? She totally should have set up one of those password locks. "Thanks. I don't know what came over me. I just crashed, I guess."

"I'm thinking you've had a rough couple of days and probably needed the sleep. Besides, it made the trip super fast for you." Mark smiled.

Which was supposed to be a good thing?

Joy's eyes instinctively hunted for Silas. There he was, tucked behind her feet, almost under the seat. What would he do when they arrived at Diamond Estates? As long as he stayed on her side, it would be fine. At least that's what she kept telling herself.

§

"Hop on out. I'll grab your bags." Mark opened the back door of the van and reached in for the two suitcases Mom had packed. Joy shouldered her backpack and picked up her carry-on. She climbed from the vehicle and planted her feet on the crunchy snow.

Her eyes were drawn upward as she gazed at the elaborate stone structure that stood before her. And that had probably stood there for centuries. "This is it? This place is amazing."

Mark nodded and smiled. "Welcome to Diamond Estates."

Joy turned in a complete circle. The forest to her back. The snowy mountainscape that spread for miles in every direction. Then back at the place she'd call home for the next little while.

She took a step closer, taken in by the stained glass windows, each depicting a scene from the Bible. "Those are beautiful." She stepped among the shrubbery near the front window and reached a hand up to touch the colored, hand-laid glass. Her fingers danced over the flowers and greenery of the Garden of Eden then rested on the shards that formed the serpent. The sunlight bounced off the amber, giving the snake a golden glow. Mesmerizing. . .

Joy snatched her fingers away and glanced at Mark. Had he seen?

"Yeah." Mark stared at the rainbow over the arc at the top of the window by the garden scene. "They're my favorite part of this whole place." Mark gestured her toward the front door.

Joy stepped up onto the porch, Silas glued to her side.

"Now just so you know, this is the main house, but you won't be staying here right away."

Joy eyed him. So, she'd be in solitary confinement?

"We have a new outbuilding that we use for newcomers and people who are in need of some intense or more individualized time with us. You'll be camping out there for a little bit, but you'll move over here sooner than you think." He swung open a wooden door that had to be twice as tall as him. It creaked as it opened. Creepy.

How awesome. Joy turned and took in the wall sconces and the ornate chandelier. The portraits on the walls reminded her of a haunted mansion—if their eyes moved. . .she was out of there.

The entire place was right out of some kind of old horror movie. Looked like Joy may have jumped right out of the frying pan into the fire when she arrived at Diamond Estates.

"What's that room there?" Joy pointed at a cavernous space surrounded by stained glass windows on all sides, beanbag clusters throughout the room, and mats on the floor. She moved into the entrance and gazed up at the wooden candelabras that hung from the ceiling.

Mark smiled into the room and patted the framed entryway. "This is where the magic happens."

Joy leaned her shoulder against the arched frame. The stained glass windows captivated her. The crucifixion scene, the garden scene she'd examined from the outside, all the stories she'd been told as a child in Sunday school, in beautiful stained glass. Amazing.

And there was the Nativity. Baby Jesus lay in the center window, pure and proud, while His parents looked down in awe from just behind Him. Gazing at their son, who would claim to be the Son of God. Did they know that then? Joy felt herself drawn to that window, to that baby. She took a step forward. . . . How could she have been a part of that burning? The sacrifice of something so innocent. Symbolic or not.

She felt a tug on her sleeve. Silas uttered a low growl. Just enough to let her know he wasn't happy. He pulled back on Joy's shirt.

What if Joy refused to go in? Would Mark notice?

Joy hung back and smiled into the room. "It's awesome. Love the windows." She turned toward the front door. "Can we go outside now?"

Mark's eyebrows furrowed. "Um. Well, we haven't gotten very far on our tour. How about if we—"

"Well, hello!" A voice boomed down the massive staircase. "You guys made it up the mountain a little faster than I expected." A stately man with plenty of silver in his black hair descended the staircase to the foyer like an old butler.

He paused about halfway down. His eyes twinkled, and a grin spread across his face as he hopped up sideways onto the banister and slid to the ground.

Um. . . Joy stepped back. Who on earth was that?

He stuck out a hand. "I'm Ben. Ben Bradley, the director here at Diamond Estates. Welcome."

What was this guy all about? He'd either be super weird or kind of cool. Joy leaned toward weird for the moment. "It's nice to meet you. I'm Joy Christianson."

"Joy. Christianson." Ben closed his eyes and smiled like he listened to a piano piece playing in his head. "That name. Oh, it's pure luxury. It's. . .divine."

Yeah. Weird. Definitely.

His eyes flew open. "Well. I'm going to get Ginny, who happens to be Mark's wife, over here while you finish up with the downstairs tour. Ginny's going to be your one-on-one companion for the first couple of weeks you're here. I'm going to have her show you around the rest of the place and get you settled in." He spun away on his heels, pulled out his cell phone, and pressed a number.

"Trust me. You're going to love Ginny." Mark smiled. "She's a gem."

"Uh-huh." Now if only Joy could see into the future and know how the whole thing was going to play out. Certainly this wasn't going to be a walk in the park. Would they expect her to do things that would upset Silas? Joy looked down at her side. When it came to her following through with the plan, Silas would definitely have something to say about it.

Mark steered Joy around the corner and pointed down a dark hallway. Swinging doors flew open as they passed, and three blurs flew out.

"Hey. No running."

Three girls turned and muttered apologies, but tore off as fast as they could.

Mark's eyes glinted with laughter. "Some birds just don't like to be caged."

If he truly embraced that truth, they'd be just fine.

"This over here on the left is Ben's office. Hopefully you won't spend too much time in there." He laughed. "No, I'm kidding. You're going to love Ben. He's got a big heart and a passion for seeing girls come to Christ."

Joy nodded. Lovely.

"In here is the kitchen, beyond that the dining room. And the next room down is the library where you girls have your school day." Mark took his cell phone out of the front pocket of his jeans. He glanced at the display. "Oops. Have to take this. Go ahead and poke around. I'll be right with you."

Joy pushed on the door and stuck her head into the kitchen. Eh. Nothing major. Cold and chromey. . .industrial. Hope they wouldn't expect her to work in there or anything. Please say there was a staff for that sort of thing. She pushed the swinging doors into the dining room and walked inside. It reminded her of Common Grounds at church. Bright light from the sun reflecting off the snowy mounds outside shone in from the bank of windows, bathing the plants and tables with a crisp gleam.

The room was divided with one of those sliding walls, so she had to exit and step around in a U to get into the library next door.

Oh, now that was a cool room. High shelves of all kinds of books. Tables clustered in the center. Let's see, six chairs at a table, five tables. . .enough for thirty girls. Was that what she was facing? Thirty troubled girls with major baggage? Should be fun. Talk about a horror.

"You finding everything okay?" Mark approached from the hall.

Joy nodded. "Is there some kind of system for finding things like the section. . .say. . .on animals?"

Mark's eyebrows raised. "You interested in animals?"

"Yeah. A lot." Time to resurrect her old dreams for her future. They'd been dormant for too long. Maybe that would distract her from everything else.

"Well, the research section is over there." He pointed to the far wall. "There's actually a setup just for the animal books right in front of that wall." He pointed to the three-shelf unit standing alone.

Perfect.

"But there's a computer over there by the desk in front. Whoever teaches on your first day will show you how— Oh look, there's Ginny now." His eyes softened.

A forty-something Kardashian look-alike in a midnight blue, designer tracksuit, perfect makeup, with hair pulled back in a sleek ponytail appeared at the swinging doors.

Joy glanced up at Mark who stared at his wife, the corners

of his mouth turning up. Someone was in love. Cool they still felt sparks after all that time.

Ginny—that's what Mark had called her, right?—reached out a manicured hand for Joy's completely unmanicured one. "Wonderful to meet you. I'm Ginny Stapleton. I'll be hanging out with you for the next couple of weeks."

"I'm Joy. Nice to meet you." Ugh. When would all the politeness end? She wandered to the bank of windows facing a snow-covered pasture. "Is that where the horses are?" She nodded her head toward the barn. Brilliant question. Where did she think they were?

Ginny grinned. "Yep, they're out there. Five of them now. Do you like horses?"

"Like? No. I love animals. Horses are amazing creatures. I want to be a vet one day, but I can't decide if I want to be a small animal vet or if I want to take care of large animals like horses and cows. Maybe even zoo animals. I don't know, but I love horses."

Ginny grinned. "Note to self. Talk of animals brings Joy to life." Her warm brown eyes sparkled.

Don't give away your secrets, lady. Makes it too easy to resist.

"Okay, well, we'll finish the tour later." Ginny gazed at Mark. "Thanks for getting us started, hon. Now we'll go out to the back house and have our first counseling session."

"Already?" Boy they didn't mess around here, did they?

"Yeah. We believe in jumping right in. It's the best way to set aside the past and set up the future."

She held the back door open for Joy to pass through. "That's what we're going to do today. We'll make some goals and some plans. We'll talk about what you feel you need, what you're worried about, what you're afraid of. I'll share some things with you, and we'll move on from there. How does that sound?"

"Like we'll be talking for the next month."

Ginny laughed. "No, seriously. Sound okay?"

Um. . .did she think Joy was kidding? It sounded pretty intense to Joy. A lot to expect for a first day. But she was game. That's what she was there for. . .right?

Joy shrugged. "Fine by me."

They turned right as they exited the library.

"What's this door?" Joy tried the handle. It was locked. Oops. Probably shouldn't be trying to open random doors.

"Oh, that's an old coat closet. We never use it."

Why would someone lock a coat closet?

Chapter 26

Joy followed Ginny down the path toward the stable, each carrying a suitcase. The snow crunched beneath her feet just like at home. Why did snow surprise her? She should have realized that some things would be the same everywhere. She looked at the mountains stretched as far as she could see. Even still, the snow looked different among the evergreen trees. Healthier, if that were possible.

She turned the corner and faced the entrance of the barn. Ginny hung back, letting Joy go ahead.

She approached slowly, set her suitcase down, and let her backpack slip to the ground.

The smells hit Joy's senses like when she passed Abercrombie and Fitch at the mall. Except the barn smelled better. Hay. Saddle leather. Manure. Earth. Joy closed her eyes and drank it in.

The shuffling of horses' feet begged for freedom. Joy listened for a moment. Giving them time to catch her scent. She heard a blow from a horse's nose, signaling curiosity. Time to go in.

Joy slid the barn door aside and stepped in. She approached the first stall and reached out her hand. The gelding shied away then moved back in for a pat. "There. Good boy." Joy rubbed the horse's nose. Too bad she didn't have a carrot or some sugar. She'd be a friend for life.

Where was Ginny? Joy glanced back at the entrance. Oh, there she was. Just hanging back letting Joy get acquainted with her new friends. Who needed BFFs when you had horses? Silas bumped against her leg. Oh, and of course, Silas. Joy smiled to herself. If only she could stay outside and mingle with the animals all day.

"Well, who are you, sweetie?" Joy reached out for the rust-colored mare. The sign on the stall said Buttercup. "Aren't you an angel?" Joy patted and rubbed. "You're such a pretty girl. I'm going to come back and bring you some carrots later." She looked into Buttercup's eyes.

The horse nuzzled Joy's arm. Joy leaned in and pressed her lips to the space just behind Buttercup's eye. "What do you think, girl? Am I going to make it here?"

๑

"What is this place?" Joy looked over the outside of the small-scale, stone replica of the big house. "Or, I should say, what *was* it?"

"It used to be a small infirmary for the monastery. We're reallocating it for our use." Ginny gazed up the front. "It's a brand-new renovation actually. You're among the first group to have the opportunity to use it."

Oh goody.

"Mark might have mentioned this, but we're using this space for most newcomers. Just to give you a place to decompress and get a handle on life before being faced with everyone else's problems and stories."

"How long?" Seemed isolated to be set apart from the main happenings at Diamond Estates. Then again, maybe the alternative of being in a house with thirty teenage girls 24-7 was far worse.

"Probably only a couple of weeks, but there's really no set

amount of time. We're working out the details of integration, but it'll definitely be on a case-by-case basis."

Did she always use such big words?

"Okay, come on in. Welcome home." Ginny opened the exact same brand-new door Dad had recently installed at the lake house. That was weird. What were the odds? She stepped aside to let Joy go first.

Joy stepped into a tile entryway, her suitcase banging on the doorframe. Minuscule compared to the main house. She set her luggage down against the wall and glanced to her right where a bank of doors faced each other on both sides. Then to her left—where an open area was divided by mint-green curtains into cubicles.

"Okay, you can poke around here later. We've got bedrooms on that side." She lifted her arm and pointed to the right. "The infirmary's over there." She swung her arm to the left. "Alicia and I run this place together. We're both nurses, and we're both counselors. So I live here half the week, and she does the other half."

"What about your husband? Does Mark live here, too?" Joy let her backpack slip to the floor beside her suitcases.

"No. That's part of the sacrifice we make as a family. We really can't have a man sleeping here, so Mark stays down the mountain at our house alone on the nights I'm here. Alicia and Ben live just beyond the property. So Ben's at home nearby when Alicia's here. It works out fine."

So weird. Who would want to do that? Joy couldn't imagine caring about a job enough that she'd be willing to stay away from home several nights a week. Hmm. Maybe Mark and Ginny weren't as happy a couple as she'd first thought.

"Here's my office. Come on in and have a seat." Ginny gestured through the doorway.

Joy stepped into a garden wonderland. Floral wallpaper and curtains. Huge flower arrangements all over the room. Chairs with delicate stripes to coordinate with the floral. Definitely a feminine haven.

But that smell. Joy fought the urge to plug her nose. What *was* that?

She searched for the source. The garbage can stood empty. No rotting food anywhere that she could see. Oh wait, the candles. Two rust-colored jar candles burned on the back wall, and two votives flickered in little glass jars on the corners of Ginny's desk. She wanted that stench in there? Gross.

Ginny sat in the desk chair and pulled it close to the desk. "You okay? You look kind of sick."

Joy waved her hand in front of her nose. "I'm just getting used to that scent of your candles. It's really strong."

Ginny laughed. "I know. It's a sick obsession of mine. You'll love it once you get used to this. This is one of my favorites. Pumpkin spice. I use it all winter."

Joy nodded. "It's nice." If she had a gas mask. "There's something about it. . . I can't put my finger on it." She shrugged. "I'll get over it."

"Well, just let me know if it gets too strong. I'll put it out."

Hadn't Joy already let her know? Wasn't the look of disgust and the hand waving the air from her nostrils hint enough? Looked like Ginny had no intention of dousing the flames.

Whatever.

"So." Ginny leaned forward and rested her elbows on her desk, her chin in her hands. "I'm really glad you're here."

Hah. That's what she thought. "Thank you." Joy shrugged. "Am I supposed to say I'm glad to be here?"

"No. If you said you were, I wouldn't believe you. This place is hard work. There's nothing easy about making a life change.

Nothing at all easy about taking control and responsibility for yourself and your life. . .your choices, your future." Ginny shook her head. "It's huge, and I won't pretend it's going to be a piece of cake. It's not."

Joy never expected it to be. What was it about this woman that made Joy want to roll her eyes?

"Okay. Let's jump right in. Why don't you go back to the beginning and tell me what happened leading up to this point."

Was she serious? Neither Mark nor Ben told her anything before Joy arrived? Why did these people insist on making Joy stay rooted in the past by rehashing it so often? She wanted nothing more than to just forget it. "Look, Ginny, can't you just tell me what you know, and I'll fill in the gaps rather than making me go over everything. We can build from there."

Ginny sighed. "I understand that it's tough to talk about, but it's really important we go back to the beginning. You can just give me bullet points, if you'd prefer, of what happened to lead you to this point, the way you see it."

Wait. "What do you mean by 'the way I see it'? The way I see it is the way it happened. I mean, my boyfriend and my best friend were kissing in my family room on Halloween night, and my best friend went home soon after and committed suicide. I don't think I've been embellishing those facts. That *is* what happened."

"I know it is, sure. But what about the in-between? What went on? What triggered you to want to search, that led you down the road you've been walking?"

How was Joy supposed to know? Wasn't that Ginny's job to figure out? It was going to be a long day.

Ginny stared at Joy. Waiting. . .for what? What did Ginny want from Joy? She wanted answers. Well, join the club. So did Joy.

"What triggered me? I wanted answers. But I don't have them." Joy shrugged. Why was she so snarky with Ginny? What had Ginny ever done to her? "I don't. All I know is when Melanie committed suicide, my friend Raven helped me reach out and contact her. That totally opened my eyes, and I began to question everything I ever knew. Nothing stayed the same because I had to look at it through a different lens. It was like everything I ever knew or believed, everything that was important to me, just totally blew up in my face."

Ginny tapped a pen on her desk. "So you wanted answers. It's okay. What next?"

"Melanie committed suicide and I called 911, and then I had to let her mom know. It was all on me, Ginny."

"I'm really sorry about that. A seventeen-year-old girl shouldn't ever have to face something like that. *Ever*."

Yeah. But she had.

"So the funeral. How was it?"

"Awful. The second-worst experience of my life, next to discovering Melanie. And I'll never forget that Melanie's mom had spread candles all around the casket. . .ugh, pumpkin spice. I guess that smell has just stuck with me." Oh, no wonder Ginny's office was choking her.

Ginny's eyes widened.

"Yeah, I didn't put the pieces together until I started talking about the funeral, but that's why that smell is hitting me so strongly. It's bringing me back to those feelings. It's making me feel the way I felt that day."

"Yep. That's what senses do. A song, a smell, a touch, they can all bring back memories and conjure up emotions and feelings." She looked around her office. "Okay, so we need to get rid of the pumpkin spice. That's clear, but let's replace it with something else. What about vanilla?"

"Vanilla?"

"It has a soothing smell. Do you have any association with that scent?"

"No, not at all."

"I'm going to start burning vanilla candles every single day. I want that scent to become a benchmark for you, a replacement memory. Every time you smell it, I want you to remember the journey you embarked on here. You can claim it so when it hits you, it triggers that feeling of hope. Okay?"

Joy smiled. "Okay. I like the sound of that. I think that's cool."

Ginny jumped up from her chair and picked up her bell-shaped candlesnuffer. She put out each candle, one by one. When the last one remained, she handed the snuffer to Joy. "Here, you extinguish this final flame."

Joy reached forward and lowered the bell over the flickering candle flame until it went out. Afterward Joy thought she was probably driving Ginny crazy with her questions, but she couldn't help it. She wanted answers. She just wanted to know.

"Whoops." Ginny looked at her watch. "Our time is up for today. Ready to go meet the girls?"

Joy's stomach clenched. Um. . .no? "Ready as I'll ever be."

Chapter 27

Silas stayed pressed to Joy's side as they reentered the big house. He glanced in every direction, keeping his head just in front of her body. Protective. Alert.

Ginny led Joy right to the dining hall and pushed open the screen door for her.

Hmm. Was it her imagination, or did the room go silent when she entered? Yes. A new girl. Let's all stop and stare. Sheesh. Joy's body tingled under the scrutiny as the girls checked her out head to toe then returned to their conversations as the noise level rose.

Except for one girl.

What was *her* problem? She had attitude written all over her from her blond spikes, eyebrow piercing, and tattooed forearms crossed on her chest. Her empty dinner tray sat on the table in front of her, her scowl enough to stop a weaker person in her tracks.

Joy glanced at Silas. He stared at Blondie as though even he noticed the little daggers being shot from across the room.

Drama. Drama. Drama. It had always existed everywhere, but how much more so when thirty messed-up teenage girls where thrown into a pot and stirred up? Joy wasn't going to let it bother her. She had bigger things to worry about.

Following Ginny's lead, Joy grabbed a dinner tray and slid it along the rails like in the cafeteria at school. Several girls stood behind the counter serving up helpings of lasagna and garlic bread. Please say they were hired help. . .but something told Joy they were residents doing chores. Which would mean. . .she'd have to do time in the kitchen. She'd rather clean bathrooms than cook. Well—she glanced around the bustling room—those toilets probably got pretty nasty, so maybe not. But close.

"You new here?" A plump woman in a chef's apron smiled as she scooped some salad into a bowl. Her jowls shook as she spoke.

"Yeah. Just got here. I'm Joy."

"Well, good. We could use some of that around here. I'm Marilyn. It's nice to meet you, Joy." She gestured to the salad bar area and handed Joy a plate of lettuce.

"Thanks." Joy paused for a moment and listened to her body. Was she hungry? Did she want this food? Her stomach rumbled. She actually felt famished for once. It had been so long since she felt this hungry.

She used the tongs to sprinkle some cheese on top of her lettuce and then added French dressing, a hard-boiled egg, bacon bits, sunflower seeds, and croutons. No one would call that a particularly healthy salad, but it sure looked good. Joy slid her tray on to the dessert section. Maybe she should skip that.

Ginny nudged her. "Go ahead. You only live once."

That's what Ginny thought.

But really? Who could resist Oreo pie? Joy selected a small piece, added silverware to her tray, and filled a cup with Diet Coke from the fountain. Hah. Diet Coke. . .that was a laugh. She probably had three thousand calories on her tray. But at least she wasn't adding two hundred more. Not that she cared.

So now what? She surveyed the dining room as it bustled with clusters of people eating, talking, and laughing like old friends. Any of the pairs could have been Joy and Melanie huddled over a pizza or a magazine. Loneliness punched her in the stomach as her status shone in vivid relief. Friendless. Alone. Pathetic.

A few tables had openings, but there was no way on earth she was going to just walk up to strangers and ask if she could eat with them. She'd never had to do that at school. Always had Melanie and Austin. Then. . .when she didn't. . .she ate with Raven. Here? Here it looked like she'd be all alone.

Wait. Where had Ginny gone? Weren't they supposed to be, like, strapped together at the hip for a while? She let her gaze rove over the tables again. Finally it landed on Ginny, waving wildly from a spot across the room at a table with another girl. The only empty seat at the table was directly across from Blondie. Of course.

Who said there was no such thing as karma? If someone had asked her, she would have said of course that would be the table Ginny would have been sitting at. And, of course she'd leave the seat open across from the one girl who hated Joy for sure. How could it be any other way?

As Joy approached the table, Ginny stood up. "Come on over, Joy. This is Savvy. I have to take off for a few minutes, but I wanted to get you acquainted with someone. So you girls get to know each other a little bit. I'll be right back."

The tough girl with the spiked do and tattoos was named Savvy? That so did not fit her.

Joy set her tray on the table and perched on the edge of her chair.

She could open with a question. "So, what are you in for?" Hopefully that hadn't come across as a rude way to open a conversation, but then what else was there to talk about? Silas slumped on the floor beside Joy, his presence comforting. She glanced around the room. How many others had a special friend with them? If only she could see into the spiritual whenever she wanted to.

"Just stuff. Causing trouble. You know." Savvy shrugged.

Joy jerked back, stunned by the Southern accent. She'd assumed the girl was fresh off the streets, not plucked off some cotton plantation. Weird. "How long have you been here?"

"Just about a week."

Oh, she was new, too. That explained the attitude—partly, anyway.

"Hey, mind if I join you?" A tray appeared at the spot Ginny had vacated, carried by a tall girl with long auburn waves.

"Go for it." Joy swallowed her Diet Coke and nodded. "I'm Joy." There was something familiar about the girl.

"Nice to meet you. I'm Paige." She cast her deep brown eyes down at her food.

Wait just a minute. Paige? "Paige McNichols? Are you Paige McNichols, the actress?"

As Paige tossed her auburn waves over her shoulder, the dark black underlayer fell in front of her shoulders. "Yep, that's me."

"But I heard you were in drug rehab."

"Hah." She laughed. "Don't believe everything you hear. . . or read. Especially read. But I guess you could say drugs are one of the reasons I'm here. This might not be a medical rehab, but I'm being healed from the inside out. Even better."

Oh, she was an old-timer at Diamond Estates. "How long have you been here?"

"About five months."

Wow. Five months. "Surprised I haven't read about it. The news has been pretty quiet. Usually you're splashed all over every magazine. But now that I think about it, I haven't seen much about you lately."

Paige flashed a movie-star smile. "Just the way I prefer it." Her grin wavered, belying her last statement.

Ginny appeared at Paige's back. "You girls getting acquainted?"

Oh, the Paige McNichols thing had been a setup. Ginny sent her over to make sure no one was suicidal or anything. Jury was still out on Savvy.

Ginny slid another chair up to the table and sat down. "How are the rest of the girls treating you, Savvy?"

"Does it matter?" She shrugged.

Boy, this girl really did have an attitude. But it was a good question. What did it matter, really?

Ignoring the questions, Ginny glanced at Savvy's tray. "Where's your dinner?"

Savvy looked at the empty tray like it was the first time she'd seen it. "I'm not hungry. Not even close."

Ginny nodded. "I get it, but you have to eat."

Savvy's eyes narrowed. "You're going to force me?"

Joy forked a bite of lasagna into her mouth. Funny. She wasn't having a bit of trouble. Judging by her own dinner, they'd have to pry the food out of her cold dead hands.

"Yes, some sort of meal is required three times a day. There are plenty of offerings up there. I don't care if you just make a salad or get a cup of soup, but you have to eat something."

Savvy gritted her teeth and huffed away to the food line.

Ginny took a deep breath and exhaled slowly.

Paige sure would be interesting to get to know. Melanie would have freaked out. Joy gasped. She'd forgotten about Melanie. It happened more and more lately. Some friend.

Savvy returned to the table and plunked her tray down.

An apple and a Snickers? Looked good to Joy. She took a bite of pie, trying not to smile. What would Ginny do about this one?

Ginny looked from the tray to Savvy's smug smile. Then she looked away.

Ah. Seemed as though Ginny didn't sweat the little things. She picked her battles and chose carefully which ones to fight.

That would come in handy.

Chapter 28

Lights out at nine thirty? Were they kidding? What was she supposed to do for the next three hours until she could coax her body to sleep? And prayer time at six in the morning? That was going to be a challenge in more ways than one. She couldn't control Silas's reaction, and she couldn't control the movement of the clock. She'd just have to worry about it as it happened.

Silas stood and turned in a circle two or three times and plopped down at her feet. She'd gotten so used to the weight of his body pressing down her feet as she slept, it was somehow comforting. Grounding. Almost like if he didn't hold her down, she could be carried away.

Sleep. Joy closed her eyes and tried to shut out the questions. Would be interesting to see her life now as a sort of side by side comparison with her life a year ago. How could so many things change so quickly? In the blink of an eye, almost everything she knew, everything she was, morphed into something completely different. Now here she was living in another state, on the grounds of a monastery with horses roaming outside her window and a spirit wolf sleeping on her feet.

Wonder what Mom and Dad had done since she'd left. Had it only been this morning when she'd stood in front of that fire with them? Did they miss her, or were they just relieved she'd taken her troubles and turned them over to someone else?

They always felt guilty about how much time they spent working. Now they wouldn't have to. Would they finish the lake house before Joy got back? It never occurred to her when she stepped off the porch to leave with Mark Stapleton that she may never return to the home she'd lived in since birth. Would she have done things differently if she'd realized? Maybe one last tour, a good-bye to her room. . .ah, it was probably better this way. Too many memories. She'd make a whole mess of new memories here. If only she could see into the future to look back knowing this would be a good experience. If only.

If only Melanie were here. Joy closed her eyes as words from *The Way We Were* filled her heart.

"You're the best friend I ever had, and it would help me so much if you could just come over and see me through tonight."

Joy grabbed the covers and rolled over. She scrunched her eyes closed. Just sleep. Morning would come soon and everything would make more sense.

🌀

She hovered over her bed.

The form of her body lay alone, under the covers. Silas's body still covered her feet. Joy knew she should stop this, yet she was powerless. If she cried out, would Ginny hear her and come to help? But then again, did she really want to be heard? The last time something like this had happened, she'd taken a little trip and learned so much. Maybe this time would be no different.

Joy's body hovered higher and sailed through the air above Diamond Estates. She glanced down as if in an airplane looking at the earth below. From up high, it looked serene, almost insignificant. Her body dropped until she floated outside the bedrooms and was magnetically drawn to one.

She flitted like Tinker Bell into the space where two girls

slept soundly in their beds and two beds stood empty. Moving closer to one of the bunks, Joy peered at the face of the sleeping girl. Oh, she was one of the three who came running out of the kitchen when she was with Mark. The young black girl— what was her name? Tonya?—had a Bible open on her chest as though she'd fallen asleep reading. That was a little extreme, wasn't it? Well, if the Bible were any indication, she'd probably be going home soon.

The other bunk?

Ah. There lay Paige on the top. Sleeping beauty. How strange to see her in that setting when photo spreads of her actual home—make that *homes*—usually filled four or five magazine pages. Her closet alone was big enough to engulf Joy's bedroom at home.

Joy moved back toward the doorway and surveyed the space above the beds. Peaceful.

But, wait, there was something there.

Joy trained her eyes on one spot and allowed them to fall in and out of focus like she was looking at one of those pictures where staring intently enough pops an image out of the confusion. She fixated on the scene until she could zero in on what she was trying to see.

Oh. She fluttered back a few inches at the glorious sight.

Standing watch over Paige's bed was an angel. She almost couldn't make out the form, but she sensed its presence. One thing she knew for sure, it wasn't like any angel Joy had ever seen before. There were no big white wings, no halo, no white flowing robes. Just peace. . .if peace could be worn like clothing.

The angel shifted his stance. Oh, the angel was a man. A powerful one. The peaceful feeling came from the protection his stance promised. He held a sword in his hand, high, drawn, ready. A shield in his other. He was a warrior.

Why hadn't she seen it all right away? Maybe because it was revealed to her a little at a time so she could process, so she'd believe. Was that how all matters of faith were handled? *Hmm.* She'd have to consider that more later.

Did the angel see her? Of course he did. How could he not? Yet he'd barely flinched in acknowledgment of her presence. Instead, he stared down at Paige's face like a newlywed—or a new father. Yeah, that was closer. His gaze caressed her as if a father standing watch over his beloved newborn baby.

Joy dove to the ground as the sword flashed. It swung in the air above Paige's sleeping form, cutting through the air like a whip. What was happening? Who was the angel fighting? Joy strained to see.

With a blink, she floated over the tile floor in the foyer, facing the prayer room. Disappointment washed over her. She'd wanted to see the battle the angel was fighting over Paige. Was it *for* her? Who won?

She shook her head to clear her focus as it was obvious her attention was meant to be on the scene in front of her. Somehow even in the semi-dreamlike state, Joy knew she'd be back there in that prayer room in just a few hours, yet there she was in her spirit. What was she meant to see?

She inched herself closer and closer to the arched opening. It was silent and dark inside. No movement at all. It made no sense to go in there. Maybe she should just go back to bed.

Joy shifted the weight of her body as if to propel herself from the house and back toward her bed, but she felt herself being shoved the other way. Or was it pulled? Or both? Someone, or something, wanted her in that prayer room.

Where was Silas? What would he do if she entered the prayer room? She would've found out in the morning, but it looked like she would be a little early.

Joy surrendered to the wishes of the unseen and inclined her head forward as she directed her body through the opening. She lingered over the threshold then pressed through.

What? She clasped her ears and curled into a ball, trying to drown out the sounds of screaming and war. She scrunched her eyes closed, desperate to seal out the sights she already saw. Death.

Joy turned her body away and reached toward the doorway. Toward the peace that waited on the other side. She had to get out of there. Please, move. Please.

But she remained tethered to the floor like a hot air balloon. As she fluttered through the air space in the room, she encountered a battlefield where a war waged and blood was spilled.

She was pummeled from every direction with sounds and sights. She was battered around the room, physically moved by the scuffles and scrimmages of spirits as they bumped into her. She ducked to avoid a swinging sword. Could it actually hurt her? She'd rather not find out.

Joy squinted, trying to focus on the spirit realm. Was this the other half of what she'd been shown in Paige's room?

Was that real blood? She needed to know what they were actually fighting for so she could decide whose side she wanted to be on. Was it some kind of senseless war?

Or was it the battle for souls?

Her eyes began to ache as brightness filled the room. Where was the light coming from? She searched the space, tracing the source. The swords. The light came right from the swords of some of the warriors. Their opponents seemed to crumble as the light grew in intensity.

Joy clamped her hands over her ears. The screams. . .they were too much. How could she make them stop? She dropped to the floor and fell to her knees. She pressed her hands harder over her ears and squeezed. "Stop!"

Her vision grew fuzzy. She couldn't make out the shapes any longer. The sound muddled together into one loud scream. Whose was it? Who was the winner?

Her head. "Stop!"

Would someone hear her screams and come to her?

"It's okay, baby. It's okay." A feather tickled Joy's forehead. "Joy? It's Ginny. Open your eyes."

Joy blinked as Ginny's hand brushed the hair from her eyes. Ah, that was the feather. Where were they? She felt beside her body, patting the soft blanket. Oh. Back in bed? Well, then, where was Silas? Why had he allowed her to go through that? Unless. . .

Had he caused it?

"It's okay. You're here in bed. You had a bad dream."

Joy tried to shake her head, but a migraine headache clutched her skull in a vise.

"Joy, come on. Snap out of it. It was just a nightmare."

That was no dream. Not that she could tell Ginny that. Her eyes blinked open and focused on Ginny's face. She'd never be able to help her. No one could.

"You okay, sweetie?" Ginny rubbed her forehead.

Joy nodded. More like a living nightmare. How would she ever set foot in that prayer room tomorrow?

§

". . .free to worship. . ."

Music blared from Ginny's room across the hall. Joy glanced at her bedside clock. Five thirty? Didn't the woman know what time it was? Joy grabbed the sides of her throbbing head. When would the pain stop?

The music played on.

Oh, must be Ginny's alarm clock. That's right—prayer time. Joy's heart sank.

She'd have to face the music and return to the battlefield in the prayer room mere hours from the devastation she'd witnessed the night before. But after what she'd seen, how could she possibly go in there? Joy glanced down at Silas. Where had he been last night?

He looked up at her, panting, smiling, begging her to need him.

Joy lowered her feet to the cold floor and searched for her fuzzy slippers with her toes. Her legs screamed in pain with every movement. Why was she so sore?

As she stood to her feet, Joy thought she'd crumple to the floor. Every inch of her body hurt as though she'd been pummeled within an inch of her life. Had she?

She moved as quickly and gingerly as her injured body would allow until she stood before the mirror.

She gasped in horror. Her arms and legs were covered with bruises, and her face looked like it had been punched. What had happened to her? No, she'd have to figure that out later. For now she needed to cover her body.

Scrambling in her suitcase, Joy grabbed the first thing her fingers touched and pulled it over her head. Her favorite sweatshirt settled over her body like a soothing massage. Now for her legs. Denim would only irritate her injuries. Ah, yoga pants. Perfect.

Joy shuffled to the bathroom and pulled the door closed. Ugh. Another mirror.

Maybe she should tell someone about the bruises all over her body—they'd let her rest and heal. Maybe they'd even be able to help her. Or they'd think she was crazy.

She probably was.

She brushed her teeth and ran a brush through her hair. She'd have to wash it tomorrow, but she could get by one more day. The thought of raising her sore arms above her head. . .no thanks.

She yawned and covered her mouth with her hand. Would there be time in the day for a nap, or was she locked into some schedule from sunup to sundown? Then again, if she slept. . . Sleeping was out of the question after last night.

Ginny knocked on the doorframe. "You about ready?" Her jaw dropped as she saw Joy's face. "What on earth?" She rushed over and touched Joy's swollen lid. "What happened?"

Tell her, or not? She looked at Ginny's concerned, yet clueless, face. Definitely not. "I bumped into the doorframe when I went to the bathroom last night."

"Oh, hon. Do you need ice?"

Aren't you the nurse? You tell me. "No. I'm fine." Change the subject. "I'm ready."

"Good, I don't want you guys to be late, especially on your first day."

Joy stepped into the hallway where Savvy stood waiting. She gasped at Joy's appearance.

"Hey." Joy averted her eyes. On second thought, Joy looked back at Savvy. "You should see the other guy."

Ginny pulled her office door closed behind her. "Ready? Let's go." She opened the front door with a key.

They'd been locked in? Seriously? Was that even legal?

Joy pulled her hands up into her sweatshirt. It was too short a walk to mess with a heavy coat, but shivering just made her body ache more.

They trudged through the snow in the dark toward the brightly lit house with the smoke coming from two chimneys. Sure was inviting from back here. At least from the ground, while conscious. On the back stoop, they banged their shoes against the concrete and watched the snow fly off in clumps. Joy winced as every bang of her foot sent a hot poker through her body.

"You guys all set?"

What if she ran into the bathroom and pretended she was sick? Joy glanced down at Silas and locked eyes with him. If only she could convey her intent. She wasn't going in there to pray to God, but she had no way of letting him know that. If he would just keep looking into her eyes, he would know.

The girls tried to squeeze past each other to get in the prayer room. If they'd been through what Joy had. . .

She watched as the bottleneck cleared and everyone scattered to a beanbag chair or cushion. Many sat in groups of three or four where they'd supposedly pray with their friends. Big *if* on that one.

As the group filed in, Joy took a deep breath. It was almost her turn to enter. Avoiding the stares at her bruised face and swollen eye, Joy shuffled toward the opening as the line diminished. She arrived at the doorway and lifted her foot, raising it over the threshold. Her body revolted against entering that room, like a lamb suddenly aware it's being led to slaughter.

No more stalling.

She put her toes down on the other side.

So far so good. Here goes.

Joy let her entire foot make contact with the floor.

Nothing happened.

No flash of lightning. No clashing of swords with lightning from their tips.

Hmm. Okay. So it was no big deal. And thankfully, Ginny didn't seem to have noticed her trepidation. Joy lifted the other foot in a similar way up over the threshold and planted it firmly in the room. Still nothing. Even Silas behaved at her side. She locked eyes with him and nodded. Good boy.

Now, where should she go? She'd take a private location, thank you very much. Joy walked to the supersize beanbag chair on the floor beneath the Nativity window—she chuckled at the irony. She'd been involved in a baby Jesus burning. Now she sat near Him in a prayer room.

She sank into the beans. At first her body cried out at the contact, then it relaxed and settled down in the soft comfort. Ah. Even better than standing. Soothing, like a bandage.

Glancing around the room, she locked eyes with Ben Bradley standing on the other side, watching. How much had he seen? Joy would have to be on the lookout for him. That dude was a little too smart.

Soft recorded music filled the room. Was that. . . ? Yeah, George Winston on the piano. Shocking it wasn't some kind of churchy music. Cool.

Silas curled up by her feet, content.

All around her, sounds of whispered prayers reverberated off the walls as the girls prayed for their families at home and for each other. Some prayed silently. That would work for Joy.

She closed her eyes and moved her lips. Hopefully no one would look closely enough to see she mouthed the words of her favorite songs, one after another.

Silas inched closer. She felt his body pressed against her leg. Looked like if she stayed true to him, he'd stay true to her. If she were happy, he'd be happy. As long as she didn't turn her thoughts or—heaven forbid—prayers toward God, Silas was fine. She could live with that. At least until she figured out what was going on.

Chapter 29

"After breakfast, do you mind coming to my office? I'd like to talk with you, get to know you a bit. I've already told Ginny." Ben spun around and speed-walked away.

Well, he'd *phrased* it as a question. Funny, Joy didn't feel like she had a choice. That Ben Bradley had approached her like a stealth bomber. An impeccably dressed stealth bomber.

So was Joy in trouble for not actually praying that morning? But how could he know? She hoped these people didn't think they could even begin to legislate thought.

Ginny waved from the usual table.

Joy walked over to her, ignoring the rumbling in her belly, being careful not to cry out in pain as her body reminded her of the war she'd been in the middle of the night before.

"So how's your day going?" Ginny looked her over.

Joy shrugged. "Well, it's hardly begun, but so far so good, I guess."

"I'm really sorry about your. . .um. . .face. Mark is bringing a night-light up from town today. We'll make sure that won't happen again."

If only a little bulb was all it would take to stop the powers of good and evil. Something told her it would take more than a tiny little glow. It didn't seem like Ginny suspected the real source of Joy's injuries, but there was no way to know. She'd never let on unless she wanted Joy to know. Besides, if she did know the truth, she'd have to deal with it. And how would someone deal with this? They'd be facing an impossibility. Just like Joy was.

"You hungry?" Ginny tipped her head toward the breakfast line.

"I'm desperate for coffee." Joy clasped her hands together. "Please tell me there's coffee."

Ginny laughed. "Yes, trust me, we wouldn't get very far in this house without coffee." She leaned in close and whispered. "In fact, I'm always worried somebody's going to talk to Ben about the addictive nature and the notion that caffeine to you girls might be counterproductive, because he'd remove it, and then what would we do?"

Joy laughed. Hmm. That was pretty cool. Joy wouldn't have expected that from Ginny. Definitely way cooler than Ben, so far anyway. "Speaking of Ben, he wants to see me in his office after breakfast. Any idea what that's about?"

"Oh, I doubt it's anything to worry about. I'm sure he just wants to get to know you. He does that with everyone within their first week sometime."

Joy raised her eyebrows. *Ow!* She needed to pretend her face was full of Botox and not move a muscle.

Ginny gave a dismissive wave. "Trust me. You're going to love him. Ben's got a heart like no other. He works like a maniac and pours himself into this place. . .into the girls. He's an amazing guy." Ginny's eyes grew misty. "When I think of what he did for my Olivia. . .and for me. . ."

Funny, that wasn't really the impression of Ben Joy had, but she'd stay open-minded.

"Now. You go get some breakfast before you run out of time."

Joy moved through the breakfast line, chattering girls all around her. Odd to be in such a packed room, yet feel all alone.

A few feet ahead, Paige stepped out of her place in line and moved back by Joy. "Mind if I join you?"

"Course not." But did Paige really want to, or had someone given her the challenge of befriending the new girl? Either way, the end result was that Joy got to hang out with Paige McNichols. Life had a funny way of throwing a curve ball at the weirdest times. Maybe she and Paige would be BFFs before the whole thing ended.

Melanie would have loved that story.

Paige inched ahead as the line moved forward. Joy followed at her heels. "So what are our choices?" She read the menu board. Cereal. Scrambled eggs. Biscuits and gravy. Bagels. . . Ooh. A bagel. That's what Joy wanted. She moved to the toaster section and slipped a blueberry one into the slots and pressed the lever down. She opened the little door to the refrigerated case where the single-serving cream cheeses were lined up. Strawberry. Perfect.

She grabbed a knife and added it to her plate.

The bagel bounced when it popped up, and Joy pinched it with the tongs then dropped it onto her plate. Now where had Paige gone? Oh. She was waiting for gravy. Paige shrugged and mouthed an apology.

"I'll save you a seat." Joy turned around to the juice machine and filled a cup with crushed ice and cranberry juice cocktail. Then she arrived at Nirvana. The coffee machine. She placed a coffee cup under the nozzle for french vanilla cappuccino, filled it halfway, then poured dark roast plain coffee to top it off. That way it wouldn't be quite so sweet.

"What do you think you're doing?" a voice whispered into her ear.

The coffee sloshed over the sides of Joy's cup as she flipped around. No one was there.

She stood like a marble statue and searched the people near her. No one was close enough to have spoken and gotten away fast enough that she wouldn't have seen anything. So it wasn't Paige. Or Ginny. Or Savvy. Or any of the other girls in that place. Then who had spoken to Joy?

What did she think she was doing? About breakfast? Or about life?

Joy flinched. Would she be hearing voices on a regular basis now? She would wind up in a mental hospital before the month was out.

Paige joined her. "Everything okay?" She looked out at the crowd, too.

Joy shrugged. "I don't know. I just zoned out for a sec. No biggie." She followed Paige to the table Ginny had saved. No one said a word for a few minutes as they set their breakfast trays down. Joy had better get a grip, or they'd start asking questions. She forced a smile and set about spreading cream cheese on her bagel.

"That's it. Act like nothing's wrong." The Voice.

Joy searched for Silas. He was right by her side, wagging his tail.

Okay. She needed to ignore The Voice. Paying attention to it would do nothing but encourage it.

Savvy approached. "Mind if I sit down?" Her eyes lowered and her mouth in a frown, she looked like she'd rather be anywhere else but had to sit somewhere.

Paige gestured to an empty seat. "Of course."

Savvy slid into it.

Joy smirked. Quite the unlikely trio they made. The silent, brooding, tattooed girl; the drug addict movie star; and the girl who heard voices and talked to dead people.

🌀

The door was open, but the office was empty. Joy would leave and come back later. Gladly. She turned to walk away when she heard a thump.

"Joy? Is that you?" A voice with no body. But it sounded like Ben. . .not The Voice.

"Ben? Are you there?" She searched the room for a closet door or somewhere he could be hiding. But *why* would he be hiding?

Another thump and some rustling then the desk chair slid back. Ben crawled out from under the desk, held up a pen, and grinned, flashing his white teeth. "Found it."

Okay. That dude was weird.

He ran his fingers through the pepper part of his salt-and-pepper hair and scrambled to his feet. He smoothed down his flat-front khakis and adjusted his sweater. They had names for guys like him at school. But she wouldn't go there.

"Have a seat."

Joy perched in the red guest chair, ready to bolt the moment the opportunity presented itself.

Ben hurried around his desk and claimed his chair from where it had rolled. He sat down and slid into position behind his desk. He clasped his hands on the wooden surface and leaned forward. "Joy. It's truly wonderful to have you here. You know, Mark Stapleton came home from the meeting he had with you and your family a week ago and told us all about you. Since then, we as a staff—me and my wife, Alicia; Mark and Ginny Stapleton; the two other counselors you haven't met yet; and even Marilyn, the cook—have been praying for you."

Uh. . .what did he want her to say? "Thanks." How weird to hear strangers across the country had been saying her name and talking about her deepest problems.

"I don't believe in coincidence, so I feel safe in believing our prayers have been answered by you being here with us."

Joy nodded. "I don't know about answered prayers, but I am here." She shrugged.

"Now, I know your story. I know what you've been going through and what you've been involved in. And if it's all right with you, I'd like to start off by talking to you a little bit about the foundation for what we believe regarding all the spiritual things you've been dabbling in. Sound okay?"

Dabbling? Right. Pretty mild word for what she had been into lately. Her swollen eye twitched. "Sure. Go for it." Not that it could help. Whether or not she understood why they believed what they did, it wouldn't change her thoughts at all.

"We're talking about the occult, which is everything that relates to satanic spiritual things like contacting the dead or praying to or sacrificing to Satan or demons. All of those things fall under the umbrella of the occult, and when we're talking about that, we have to look to the apostle Paul who tells us about idolatry and witchcraft."

When he put it like that, it sounded so sinister and evil. There was no way that was what she was involved in. There'd been no talk of Satan or secret demons.

"When people try to become a part of the spiritual world outside of what God has authorized us to do, they're opening themselves to demonic oppression. Does that make sense?"

Joy couldn't battle him the whole time or he'd wonder if she was a hopeless case. Maybe she was, but that was something she'd have to figure out for herself. "Yeah. I mean that's pretty much what happened with me, I guess."

"Yes, absolutely. We see this spelled out for us in First Corinthians where it says that the sacrifices of pagans are offered to demons, not to God. That's talking about when people bring a sacrifice to an altar to earn favor with Satan. When people try to tap into the spiritual world in an unauthorized manner, then they are opening themselves to demons."

"You said idolatry earlier. What does that have to do with all of this?"

"Good question. All the way back in the Old Testament, the occult started with idolatry. Building towers to worship other gods, making statues, often golden. . .those can all be idols. Idols can also be found in your heart, but for this biblical reference, they're symbolic things that are worshipped."

Wow. Did he ever give a simple answer? Joy might be more confused now than she was before.

"Sometimes, back then, and now, people would burn down the gold or another substance and form it into something that would represent and receive the worship. That's all occultic. That's what idol worship is."

Ben waited. He watched for a response from Joy. What could she give him? Another question would probably thrill him right out of his pristine but off-brand shoes. "You made it sound like Paul had several places he addressed this. Are there others?"

Ben flipped forward in his chair, the back legs lifting. He yanked his Bible across the desk.

Simmer down. Don't want to fall now.

"Yes. In the book of Acts there was record of a slave girl who got paid a lot of money by a fortune-teller. She chased after the followers of Christ and shouted things at them. Her spirits of evil could not coexist nearby their spirits of good. Eventually it bummed Paul so much, he stood up in front of all those people and demanded that the evil spirit flee in the name of Jesus."

So where could she find this Paul guy. . .or at least someone like him who could do that for her? Then again, did she really want that? The thought of being all alone again. . .not a great alternative. "So what happened?"

"As soon as he told the spirit to leave in the name of Jesus, it left her." He held up his finger. "But it wasn't over yet."

That was supposed to shock Joy? Of course it wasn't over yet.

"Because of that demon this girl had the ability to foretell the future. Her masters made lots of money off her skills, and they weren't too happy. So Paul and Silas got arrested 'cause they ruined this slave girl's ability to make money for her master."

"Wait a second. What did you just say? Paul and who?"

"Paul and Silas. Silas was his companion on his missionary journeys. They basically served God together. Paul mentored him, and Silas was his companion, like his best friend."

Joy sat speechless. She looked at the floor by her feet where Silas sat watching her. His tail lay limp and motionless. He didn't look angry though. More like neutral—like he was just watching, waiting for her reaction.

"What if it hadn't worked?"

Ben rubbed his chin. "What if what hadn't worked?"

"Well, what if Paul had said what he did about the demon leaving the girl in the name of Jesus, but then it didn't leave. What if it turned on her?" Joy looked away to avoid eye contact. She didn't want to give too much away. "Don't evil spirits get angry at being sent away?"

"Well sure. They want to test the power behind the order, like if you tell somebody to leave your presence and they don't want to, they're going to battle back until they see how strong you are. It's just natural. The only way to combat that is through complete faith that the name of Jesus is more powerful than any demonic being whatsoever. . .even Satan himself."

Joy tried to hide her skepticism. Ben sounded smart,

but unless he'd already gone through what she was currently experiencing, how could he truly know?

"You're probably wondering how I believe this. Number one,"—he held up one finger—"all the answers a person needs about God are found in His Word, and I have complete faith that He's true to His promises." A second finger shot up. "Number two. There's not a single thing you could conjure up that hasn't passed through these doors. We've seen it all, and time after time after time, the truth and the power in the Word of God has proven true. Every single time. Without exception."

So what would it take? What did she have to do? She wanted to ask, but she couldn't come right out with Silas right there in the room. He couldn't know what she was thinking. If he realized what she wanted to know, he'd make sure she never found out. That was the scary part.

Ben squinted at Joy. "Was there something else you wanted to ask me just then?"

Wow. He was good. Joy shook her head. "No. I'm just taking it all in. I honestly do appreciate the explanation though." She wiped her sweaty palms on her legs.

Ben sat back in his chair and clasped his hands behind his head. He eyed Joy, the skepticism narrowing his gaze. "Okay. I have one more thing to say, and then I'll let you go about your day and get more acquainted with Ginny and her practices here at Diamond Estates. . . . Oh, you start your schooling today, too, right?"

She nodded. What was he going to say? Hopefully something she could use.

"I want you to know that when you're a Christian, a follower of Christ, when you stand on the promises of God found in the Word of God, you have nothing to fear. In Proverbs twenty-six we're told that a curse without cause cannot alight."

Sigh. He'd been getting somewhere, but now he'd lost her again.

"Which means if you've circumvented the power, the curse can't take hold. It can't stick. Like unplugging a hair dryer. . ."

Now *that* she got.

"If you unplug it, will it dry your hair?" Ben shook his head.

"No," Joy whispered.

"The same is true with the power of evil in your life. If you unplug it from the source and remove its power over you, that evil can exist around you without being able to affect you."

Joy nodded. Good words. . .hard to believe, but nice to hear.

"Can I give you an assignment?" Ben smiled.

"You're the boss." Joy shrugged.

"Okay. What I want you to do is to say this phrase over and over, out loud, in your head, as you walk the halls, as you lie in bed." Ben raised his eyebrows. "Okay?"

"What's the phrase?" Only an idiot agreed before hearing the details.

" 'I'm setting my sights on You.' I want you to say that over and over and over, to Jesus." Ben sat back and watched Joy's face.

Was it true? Was she setting her sights on God? She leaned in that direction, but. . .to say that out loud. . .even thinking it was scary. Ben obviously had no idea what kind of fire he was playing around with.

"I'll give it a try."

Chapter 30

I'm setting my sights on You.

Ben had said it would take hold eventually. So far. . . nothing but words. *I'm setting my sights on You.*

Silas shifted on her legs.

I'm setting my sights on You.

Silas yawned and stretched.

I'm setting my sights on You.

She didn't feel any different. But it wasn't supposed to be a magic trick. How should she feel? She could recite the phrase a thousand times in her head, but it didn't seem like anything would change because of six simple words. Maybe she needed to say them out loud. But was she ready to make a declaration like that? Especially without knowing what the consequences would be.

Trapped between two worlds. If only she could have the best of both of them.

She watched Silas's chest rise and fall with his heavy breathing.

I'm setting my sights on You.

Okay, here goes. Out loud. At least a whisper. "I'm setting my sights on You."

Joy whispered the words again then waited.

Silas lifted his head. He stared into her eyes.

"It's okay, boy. It's all right."

He let out a low growl and stared with a powerful gaze.

Joy slowly lowered her body, inch by inch, until she was flat on the bed, head resting on the pillow. She pulled the covers up to her chin. She had better be careful. In fact, it was time to think of anything else.

Nice try, Ben, but that was a total fail.

❧

"Fire!"

"Fire!"

The alarm screamed along with the human wails coming from the hallway.

Joy pulled her body upright and found it difficult to focus. And to breathe.

"Joy, get up." Ginny inched the door open and threw a wet towel at Joy. "Come on. Cover your face with that. Let's go."

Coughing and gagging, Joy put her bare feet on the floor and searched for her slippers with her toes. The smoke billowed in through the cracked door. No time.

She pressed the towel to her face and stumbled for the doorway, hacking and gasping for air. Her lungs burned like a fire roared within. Would she make it outside fast enough to douse her internal flames with fresh air?

Ginny stood at the main door. She motioned for Joy to hurry as she shoved Savvy into the snow outside. Massive blue and orange flames licked at Joy as she stumbled past Ginny's office. She ducked and pressed the towel harder against her face.

"Go out! Don't wait. I'm coming," Joy screamed through the smoke at Ginny.

"No way! Come to me. Hurry."

Joy stumbled about two feet from Ginny—from the promised land. She reached out to grab at nothing. . .her visibility gone, her eyes burning from smoke.

A hand clamped on to her arm and pulled until Joy was free of the burning building. Her body flopped into the snow like a rag doll.

Air!

Joy gasped and sputtered as she sucked in as much as her lungs would allow. She coughed and gagged. Her stomach. . . She rolled over to the side and vomited into the bush beside her.

Better.

Her skin tingled. Joy looked down at her body. Of course her skin tingled, she was sitting practically naked in her thin T-shirt and boxer shorts in the snow. She scrambled to her bare feet and looked around for somewhere else to step.

Firemen bustled through the yard, pulling hoses and carrying extinguishers.

People shouted orders.

Alicia clung to Ben, her face buried in his chest, shoulders heaving from sobs.

Ben's lips moved in prayer.

Ginny rushed over to Joy. "Are you okay? We need to get you some treatment. An ambulance is on the way. For now, let's get you into the library. Can you walk?"

Joy looked down. Run was a better idea. She set off to jog, but her body couldn't move more than a few inches. Ginny lifted Joy's arm and laid it across her own shoulders then placed an arm around Joy's back. They lumbered as fast as Joy's legs could carry her. With the smoke inhalation, on top of her bruises, on top of her black eye. . .she was a mess.

She was losing the battle.

Chapter 31

Joy stumbled onto the deck, her feet numb from walking barefoot in the snow, and entered the library. Ginny helped her to the overstuffed sofa and laid her down.

Wheezing and coughing, Joy's lungs burned. If only she could grab handfuls of snow and shove them down her throat into her chest to put out the fire.

Breathe. Breathe. She closed her eyes and tried to concentrate on oxygen airflow.

Ginny leaned close to her ear. "Joy honey, you're suffering from smoke inhalation. You'll be fine. I know it's scary, and it feels like you can't breathe. The best thing you can do for yourself is to relax."

Joy looked into Ginny's eyes. "Can't you help me?" She gasped. "Is there medicine for this?"

Ginny nodded. "There are things, but they are—or were— in the infirmary. It's all gone." Her voice caught, and her chin trembled.

Joy closed her eyes. Figured. Okay, just concentrate on breathing. "I can't. . .believe I slept. . .through it all. I really couldn't hear. . .it in my room." She sucked in air and watched the red lights from the fire trucks outside swirl on the walls.

"Shh. You shouldn't try to talk. Just let your lungs rest." Ginny squeezed Joy's shoulder. "Where is that ambulance?" She wrung her hands together. "This is ridiculous."

A siren drew closer. It sounded different than the fire trucks.

Ginny exhaled a sigh of relief. "That would be the ambulance." She sped from the library to the front door.

Joy heard the door open, and boots clomped on the tile floor.

"She's back here in the library." The words rushed out of Ginny's mouth.

Now that Joy thought about it. . .where was everybody? Thirty girls, you'd think somebody would be interested in some gossip. But no one had come to see if she'd been burned to a crisp.

"Okay, ma'am, is she the only one injured? Where are all the other residents?"

"Other than me, there were only two in the fire, and Savvy is fine. The others were all here in their rooms. This house wasn't affected. They're now in the prayer room, praying."

Ah. That figured. The paramedic knelt beside Joy and placed two fingers on her wrist. He listened to her breathing with a stethoscope. "We're going to pack you up and take you for a ride, hon. Just hold on for a minute." He stepped away from Joy and spoke into his radio.

Joy shook her head. "Oh no! Please not the hospital. Anything but that." There went her never-been-to-the-hospital brag. Up in smoke. Literally.

Ginny patted Joy's arm. "If you need to go, then you'll go. Just relax. Lots of people are praying."

Was that supposed to make her feel better? The way she'd been living, their prayers might make things worse for her.

Joy closed her eyes. Just focus on breathing. In and out.

Where was Silas? He hadn't been there when she woke up. Why hadn't he warned her of the fire?

The back door opened, and wet footsteps slapped the floor

toward her. She was too tired to find out who it was.

"They're saying the fire originated in your office."

Ben's voice. Talking to Ginny?

The paramedic was at Joy's side again. What was he going to do to her? She peeked through slits. On second thought, she didn't really care. She let her eyelids flutter closed again.

"It must've been my candles, but I'm positive I put them out. Maybe one of them didn't go all out?"

Joy's heart sank. She lifted her head to look at Ginny and parted her cracked lips. "You did put them out. This wasn't your fa—" Her lungs clenched the end of the word. Joy gasped for air, but she had to let Ginny know. It wasn't her fault. It was Joy's. They were after her, and anyone who got in the way was in trouble.

"Shhh." A second paramedic reached over Joy's head and put a finger to her lips. "Stay quiet and restful."

Ginny shook her head. "I know I did," she muttered to no one in particular. She whipped around to look at Ben. "Will we lose the whole place?"

"I don't know about that. I doubt it. But there's definitely going to be some damage."

It was another warning. What was Joy going to do? Every step she took toward God ended in complete disaster. Someone was going to get seriously hurt. Maybe she should just leave Diamond Estates forever. This was her problem, not theirs.

Where could she go? She couldn't bring this home to Mom and Dad. She'd be all on her own.

Or. . .

She could just live with it. She could fake her way through the program and stay put spiritually. Keep the demons at bay— literal ones and figurative ones—by staying as far from God as possible.

Silas appeared at her side and nuzzled her hand.

🌀

Joy sank back in her beanbag, exhausted from her trip down the mountain to the ER. An inhaler tucked safely in her pocket, along with the order to consume tons of fluids—she would bounce back in no time, they'd said.

Now what? So. . .she'd decided to fake it. She'd have to let Silas know so he didn't get angry when he saw things he didn't like.

Ginny paced from one side of the prayer room to the other. The other girls were long since in bed except Savvy. She had her eyes closed, her face black with soot except for white rings around her eyes. She wiped her upper lip with the side of her hand and created another white streak. Why hadn't she showered already? Surely someone would loan her some clothes.

Unless. . .did Savvy feel as alone as Joy did?

A spasm clutched at her chest. Joy grabbed the soft dishrag Marilyn had brought her and coughed into it. The clamps squeezing her upper body were like nothing she'd ever experienced before. The meaning of hacking up a lung became all too clear to her.

Ginny strode across the room to Joy.

Joy waved her hand and forced her body to stop retching. "I'll be fine. . . . They said it would be like this for a while."

Silas sank onto the floor beside her and rested his chin on her leg. Had he been worried? Or was this his doing?

Ginny shook her head. "I feel like I should have agreed with your mom."

"No way. I didn't want to spend the night there at all." Joy shrugged then winced. Right. The bruises. "Besides, what could they have done?"

Ben appeared as a shadowy figure in the doorway.

"Everyone all right?"

Joy nodded and coughed into her rag.

"How about you, Savvy, you ok?"

She shrugged. "It's not the first fire I've lived through."

"Oh?" Was it rude to press for info? But Joy had to know something, anything, about Savvy.

Ben sank to the floor and crossed his legs, looking at Savvy. He was in.

"Yeah, my house burned down when I was ten." Savvy shrugged and picked at the thread on her beanbag. "I tried to get my mom out, but. . .she was passed out and I couldn't lift her."

Joy gasped. "How awful."

"Passed out from smoke?" Ben whispered.

"No. From vodka."

Joy scrunched her eyes shut. So much pain out there in the real world. A world she'd never known existed until it was dumped on her full force a few months ago. Maybe if she'd had tastes all along it wouldn't have been such a shock to her system.

Savvy took a shuddering breath. "Does anyone know what actually happened tonight?"

"Speculation is it was a candle, but Ginny believes she put them out. So"—Ben shrugged—"we don't know yet. The insurance company will investigate, I'm sure."

"I've been thinking. . ." The words flew from her lips before Joy could stop them.

Ginny stopped pacing.

Silas raised his head and eyed her. Warning.

Ben spun around to face Joy. "Yes? What is it?"

"Well, actually, I just. . ." Joy bit back her thoughts.

Ben's eyes looked hopeful and bright, like he wanted to coax the words from her.

She glanced at Silas, then back to Ben. Never mind. "It's

just that it could have been anything, like, well, I don't know, a curling iron or a hair dryer." Would Ben notice?

His eyes narrowed. He stared at her for a few seconds. "Well, did any of you three use any of those things yesterday?"

Joy shook her head.

Savvy scoffed. "Yeah, like I use a curling iron."

They turned to Ginny.

"Yeah, not me either."

Ben nodded. "Then I think it's safe to rule those things out. Besides, the fire didn't originate in the bathroom." He leveled his gaze at Joy, eyes imploring her to open up. He knew. "Was there anything else?"

She shook her head. "No. Not that I can think of."

⑤

"Good news."

Thirty diners looked up from their breakfasts as Ben clapped for their attention.

Joy smirked at Paige. "Good news? Maybe last night was all a dream."

"Wouldn't that be nice?" Paige smiled.

Joy sipped on her hot tea, the honey soothing her singed throat as it went down.

"There will be no school today."

The room erupted with cheers.

Ha. Not so fast girls. It was pretty clear what was coming. Even the new girl could see there was another part to this announcement.

"Bad news."

The cheering stopped.

"Bad news is, you're all on fire-cleanup duty." Ben held up his hands to silence any coming protests. "Everyone in old clothes after breakfast. Then meet us right out at the old house to get this thing straightened out today."

The dining room filled with a chorus of groans. Forks tinked as they were dropped on plates, and a couple of napkins flew into the air where girls tossed them.

"What had they expected? A day at the mall?" Savvy scowled. "All hands on deck."

A chorus of groans filled the dining room.

"Really." It was way better than kitchen duty as far as Joy was concerned. If only it hadn't been totally her fault. Reminded her of those army movies where one dummy's mistake sentenced the whole troop—or whatever they called it—to a thousand push-ups. Well, probably not a thousand.

". . .and then we're bringing in some crews to clean up the mess." Ben lowered his hands. "See you over there in about twenty minutes."

No sense wasting any more time. Joy wobbled to her feet and dumped the contents of her tray into the trash. She was dying to get over there to find out what she could salvage from the damage in her room.

Chapter 32

So we'll be moving you girls over to the big house now."
Ginny grinned at Joy and Savvy like she'd just given them a
surprise.

Really? Did she *really* mean they weren't going to make her
and Savvy stay in the ashes? Joy fought off the eye roll.

Oh boy, the snark was in full force today. Well, anyone
would be a bit testy if they had her injuries and had gone
through all she'd been through. Wouldn't they? Still, Ginny
hadn't hurt her.

"So where will we go?" Savvy lugged her suitcase into the
hallway and hefted her backpack onto her shoulder. Most of
her things would survive after a heavy laundering. What a relief.
Ginny and Joy? Not so lucky.

"You'll both move in with Paige and Tonya."

Joy nodded. "Makes sense." That's where the most
recent openings had appeared. Roommates would be good.
Companionship.

What would Mel have said about Joy being Paige
McNichols's roomie?

"So, I want you two to go get settled. And Joy. . ." Ginny
looked Joy up and down. "I want you to take a nap or rest in
bed for a while. You need to let your body heal."

Joy nodded. No strength to argue. . .or even speak.

Savvy led the way, dragging her things.

Everything Joy could salvage fit into her backpack. Half full, it still dragged her body down. She felt. . .um. . .depleted. That was it. Depleted of energy and health. Life. She had no life left in her. A nap would help.

Joy followed Savvy into Paige's room. "Hello? Anyone in here?"

Tonya poked her head out of the bathroom. "Yeah, I'm in here, and Paige will be right back. Make yourselves comfy and grab an empty bed. The dresser at the foot of each bunk is shared, so fight for your drawer space."

Savvy chuckled. "Want to arm wrestle for it?"

Joy held up her belongings. "Pretty sure we'll be fine."

Tonya stepped from the bathroom, rubbing her dripping hair with a towel. "I hope you guys don't mind, but Paige and I already have the bottom bunks, so you guys are stuck with the tops. At least until we leave."

Joy slung her bag onto the bed above Paige's. "Works for me. I was terrified of sleeping on the bottom. Claustrophobic, you know." She reached for the crisp white sheet folded on the bare mattress.

Ha. Not only was she Paige McNichols's roommate, but now they were bunkmates. She'd have to get pictures. Someone would care to see them one day. Maybe.

Where was Silas? Joy searched the floor space. Ah. There he was, right at her heels. Would he be able to get into the top bunk? Or would he have to stay on the floor? She turned back to her bed to tuck the sheet around the mattress, and there he was, curled at the foot of the bed. Well, that answered that—he'd sleep at her feet like always.

Did Silas actually sleep? Heh. Joy looked into his eyes. What do you do all night, boy? Did they have some late-night spirit poker game on the roof?

Savvy cleared her throat.

Had she been watching? Savvy must think Joy was nuts.

Savvy opened her suitcase, and the room filled with the smell of smoke.

Tonya wrinkled her nose and waved her hand in front of her face. She ran to the bathroom and came out spraying an aerosol air freshener.

Joy froze. "What is that smell?"

Tonya looked at the label. "Pumpkin spice. Isn't it yummy?"

Mm-hmm. Joy closed her eyes. Too tired to get into the story. She'd have to deal with the smell for now. And destroy the can later.

Savvy piled her clothes in a heap in the hallway then stepped back into the room. "Okay. So anything we need to know?"

"Well, while she's out, I'll warn you. Paige snores." Tonya laughed.

Joy could see the exaggerated tabloid headlines. YOUNG STARLET SNORES AND DROOLS. "Won't bother me a bit. I'm a really sound sleeper—obviously. About slept through a building burning down on top of me."

"Cool then. How about you, Savvy?" Tonya flashed a grin.

"I'll be fine. How about shower time?" Savvy tipped her head toward the bathroom.

Joy opened her mouth to beg for a time slot for bedtime showers. Her hair took too long to dry to wait for morning. The door crashed open, and Paige sailed into the room.

"Hey! Guess we're going to be roommates now." She grinned at Joy.

Savvy cleared her throat. "I'm really sorry to interrupt, but I have to know something, especially since we're going to be rooming together." She turned to Joy and took a deep breath. "I have to know. What's the deal with you? Why are you here, and what's up with that ring around your neck?"

Joy felt the color drain from her face. "Why do you ask?" *Think of something. Quick.*

"I'm just saying. . .I feel like. . .well, I need to know if anything is going to be going on in here."

"Anything like what? What are you talking about?" Paige's grin had disappeared as she looked from Savvy to Joy and back again.

"Look, no, everything is cool. I'm totally cool. I'm here because, well. . ." She hadn't really had to answer that question yet. What to say? "I'm here because I turned to some dark things looking for answers about light and life. I didn't find what I was looking for." Come on, Silas. Figure it out. She was just saying what she needed to say. Don't take this out on the other girls.

Savvy nodded, her eyes clouded with skepticism. "That doesn't sound very convincing. Are you into all that kooky stuff. . .like, are you going to be talking to spirits?" Savvy's voice softened. "I ask because that's how my parents are. . .my dad now, and Mom, well, before the fire." She inhaled sharply. "And I really don't want to live with that right now."

Joy shook her head. "No, I promise, neither do I. That's why I'm here. I'm healing and trying to move on."

"Good." Paige nodded and rubbed Joy's shoulder.

Ow. Would people please quit touching her?

Paige dropped her arm "That's all we need to know. We'll support you however we—"

"Not quite. I just want to know about that ring." Savvy pointed at Joy's chest.

"So what? I have a ring on a chain around my neck. It was a

gift. Why do you care?"

"Like I said, I've been around the occult my whole life. I know what a ring like that represents."

"Well, it's got nothing to do with the occult. I was given this ring by friends." Joy shrugged. Enough already.

"I'm sure you were. But in what setting was it given to you? I know you're not going to shoot straight with me, but I'll tell you for sure—it was a spiritual thing. I can tell."

Tonya came back with four cans of Dr Pepper. She stopped short as she took in the somber scene. "What's going on?"

Paige held up a finger. "Just a sec."

"Okay, yes. It was a spiritual thing. It was given to me in the middle of a ceremony, like a séance."

Tonya grimaced. "Lovely."

Paige gasped and shivered. "Freaky. But so what? We've all done things we regret. Haven't we? I know I have. Why all the drama?"

Savvy shook her head. "That's different. Mistakes, we just leave behind. This. . .having a foot in the world of the occult. . . you don't just leave that behind. It's not that easy."

She could say that again. Joy crossed her arms. "What do you want from me? I'm doing my best."

"You can't come in here in this room with that ring." Savvy planted her feet like she was ready for a fight. Did she think Joy was going to punch her? *Get over your bad self.*

But what was she saying? Did Savvy actually think she would be able to make Joy turn the ring in to Ben? Yeah, like that was going to happen. "Look, I've removed the power from this ring. And if I don't give this ring any authority other than it being a gift from a friend that I care about, then that's all it is. I use it to pray for her." That was a good one. As long as Silas knew her intentions. Joy didn't dare glance his way for fear

Savvy would catch on. But she heard no growls and sensed no movement. He must approve of her facade. That was a huge relief.

Savvy eyed her. She crossed her arms on her chest.

Joy shrugged. "I feel like it connects me with her, not with anything spiritual. It's something special to me. It's a little sentimental, that's all." Not that it was up to Savvy.

Savvy nodded. "I guess I get the prayer connection. And the Bible talks about taking what the devil meant for evil and using it for good."

Ooh. Joy had forgotten about that. Perfect.

"But I'm going to be keeping an eye on you, Joy. I don't have room in my life for the kind of trouble you've been messing around with. Not anymore."

Silas growled.

Savvy might want to sleep with that eye open.

Chapter 33

Something tugged on the sleeve of her denim jacket. Joy looked down, expecting it to be Silas. No, no Silas. Not really a surprise since he seldom accompanied her into the youth room at church. Then who pulled on her shirt? She looked into the row behind her. Everyone behind her swayed to the music and had eyes closed as they sang. Didn't seem like it could have been any one of them, and it was just too dark to see beyond them.

She felt the tug again. What on earth? She tipped her head down and looked under the seat. No one, nothing there.

"Joy? Are you Joy?" a voice whispered in her ear.

Joy squelched a scream and whipped around again. She had to find the face of the voice. Was it the same voice she'd heard before?

"No. Don't turn around. Don't draw attention. Are you Joy?" The voice sounded irritated. If Joy could just see where it was coming from.

Should she answer? Was it even a human? It sounded like a male voice. Joy nodded. Oh, no way the nod would be seen in that room. She'd have to speak audibly. "Yes. Why?"

"You need to go to the bathroom. Go all the way to the back, and enter the second stall from the wall. Behind the toilet you'll find a cell phone. Someone wants to talk to you."

"Who is it?" Joy hissed into the dark. Good thing the music blared.

No answer.

Seriously? Some unidentified stranger whispers in her ear and then disappears after telling her to sneak off into a private bathroom stall. Right.

No one but a ghost could've disappeared that quickly. Joy searched the darkness around her. Which meant it probably wasn't a real person. Even more reason not to go to the bathroom.

But. . .who wanted to talk to her? Would Joy be able to sleep if she didn't find out? Maybe she should just go find the phone and get it over with. She could handle whatever she found in there. After all, it wasn't like she was alone. Couple thousand people in that church building at that very moment.

She glanced at the stage. The worship team was just getting into it. The drummer was going crazy, and the singers were lifting their hands and swaying with their eyes closed. It would be another fifteen, maybe twenty minutes until the lights came up.

But what if she went in there and got attacked by somebody? Yeah right. Attackers didn't usually use first names. Did they?

No. She had no choice. She had to find out.

Joy leaned in front of Paige and tapped Ginny's arm. "I'll be right back. I have to go to the bathroom."

Ginny nodded and opened her mouth.

Nope. Joy was out of there. If she stuck around, Ginny would make her bring someone along. How would she explain to Paige that a headless voice gave her an order and she followed it?

Joy made for the aisle, stepping over feet and purses and

weaving around bodies, nudging the closed-eye worshippers aside to let her pass. She passed through the double doors into the bright lobby.

Now for the bathroom. She hurried in and swept past the sinks and five stalls on each side. No feet. She arrived at the second stall from the wall, just like the voice had said.

She looked both ways. All alone. It was time.

Joy pushed the door open and winced, expecting to see someone crouched on the toilet ready to pounce. It was empty. Phew.

Okay. Breathe.

Joy moved to the toilet and reached behind it. Gross!

A phone lay right there on the tile just like the voice had said.

Should she talk? Oh no. What if it was a trick? Maybe Ben had set this up to see if she would sneak around. Now that she thought about it, that was a real possibility. . .if not a probability. She was on thin ice already. . . .

Okay. Options? Speak and risk it being a trick. Or don't speak and never find out who's on the other end of the call.

No contest.

"Hello? Is someone there?"

"Joy, is that you?"

"Raven? How on earth. . .how did you find me? How are you calling me?"

"I've been there before, remember? I have friends."

"But how. . . ?"

"I just got in touch with someone and had him track you down. How are you?"

Why had she gone through all that trouble? "I'm good. So that voice. . .it was a real person?"

"I see your perception of reality hasn't fully expanded yet. It will if you allow it."

Was that an answer to the question Joy had asked? Looked

like Raven wanted to stick with the mysterious.

"Have they brainwashed you yet?"

"Brainwashed? Naw. I'm holding strong here." No way Joy could be honest with Raven about her fears and the dangers she'd been facing. If Raven hadn't figured it out for herself already, then she was in far too deep and wouldn't be of any help to Joy. Joy couldn't break herself free, let alone Raven.

"You sure about that?"

"Oh yeah. I'm doing good." Silas bounced against her leg. Joy giggled. "It's like Silas can hear you. He must recognize your voice. . . . He's going bananas."

"Oh cool. Silas is there?"

"He has barely left my side." Which had its pros and cons, for sure.

"Good boy."

Joy was out of responses. What could she say to Raven anyway?

"Well, you lasted there a lot longer than I did. How are you doing it? I mean, if you haven't given in to the program?"

"Well, they don't know that part. A lot has gone on since I got here, a fire. . .all kinds of stuff, and I've just been able to fly under the radar."

"Good for you. That's really great!"

"Yeah." Joy guessed it was good. Didn't feel all that great.

"Well, I'm going to let you go so you don't get into trouble, but I just wanted to let you know we're home pulling for you and anxious for you to get back."

"Wait. How's Austin?" Joy chewed her lower lip. Did she really want to know? Raven's answer might include the words *new* and *girlfriend*. Could Joy handle that?

"Hoo boy. That dude hasn't looked at another girl since you left."

Why did that make Joy happy? She shouldn't care. Shouldn't have even asked. He'd kissed Melanie—she needed to remember that. But what if her vision had been accurate and he'd been trying to push Melanie away? Joy would have to find out one way or another.

"Well, thanks for getting in touch with me. I'd better go."

" 'Kay. Bye, girl."

Joy touched the STOP button and stood staring at the phone. What should she do with it now? Set it back under the toilet or take it with her? It made more sense to put it back. Its owner would claim it.

Then again. She had a phone in her hand. She was calling Mom.

She pressed the familiar numbers and waited for that voice. "Hello?"

Sound bright. Happy. Don't make her worry. "Hey Mom."

"Joy? Is that you? Are you okay?"

"Oh yeah. I'm great."

"Phew. I don't usually hear from you on Sunday."

"I'm fine. I'm actually in the bathroom at church using a friend's phone. Just wanted to hear your voice. Nothing major."

"No problem. I'm so glad to hear everything's going okay for you. I miss you."

"Miss you guys, too. I would love to be sitting there playing Yahtzee with Grandpa."

"Oh, your grandfather hasn't been playing too many games lately. He hasn't really been feeling well. Had pneumonia and now he's having a hard time bouncing back. But by the time you get home this summer, he'll be raring to go."

"I'm counting on that. Would you tell him I love him?" Joy waited. "Mom? You there?" Joy looked at the phone. Oh no. The battery died.

Hope she heard the last part.

Chapter 34

The forest stretched on for miles, but the library. . .not so much. The walls were closing in. Joy had to get out of there. Too bad Ginny wasn't the teacher today. Joy wasn't sure about Tammy yet. Three weeks at Diamond Estates, and Joy still hadn't had enough time with her to know which buttons to push to help her get her way. With Tammy being deaf, it was a bit more difficult to read her.

Joy approached the desk and put her workbook down in front of Tammy. "I finished everything I'm supposed to get done for the whole week, and it's only Wednesday. I'd really love some fresh air. What would it take to get some time out on Buttercup? I mean, am I allowed to go by myself, or how does that work?"

Tammy reached for Joy's schoolwork and flipped through the pages. She raised her gaze and enunciated carefully. "Nice job on this. Sure, you can definitely go for a ride. But not alone. You'll either need to find a riding buddy whose schoolwork is far enough ahead, like you, or I can find one for you. I'm sure there are plenty of girls in this room who would jump at the chance to get out on the mountain."

Joy turned around and looked at the twenty-eight girls scribbling in their workbooks, taking tests, or reading a book. Yep. They definitely would prefer it. But Joy wouldn't choose to spend the next couple of hours with most of them. "How about Paige? I know she's worked way ahead."

Tammy laughed. "No, no. Paige is terrified of horses. She'd rather be in school."

Oh right. How had Joy forgotten?

"I think Savvy is your best choice. She loves to ride."

Joy took a deep breath. But would Savvy want to go off with Joy? She still seemed odd at times. Like she didn't quite trust Joy. "Okay. I'll go ask her."

Tammy nodded. "Go for it."

Joy crept around the girls working at their tables and headed for the back where Savvy sat reading by the research section. She approached and dropped her voice to a whisper. "Hey, Sav. Up for a horseback ride? Tammy said we could go."

Savvy dropped her book and raised her eyebrows. "Seriously?"

Joy nodded. "I know. I was shocked, too. Let's go before she changes her mind."

Tammy smiled and waved at both girls.

"I'm in." Savvy jumped up and followed Joy out to the barn.

Buttercup pranced and snorted while Joy saddled her, like she sensed she was about to be freed.

Joy surveyed the barn. Smoke had damaged the far wall and melted the windowsill and frame. Thank goodness the horses hadn't been hurt.

"That would've been awful. Wouldn't it, girl?" Joy patted Buttercup's neck.

"Okay." Joy put her foot in the stirrup and swung her leg over. She turned to Savvy. "You ready?"

Savvy gave a nod from atop Jupiter. "Absolutely. Let's go." She pulled on the reins and turned Jupiter's head to face out the barn door then clucked her tongue and flicked her reins. "Come on, boy." He clomped toward the grazing field.

Buttercup followed Jupiter through the pasture and then beyond as they headed up the trail.

"I'm kind of surprised they let us hit the mountain without any supervision. That shock you?"

Savvy shook her head. "Not really. I mean, what we can do up here? Where we going to go? Are we going to take off on horseback?"

Sounded like a pretty good idea to Joy.

The sun sat high in the sky, beating warmth onto their heads though the air was brisk and cool. Perfect. The horses clumped along the trail. They needed no direction as they headed right up to the apex of the mountain. Joy planned to take the horses up as far as they could and then head back. Similar to the plans she had with. . .

Joy shuddered.

Savvy studied her. "What was that about?"

"Oh, being out here took me back to a tough memory for a moment. Thought I was over it. . .guess not."

"You want to talk about it?"

Joy shrugged. "It's nothing big, just involves me bringing my cousin on a hike. We got stuck in the snow, and it was my responsibility to get her back. We had lots of trouble."

"Why was it your responsibility? Was she little?"

"Beatrice? No." Joy glanced up at the sun. "She has Down syndrome, and she relies heavily on our help. I felt responsible for having her out there and not being able to care for her."

"Wow. Yeah. I could see why that would be so upsetting. So how did you get out?"

Now that was a convenient skip over the prayer debacle. "Oh, the rescue guy showed up. We hopped on the back of his snowmobile, and he drove us out of there."

"Oh. Well that wasn't so bad then."

"Well, after about six hours of freezing in the snow, and low to no visibility due to the blizzard. . ." Joy chuckled.

"Oh yeah, never mind. That sounds pretty tragic."

Silas was nowhere to be seen. Maybe he didn't like horses, or maybe he trusted her to be alone with Savvy. Whatever the reason, it felt free. Even for just a few minutes. Maybe she could open up to Savvy a little bit. A very little bit.

"A whole mess of things happened in those six hours. When we finally surfaced, I decided to start looking for a way out." Joy shot a glance at Savvy.

"A way out of what?"

Should've known. No one would leave a statement like that hanging. "You know. A way out of my life. You were right about a lot of what you said about me. And I'm stuck." The tears coursed down Joy's cheek.

Wait a second. Had she said she *is* stuck? Present tense? Please say Savvy hadn't caught that.

Savvy locked eyes with Joy. "What do you mean you're stuck? Still?"

"Oh no. I misspoke. I just meant then. I wanted to be free from the hold on me, but couldn't find a way. Until. . .well, you know. . .until I came here." Don't search for Silas. Just act natural.

Savvy shook her head. "Not buying it. It's pretty clear what's up."

Should she fight the issue or drop it? Or admit to it. Joy had no idea what her best move was—she'd never had to live like this before. Her biggest worry in her past was making sure she was the life of the party. Everywhere she went. Now? Now her biggest worry was survival.

Sigh. "I mean, I can't get out. Every time I try, something

really bad happens, and I'm afraid I'll be stuck forever."

Savvy nodded. "And. . .the fire?"

Joy shrugged. "I mean, I can't be sure, but it sure looked like it and you know what? That fire started just a couple of hours after I said a simple little prayer." Six words of fateful surrender. "Went to sleep and woke up to the fire. See what I'm saying? I'm so afraid that if I keep pressing forward something really, really horrible is going to happen. They're testing me to find out how far I can be pushed, and the stakes get higher and higher."

"Who's testing you? Who are *they*?"

"I wish I knew."

Savvy shivered. "I don't know. I think this is too much for us to handle. You need to be honest with Ben."

"Look. I opened up to you in confidence. You can't say anything about this. People's lives could be at stake. My life could be at stake. Just pretend we didn't have this conversation."

Savvy remained silent.

"Please. Please promise me." Joy sounded a little desperate, even to herself.

"Just think about what I said. Some things look impossible to us until you ask someone else to come in and take over."

No way. "Just trust me. Promise me. Please."

Savvy slowly nodded. "I promise."

૭

"Ben wants to see you in his office." Paige slapped a yellow sticky note on Joy's bedrail as she sailed through the room toward the bathroom.

Huh? What did he want to see her for unless. . .Savvy? She couldn't have. She'd promised.

Joy stood up and planted herself right in Savvy's line of sight. Joy stared and waited. "Did you tell Ben what we talked about?"

Savvy shrugged. "My mom always said, 'Savannah, there are some promises you just can't keep.'"

How could she do that? Savvy had no idea the level of trouble she may have just unleashed on this place. Would she have done it if she had understood? Maybe Joy should have explained better. She'd been willing to carry it all on herself, without help, so the others wouldn't be put at risk. But now. . . Ben would force her to open up. And what Ben wanted, Ben seemed to get.

Joy headed down to the office, rehearsing what she could say. This was not going to be pretty. She approached the door and heard voices inside. Peeking from around the corner, hoping no one would see, she saw the sleeve of Ben's dress shirt. Mark stood at the window, his back to the door. Ginny and Alicia sat in the guest chairs, and Tammy slumped on the floor, leaning on the wall.

Oh great. Another intervention. She was toast. They all were.

There stood the front door before her. She could just leave. Who would stop her? Just walk right out and save them all from paying the price for her own mistakes. She lifted her foot, ready to bolt.

"Joy, is that you?" Ginny leaned out the doorway and turned her head to find Joy standing poised to flee. Not that Ginny needed to know that.

Joy breezed into the office and sat in the only empty chair. "What's up? Paige said you wanted to see me? You planning my birthday party? It's not until April, you know." Not a care in the world.

Ben leaned forward and stared at her face. "We're going to lay it all out on the table right here and now. I want a straight answer. Are you still connected to the occult? Do you still feel connected to demonic, paranormal activity?"

Moment of truth? Or lie?

Joy's insides churned over the decision. If she told the truth, they'd help her, but then. . .who knew what? If she lied, they'd leave her alone and everyone would be safe, but she'd be stuck forever.

Joy shifted her shoulders back and raised her chin. Might as well look confident. "What? No. Not at all. I'm totally good. At peace with where I'm at. I mean, I have some growing to do, but I'm on my way." Perfect.

Silas stood tall and proud beside her. His nose lifted in the air as if in victory. Joy imagined him howling to his wolf pack, letting them know his latest conquest lay bleeding in the snow, waiting to be ravaged by the pack.

"Well, Savvy told me that you're still struggling with some things, and that you have fears."

"Hmm. I wouldn't exactly say fears. More like memories. They bug me sometimes. You know, it's hard to let go of the past sometimes."

He stared. "How has your time here helped you?"

"I'm really glad I came here because it gave me the opportunity to get away from everything associated with my problems." Joy shot a look at Ginny and lifted one shoulder. Come on, help a girl out.

Ginny nodded. "She is doing well. She's studying and learning. She's an active participant in our counseling sessions and has shown a lot of growth. She takes part in prayer and, well, you know, it's going well even though a lot has happened since she got here. But Joy has really taken it all like a trooper."

Joy kept her mouth shut. It was one of those times when talking could only bury her deeper.

"Speaking of that. How did you feel after the fire? Being

ripped out of your room in the back house and shoved in with everyone else?" Ben tapped a pen on the desk as he stared.

Ah. Her chance to totally change the subject. "Can I be completely honest?"

Ben nodded. "Yes. Please do."

"Well, I think it's much better in here. I was kind of depressed out there. It felt too isolated. Like I wasn't good enough to be with everyone else. I get why you wanted us to start off out there, but I think it might have been counterproductive."

Ben's eyebrows shot up.

Mark raised a hand. "If I may?"

Ben turned to him and nodded. "Do you have something to add, Mark?"

"Yeah. Ginny and I feel the same way. We think it felt like a punishment or a leper colony. That maybe we should consider turning it into a rec center when it's rebuilt."

"Hmm." Ben looked up at the ceiling. "That is excellent feedback from you both. Thanks so much for sharing that. We'll have to start some dedicated praying about that decision then."

Joy nodded. She was almost home free.

"So you're good then?"

"I'm good."

Ben leaned back in his chair, his hands clasped behind his head like he did when deep in thought. He'd never doubt her. Or maybe he would. Maybe, more than anything, he wanted to believe that all was well. If so, she'd just handed him the lie he sought.

Ben dropped his hands and leaned forward as far as he could across his desk. "Then Joy, you won't mind answering a simple question. Will you?"

"No, course not." *Don't look for Silas.*

"Who is Jesus Christ?" Ben narrowed his gaze and trained his eyes on Joy's face.

"He's the Son of God." That was easy. Even Satan knew that and said it in the Bible. Joy ran no risk of trouble with a factual answer like that. She'd be out of there in five minutes, max.

"Okay, good. One more question, and then we're through."

Joy took a deep breath.

"Who is Jesus Christ to you?"

Chapter 35

Well, that was it. Joy was dead. Silas would never stand for a real answer to this question, and Ben couldn't handle either the truth or a lie. And Jesus, Himself? Yeah, Joy couldn't lie about where she stood with Him directly. She was toast. Period.

"Ben. I'm so sorry to interrupt." Ginny held up her cell phone and scrolled up. "I've had my ringer off, and now I'm getting a 911 text. You should see this." She stretched her arm across the desk and bit her lip.

Ooh. Saved by the bell. So to speak. 911? She wouldn't even need to come up with an answer at all.

Ben frowned and accepted the phone. He held it at arm's distance and squinted at it. His frown deepened. He rubbed his temples then looked at Ginny and shook his head.

Ginny nodded.

Sorry for the poor sucker who was getting bad news, but she was free and clear for today at least.

Ginny exhaled and closed her eyes. Her lips moved ever so slightly.

Something was definitely up. It was Joy's chance. "You guys need me to leave?"

"No." Ginny looked at Ben. He nodded his encouragement and stood up. He moved to the front of his desk and perched on the corner.

Ginny took Joy's hand. "Sweetie, this is about you."

"About me? That text is about me?" Joy's eyes roved from Ginny to Ben.

Mark stood up. "Should the rest of us leave?"

Ben nodded. "Probably best." He held the phone for Mark to see.

Mark read it, nodded, then ushered Alicia and Tammy from the room.

Joy's heart thundered. The sound of rushing water filled her ears. Somebody had better spill it in a hurry, or she was grabbing that phone herself.

Ginny took a deep breath and knelt in front of Joy. She grabbed Joy's other hand and squeezed them. "Sweetie, your grandpa had a heart attack and. . .well, it doesn't look real good for him."

Air whooshed from Joy's lungs. She put her face in her hands. What if he died? Joy would never forgive herself.

Wait a second. He was an old man. The voice on Joy's other shoulder spoke reason. She didn't need to claim the guilt for this. Did she?

Guilty or innocent, Joy couldn't lose her grandpa. No way.

Ginny waited until Joy looked up. "I'm going to call your mom back so you can talk to her." She held her phone to her ear and waited. And waited.

No answer? How could Mom not answer at a time like that? Joy's brain screamed. *Just make it stop. The pain. The fear. The loss. Not Grandpa! Not him.* She needed him there to go home to. He was her rock. He loved her like. . .well, it was the unconditional love she'd always heard about. She's seen it personified in her grandpa.

Please don't take him. Please.

Ginny lifted from the floor and sat on the edge of the

seat beside Joy. She gripped one of Joy's hands. "It's okay. Just give her a second. Maybe they're talking to the doctors or something."

Joy nodded. *Please. Please let him be okay.* It was the closest to praying she could manage. But it was a prayer. Did God hear her?

Ginny's phone went off. Finally. Was probably only two minutes, but those two minutes stretched on for a lifetime.

"Hi. I have Joy here for you." She looked away as she listened. "Yeah, I'll let you. . ." Ginny reached the phone out to Joy. "Here you go, sweetie. It's your mom."

"Mom? Are you there?" Joy scooted forward and gripped the phone with one hand and the arm of the chair with the other.

"Hi, baby. Listen to me. Everything's going to be all right." Mom gulped. "I want you to believe that."

Her voice. It. . .it was so. . .warm. Joy collapsed into the chair. "Tell me. How is he?"

Mom drew in a deep breath. "Sweetheart, Grandpa passed a few minutes ago."

Joy dissolved. Her body crumpled, and the tears poured from her eyes. She tried to speak into the phone, but couldn't croak out the words. She handed it to Ginny. This couldn't be happening.

"Mrs. Christianson?" Ginny spoke into the cell. "She'll be okay. Why don't you let me calm her down, and we'll call you back in a few minutes? Okay?"

Calm her down? How exactly did Ginny plan to do that?

Ginny put her arms around Joy and pulled her in. "It's okay, love. It's okay. Your gramps was a believer, right?"

Joy nodded. Was he ever. She took a shuddering breath and wiped her eyes. "I need to talk to my mom. Can we call her back now?"

"Of course. I need to get info to Ben about getting you home for the funeral, too. Maybe you could ask your mom about that so we can start making arrangements."

Joy gasped. "You mean I can do that? I can go home for the funeral?"

"Well yes, hon. You're not imprisoned here. And this is a life-altering event for your family. Sometimes it's more important to respond to circumstances with flexibility than it is to live by the letter of the law."

Joy nodded. Still not believing it was true. Or not wanting it to be. She hadn't decided which.

"In this case, of course we're going to let you travel home if you want to. On the other hand, it's completely your choice not to if you think it's too much for you. But we'll leave that decision up to you and your parents."

It was scary to think of going home even for a couple of days. She wasn't strong yet. What if going home exposed her. . . reopened the wounds that hadn't even healed yet. What if she brought trouble home to her parents?

Then again, what if she could prove to herself that she was strong enough to handle whatever happened?

"Can I talk to my mom?" *Now*.

๑

Ben's car came to a stop beside Dad's Cherokee.

Joy closed her eyes. In mere seconds, she'd climb into the Jeep and finish the journey that would force her to come face-to-face with all she'd left behind.

It would be okay. She was only staying for two nights, a brief moment. She'd make it through and be back in Colorado before she knew it. But first she had to say good-bye to her grandpa. And her past. At least as much of her past as possible.

Joy stood still for Mom's hug while Dad threw the single

suitcase into his trunk and shook Ben's hand. "Thanks for bringing her this far, man. Appreciate all you've done."

Ben clapped Dad on the shoulder. "Our prayers are with you and your family. We're all so sorry for your loss. But we don't grieve like those who have no hope, do we?"

Uh-oh. Better get out of that rest area before Ben started preaching. Joy climbed into the back seat and pulled the door closed.

Mom and Dad got in, Dad behind the wheel. They looked older somehow, if three weeks could do that. Had it only been three weeks? Wow. So much life had happened—and death.

Joy glanced beside her at Mom. She stared straight ahead. No emotion.

Dad? He watched the ground pass under the car.

Not really the rousing homecoming Joy had expected to receive on her first trip back home. Then again, she'd also expected Grandpa to be there to celebrate her return.

Wouldn't they speak to her at all? So awkward.

Should she start a conversation? Ask a question? Make a comment? Or was it better to leave them to their thoughts?

Joy looked out the window as they rode in silence past the familiar landmarks. It felt so weird to be home. Then again, she felt so removed from that place, like it wasn't even home anymore.

Mom turned around and glanced between the seats. She plastered on a fake grin. "So what's it like to be back? Excited you got to come home for a visit? Well. . .barring the circumstances of course."

"Yeah, it's hard to be excited considering the reason I'm here, but it's cool in a way. I mean. . ." Joy shrugged.

"What? What were you going to say?" Dad glanced in the rearview mirror and locked eyes with Joy.

"Well, it's just. . .it's scary. You know, it hasn't been that long that I've been at Diamond Estates. I don't feel strong yet. I'm definitely not confident in anything. Not that this trip is about me at all." She sighed. "I guess I'm just kind of paranoid. I feel like I'm treading water, and to be thrown into the deep end again so soon is just a little unnerving."

"I could see that. That's a really honest take on it." Dad nodded. "So would you say you are glad you went to Diamond Estates?"

Joy chuckled. "Glad? That's a tough word to use to describe all that's gone on. But I'm totally grateful that I had the opportunity to go."

"Are you dreading going back?" Mom spoke softly. Like she was afraid of the answer.

Joy shook her head. "Oh no. Honestly, I can't wait. I really need to be there, and until I'm safe and sound back to my little room in that monastery, I'll be nervous."

Dad held Joy's gaze in the mirror reflection. "We're here for you, sweetheart. Just be honest with us about what you need while you're home. We want to help you through this."

Mom reached back and patted Joy's leg. "Yes. Please let us know how we can help you make sure that this visit doesn't set you back."

Dad pointed the car down their street and pulled into the driveway.

"Whose car is that?"

Mom shot daggers at Dad. "Stella is staying with us until after the funeral."

Frying pan, meet fire.

Chapter 36

Joy was ready for anything when she walked in the front door.

She expected Stella to be flat on the floor sobbing in grief, but what she wasn't ready for was to find Stella bustling around the kitchen, broom in one hand, oven mitt in the other, singing off-tune and off-beat a quippy, quirky song Joy had never heard.

What on earth?

"Stella?" Joy stepped into the kitchen and let her backpack slide to the floor.

Stella gasped. "My Joy. You're here." She rushed over and pulled Joy into a tight embrace. "I'm so glad to see you."

She pulled Joy back and looked into her eyes. "Baby, you okay? As soon as this happened, you were the first face that popped into my mind. I knew this would break your heart. . . losing your granddaddy like this."

Tears filled Joy's eyes, and her chin quivered like a baby's. "Yeah, it's awful. I miss him so much." She'd missed him before this, but now. . .

"Me, too, baby. Me, too."

Stella sat down at the dining table with two mugs of steaming hot cocoa. She patted the seat next to her, her bangles tinkling. "Here. Sit with me. Let's talk about him."

Joy nodded and slid into the chair. "That sounds really good to me." She blew the steam away from her hot cocoa before she took a sip. "Tell me how it happened. I mean, if you can. If it's too hard, I can find out another time." Joy gazed into her cup. "But nobody wants to talk to me about it, and I've been dying to know." Joy put a hand over her mouth. "Oh, sorry. I didn't mean to say dying."

"Oh baby. Don't worry about that. We're all dying, you know? That's why I'm trying to be in good spirits about it all. Baking and cleaning."

And singing. Joy smiled. "That's good."

"Your mama didn't want me here because she's afraid I'll talk to you about something she doesn't approve of—in fact, she's probably back there yelling at your daddy about me staying here."

Ha. Stella was probably dead on.

"But, I'm not sure if you believe in"—she lifted a finger to her lips and whispered—"reincarnation. But I do. I believe your grandpa will come back even better than he was before." Stella's eyes grew misty. "You know, of all the souls that have walked this earth, your granddaddy was the finest. He wouldn't hurt the most vile of people. . .never said a bad word about nobody. Never even looked cross-eyed at them. We could all take lessons."

"Tell me about it. I've known that to be true my entire life." Joy's breath caught. "He was my favorite person."

Stella nodded as though it was assumed. "So you want to know how it happened?"

"Yes. Please. If you can talk about it."

"Here's the deal. He'd been sick. He had pneumonia and his ol' body just wasn't coming back strong like it had in the past. And his lungs were still a little frail." Stella's lip twitched.

"It's okay if it's too much right now." No sense adding to the poor woman's pain.

"Actually, it feels good to say the words. Let me, okay?"

"Of course."

"So we had a big snow, and he insisted on shoveling. I was so angry. I begged him not to. I even called your dad."

"You did?" Joy chuckled. Stella ratted out Grandpa to his own son. Way to go.

"Your daddy said, 'Dad, now you just wait till I get off work. I'll come straight there and take care of it for you.' I think that bothered your granddaddy more than anything." Stella pulled a hanky from inside her shirt and dabbed the corners of her eyes. She shook her head. "He wouldn't hear of it, you know?"

Joy nodded. Sounded just like Grandpa.

"The thought of leaving the driveway covered in snow. . . well it was embarrassing to him. You know, his pride. Man of the house." She looked up at the ceiling and blinked back her tears. "He would take care of it, he said. He worried that the neighbors would think he didn't care or wasn't able."

Stella laughed. " 'You aren't able!' I told him. I even offered to call the neighbor boy and pay him twenty bucks to come do it. That kid has a snowblower for crying out loud. He'd have had it done in ten minutes. Quickest twenty bucks that kid ever earned, I'm sure."

Joy chuckled. "Most definitely."

"So John went out and shoveled for a little while. I watched from the window and saw steam billowing from his face with every breath. But then the puffs came out slower and slower. He was running out of energy, and his lungs couldn't keep up. I scrambled to get my coat on, keeping one eye on the driveway through the foyer window."

She paused and lowered her gaze to her cup. "Then the shovel fell. He couldn't hold it up anymore. I reached for the phone and ran outside. I knew."

Joy nodded. Poor Grandpa.

"He clutched at his chest and fell to the driveway before I could get to him."

Joy choked back a sob and took a sip of her cocoa. She tried to cover her emotions, but Stella covered Joy's hand and squeezed. She knew.

"There I sat waiting for the ambulance. I mean, I couldn't bring him in the house, and I don't know if you're supposed to move a heart attack victim. Then I remembered something I read in one of those e-mails that go around. I didn't have time to check Snopes, but at that point, what could it hurt? I ran into the house and got an aspirin. I shoved it in his mouth. Under his tongue and then just sat there with him in the snow. The ambulance came and drove him off."

"Was he. . . ?"

"They said he was alive, but he wasn't conscious. Still, I hoped. Who wouldn't?"

"I would have." Joy sighed. "Did they let you go with him?"

"No. I had to follow in my car. So when the ambulance drove off, I went into my room and touched all of my little trinkets. I said a prayer to the universe and followed him to the hospital. He never woke up."

Joy looked into Stella's eyes. "Do you feel like the universe failed you?"

Stella shook her head. "No. Life and death are natural, and the cycle can't always be broken."

Mom breezed into the kitchen. "So what's everyone talking about?" She locked eyes with Stella, the warning clear.

Joy shrugged. "I wanted to hear the story of how Grandpa died."

"Oh honey, don't talk about that. It'll just make you sad."

"I am sad, Mom. A story won't change that."

🌀

The window flew open. "Joy, it's one o'clock in the morning. What are you doing here?"

"I know. I'm sorry to wake you up. I needed to talk to you, and I wasn't sure if I'd have the opportunity after tonight."

Austin nodded. "I'm really sorry about your grandpa. He was an awesome man."

"Thank you." Joy stared at that face she'd loved for so long.

"Okay. Let's talk. I'll come outside—no need to do it through an open window in the middle of winter. Hold on." Austin backed away then came right back with a gleam in his eye. "But only if you put the rocks down. You're scaring me."

Joy opened her hands and let the stones rain to the ground. "Sorry. I was just prepared to throw a lot of pebbles to wake you up."

"Um, from the looks of things, you'd have broken my window in about a minute." He disappeared.

Joy laughed. It felt so good to laugh. If she stuck around, maybe she and Austin could laugh together a lot more. She shoved her hands deep into the pockets of her red jeans— purposely not wearing anything black.

He approached from the front, shrugging into his Columbia jacket. "Now what's up?"

"I have to know something." Joy took a deep breath. Don't think about how good he looks. "When I walked in on you and Melanie, were you trying to push her away? Did she kiss you, and you resisted?" *Tell the truth, Austin.* Joy stared into his eyes. She'd know.

Relief flooded his face as Austin nodded. "Yeah, that's how it happened."

Joy let the pent-up anger whoosh from her body. "Why?

Why didn't you ever tell me that before? I mean, I've been living with this anger and this feeling of betrayal. . .a simple explanation would have at least helped."

"I tried a couple of times. But first you wouldn't listen, and by the time I might have gotten you to listen to me, you were. . . different. By that time, you'd never have believed me in a million years. And it just would've made things worse."

"What if I really do believe you?" Joy's heart thumped.

"What do you mean?" Austin cocked his head. "What are you asking me?"

What did she want from him? What was she asking? She had to be careful not to lead him on. That wouldn't be fair to him after all this time.

But what if she did stay home? Would the sky fall or the earth quake? Or would she just be like every other teenager with a problem she'd have to learn to live with, but she'd have Austin. Worth a shot. "What if I could put it back like it was? I don't have to return to Diamond Estates. It's my choice."

Austin whipped his head from side to side. "Oh no. I'm not going to be the cause of you making a decision like that. If this is something *you* need, then it's something we *both* need. I mean, I can't have it on my conscience that you didn't get the help you required because I was selfish and wanted you here with me."

She'd been afraid of that response. "But. . .it wouldn't be like that."

"No, Joy. Now I'm not saying it's a requirement that you go through Diamond Estates in order for us to be together one day. But I wouldn't think very highly of your decision if you quit. I really want you to finish it out." He smiled. "I'm a big boy. I can wait."

Can? Sure. But did that mean he *would* wait? "Okay." Joy

nodded. If anyone could, it was Austin.

Joy sighed. He was probably right. As much as it was painful to realize—as much as she knew it, too. "Boy, I really made a mess of things, haven't I?"

"Oh, we all have. This has been crazy. First Melanie, now all you've been through. Oh, and now your grandpa. It's been a rough year."

"Yeah. You can say that again." Joy bit her lip. "So what can I expect?"

Austin furrowed his eyebrows. "What do you mean?"

How did she come out and ask him this? But they'd been together for so long, she should be able to be honest with him. "Well, I guess what I'm asking is, if I go and come home, what am I coming home to?"

The light dawned on Austin's face. "Oh. You're asking me for a commitment."

"I don't know. It seems really selfish to ask for some kind of a commitment, but I guess I'm wondering if that's your intention."

Austin took her hand. The warmth of his skin sent electric shocks up her arm. Austin knew her better than anyone on earth. If he accepted her. If *he* loved her even knowing her as well as he did, then maybe there was hope for her. But if he rejected her. . .then. . .

"Joy, I love you. It's always been you. I will wait for you. That was always my intention, you know. From the minute we broke up until the minute you pelted my window with rocks, I was waiting for you. And I will continue."

Joy exhaled in deep relief and nodded. "Me, t—"

He silenced her lips with his finger. "Don't say it. Don't make any promises. Let's just leave with expectation and hope."

Joy nodded. "Will I see you at the funeral tomorrow?"

Austin shook his head. "If it's all right, I don't think so. I want to leave things as they are and let this be our temporary good-bye."

Chapter 37

Jonathan Christianson treasured his children, cherished his grandchildren, and adored his wife. And he served his God."

Stella dabbed her eyes in the front row, her shoulders shaking with sobs.

"None of us who knew him expected to be sitting here today, but Jonathan Christianson would have told you he was ready. He would have told you, if he had the opportunity, that not a single one of you is guaranteed tomorrow." Pastor Scott looked out into the crowd of mourners and made eye contact with as many who looked at him. Joy cast her gaze away.

"He would stand up before you right here and now and tell you what Jesus Christ did in his life and that before he died his greatest wish was that every one of you would turn your heart and life over to Jesus as he did."

The pastor grabbed the corners of his podium and leaned over it. "Jesus is the reason Jonathan Christianson was ready to let go of this flesh, to let go of this world, and enter into eternity." He took a deep breath and grinned. "I love this next part. Three days ago at 'time-of-death 3:54,' February the tenth, Jonathan Christianson came to life. He stood before his Savior and heard those beloved words." He looked up with the longing evident in his sparkling eyes. " 'Well done, good and faithful servant. . . Enter into the joy of your Lord.' And so he did."

Joy wiped the tears from her cheeks. She could only imagine how Grandpa felt at that moment. Wait. Did that mean she believed that's how it happened? If it's real, how could she not want that for herself one day?

"Now,"—Pastor Scott dropped the smile—"how about you? Are you ready to face Jesus Christ today? Are you ready to stand before Him and hear an assessment of your life?"

No way. Joy looked down at her feet. Anywhere but at the pastor. He seemed to see right through her.

"Followers of Christ get to have their life assessed according to what He did. Everyone else has to rest on his or her own deeds and misdeeds. How will you measure up? Consider carefully, because that would have been Jonathan Christianson's last wish. I promise."

Joy stood to her feet and shuffled in a line behind her parents, following the casket down the aisle. How many times had Grandpa walked that aisle in his life? She'd always thought he'd watch her walk down this very aisle on her dad's arm one day.

Only five days before, he'd exited the church down that very same aisle. Had he known? What if he'd carried the knowledge of his impending departure with him for days? Weeks? Months? Would he have done anything differently? Or had he lived with no regrets? Yeah. That was Grandpa. No regrets.

With Silas right by her leg, Joy stood next to her mom on one side and Stella on the other at the snowy graveside while Dad stood with the other men around the casket.

Daddy. His face was drawn, pale. He'd soon be walking away from his rock and his best friend. . .forever. Would this change him? Maybe he'd try to relax, work less, and be home more. But Joy wouldn't be there with him.

Grandpa. Her throat clogged as the pastor read from his Bible. Joy would never see him again. He'd never know if she managed to get her life together. The last time he'd seen her, she was shaking her head, telling her parents and Mark that she couldn't let go. He took the memory of that disappointment to the grave. And Joy had to live with the memory.

Hopefully he could see her now. If Melanie could see her and Grandma had been with her that one night, maybe he could. Then again, maybe it was like Ben said. It was all demonic, and they weren't real manifestations of the people. If it wasn't real, then maybe Grandpa couldn't see. She may never know the truth.

She shook her head. None of it mattered. Her goal had to be that she would meet him one day in eternity. She had to make that happen. She had to find a way.

Stella snaked her hand around Joy's arm and clutched her fingers. It had to be so difficult for her to stand at the grave of her beloved husband and watch him being buried beside his first wife. How uncomfortable, humiliating, and devastating this day must be for her. She could have fought back and gotten a different gravesite. She was his wife, after all. But thank goodness she hadn't.

Joy squeezed her hand and put an arm around Mom as the service headed toward a close. Those who wanted to bent to scoop up some dirt and drizzle it on the casket. Joy couldn't do it.

Pastor Scott raised his eyes toward heaven. "Father, thank You for this life, thank You for Jonathan Christianson, and for allowing him to touch so many countless souls with the truth of Your Gospel. Let each of us live as a legacy to his heart. Let our own hearts continue to beat with the passion he had for knowing You and making You known." He looked at Joy and caught her gaze before she could glance away. "And if there is one among us who has not surrendered to You, Holy Spirit, in honor of the legacy of Jonathan Christianson, let that heart turn to You."

Joy's knees wobbled.

Silas moved in closer and pressed hard against Joy's leg.

The tug-of-war over her soul raged on. And on.

※

Church potluck? Really? What a cruel thing to do to a family. Drag them through their darkest moment and then drop them into a party where they were meant to be the hosts. Time was, Joy loved a good party—not anymore. Too much attention, too many expectations.

"Mom?" Joy interrupted the silent drive from the cemetery to the church.

"Hmm?"

"Would you mind if I just jumped out as you passed by the house? I'm not in a very social mood." That was like saying Paige McNichols had made a buck or two in Hollywood.

Mom whipped around. "What? No! You can't mean that. Your family needs you. . . . We need each other. It's important."

"Okay, sorry I asked." Sheesh.

"No, I'm sorry. I didn't mean to jump on you. Honestly, I think we'd all prefer a nap and some quiet today. But this luncheon is an important part of the grieving process."

Joy nodded. She didn't see how, but whatever.

"Besides, sweetie. Beatrice needs you there."

That did it. "Okay. You're right. How is she?"

"She's taking it pretty hard. Sue didn't think she could handle the funeral. But she'll be at the potluck because we figured it wouldn't be as sad of an event."

Total mistake, not that they asked Joy. Bea loved Grandpa and needed closure just like everyone else. They assumed she didn't understand, but that girl saw more than they realized.

And since when was sad a bad thing? Of course Beatrice would grieve. . .she already was grieving. And now she was left out, too.

Yeah. She needed Joy.

The car stopped in the church parking lot, and they climbed out. *Just take a deep breath. You'll be fine, and then it'll be over.*

People dressed in their Sunday best overflowed the fellowship hall. As the Christiansons arrived they parted like the Red Sea in front of Moses.

Turn polite on autopilot. Joy plastered a smile on her face. Not too big of a grin—don't want those people to think she was cold and unfeeling. But big enough they'd think she was poised, mature, and friendly. Perfect. Now where was Bea?

Joy moved in line slowly with her partitioned cardboard plate and can of Dr Pepper. She passed the Jell-O, homemade macaroni salad, store-bought potato salad, and all sorts of one-dish wonders brought in by the church ladies.

She added a small spoonful of whatever, just so people wouldn't bother her to eat. If she went the rest of her life without someone telling her she needed to eat, she'd be thrilled.

"Bea?" Joy spoke across the table. "Do you need some help?"

"Nope. I'm good." Beatrice chewed on her tongue as she concentrated on making room for a little bit of everything.

Where was Stella? Joy searched the room. Oh, there, all alone at the table in the center of the room, right where Mom had parked her when they arrived. Poor Stella. She'd been going downhill all day. The songs had long since disappeared, so had her smile. She seemed to have given up trying to be positive.

Would she make it through? Maybe she needed to eat. There was no plate in front of her. Was Mom getting it? Joy looked up and down the buffet line. Nope.

Well, Joy'd just make up the plate in her hand for Stella. She added a roll, pat of butter, little bit of green bean casserole, then took the last two deviled eggs off the serving dish. She could get away with it. They were Stella's favorite.

"Hey Bea?"

Beatrice looked up with a scowl at being interrupted.

"I'm taking this plate over to Stella. Come sit by me when you're done, okay?"

Bea's eyes brightened. "Okay. Save me a seat. I might be a minute—need more eggs." She held up the empty platter.

Oops. "Okay. No problem." Joy hurried to Stella and slid into the chair across from her. Joy slid the plate toward her. "Here, eat something."

"Oh baby, I don't know. I don't know if I'm hungry or if I'll ever be hungry." She dropped her head into her hands. "What have I done?"

Joy rubbed her forearm. "What do you mean? You haven't done anything. But you have to keep up your strength." Joy almost chuckled, and she heard the countless concerns voiced by people who'd wanted her to eat over the past few months come from her own mouth. Ironic.

Stella picked up the fork and lifted a bite of green bean casserole to her mouth. Her face showed no emotion.

"There. That's something. How about some bread?" Joy reached for the roll and lifted the butter with the knife.

"No. No." Stella batted her hands away. "Help me." Stella stared down at her plate.

"I'm trying to. Want me to cut up your meat?"

A single tear dripped onto Stella's egg. "Not what I mean."

"What then? What can I help with?" Was Stella having a nervous breakdown? Should Joy call a doctor?

"I need help. I need to talk to Pastor Scott. He's right about it all. I wish I'd never. . ."

Joy nodded then searched for Silas. He wasn't there, at least that she could see.

Stella locked eyes with Joy. "I'm scared. Will you get the pastor? Right now. Please hurry."

Joy saw stark terror in Stella's eyes. What was she so afraid of? "I'll be right back." She stepped back from the table.

Stella groaned. "Never mind. I can't do it." She waved with a trembling hand.

Joy stopped midstep. "What? What do you mean?"

"I know you don't understand. I'm really scared. I need to. . . I can't get out." Stella's hands shook as they twisted the napkin Joy had set before her.

Oh boy. Joy knew exactly what Stella meant. "Do you want out?" They locked eyes.

Stella closed her eyes for a moment then nodded, her shoulders sagging.

Time to move fast. They needed reinforcements. "Then you stay right here. I'll be right back." Joy backed away, her eyes locked on Stella. She looked away and moved toward the pastor who stood on the other side of the room talking with Dad. He would know what to do.

But where was Silas? Where had he taken off to?

Joy looked out on the group of people. Her vision grew fuzzy as new images crowded the old. She sniffed. What was that stench? It was rotten—like the smell in Raven's room that day—only magnified times one thousand. It smelled like Hell.

Fear gripped Joy as she looked on a room full of oblivious people with a layer of the spirit world draped right over them. A different dimension existing in and among them as they chatted and ate from their foam plates.

Joy was ripped from the present flesh, from existing in that room with them, as one of them, to hovering between the flesh and the spirit and watching both at the same time. Between the real and the spiritual. Or maybe it was all equally real.

A vicious battle raged in the space around Stella's body. On the outside, she looked mostly normal—like a widow. But in the spirit, Stella was being ravaged from all sides.

How could she not feel the vile creatures clawing at her? They whispered lies into her ear and shouted insults at her body.

"You're worthless."

"You shouldn't be allowed to live."

"He's with his better wife."

"That preacher was wrong."

But bright beings, though fewer in number and in a weakened state, spoke truth.

"You're beautiful."

"Jesus loves you."

"You're an amazing, worthwhile creation of God."

Listen to them, Stella. Listen to the good voices. By why were there so few? And why were they losing? They were batted away or pummeled by the evil spirits whenever one got too close to Stella. Yet they persisted.

Stella took a bite of egg. Trying to look normal, though Joy watched her hands shake. Her head lifted, and she searched for Joy, her eyes wild with fear.

Blood flowed in the battle for Stella's soul. Good had taken blow after blow. Powerful, mighty angels, like those she'd seen in the prayer room at Diamond Estates, fell to the ground in defeat.

Evil grew and its strength intensified as Stella pulled at Joy's consciousness from the flesh. "Never mind. I changed my mind."

"No!" Joy shouted to Stella. "Fight back."

No one in the room flinched at the sound of Joy's screams

that merely blended in with the battle cries filling the room. Were her shouts audible to Stella?

Was Joy destined to watch this war until its bitter end? How to get a message to Stella? If only she'd fight.

The remaining warriors, with their vicious faces, glistening with sweat and blood, parted and bowed their heads.

What was happening? Joy frantically searched the air, looking for the head demon.

Joy gasped.

With slow, regal steps, the grandest, most beautiful tiger Joy could ever remember seeing approached Stella. He watched her spirit weep and tremble. The gleam in his eyes revealed the pleasure he took in her misery.

The tiger circled Stella like stalking its prey. Could she see him?

With all of its muscular glory, the tiger reared back and roared inches from Stella's ear. Her hair waved in the breeze from the tiger's breath. Couldn't Stella hear that?

But she didn't move. No one noticed.

Joy lifted her foot, but couldn't. She was paralyzed in-between.

Stella locked eyes with Joy and shook her head. "Never mind, Joy. I didn't mean it."

But she *had* meant it. Joy saw the truth in her eyes when she'd asked for help. Would they leave her alone if she backed down? Exactly what Joy had been trying to do.

Stella lifted the deviled egg to her mouth, and she took another bite, pretending all was fine. Unaware of the bloodthirsty predator at her back. Stella's eyes flew open. She shook her head.

The tiger crouched low to the floor then leaped with a mighty roar. It dove for her neck and sank his long teeth into her artery.

Stella grabbed her throat, coughing, gagging, her eyes wild with pain and fear.

"Someone help her. She's choking."

"Anyone know the Heimlich maneuver?"

"Pound on her back."

Sue rushed to Stella's side and slipped her arms around from behind. She squeezed with all her might.

The tiger didn't let go. Blood and saliva dripped from his mouth. He twisted his head and clamped tighter one last time with his powerful jaws.

Sue squeezed again, short, tight bursts against Stella's sternum. "Maybe we need someone stronger over here. Has anyone called 911?"

Stella locked eyes with Joy.

In one world, the tiger let go, and Stella slumped to the spiritual earth in a pool of her own blood.

In the other world, Stella fell into her chair, clutching her throat as she convulsed.

A plate of deviled eggs clattered to the floor.

Bea covered her mouth and screamed.

Chapter 38

That's it. That's it. That's it. Joy searched for the quickest way out that would require her to plow down the fewest people.

Joy took one last look at Stella then shifted her gaze to Beatrice being ushered out the side door by her mom and a few of the aproned church ladies. No one was looking at Joy. It was now or never.

She speed walked to the fellowship hall entry then bolted down the hallway and up the stairs toward the front doors. She tumbled against the crash bar, threw the doors open, then ran across the parking lot. Her legs pumped, and her chest heaved as she sprinted toward nowhere.

Silas stayed right at her heels. Joy glanced back every few seconds to make sure he wasn't getting angry, but he simply ran. Anyway, if he were chasing her, it would have been over by then.

She could never turn back to God. All Stella had done was look toward Jesus. That was it. And it cost her life in the most vicious way Joy could imagine.

Joy was guilty of the same search. She'd experienced the same longing. But she had to put that out of her mind for good now, or the same thing would happen to her. She'd already had some close calls. No, she could never go back.

But where could she go? She ran past Hoke's. No, they'd

look for her there. She passed the street to Melanie's house. Mom said Maggie had moved. The memories must have become too much for her. Joy would have moved, too. In fact, she had.

She could go to Austin's, but he played too much by the book. He wouldn't turn her away, but he'd turn her in. No. Worse than that. He'd convince her to turn herself in.

A fugitive running from everyone, hiding both flesh and spirit.

She came to a stop on a familiar patch of sidewalk and looked up at the movie theater marquee. Why not? It sure wouldn't solve all her problems and she couldn't live there, but it would buy her a couple of hours to sort out what she could.

Let's see. . .what was playing? Anything lighthearted, a little funny. Nothing heavy, scary, or sad. Ever again.

Joy bought her ticket and entered the theater. She picked her favorite seat, three quarters of the way to the left and three quarters of the way back.

What was she going to do?

One part of her screamed to try to fight her way out. The survivalist in her demanded that she find a way. That there had to be someone out there who could help her. She wasn't the first person to go through something like this, and she wouldn't be the last one. It had been going on since Bible times, and it would continue on forever.

Why couldn't she talk to someone she trusted and just turn the whole thing over? She could say, "Here, Ben or Mom or Ginny. This is what's going on with me. I'm scared. I need help." And then sit back and let the help come. But she'd never do it because they'd all be at risk, too. No matter how many times Joy tried to devise a new scenario, she arrived back at the same conclusion.

And the fatalist inside her brain simply laughed at the survivalist.

The credits rolled, and the lights came up.

She watched people gather their empty popcorn buckets and cups of soda and shuffle out of their seats, squinting as their eyes adjusted to the light.

Time for her to go, too. But where could she go that she wouldn't be putting others at risk? Best to just watch another movie, buy a couple more hours. She gathered her things to move to another theater, maybe something a little longer.

"Joy?"

"Mom?" Joy spun around. "How did you find me?"

Silas appeared under Joy's feet.

"Oh, a little birdie told me where you might be. Even the seat you'd have chosen." She offered a worn smile.

Joy nodded. Austin. "Did he come to the funeral?"

"No, I went to his house. He's worried about you."

"Yeah."

Mom took a step closer. "Why did you run?"

"I just can't face any more, Mom. Death and loss, the fear. I'm tired of being afraid. I just needed a break."

She nodded. "Makes perfect sense to me." She moved in one more step. Like she was cornering a skittish rabbit. "Tell me. What can I do for you? How can I help you?"

Joy eyed her. Could she be honest with her mom? No. For Mom's sake, Joy had to get rid of her. She had to. "At the risk of sounding completely ungrateful and rude, could you leave me alone? Just let me be here by myself and figure out things by myself. No offense, really."

The corners of Mom's smile drooped a bit, but she recovered quickly. "Sure, I can do that. I actually expected you to say it." Mom dangled Joy's keys. "Dad's waiting for me outside.

We brought your car."

"Thanks, Mom." Joy pocketed the keys.

Mom left as the lights dimmed.

If she could just figure out what had happened in those last moments with Stella. When she was trying to bring Joy back, saying she'd changed her mind after crying out for help, why didn't they let her live? They must have known her heart wasn't true—that was the only explanation. So if Stella wasn't matching her actions up with her heart and mind, and they knew, and they killed her for it. . .then Joy was doomed.

Joy slouched down in her seat as a new batch of moviegoers entered the theater. No one knew she was there. Hey, maybe that's what her tombstone should say. No One Knew She Was Here.

Maybe it should say that sooner rather than later.

Joy had watched Stella die. Sure it had been painful, probably, but it didn't last very long, and there were other ways. She didn't have to pick suicide by demon tiger, but maybe some pills or a rope.

She felt the roots of an idea spread through her body as the layers of logic grew. Yeah. That's what she'd do.

Joy would kill two birds with one stone. . .or three if she counted herself. Silas inched closer.

Where could she buy a rope this time of night? Oh, no need. She'd go to Grandpa's.

Chapter 39

Joy steered the car onto the half-shoveled driveway. The lights were off at the house. Of course they were.

She looked at the ridges in the snow where Grandpa had last pushed the shovel. The mounds of snow he'd scooped to the side. The scuffled area where he'd fallen.

She walked past the house to the garage out back and used her key to open the seldom-used side door. She batted away the rake handles and roasting sticks that fell toward her as she pulled the door open then stepped inside and flipped on the light.

As her eyes adjusted, Joy searched for a ladder. Oh. Easy. Right in front of her. She popped it open in the center of the space.

Now, where was the rope? Grandpa had plenty; she'd seen him use it a ton of times.

There it was. Coiled on a peg on the wall opposite the door. Too high to reach, she'd need the ladder. Or. . .she grabbed a rake. This would work.

Joy stuck the rake handle through the coil and lifted it off the peg. It slid the length of the handle until it circled her arm.

Okay. Now. She had to think about knots. She used to know all that stuff, but not anymore.

Oh, her phone. So long without it, she'd almost forgotten

that she had it. She pulled it out of her pocket and looked at the display. Could Google tell her how to tie the knot?

How to tie a noose. SEARCH.

Apparently so. Dozens of references popped up. She'd pick the one with the diagrams.

Joy looped the rope and wrapped the end around the loop just as the diagram showed then threw it over the beam across the middle of the garage and secured it just like in the picture. She wiped the tears from her eyes as her vision blurred.

She needed to rehearse the words she'd pray. She'd call out to God. That would bring forth the evil spirit. Silas would turn on her and then war would rage on. But it wouldn't be over yet. She would pray, give her life to Jesus, and ask Him into her life. The question was, how much time would she have between that moment and when Silas attacked? Not *if—when*. Because, if she was going to die, it was going to be on her terms.

Silas watched her closely, his tail wagging. He seemed happy to see what Joy was doing. As though he understood. Was that good or bad? She had no idea what the difference was anymore.

She moved the ladder into position and got ready to climb. Wait. Should she leave a note? She really had nothing to say. But, then again, the note wasn't really about her, it was about them. . .the people she'd leave behind.

Joy rummaged in Grandpa's drawers and found a stubby pencil and a paper bag from the grocery store. She ripped the bag and opened it flat.

Mom and Dad, I love you. I'm sorry for what I've done that has hurt you. I'm sorry for how my choices have cost you so much. Thank you for being great parents and for loving me.

She drew a line on the paper and moved her pencil beneath the line.

Austin, I still consider this a temporary good-bye.
I love you.

Love, Joy

Okay that was it. Nothing left. Joy put the letter on the workbench and shifted the ladder a few inches. She climbed to the third step, tears pouring from her eyes. Her hands shook as she slipped the noose over her head and around her neck. She tightened it just enough to feel it.

Time for her prayer. Was she ready for this? There would be no turning back.

She clenched her fists and opened her mouth. Here goes. . .

Lights flickered through the tiny window over the workbench, and a car squealed into the driveway. The garage door began to rise.

Joy stared into the night as headlights from Dad's car shone spotlights on the scene. If only it were a scene in a movie, rather than real life. She'd receive an Academy Award for sure. She'd stand on that stage, with the Oscar in her hand, and thank her parents for not coming unglued in this moment. Why was no one moving?

The bright beams prevented Joy from seeing their faces, but she could imagine. She had destroyed them. There was no doubt. They were forever changed. All of them.

Dad climbed slowly from the car, expressionless. He stepped toward Joy.

Joy lifted the rope over her head and shot a look at Mom as the car door opened.

Mom stepped out of the car wearing her ratty flannel

comfort-pajamas, phone pressed to her ear. Was she calling the cops? Would Joy be checked into a mental hospital?

"We'll have her there as soon as possible. We're leaving now." Mom pressed a button and dropped the phone into her front pocket. She turned to face Joy.

"First I was scared. Then I was sad. Now?" Mom shook her head, looking like she was ready to breathe fire. "Now I'm just mad."

Dad clenched the steering wheel, his knuckles white and his face ashen. Joy knew he'd never forget the sight of his daughter with the noose around her neck, about to kick that ladder aside.

Mom rubbed her head. "Joy, we've done all the talking there is, I think. You're going back. Now."

"What do you mean, *now*?" She knew where.

Mom took several deep breaths. She closed her eyes. Counting to ten? Or praying?

She opened her eyes and leveled her gaze at Joy. "Look, I don't understand the level of your pain, obviously."

"I feel like we did you a disservice by letting you come home right now." Dad shook his head. "You even said you weren't ready."

"And Stella. . . ?" Mom eyed Dad. She'd probably make him pay for that one for a long time. She'd lay much of the blame there. An easy scapegoat. Mom was only human.

"If you stay here, you won't make it through this year." Mom sobbed. "If you go back, you have a shot."

Joy's shoulder slumped. She nodded. "I had planned on going back, not this way of course. But I guess everything's different now."

"Yes. Everything is different." Dad stared straight ahead.

"Look. Joy, I don't want this to sound cold. I don't want

you to be fifty years old talking about how your mom sent you away. But as a mother who will stand before God one day to answer for you, and answer about what I did to protect you, I have to send you away. Today. Right now."

Joy leaned her head on the headrest in front of her.

"It feels different this time, Mom." Joy sighed. "It feels like there's no hope. Like you're kicking me out and don't expect me back."

"No, it's not that. I'm desperate for you to come back. But for *you* to come back. The you I know and love. You're barely a shadow, a dim reflection, of the Joy we once knew. I want *her* back. I'm terrified, and I have no idea how to help you."

Mom swiped at a tear with the back of her hand. "And you know what?" She whipped around to look Joy in the eye. "I'm so angry at the enemy of our souls who has his claws in you. You're under a cloud and can't see a way out. And I'm mad."

Dad nodded again. "So, yes, we're going now. There's not a moment to waste. Ben is meeting us in Sterling."

"You mean right now? What about my stuff?"

"We'll swing by the house and I will go in to grab what you need. But yes, we're going now." Mom stared straight ahead.

"Why does it all have to be so hard?" Joy leaned back as the words from *A League of Their Own* fluttered through her brain. *"It's supposed to be hard. If it wasn't hard, everyone would do it. The hard. . .is what makes it great."*

"What about Stella's funeral?" Joy whispered as the car hurled down I-76.

"I think we've had enough funerals around here. We're going to skip it this time."

Could they do that? Just not give someone a funeral? Especially when that someone had no one else. "You sure you won't regret that decision later?"

"We'll memorialize her in our own way." Mom's jaw clenched. "But no. We won't regret it."

Exits passed and the distance narrowed. The mile markers flew by like taunts. Finally they pulled off at the rest area where Ben waited.

Mom climbed out and opened the door for Joy.

Dad raised a hand toward Ben.

Ben nodded but kept his distance. Probably giving them a moment to say good-bye.

"Okay, Joy baby, give us a hug." Mom pulled Joy tight and held on with all her strength. "Hey." She pulled her daughter back so she could peer into her eyes. "Please be safe. Please promise me you won't hurt yourself."

"I promise." Joy hugged Mom again.

"I love you, I'm praying for you every single moment of every single day. Please embrace the program with all your heart when you get back. Let it in." Mom raised her hands to Joy's face and pulled her close. "Let these people help you. Please promise me you will."

Would she ask that of Joy if she knew what the consequences would be?

"I love you, Daddy." She leaned forward to accept his strong hug.

"I love you, too, princess." He hadn't called her that since she was a little girl. She rested in her father's embrace as long as she could.

"Love you guys." She turned and walked away.

Would she ever see them again?

Chapter 40

Time to get down to business. Joy, come with us."

Joy followed the team to the prayer room without a word.

Mark reached out for Ginny's hand. Alicia moved nearer to her husband.

What was happening?

Ben moved to the center of the room. "Please, everyone, form a circle. Joy, you come stand in the center. We've gathered here today because, well, we're tired of this nonsense. If you are in agreement, we are going to pray once and for all, with the authority given to us by Almighty God, and release you from the strongholds on your life."

Joy's knees wobbled. She reached out for support. "Can I have a chair?"

Mark rushed to the side wall and grabbed a folding chair. He popped it open and slid it up to her legs.

Joy collapsed into it and took several deep breaths. "Do you guys have any idea what you're up against?"

Ben smiled. Alicia nodded.

Mark punched the air. "Yes. We know. And we're sick of stepping aside, waiting for you to figure out what needs to happen. We should have done this a long time ago, but we're going to make up for it now."

"Mark's right about one thing." Ben stepped forward. "We are sick of stepping aside and letting evil win. But I don't agree that we should have done this sooner. It won't work without you, Joy."

Mark nodded. "Very true."

She looked down. They were going to make her say it.

Silas moved so he was in view. She looked away.

He shifted into view again.

He wouldn't give up. Joy looked into his eyes. They held a message. Those piercing blue eyes she'd once loved so much said: *I. Dare. You.*

Ben crouched down. "So. It's up to you. Do you understand what's been happening to you? Do you understand what we're asking you to do?"

She nodded.

"Do you believe in your heart Jesus Christ is Lord?"

She nodded.

Silas snarled.

Oh no. She might as well have finished the job in Grandpa's garage. It would have gone better that way than how this would end.

"I need you to say it out loud, Joy. Romans ten tells us to confess it with our mouths. Do you believe in your heart God raised Jesus Christ from the dead and that He wants to do the same for you?"

Silas gnashed the air. The hair on his back stood straight up.

What could she do? Yes! She believed. But. . .

Silas lifted his face and howled.

Joy's hair swirled back from her face. "I don't know if you understand, but I'm in actual danger right now." Her voice trembled. "Actually, we all are."

"Yes, Joy, you are in grave danger. We get that." Alicia rubbed her shoulder.

Joy shook her hand off. Not the time for comfort. "No! I don't mean spiritual danger. I mean real physical danger. All of us."

Alicia stepped back as Silas was joined by some friends.

"Only you." Ben sighed. "You see, when I put my faith in Jesus, then He became a shield about me. . .and Ginny and Alicia and Mark and every other girl in this place who has surrendered to Him. We need not worry about the battle that rages all around us. We know the winner. Our God is mighty to save and shield us as our protector."

Ben's words made sense, but his voice droned on and on as Joy watched Silas assemble an army.

"That protection is assured the minute you surrender to Jesus."

"Fine. But it's that minute between saying I want to and actually doing it that terrifies me. Like right now." Joy trembled. Her whole body shook, and her knees knocked together. "They're coming for me."

"Then do it, Joy. No more talking about it. Who is your Savior?" Ben grabbed her hands. "Who's your Master? Say it!"

Silas roared. Foam flew from his jowls. He led the pack as they inched toward her.

Why couldn't she see the rest of the battle if she could see this part? Was it possible? If she said His name?

"Say it, Joy! Who do you choose?" Ben's face strained.

The others prayed.

Silas was ready to charge.

Joy could still back out. She could still make it okay, but one more step, one more word, and that was it.

"They're coming for me."

"Then let them come, Joy, let them come." Ben put his hands on her head. "Father God, please place Your protection around this girl. Give her the freedom to turn to You. Lift the burden of fear from her shoulders. Make it easy for her to turn her eyes upon You. Shield her. . ."

Too much. Joy jumped from the chair. It clattered to the floor as she ran from the room. She glanced back. The wolves calmly walked toward her, but they didn't seem in any hurry.

She had to hide. Could she hide from Silas?

Maybe she could. It was at least worth a try. Legs shaking, ready to vomit, she stumbled down the hall.

Ben's office was locked. The library? No, no place to hide in there. The dining room? No, that wouldn't work. Ooh, there was a closet at the end of the hallway. But it had been locked last time. *Please be open. Please be open.* Joy chanted as she tried the handle. It opened easily. She stepped inside and shut the door then flipped the lock. Safe for the moment.

Stepping back, away from the entrance, Joy lost her footing and tumbled down, down, down. Like Alice. Her body bumped along a stairway. What would she find at the bottom? She slammed into a hard, flat surface and felt around for a clue. It was another door. What could be in there? Somewhere good to hide, hopefully.

She tried the handle, and the door swung open to darkness. Joy didn't care what the place was. She'd go in so she could get as far away from Silas as possible.

If only she knew where Silas was.

Wait a second. What an idiot. Silas showed up wherever he wanted to. He was toying with her right now.

She reached behind her. Should she go up? Or keep going? She couldn't see anything at all. How could she step into a room with no knowledge of what it was?

She felt the walls. Oh my. What was the purpose of such a narrow passageway? And the ceiling. . .so low, she'd have to hunch over. No way she could handle that.

Pieces of the wall crumbled off into her fingers. She sniffed the residue. Dirt. What was it, some kind of escape tunnel for the monks? Was there a secret door or another way out? Joy patted the dirt walls and inched her way deeper into the tunnel. Her breathing grew shallower as her sense of confinement grew.

She clawed at the earth above her. Nothing. She'd stepped into her own grave.

What was that sound? It came closer. Yep. There it was. Silas and his friends had found her. Well, doubtful they needed to search. But there they were.

Joy backed up. Please let there be a way out. *Please.*

She gasped for air but a cloying, decayed, consuming stench filled her nostrils and her lungs, squeezing out the life-giving oxygen she so desperately needed.

Her back banged against something. She felt behind her. A door! She reached for the handle and pulled. Locked. She slumped to the floor and curled into a ball as the snarls grew closer. She'd lost. No question about it.

She sucked rotten air into her lungs. When would it be her last breath?

There he was. Staring at her. Standing in the doorway in the midst of a green glow, like an aura. The light glinted off his eyes. He was alone. Come to claim his prize.

Joy drew her knees in tighter to her chest.

Any second he would pounce, and when he did, it was over.

She could almost hear the power exerted as Silas readied himself for attack. Every muscle in Joy's body tensed. She crunched as tightly as she could.

What did she have to lose? Her reason and desire pushed through the shroud of darkness and broke down the lies she'd been told.

Pray. Now. "Jesus! God, please protect me! Jesus, Jesus, Jesus." Joy shouted His name over and over. She couldn't think of anything else to say. Hopefully it was enough.

She waited for the attack. The battle was on—all around her. Anything could happen.

When would it come? She listened. The space around her was silent except for her own gasping for air. And the repetition of one word. *Jesus. Jesus. Jesus.* Her hands sweated as they clenched her hair and held her body curled into a ball.

Maybe the attack would never come. "Jesus. Jesus. Jesus."

A light flashed through the doorway.

"Joy? Are you down there?" Ben's voice carried hope.

Maybe—just maybe. If only she could see.

The tiny passage filled with the light of several flashlights. Ben stumbled to Joy and reached out a hand.

"Wait. Don't move. Somebody give me a light." Joy had to know. She had to see.

Ben handed his to Joy, and she shone it down at the ground.

There lay Silas, her darkest enemy, slain at her feet.

§

"Okay, come on. Let's go." Ben flicked the light toward the doorway. "Let's get out of here. You can tell us all about it upstairs."

"D–do you see that?" She pointed the flashlight at the ground. Silas was gone. "Never mind. I'll t–t–tell you about it in a minute. I'm so cold."

Joy trembled her way up the stairs, her teeth chattering.

Ginny slipped her arm around Joy's back and squeezed. "You're in shock, sweetie. You'll warm up soon."

Alicia wriggled out of her sweatshirt and laid it across Joy's shoulders.

Ben plodded up the stairs in front of the pack. Humming. Was Ben crazy? How could he be humming like nothing had happened? He was happy, satisfied, and at peace. Joy wanted to live like that. Even in the darkest time.

But she still had questions. Why had she lived and Stella died? And how could she get Raven out? How could she reach the countless others who were stuck between two worlds?

"Ben?"

He held the office door as everyone entered then shut it. "Yes?"

"Will you teach me how to help other people get away?" Joy jerked her head back the way they'd come. "Like that."

"Of course I will." Ben beamed at Alicia. Then he looked at the group. "Let's finish this thing, shall we?"

Mark, Alicia, Ben, and Ginny placed a hand on Joy's head.

Ben lifted one arm and closed his eyes. "Father God, we thank You for protecting Your child and for embracing her and forgiving her. Please place Your permanent hedge of protection around Joy—her heart and her mind."

Joy felt the warmth course through her body. A healing heat. Possessing her.

"Let her go from this moment and use her experiences to lead others from darkness and help her tell them about You. May her face be so bright and shiny that the Spirit of God will be evident to all she encounters."

Joy felt her hands shake, her body trembled, and her stomach flopped. So that's what all those people felt when they couldn't resist the urge to worship. Joy raised her hands up to her heavenly Father, her Savior, her Master. "Thank You, Jesus."

Ben closed his eyes and breathed a sigh. "It is finished."

Chapter 41

Joy gasped, and her hand flew to her mouth. "I have to call my parents."

Ben nodded. "I'm pretty sure that can be arranged. Ginny, can we get them up on Skype?" Ben handed Ginny his MacBook. "I think it's best face-to-face."

"Great." Ginny popped open the laptop and brought up the Skype application. "What's their user name?"

Joy chuckled. "You can't laugh. It's *Homes4u*."

Ginny smiled and entered the new contact. "Now we wait to see if they accept the add request."

"Hon." Alicia stepped up to Ben. "Do you need me right now? I really should go help Tammy hold down the fort. It's dinnertime."

"Absolutely. Good thinking. We'll see you later." He bent down and gave her a kiss on her forehead.

How sweet. But now that she mentioned dinner, Joy was famished. Fighting demons took a lot out of a person, she guessed.

"Okay if I stay?" Mark asked. "I'd like to see how your parents react. And it would be cool to talk to your mom and dad if it's okay. I felt a connection with them when I met them."

Joy shrugged. "Why not? It's a good phone call."

"Sure is." Ben grinned.

"Oh, cool." Ginny hit the ENTER key. "They accepted it already. We're connecting now."

Joy stretched her legs out and yawned while the sounds of the Skype connection floated over the airwaves. "Wow. What a day. I just wish Mom and Dad could have actually been here to see it."

"But they'll see it now." Ben grinned down at Joy from his perch on the corner of his desk.

How was it possible his pants still had creases in them after all they'd been through? Joy was sure she looked a mess with mascara-raccoon eyes and hair all wild. Ooh, maybe she should have thought of that before agreeing to a video call.

"Hello? Joy, is that you? Is everything okay?" Mom looked a little high strung with wide-eyed panic.

"Hey Mom. Everything's great. Is Dad there, too?"

"Yep. He's here." She scooted over a few inches, and Dad stuck his head in the path of the webcam.

"Hey Joy. Good to see you." His eyes wore a questioning look.

"Here, let's put the laptop just a little farther away so you can see us both." Her arms filled the camera space and fumbled around. "There, how's that?"

"Perfect." A more annoying start to the call than Joy had hoped, but fine. "I'm here with Ginny, Ben, and Mark. And we have some things to tell you."

Now, what to say? "I honestly don't want to go into all the details because it's a little too fresh. But I will tell you I have been under heavy, heavy spiritual attack. Basically, I've been stalked by a demon." Any reaction from Mom or Dad? Nope. They kept straight faces. Either because they weren't surprised, or they were trying to reserve emotional reaction.

"Because of his presence in my life, which at first I

welcomed, I haven't been able to make any connection with God or with the true program of Diamond Estates since I got here."

"Which we knew." Ben jumped in. "But we always want to give each girl the time she needs to make a free-will commitment."

"That makes total sense." Dad nodded.

Joy sighed. "That connection led me to do some crazy things."

Mom's eyes widened. "You mean like at Grandpa's house?"

"Yep. And I tried to break away. So many times, in so many ways. But every time I did, something really bad happened, like the fire here and Grandpa dying. It just kept on and on and got worse each time." Joy shrugged. "I was afraid for my life and for the lives of everyone around me."

Dad searched the space he could see. "Ben? Are you still there?"

"Right here." Ben slid into view.

"Is what Joy's describing even possible? Not that I think she's lying—not at all. But could it have been something else?"

Ben's expression turned grave. "It's entirely possible, Mr. Christianson. The spirit world is a very real and very dangerous place. Dabbling, testing, experimenting. . .those things only open a door no one should walk through. And it often, in fact usually, closes behind a person who takes that chance."

Dad nodded and turned to Mom. "Stella?"

Mom sighed. "That's what I kept trying to tell you."

"Okay. We'll talk about her later. Off camera. I don't like my apologies recorded."

Everyone laughed.

"So, anyway. They prayed for my protection today and walked me through. And I surrendered my heart to Jesus." Joy sat back with a grin spread from ear to ear. "Not that it was easy. But I'm too exhausted to go into details. Maybe I'll write a book about it someday." Joy laughed.

"Sweetheart. That's wonderful." Mom wiped away a tear. "I can't even begin to tell you. . ."

"Yeah. You couldn't have given us better news." Dad beamed.

Ben leaned in again. "I feel privileged to have been here and be a part of this. She's a changed girl."

Dad nodded. "I can see it written all over her face. Her eyes are sparkling again." He turned to Mom. "Peg, I do believe we have our Joy back."

They signed off the call, and Ginny moved to close the laptop. Joy reached out a hand to stop her. "I was thinking, since we have the Skype opened, what would you guys say about me making another call?"

Ginny narrowed her eyes. "Who do you need to call?"

"My cousin, Beatrice. She's the one I went through a lot of this with—she was the one in the blizzard with me."

Ben shook his head. "I'm not sure I can let you contact a friend from your past. Not just yet."

"No, no. Remember? Bea is the one who has Down syndrome, and she's had a really hard time. Just me being away would have been hard enough for her. But to lose Grandpa, and then to witness Stella's death. Ugh. I can't even imagine what she's going through."

"Oh, the poor thing. That's awful." Ginny rubbed Joy's arm.

"Plus, I ran out of the church this morning and never went back. So I never got to say good-bye to Bea. I'd really like to make it right with her."

"I think we can make an exception this time." Ben stood up and stepped toward the door. "But I'll leave this one to you two. I've got to make sure everything's holding up out there." He gestured down the hall to the rest of the house.

"Ben?" Joy gazed up at him.

"Yes?"

"Thank you. Just. . .well. . .thank you." Joy wiped a tear from the corner of her eye. "You saved my life."

He smiled and shook his head. "Nope. Jesus did that a long time ago. You just had to realize it." He spun away and strode from the room.

Ginny poised her fingers over the keyboard. "Okay, let's see what we can do. Do you know her Skype address?"

"Sure, it's easy. B-E-A-O-M-A-L-L-E-Y."

Ginny typed the information and requested to add the contact. "Now we wait."

"I'm not sure they'll be online though. If they're not, can I use a regular phone? Or try this again later? Maybe I could send a text or e-mail to have them meet me here at a certain time?"

"Sure. That's fine." Ginny pointed at the screen. "Not going to be a problem though. Someone accepted our request."

"Hello? Who is this?" Sue's concerned face appeared.

Oh, naturally she'd want to see anyone new who tried to contact her daughter.

"Aunt Sue. It's me, Joy."

Her mouth broke into a grin. "Joy? I can't believe it's you." Her face fell into serious mode. "How are you? Your mom and dad told me what's been going on. I don't even know how you're handling all of this. Are you okay?"

"I'm really good." Joy grinned. "Trust me. Everything's changed. Mom can fill you in. I'm actually on borrowed time right now, and I'm desperate to talk to Bea. The last time I saw her. . .well, you know. Is she still up? Can you put her on?"

Sue smiled to her side.

"I'm here." Beatrice nudged her mom a few inches then plopped into the chair as she chewed on a Twizzler.

"Hi, Bea. It's so good to see you."

Bea leaned forward and stared into the camera, smiling at herself as she watched her face change in the little picture up in the right corner.

Joy waited. Whatever made her happy.

Bea stuck her tongue out and made silly faces.

A minute went by. Joy smiled at Ginny. "So, Bea, how's school?"

"It's good. I'm doing really good. They tell me I can go to the next grade. I'm really happy." Her smile disappeared. "But Joy?"

"Yes." *Here it comes.* Joy would have to answer for everything. She was ready.

"I don't know. So much happened. . .I just asked Jesus to help me put it back in the past. He did, so now I don't think about any of it." She shrugged a shoulder. "He'll help you do the same thing, too. You know, put it all behind you."

"That's wonderful. He's really good at that, isn't He?"

Beatrice nodded.

"Bea? Can I tell you a good thing?"

"Yes. You can tell me a good thing anytime."

"Well, my good thing is that I only talk to Jesus now." Joy grinned.

Beatrice threw both hands up to her cheeks. She squealed. "I'm so happy, Joy, and Jesus is happy, too."

"I know He is."

Ginny pointed at her watch face.

"Bea, I'm about out of time to talk on the computer. But, we can do it again, okay?"

"When?"

"Well. . . ?" Joy looked at Ginny and whispered, "Next week?"

She nodded. "Sure. Four o'clock."

"How about if we talk at four, next Friday?"

Beatrice rummaged in the drawer and pulled out a pencil then grabbed a sticky note. "When?" She poised to write, serious as if Joy was about to give her nuclear launch codes.

"Next Friday at four o'clock."

Beatrice chewed on her tongue while she wrote. "Four in the afternoon, right?"

"Yep. Unless you want me to wake you up at four in the morning."

"No." Beatrice laughed. "I don't want that." She read the paper and then counted on her fingers. "Seven days?"

"Yes. I'll talk to you again just like this in seven days. Sound okay?"

"Sounds great. I love you."

"I love you, Bea."

Joy exhaled her tension. It had been a long day.

⟳

"I bet you're wondering why we've brought you all here today." Ben stood on the stage in the prayer room and looked out over the girls sitting before him. "Once in a while someone comes here and has difficulty shedding the ties to the past. It can make things really hard to surrender to what God has in mind. Anyone here know what I'm talking about?"

A chorus of groans and a few lifted hands were offered in response.

"Yeah, I thought so. And once in a while we get to see a miracle. We get to witness the hand of God miraculously intervene in a humanly impossible situation. Someone, one of you actually, has a little story to tell. Anyone want to hear it?"

He clapped his hands, and the group followed suit. Joy could see the question on their faces: who was he talking about?

Ben grinned. Boy, he liked to go for the suspense reaction. "Joy?"

Joy stood and walked to the front amid whispers and stares. She looked over the girls. "I know what you're thinking. Believe me, I'd have thought it, too. But how about you hold your judgment for fifteen minutes and let me tell you my story. Okay?"

Joy plunged in. "I came here because I was stuck in a life of the occult and the paranormal. I dabbled and then later immersed myself in it. It all started innocently because my best friend had committed suicide, and I missed her. I had so many questions. Someone came along and offered me a way to talk to her."

Joy saw several girls nodding along with the story. Including Savvy.

"It started with only contacting Melanie, but then my grandmother, too. Then I had some out-of-body experiences."

Joy took a deep breath, trying not to notice the shock on some faces.

"This part is hard to talk about, but my friend gave me a guardian spirit, a protector. His name was Silas, and he was a white wolf. He protected me constantly and was with me always. Even here."

Several girls gasped.

"That's right. While we were having dinner, he was right there by my feet. Or while we were here in the prayer room, he was circling me, making sure I didn't get sucked in with the God stuff or become affected by your prayers. It totally worked. I was trapped."

Joy looked at Ben.

He nodded encouragement.

"Over time, our relationship changed as my heart strained

toward Jesus. The spirit within me craved companionship with its Savior. But my flesh was committed to another master."

The girls were leaning forward, hanging on to every word Joy said. How far should she go into the story? How much was too much?

"Every time I tried to pull away from evil, something bad happened or I was threatened. Without giving Satan too much credit, what I'm trying to say is that the spirit world of good and evil is real, and it's happening all around you right now."

Joy took a deep breath.

"I had flashes of visions where I got to see the battles that rage over your beds while you sleep."

Mouths dropped open.

"Yes, you. Tonya, Paige, Holly. . .all of you."

"I even saw into the intense war you guys fight with your prayers in this room. It sets the spirit world on fire. You should feel some holy pride for that."

Ben laughed. "Not that we're encouraging pride now, girls."

Joy rolled her eyes.

Everyone laughed. Nice tension breaker.

"We might not know exactly what is happening or why, as long as we know that to win the battles, and ultimately the war, all it takes is the name of Jesus." Tears coursed down Joy's face. "The power is in that name, and it was only when I took a chance and cried out to Him that I was freed the instant of the final attack—the one that would have taken my life."

Paige and several others dabbed their eyes.

"Then, you want to know the coolest part?"

They nodded. Every single one.

"The Lord opened my eyes, and I was able to see into the spirit realm. My enemy laid at my feet, slain by the blood of the Lamb.

"Each and every one of you has that very same power right in the palm of your hands. The Bible says that at the name of Jesus every knee will bow. Every knee. That means every enemy of yours. Every force that comes against you. Every spirit of doubt, worthlessness, or guilt. Crushed."

Joy shrugged. Had she really said all of that? Where had it come from? She looked at Ben. "I guess I'm done."

Ben moved to the front. He turned to Joy with authority in his eyes. "Joy Christianson, there's a calling on your life. You are going to be a powerful voice on issues of spiritual warfare. What Satan has meant for evil in your life, our holy God has turned around for His eternal good." He swallowed a few times to compose himself. "You will be a light of hope to young people. They will hear you and believe then turn their hearts to Christ because of your words." He stood silently, lips moving in prayer.

It almost felt like those words were from God Himself. Could that be? She'd talk to Ben about it later. In private.

Ben looked over the group. "Girls. There's an old Cherokee legend. . ."

Thirty groans filled the room.

Ben laughed. "No, no. Hear me out. The legend has it that an old Cherokee granddad tells his grandson that there are two wolves inside everyone. One is evil—pride, jealousy, anger, rage. The other is good—love, joy, peace, patience. They battle over control in the heart and minds of every person."

Ben strode across his stage. "So the little boy thinks about it for a minute, then asks, 'Granddad? Which one wins?' The wise old man looks at his boy and says, 'The one you feed.' "

๑

Mark stepped beside Joy into the lunch line. "Mind if I cut?"

"Hey!" Paige teased. "Get in line like everyone else. Thinks he's something special just because. . .well, why is it, Mark?"

"Ha. Ha. I just want to chat with Joy for a sec. Okay?" Mark winked. He could get away with anything with those girls. And he knew it.

He turned to Joy. "So, I wanted to talk to you."

"Sure. What's up?" Joy pushed her tray along the rails and took a sip of her Dr Pepper and added a brownie to her tray.

"I'm curious about something. How do you feel about your tattoo? That was a bit of an issue when I first met you—you felt like it connected you to the wolf. So what now?"

"It's awesome. I still love it." Joy shrugged. He might not understand, but it didn't matter.

"But it's a permanent reminder of the darkest days of your life. You don't regret it?"

"Oh no. Not one bit. It's my journey. It's a benchmark to remind me of my turning point. Jesus and I? We slayed that wolf." Joy smiled. "There's another side to it, too. Remember that Cherokee legend Ben talked about?"

Mark tilted his head. "Yeah. The one with the little boy and his grandpa. . .oh, and the good and evil wolves?"

"Right. Well, for a long time, I fed the evil one. Now I'm feeding the other one."

🌀

"Happy birthday to Ben!"

"Happy birthday to Ben!"

Joy looked around the room while the song continued. It was like the heavens had opened and doused everything with the brightest light. The world was in high-def. Before it had been like watching an old black-and-white movie on a VHS tape. Dim, dreary. No dimension.

The divider had been slid black; the library and dining room opened into one big space. The fire roared in the fireplace; the music blared through the sound system. Tons of people she'd never seen before. So this was a party? She'd forgotten how to have fun. But it was all coming back to her—she totally had her eye on the game of Twister happening in the back. They hadn't seen a back bend until they saw hers.

Ben leaned forward to blow out his candles. Alicia dove for his tie. Thank you. No one wanted another fire. Candles out, Ben reached for the mic. "Mind if I say a few things?"

"Do we have a choice?" The words slipped out before she could stop them. Luckily the twinkle in her eye reached him first.

"Ah. Someone knows me too well. No. You don't have a choice." He winked. "I just want to tell you all that I love you with all my heart. You make my life, *our* lives,"—he smiled at Alicia as he tugged her close—"richer than you could ever realize. Thank you for being you."

He bent to set the mic down.

"Well, that wasn't so bad," Joy teased.

"Oh, I almost forgot." Ben grabbed the microphone again.

A chorus of good-natured groans filled the room.

"We have a surprise for you. Me, Alicia, Mark, Ginny, and Tammy." He paused for effect. "Construction begins tomorrow on the back house. And here's the surprise. It will be a rec center. Workout room, theater room, coffee bar, aerobics studio, stuff like that."

A cheer erupted. Perfect. No one wanted that awful quarantine setup.

"It'll go in stages. So dig out your old clothes. Pretty sure we'll be calling on our cheap labor now and then."

Had there been any doubt?

Now. She was at a party. It was time to meet someone new. Hmm. That pretty dark-haired girl with the purple streak down the side of her hair looked interesting. Joy approached her and stuck out her hand. "Hey. I'm Joy."

"Hi. I'm Olivia. It's really nice to meet you."

"Olivia? Are you Ginny's daughter?" Joy hadn't realized she was drop-dead gorgeous.

"Yep, that's me; this is my fiancé, Justin."

"Oh. I didn't know you guys were engaged. Congrats. It's nice to meet you, too, Justin." And that's how it was done. Just like normal people, making new friends, laughing at jokes.

Time for Twister. "Can I play?" Joy spun the dial and moved in for a contortionist's dream. Her foot on the yellow circle, she had to reach her opposite arm to the blue one across the mat. "Sorry, Paige. You're going down."

Joy made her move, stretching her body over the top of all the players and put her hand on the dot. So hard to stay in position with all the laughing.

Paige collapsed to the floor. "Fine. Fine. You win." She laughed.

"Let that be a lesson to you all." Joy stood like a general surveying a battlefield. "Any other takers?"

Paige grinned. "Joy, you crack me up. You're the life of the party. Who knew?"

Epilogue

Joy peeked from behind the curtain out into the sea of faces. Two thousand wide-eyed teenagers looked to her for answers. Spiked hair, blue hair, nose rings, tattoos. . .whether out of rebellion or for personal expression, they all wanted to be different. . .but inside, they were all the same. Needy. Desperate. Just like she had been.

When she'd talked to him on the phone earlier that day, Ben Bradley had said, "Just tell it like you told the story to us that day in the prayer room. Do you remember what I said? I told you that you would go on to be a voice of hope to young people, that you would tell the story of good and evil in the battle raging over each one of them. Then I said they would believe you and hearts would turn to Christ. Today is the first fulfillment of that prophecy. Go out there and give it all you've got."

Joy wiped her sweaty palms on her designer jeans. She sure had prepared for this. Public-speaking lessons, Bible training, a really good shopping trip. She was dressed to kill with a speech that would give life to those who heard it.

So said Ben.

"Father, open their eyes and ears to the truth. Let them hear You call to them from behind the enemy's veil." She shook the tension from her hands and arms then rotated her head in circles.

She flipped open her favorite Bible, the one her parents gave to her on Christmas, the year it all happened, to Psalm ninety-one and read, " 'Because you have made the Lord, who is my refuge, even the Most High, your dwelling place, no evil shall befall you, nor shall any plague come near your dwelling; for he shall give His angels charge over you, to keep you in all your ways. . .' "

"Miss Christianson, it's almost time." The stagehand with the walkie-talkie helped her up the rickety back stairs until she was standing on the stage behind the curtain.

"And today," the emcee rallied the crowd, "I have the distinct privilege to introduce our special guest. This young lady is only twenty-one years old and is recently engaged to the love of her life. She has experienced things that will chill you to your toes—but I'll let her tell you about that. She's a graduate of the Diamond Estates program and a Bible student. She also just released her first book, *Feed the Good Wolf*, about spiritual warfare. Let's welcome Joy Christianson."

Joy took a deep breath and parted the curtain. She stepped into the spotlight and lifted both arms, waving. When the applause died down, she stepped up to the mic. "We serve a mighty God. How many of you know that today?"

She stepped back and bathed in the cheers for her Savior. She nodded. No hurry at all.

When the crowd settled, she took the microphone again. "I'm glad to hear it. Now, let me tell you a story. It's a story of hope in the midst of pain, and of life and light in the midst of death and darkness. And it's a story of power. Great, great power. In living color, it changed my life, yes, but it almost ended my life. . .many times." She let the words roll off her tongue and watched the effect vividly reflected in the eyes of those who truly listened.

" 'It is finished.' That's what Ben Bradley said the moment I turned my heart to Christ. And he was right." Joy looked over the teenagers. "It can be finished for you. Right here, right now. One step. One act of faith in movement toward Jesus. That's all it takes. Come." She gestured to the altar space in front of her then stepped back and raised her hands up toward the ceiling, watching as teenagers from all walks of life streamed from their seats, tattoos and all, and raced to the feet of Jesus.

It is finished.

Discussion Questions

1. What kept Joy from surrendering to God?

2. Do you think her struggle was a valid one? Why or why not?

3. What keeps you from fully surrendering to God?

4. Discuss Austin's role in Joy's life.

5. Who or what has helped you understand God's love for you?

6. Do you believe in the powers of good and evil?

7. What was the defining moment for Joy?

8. Was that an easy time for her? Why or why not?

9. What would you have done differently than Joy did once she realized she was in big trouble? Why?

10. What is a defining moment in your walk with Christ?

11. Did change and growth come easy for Joy? Does it for you?

12. Did Joy learn more about God from the good things or the bad things?

13. How are you like Joy? How are you different?

14. Discuss the old Cherokee legend. What does it mean?

15. What have you learned about your own choices from reading about Joy's life?

Chapter-by-Chapter
Discussion Guide

Chapter 1

- "If it's nothing more than a toy, it's harmless. If it's an authentic tool to contact spirits, wouldn't you want to know?" How do you feel about that question?
- What do you think is making Joy suffer?

Chapter 2

- Do you believe the scene with the Ouija board could actually happen?
- Do you think Melanie contacted Joy from beyond the grave?
- Describe Joy's downward progression and how sin has become easier for her.

Chapter 3

- Why did Joy run to Raven?
- What made Joy so upset? Hadn't she asked for it?
- What was that rotten-egg smell?
- In what ways have you already seen God at work in Joy's life up to this point?
- What are her thoughts about God?

Chapter 4

- Why might some people think suicide is contagious?
- What did Joy feel when she realized she was laughing?
- How are Joy's feelings toward herself changing?

Chapter 5

- What did Austin do to Joy?
- Should she have listened to him longer? Forgiven him?
- Define the occult.
- Why is it wrong?

Chapter 6

- How would you have felt in those moments Joy experienced in Melanie's room?
- What does this verse mean to you in light of Joy's trauma:

  No test or temptation that comes your way is beyond the course of what others have had to face. All you need to remember is that God will never let you down; he'll never let you be pushed past your limit; he'll always be there to help you come through it. (1 Cor. 10:13, The Message)
- Was any of it her fault?
- What is it about Bea that reaches Joy's heart?
- Who is a comfort like that to you?

Chapter 7

- Heather asks if Joy and Austin might get back together. She assumes Joy will forgive him. If you were in Joy's shoes, could you forgive him?
- What might the changes in Joy's appearance signify?
- Are people pressuring Joy too much?

Chapter 8

- What is Joy's relationship with her parents like?
- Do you think they're doing a good job or a poor job?
- Do you think Joy's problems are normal considering what she's been through? Or should Mom and Dad be concerned?
- Is counseling a good idea for Joy?

Chapter 9

- What do you think of Mary Alice Gianetti?
- What does Joy think of her?
- Joy approached the cemetery wanting the truth. She wanted to make sense it of it all. How could she have achieved that a different way?

Chapter 10

- Raven wants to take Joy to the next level. The next level of what?
- What should Joy do?
- Describe Joy's dream.
- Why are "if only" two of life's most gut-wrenching words?
- How does the scene in the shop describe faith?

Chapter 11

- Who are they praying/talking to when they reach out in the lake house?
- What's the significance of the onyx ring?
- Who is Silas?
- Why is Silas angry at Austin's presence?

Chapter 12

- What's the story behind Stella and Grandpa?
- Why did Stella get the tiger tattoo?
- Joy says she's thankful for new beginnings. Why?
- Do you think it's actually Melanie talking to Joy through the Ouija board?

Chapter 13
- Is what Joy's involved in a religion?
- What's the significance of the Silas tattoo to Joy?
- Will she regret getting the tattoo?

Chapter 14
- Where does Joy fall in the stages of grief right now?
- What is the "acceptance" part of the grief process? Is it important? Is Joy there yet?
- Why didn't Austin tell Joy's parents the whole story? Should he have?
- What should Kelsey have done when she saw Joy sitting in front of the fire? What would you do?

Chapter 15
- How do circumstances spiral out of control in this chapter?
- Is Joy in over her head?
- Do you believe these things can happen?
- Should Joy take her discovery about Austin seriously?

Chapter 16
- What do you think about the drug testing from Joy's perspective and from Mom's perspective?
- Is Mom right to take Joy for the testing?
- How would you feel in Joy's situation?

Chapter 17

- What is the significance of what happened at the cemetery?
- What kind of symbolism do you see in that scene?
- How could Joy allow herself to participate?
- Why does Dad say it was worse than any of the other things she could have done?

Chapter 18

- Was Aunt Sue gossiping about Joy?
- Is a person's spiritual journey strictly a personal one, or should parents and loved ones participate?
- If you were Joy's parents, what would you do at this point?
- Has your opinion of them changed at all from the beginning of the book?

Chapter 19

- How would you feel if you walked into the intervention Joy found when she arrived home?
- Do you think the offer of taking Joy to Diamond Estates is a bit extreme?
- Why do you think they won't accept girls into the Diamond Estates program unless they want to be there?
- How does that mirror salvation?

Chapters 20 & 21

- Why does Silas get mad?
- What makes Bea so spiritually in tune?
- Is Bea's faith strong and rock solid, or is it weak and silly? In other words, is it really necessary for her to draw such a firm line between good and evil?

Chapter 22

- What kind of help does Joy want?
- Do you think she knows what she's asking? Why or why not?
- How do you feel about Raven's reaction to Joy's plea for help?

Chapter 23

- Do you think Joy's parents are overreacting?
- Is a program like Diamond Estates necessary for Joy at this time?
- In what ways is this a sacrifice that her parents are making?
- In what ways is it a cop-out?
- Has your opinion about Joy's parents changed at all since the beginning of the book?

Chapter 24

- Does it make sense that Joy would keep the ring? Or do you see it as a sign of trouble yet to come?
- What does Joy mean by this: "God and I were on a what-have-you-done-for-me-lately basis. And it didn't look good for Him"?
- What would you say if a friend said that to you?
- How do you think Grandpa feels as he sees this unfold?
- Why can't Joy follow through?

Chapter 25
- What's the significance of the stained glass windows?
- Regarding the prayer room, Mark says, "This is where the magic happens." What do you think he means?
- Why does Joy have to live in the house out back? Is that a good thing?

Chapter 26
- What's the connection between Joy and the pumpkin spice candles?
- Do you have any triggers like that? Smell, song, taste?
- Other than grief, what truly caused Joy's spiritual search?
- Are there unanswered questions in your life that leave you feeling empty spiritually?

Chapter 27
- How is Silas feeling about the whole Diamond Estates adventure?
- What about the prayer time? Do you have your own daily quiet time with God?
- Is it wise or unwise for Ginny to choose her battles and not give Savvy a hard time about eating?
- What do you think is going to happen with Joy at Diamond Estates?

Chapter 28

- Joy feels like her parents might be better off without her. Did they send her that message? Should they have been more available to her?
- What do you think about the out-of-body experiences?
- What was Joy being shown with this one?
- Why is Joy afraid of the prayer room?

Chapter 29

- Do you think anyone suspects Joy of not telling the whole truth about her injuries?
- What are some of the strange things Joy has experienced, the most recent of which being The Voice? How much of that would it have taken for you to get help?
- Joy likes the idea of getting help to get rid of the spirits that are affecting her, but then she worries that she doesn't want to be alone either. Why do you think she feels that way?
- What's the solution?
- What is idolatry and how does it apply to Joy's choices?

Chapter 30

- What upsets Silas so much?
- Was the fire natural or spiritual. . .or both?
- Who does Joy blame for the fire?

Chapter 31

- Can the fire be a punishment from God? Or is it an attack from the enemy?
- Or could it just be natural? Does everything have to be tied to the spiritual?
- What do you think it is in this case?

Chapter 32

- Why doesn't Savvy want to room with Joy?
- What is the basis for her concern?
- Do you think she's justified?
- What does it mean for God to use for good what the devil meant for evil?

Chapter 33

- What should Joy have done when that Voice directs her to the bathroom?
- What about once she hears Raven's voice?
- What do you think compelled Raven to get in touch with Joy?

Chapter 34

- What does Joy mean when she says she wants to find a way out?
- Savvy promises to keep Joy's secret. Do you think she should?
- Why kinds of problems might she be facing if she answers the question: Who is Jesus Christ to you?
- And, who IS Jesus Christ to YOU?

Chapter 35

- Sounds like Joy might be giving up. Why doesn't she have faith that God can get her through this?
- Is there any grief or pain in your life that keeps you from drawing close to God?
- What do you do about it?
- She's a little worried about being on her own away from Diamond Estates. Do you think those concerns are reasonable and helpful? Why or why not?
- Is it a mistake having Stella stay in the house with Joy? Why or why not?

Chapter 36

- Is it good to talk about grief as a part of the healing process?
- Does Joy make a mistake by going to Austin?
- Do you have a different opinion of Austin now?

Chapter 37

- How does Joy's faith begin to shift at the funeral?
- If she wants to meet her Grandpa in eternity, what does Joy need to do?
- What is it that Joy is actually witnessing take place around Stella?
- What are the other people seeing?
- How might that apply to the spiritual battle going on all around you?

Chapter 38

- Why does Joy flee?
- She determines that she can never return to God. Why?
- Joy feels hopeless. Why? What is she considering?
- Can you understand why she'd come to that conclusion even if you don't agree with her?
- What would you say to a friend who was dealing with the same sort of hopelessness?

Chapter 39

- How do you think Joy's parents felt when the garage door opened?
- What do you think happens next in Joy's life?

Chapter 40

- The battle Joy is embroiled in is intense. How could she have avoided that kind of fight for her life?
- Who wins?
- How have you been challenged through this book?

Chapter 41

- "The spirit within me craved companionship with its Savior. But my flesh was committed to another master." What does Joy mean by this?
- What does the old Cherokee legend mean to you?
- Do you believe the spiritual battle Joy witnessed is happening around you and even for you?
- How confident are you in the power of God to save you and protect you from the enemy?
- Have you given your life to Jesus?
-

Austin and Joy are getting married. Want an invite to the wedding?

How Can I Be Saved?

Everyone is a sinner:
For all have sinned and fall short of the glory of God. (Romans 3:23 NIV)

God requires payment for sin:
For the wages of sin is death, but the free gift of God is eternal life through Christ Jesus our Lord. (Romans 6:23 NLT)

Jesus paid the price:
But God showed his great love for us by sending Christ to die for us while we were still sinners. (Romans 5:8 NLT)

You need only believe and confess:
If you confess with your mouth that Jesus is Lord and believe in your heart that God raised him from the dead, you will be saved. (Romans 10:9 NLT)

It's a done deal:
So now there is no condemnation for those who belong to Christ Jesus. (Romans 8:1 NLT)

The steps of salvation are:

1. **Confess** you are a sinner.

2. **Understand** that you deserve to pay the price for your sins.

3. **Believe** Jesus Christ died on the cross to pay that price for you.

4. **Repent** by turning from your sinful life to newness in Christ.

5. **Receive** the free gift of salvation.

Congratulations on taking this important first step on a journey with Christ!

Remember, salvation doesn't mean you're perfect, it only means you're forgiven.

But through the power of God, if you allow Him, He'll help you walk in righteousness as He points you in the right direction.

Youth-culture expert, Nicole O'Dell, resides in Paxton, Illinois, with her husband and six children—the youngest of which are toddler triplets. She's the founder of Choose NOW Ministries, dedicated to battling peer pressure and guiding teens through tough issues while helping parents encourage good decisions, and host of Choose NOW Radio: Parent Talk and Teen Talk, where "It's all about choices!" On air, O'Dell covers peer pressure, dating, purity, drugs, alcohol, modesty, popularity, and anything else that comes up along the way. Nicole writes and speaks to preteens, teenagers, and parents about how to prepare for life's tough choices.

She's an author of YA fiction, including the popular Scenarios for Girls interactive fiction, which offers readers alternate endings, allowing them to decide what the main character does, and the Diamond Estates series based on her experiences as a resident at Teen Challenge as a teenager. Her non-fiction for teens includes *Girl Talk (February 2012)*, which she wrote with her two daughters based on their popular advice column.

Nicole's desire to bridge the gap between parents and teens is evident in her parenting non-fiction like the Hot Buttons series aimed at helping parents handle tough issues with their tweens and teens before they pop up in real life. Watch for Hot Buttons books on subjects like dating, Internet activity, sexuality, prejudice, friendship, politics, and more.

For more information on Nicole O'Dell or her books, or to schedule Nicole for a speaking event or interview, visit http://www.nicoleodell.com. Podcasts of Choose NOW Radio are available at http://www.chooseNOWradio.com.

Don't Miss Out. . .

Make sure you pick up book 1 & 2 from the Diamond Estate Series

THE WISHING PEARL
BOOK 1

THE EMBITTERED RUBY
BOOK 2

Available wherever books are sold.